Alex Andre

LOST & FOUND

The E Apocrypha

Book 1

Disclaimer

All characters and events appearing in this work are fictional.

Any resemblance to real persons, living, dead, or yet to be born, is purely coincidental.

To L—my muse, my first reader, my everything!

Maps

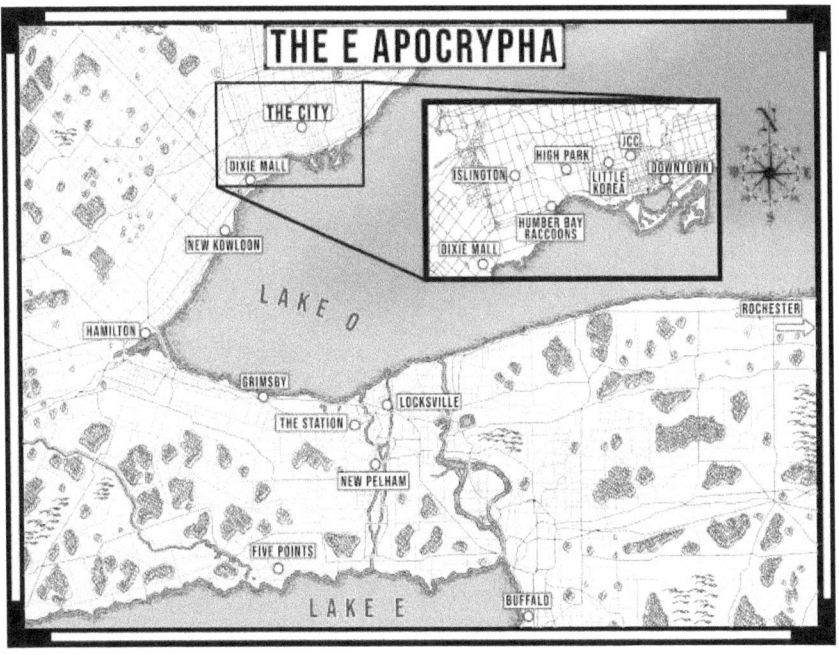

Map by Oscar Paludi "Exoniensis"

Part 1

LOST

Chapter 1

Yun-mi

September 18, 42 PE

Quiet as a subway tunnel in the dead of the winter; check. Still as pond water on a hot, breezeless day; check. Slow and shallow abdominal breathing; check. She was like a stone figure. The sharp tip did not waver.

The weapon returned the warmth of Yun-mi's sweaty palm through the well-worn cord wrapping. A spear. Really? *Really?* Heavy, cumbersome, unwieldy. A man's weapon. The worst choice for the City. But... That was her task, and she'd make the most of it. Had to, or else.

The coyote's ears snapped up, and it stopped tearing into the unidentifiable pieces of its meal. Baring bloody teeth, the beast issued a growl so low it reverberated through Yun-mi's feet.

At the crunching of concrete debris—that's what had spooked it!—the animal's muscles rippled under its fur. Damn!

She launched.

The heavy projectile hit the moving target with enough force to pierce the coyote's scruff, disjoint the vertebrae, and strike the wall, impaling the animal.

Yun-mi froze, and the coldness spread through her chest. Two holes. Imperfection. The pelt was ruined. The price? Screw the price! Her life was on the line.

She stood, unable to move, to breathe. Did she just fail her test? *The* test? Why did Joon-woo have to insist on the stupid spear? With her bow, she would've put an arrow straight through the animal's eye!

"You were taking too long." Joon-woo appeared in the doorway, his rifle casually held in one hand. He took the scene in and frowned. "How many opportunities did you have and not take, looking for a better one?"

Oh, no. No, no! An acidic wave rose from her stomach. She gagged and swallowed. The nauseating bitterness receded, leaving her throat burning. And not just the throat. Her world was crumbling down in a fiery catastrophe.

"Follow your instincts, don't overthink it," Joon-woo continued, as if not noticing her panic. "You lingered until it was too late. Then you were forced to react, and the result is—" he pointed at the coyote's limp form.

Yun-mi's teeth clenched. It was over.

Not a big deal. Only the single most important opportunity of her life. A missed chance to move to the next level; to finally join her mentor, their clan's best Rat, on a trading run. She'd been working her ass off toward this point for the last two years, and—

Joon-woo tsked. "In some situations, being smart or cunning gives you an edge. This wasn't one of those. You get a shot, you take it. Don't let perfect be the enemy of good."

She squeezed her eyes shut. Not to see her shameful failure, this disgusting room with its peeling wallpaper, the broken windows, the rotten furniture. More than anything, not to witness Joon-woo's reproving grimace. Or would it be pity? That'd be worse.

He fell silent. Yun-mi risked a glimpse. Joon-woo was studying her; as always, with an unreadable expression.

She hurried to bend in a deep bow. "Sorry, Kim Joon-woo! I was listening! The perfect is the enemy of the good, I must follow my instincts." Anything, so long as he didn't give up on her.

She cautiously peeked up and met a coy smirk.

"Maybe you were, maybe you weren't. We'll see at the West End tomorrow."

Did he just...? Yes!

A happy little sun bloomed inside her, instantly turning the world warmer and brighter.

"*Kamsahamnida!*" She bowed deeper.

"Let's go. Don't forget the coyote." He slung the rifle behind his back, waiting for Yun-mi to retrieve the spear and heave the carcass onto her shoulders.

She passed the test! Once she's gone trading, she wouldn't remain an anonymous scavenger anymore. No more disrespect. No more being the laughingstock, the teenage weirdo loner with ambitions of a grown-up man. Under Joon-woo's guidance, she was on her way to becoming the most famous Rat in the City!

A wide, goofy smile stretched the corners of her lips and refused to let go.

The dead coyote grinned back.

September 19, 42 PE

So this was the West End? Meh. Similar to home, yet very much not home.

Downtown, she knew. It spoke to her. She could disappear like a startled rat at the first sign of danger; fade into the maze of the crumbling skyscrapers and their underground levels, the labyrinths of the Path, the utility tunnels, the subway. Take her, blindfolded, anywhere between Bloor and Lakeshore, and she'd find her way home. No, she'd *be* at home!

This part of the City Yun-mi had never been to, and the foreignness pressed against her chest. The further behind she and Joon-woo left the last subway station, the worse she dragged her feet. Any rustle of a small animal or whisper of the wind, and her neck hairs stood on end. Her hand squeezed the intimately familiar, soothing riser of her bow. The tips of the fingers on her other hand twitched, ready to rip an arrow from the quiver and nock it on the string.

Get yourself together. Dixie, here I come! You won't know what hit you!

Her first trading. An opportunity she'd been looking forward to for months—and had almost blown the day before. She shivered. Yeah, yesterday was quite a day. But in the end, Joon-woo invited her, and that was all that counted.

Yun-mi stole a glance at her mentor and fought the stupid grin clinging to her face.

No one had ever given much of a damn about the oddball, rebellious little girl, her unlikely successes and predictable failures. No one but Joon-woo. He'd put his trust in her. What if she failed to meet his expectations or, worse yet, failed to meet hers?

A shiver jerked her shoulder blades.

That's right, you're just a seventeen-year-old kid with much more to learn than what you've mastered so far.

She frowned and stomped out the treacherous little voice in her head. Sadly, it had a point. So what? Knowing her limitations was important. An overconfident Rat was a dead Rat.

She diligently scanned every broken window, every pile of bricks, every alley they passed. Taut as her bow's string, almost ringing.

Everything was going to be fine.

A tall, wiry stranger materialized where no one had been a second before.

Oh, shit!

Yun-mi's arrow looked back at him in no time, the base of her thumb anchored at the jawline.

Blink, pal, and you're dead.

The man held his open hands up in the air, preempting suspicions of hostile intentions. He gazed from Joon-woo to Yun-mi and back with an affable smile and wiggled his fingers.

"Parker." Joon-woo sounded unfazed, almost indifferent. As if he were used to people suddenly appearing before him while he was slinking through questionably safe territory, carrying high-value cargo.

"Kim," the stranger greeted him with similar equanimity. "Mind telling your baby Rat to aim that arrow somewhere else? I'm pretty comfortable with the number of holes my hide's got so far."

Joon-woo signaled for her to stand down. Yun-mi lowered her bow and let it straighten up, but left the arrow on the string. In case of... just in case.

"Got yourself a fierce one, Joon-woo, huh? I already like her." The newcomer gave her a thumbs-up. "Gonna introduce me?"

Yun-mi's mentor lowered his eyelids. "Park Yun-mi, meet Jim Parker of the Humber Bay Raccoons Clan. Parker, my trainee Park Yun-mi."

Safe enough. Yun-mi slid the arrow back into the quiver.

"Park, Parker—almost namesakes, huh?" The man winked, retrieved his cargo bag from behind the concrete barrier he'd used for concealment, and approached. "Dixie?"

"Dixie."

"Come with?"

"Fine."

These two sure didn't need too many words to communicate. Must've known each other for a while.

Walking behind the two men, she examined Parker. Late twenties, same as Joon-woo. A Rat, obviously, and a veteran one. That springiness in the step came only with experience. A brown leather jacket, jeans, and a gray ball cap. A serious rifle slung over his shoulder, larger than Joon-woo's. High caliber, bolt action, powerful optics. Impressive. Parker must be one of his clan's top Rats if he could afford it. A wicked kukri in a sheath at the small of his back. A tanto knife strapped to his left thigh. A fellow leftie, huh? A push dagger handle protruding from his high-laced combat boot. This guy meant business. Then again, a Rat who didn't was a dead Rat.

A group of three Rats presented a much tougher target than one and a half. Enough to deter potential wrongdoers from doing wrong. Fewer opportunities for her to fail.

No. Can't afford complacency. A Rat that lets its guard down ends up a dead Rat.

Joon-woo and Yun-mi had taken the tunnels all the way west to Kipling, the terminal station. The fast and safe route. From there, their path lay overland, through nonaligned territories, an uninhabited area filled with abandoned factories, empty shops, and a monstrous intersection of three highways.

Why didn't the Ancestors bother to extend the subway to the Dixie Mall? Everything would have been so much easier!

Subway meant home. True Rat, Yun-mi slept and ate underground, and when the time came, she'd mate and procreate there. Indoors and tunnels kept Rats safe. Open streets were too exposed. Like now.

The knots of tension in her neck and shoulders threatened to turn into cramps. If only she could be as casual as Joon-woo and Parker... Yun-mi relaxed her back, imitating the two men's self-confidence.

I'm the man for the job, she projected to the world around her. Never mind the minor detail of her being a woman. Strong, fast, sly. Deadly. Someone for Joon-woo to be proud of, for her clan to rely on.

Parker dropped to one knee and threw his right fist up.

Danger!

His left hand reached for his knife.

Raiders? Bandits? Other Rats?

Yun-mi did what they'd practiced with Joon-woo. As the one closing the file, she turned back to secure their six, trusting the men to guard the remaining sector. She crouched to present a smaller target, with an arrow resting on the shelf of her bow.

A tense minute passed. No one was charging at them, or shooting at them, or as much as looking funny at them. Another minute. Not a movement anywhere to catch her eye. Nothing was happening at all. But there must have been a reason for Parker to raise the alarm. She wasn't blind or deaf. Maybe too inexperienced to recognize the signs of a threat?

A stifled noise behind her jolted Yun-mi's hypersensitive hearing. She started turning when someone grabbed her hair and yanked her head back. Simultaneously, a knee pushed against her back and a hard object touched her throat. Yun-mi gingerly peeked down her nose. A kukri's curved blade was hugging her neck under her chin.

Parker's suave voice whispered into her ear. "Don't be stupid. Lay down the bow. Slowly."

The absurdity of the situation made her dizzy.

If it was another one of Joon-woo's tests, she'd failed it, miserably. Her cheeks burned. With no way out, she complied.

"Good." Parker's warm breath tickled Yun-mi's skin. "Now, the knife. Very good. The other knife. Don't play games with me, Park, I said, the other knife."

Yun-mi reluctantly obeyed. No one was supposed to know about the stiletto up her sleeve.

"Okay. Down on both knees. No heroics, I'm faster than you. Good girl. Knees apart. Wider. Give me your hand."

A loop tightened around her right wrist.

"The other."

A loop, left hand. A jerk bringing her elbows together behind her back squeezed a gasp from her. Ankles, tied together and to her hands.

Yun-mi's mind vacated her skull. It refused to digest the signals her senses were sending. This was not happening. Not to her. Not to the up-and-coming best Rat of the clan.

"Joon-woo?" Her tentative, borderline plaintive call met no answer.

Parker grabbed her by the restraints and spun her around. Agonizing pain shot through her shoulders, bent backward beyond their normal range of motion, but she forgot about it a second later.

Joon-woo was there, lying on the ground.

Not the best time to take a nap.

Then the details started trickling in. The unnatural pose, knees bent out in different directions. The dark puddle spreading underneath. Something must have been wrong with Yun-mi's damned eyes, because what they were showing her could not be right. Joon-woo was invincible. Infallible. As close to a god as a mortal could get. Resigning to the inevitable, she took in the scene. With Joon-woo's throat, opened from ear to ear, being the central piece of evidence.

Her heart stopped for what must have been a fraction of a second, but felt like an eternity. A cold claw squeezed her ribcage, driving the air out with a sob, ripping her on the inside with merciless talons. She would have tumbled to the ground, but Parker clasped her shoulder.

Joon-woo. The man who had taught her and raised her. Who'd become an older brother she'd never had, and her secret crush she'd never admitted. The only person who had cared about her. The only person she had ever cared about, too. Gone.

Her life was over.

Yun-mi should've been scared, but fear did not come. If Parker had wanted to kill her, she'd be dead already, just as—

She squeezed her eyes so hard her eyelids should have bled. But the pain of the loss was the unbearable one. She was going to be sick.

Don't look. Don't think about Joon-woo. Don't think at all. No, think of something else. A distraction. Anything, just not this.

Her career was done for. There. Tragic. Who would teach her? Who would mold her into a proper Rat?

That didn't work. *No hiding from the truth. Face it.*

Someone had to avenge Joon-woo, but Yun-mi was alone in the world. So, not someone; she. It was up to her to make this right. The mourning would wait. Rat up!

"You—" Her treacherous voice trembled. "Why?! You were his friend! He trusted you!" Anger swept aside all other emotions, infusing her words with scathing hatred.

"No, and no." So civil. "No, he wasn't a friend, more of an occasional trade associate. And no, he did not trust me. No Rat would trust anyone and live to his age. Didn't he teach you? Should've been the first lesson. Anyhow, it was an informed risk calculation, not trust. This time, he miscalculated."

"But why?!" The scream escaped Yun-mi's constricted throat. Her vision inexplicably blurred.

"A powerful move to make today, that's all. Nothing personal, strictly business. There are forces—" He dismissed her with a wave of a hand. "It's a game on a different scale, you won't understand."

"Try me!" Yun-mi threw her head up with all the defiance she could muster.

"Hm? Very well, why not. A certain player wants to expand their influence. Bloor clans are in the way. Too stubborn to unite with each other, let alone accept external guidance. That player has contracted me to clear the path. With me so far?"

She growled, not ready to give him words. Not words of agreement or acceptance.

Parker smirked. "I'll take that as a 'yes'. If so, you understand why Joon-woo had to go. He is... *was* one of the best, well-known Rats in the City. And we, the Rats, are unique, maybe two dozen worth the name. Eliminate them—and you've defanged the clans. Any remaining resistance would be purely symbolic. Fierce, but fruitless. Does this answer your question?"

If only looks could burn. Yun-mi's would've peeled Parker's skin off. If only.

"Besides," he said, finally manifesting smugness, "it's a triple win for me. I get paid by my patron, I can sell your clan's goods, and"—his eyes flatly locked on Yun-mi—"you."

Chapter 2

Buck

September 18, 42 PE

The sergeant dismissed the squad two hours before dusk. Unheard of. The drillmasters knew better than to leave the rookies with idle time on their hands. Idle time eventually led to idiotic ideas and unbelievably asinine levels of dumbassery, it was known. But apparently, the most vicious instructors enjoyed an occasional break from herding cats, too. The warm and quiet fall evening could have something to do with that.

With training finished for the day, Buck fetched his cleaning kit and sat at the wooden table in the barracks' inner yard. He disassembled his rifle and lovingly oiled and wiped the parts. Then did this all over again—not for the need, but for the joy of the process.

Less than a year ago, Buck could only dream of holding a rifle. A real, functioning firearm in his own hands!

As a little boy, he fantasized how he'd become a famous warrior, leading the mighty Five Points Army to fight abominable heretics, wild-eyed zombies, and mutant monsters. Liberating kingdoms—along with pretty princesses, of course—from ruthless villains' yoke in the vast wastelands beyond the Boundary. What boy his age didn't dream of those? They all carved wooden toy guns, especially after the Army parades.

For Buck, there was an extra reason. He *had* to understand how guns worked. Beyond being powerful, most advanced weapons of war, guns were fascinating, driving that unquenchable thirst to know, to *see*. Turned out, none of the adults, even soldiers, could provide satisfactory explanations. No one knew.

And here he was, a soldier himself. A green private still, but issued with the coveted uniform. Half a year into the training, he had finally received a gun. A real gun! True enough, not all black, his Garand had wooden parts like his old toy weapons a decade ago. *Unlike* toy guns, this one fired very real bullets. And needed to be cleaned. Thoroughly.

Rookies were always grumpy. Given a subject, they'd find a thousand reasons to bitch about it. The one thing they all universally enjoyed was the live fire range. Yes, they had it only once in two weeks, and received three meager rounds each. Oh, well.

He cycled the action, listening to the sweetly smooth movement of the reliable and deadly mechanism, savoring the smell of the gun oil, and began the disassembly again.

The vision came as they always did, without a warning. The table, the yard, the rookies around him—everything froze, losing color and contrast. Instead, he saw the parts of the rifle moving back and forth, snatching a round from the magazine, chambering it, locking, firing, rushing back against the resistance of the spring. And again, and again.

Magnificent! Possibly the most beautiful thing he'd ever seen. But also terrifying, and not because of its lethality. Shit. How could this be? A rifle was, in fact... a machine? An abomination?! No, no, no, this was all wrong. Cold sweat broke out on Buck's forehead.

"Brennan! Hey, Brennan!" a distant voice pulled him back to reality.

Still stunned, Buck threw a cloth onto the disassembled parts and turned around. Hurriedly pulling his legs from under the table, he stood to attention. "Corporal Chase!"

"At ease, Private," said the corporal in good humor. Buck followed the order, but his jaw refused to unclench. "Looks like the Master Sergeant is pleased with your performance. Which, as I'm sure you've noticed, doesn't happen often. As a reward, you're dispatched to the Marketplace Peace and Order Preservation duty. Report to the guardroom tomorrow morning at oh-six-hundred. Uniform—full camo dress. Questions?"

Processing the corporal's words took so much effort, it left Buck out of breath, as if he'd run ten kilometers. His heart madly pumped blood through his ears.

"Sir," he gasped, "what about my training schedule, sir?"

The corporal's face, uncharacteristically beatific to that point, soured. "Private, you must be dumber than you seem. That's mildly disappointing because I thought little of your wits to begin with. Frankly, I can't imagine what earned you this privilege, but by the Seven Hells, I will not question Master Sergeant's decisions. Show up on time tomorrow and try not to ask too many stupid questions. Better yet, don't ask questions at all. Clear?"

"Sir, yes, sir!"

"Good. Atten-*shun*! Dismissed." The corporal departed.

A hand clapped Buck on the shoulder. "Look at you, knucklehead!"

"Yeah, what's that about?" A second hand landed heavily on the other side.

"Boy, the Marketplace duty! Are you lucky, or what? Did you bribe someone? Whose ass did you kiss?" Larry winked.

"Open your eyes and look your best! The girls at the Marketplace... M-m-m!" Sam kissed the tips of his fingers.

"Come on, Sam, we're talking about Buck here. He'll never gather the courage to strike a conversation with a girl."

The three of them had grown up teasing each other. Buck would not have been offended even if he'd cared to listen. He didn't. Thick fog filled his skull. Was this happening? For real?

Ignoring his buddies, Buck sat back, removed the cloth from the Garand parts, and absentmindedly reassembled the rifle. Too many questions. No answers. Why was he singled out? Uh-oh. Does the Master Sergeant know? But how? Did Buck give away his ability somehow? Why the Marketplace? And... rifles are machines?!

September 19, 42 PE

Buck scrambled up at four in the morning.

Since lights-out, sleep had refused to come. He had tossed from side to side under the blanket. The pictures of him in the Marketplace flashed through his mind. Especially all the things that could go wrong. Screwing up an award assignment would be a disaster, putting an end to his Army career before it began.

The revelation about guns' true nature nagged at him too, but the coming Marketplace adventure easily overshadowed the confusing discovery.

Unable to stay in bed any longer, he tiptoed to the washroom and spent twenty minutes in front of a mirror, tugging and pulling at his uniform to achieve the perfect fit.

At half-past five, he was pacing outside the guardroom door. The clock on the tower mocked him, creeping with merciless slowness. In the darkness, way before the predawn, telling the time amounted to guesswork, but Buck kept checking every few steps. At what he hoped was five minutes to six, he ran out of patience, took a deep breath, and stepped in.

Behind the tall counter, the officer on duty raised his head at the creak of the door. "Ah, Brennan."

"Sir, Private Brennan reports for the Marketplace Peace and Order Preservation duty, sir!" Buck barked in a single breath, clicking his heels.

"Good, good," said Lieutenant Jarvis, rubbing his drowsy eyes. "At ease, Private. Your first such assignment, obviously?"

"Sir, yes, sir!" Buck switched to *at ease* but remained stiff, maintaining a well-drilled implacable expression.

The officer smiled. "Relax, Brennan. You are not in any kind of trouble. Very much the opposite."

"Thank you, sir!" Buck exhaled and allowed his face to loosen up a bit.

"Here's your briefing. The Army maintains a Special Detachment at the Marketplace to ensure peace and to deal with any trouble that may arise. You are going to be a part of it, along with four other soldiers, a sergeant, and an officer. You are relieved of your training schedule for three days, starting today. You'll travel to the Marketplace with the supply train dispatched from our kitchen, which leaves in"—he squinted to consult the tower clock through the window—"roughly twenty minutes. You will receive further instructions from Sergeant Gomez, and will follow them to a T. Which I expect not to be complicated, even for a private, because your task will be to stand at your post, looking scary and making sure nobody fools around. Three days from now, another detachment will arrive, and you'll return with yours. Questions?"

"No, sir." A great lot of questions milled in Buck's head, but he followed Corporal Chase's advice and refrained from asking any for fear that some may turn out stupid.

"Fantastic. Pass me your rifle. Only cudgels in the Marketplace." Lieutenant Jarvis locked Buck's Garand in a cabinet and returned to his seat behind the counter. "That would be all. Go to the kitchen, make your presence known to the Chief Cook, and be ready to leave when he says so. Good luck, Brennan. Dismissed."

Buck clicked his heels again, bringing his fist to his chest with a snap, smartly turned around and marched out. His heart attempted to flee from his rib cage through his ears. In the yard, he bent over, catching his breath. Sweat soaked the back of his shirt, clammy in the early morning chill. One step closer. Hadn't screwed up yet.

***

Master Rodriguez glanced in Buck's direction and disappeared into the kitchen, to show up a minute later with a plate full of omelet and sausages.

"Baxter Brennan, I presume?" He set the plate on a table and invited Buck to sit.

"Yes, sir!" Buck eagerly ogled the content of the plate. Rookies were permanently hungry, tired, and horny. A fact of life. And while Master Rodriguez obviously wasn't in any position to ease the latter two grievances, his cooking made him famous well beyond the Base.

"Eat, son, we'll be leaving once you're finished."

These simple words left Buck speechless. The Chief Cook himself waited for him? Unthinkable! He'd better not test the limits of Master Rodriguez's goodwill.

Buck put his hands together in the Sign of Faith.

"Blessed be thou, Father God Almighty, and thou, Mother Earth,
For gracefully allowing us to taste the fruit of your communion.
Blessed be the hardworking farmers, deliverers of these fruits into the world
With their sweat and their labor and their simple tools.
Blessed be the kitchen and the cook that brought these onto my table.
Amen."

He rattled off the Food Blessing and gobbled the content of the plate without noticing the taste. Let's go, let's go!

"Me neither, Baxter, me neither. Can't recall the last time they sent a rookie to snoop around the Marketplace." Chief Cook Master Rodriguez clutched the reins.

He was an ancient man, probably in his fifties—older than Buck's father. Tall but not broad, with the genial face of a kindly grandpa. He wore his long gray hair in a thick braid, the subject of countless muted discussions among the young recruits. A brush of silver mustache and well-groomed sideburns were not regulation either, but who was Buck to judge?

Master Rodriguez showed no hurry and let the big black horse choose its own pace. The cart rolled lazily on its four rubber wheels. The horse needed no guidance to bypass the larger pits in the gray, cracked road.

"Did you know, son, that this hard stuff covering the road is called 'asphalt'?"

Buck didn't. *Asphalt.* He rolled the unfamiliar word on the tongue. Odd, foreign. Wrong. Like it could have something to do with engines, curse their name.

"Before the E, they knew how to make it," continued Master Rodriguez, confirming Buck's suspicions. "They didn't allow the roads to fall into such disrepair, oh no. My father told me the roads used to be all flat and smooth, and you could travel without the fear of breaking a wheel, or an axle, or a horse's leg."

Was this some kind of test? If it was, Buck wasn't failing it.

"But they used machines to make it, sir. That's what brought the E upon Humanity! It had sinned by worshipping the machines, may those forever be forgotten, and God Almighty cast the Enginocide upon them to purge all that filth from the suffering face of Mother Earth!" The words came naturally. Weekly sermons had them etched in his brain.

"Filth, um-hum," Master Rodriguez muttered under his breath. Then, louder, "Son, I was too young to remember, but my father told me many stories from the years BE, in great detail. To tell you the truth, I didn't hear about much filth, as far as I recall. Not more than in your average village street today."

"But sir, you surely understand we mean filth in the spiritual way!" Why did the elderly, respected Master argue with such basic, well-known truths?

"Ah well, you're right, Baxter. Pay no attention to the ramblings of a senile old fart."

They continued in silence for a few kilometers, each preoccupied with his own thoughts, to the accompaniment of measured hoof beats. Buck wrapped himself tighter in his poncho against the breeze.

"Instead of religious disputes, better tell me about your family. I might have known someone named Brennan back in the day. You're a Creekpointer, yes?"

"Yes, sir. But there's nothing unusual about my family." Someone showing interest in his lineage? That was a first. "Dad's a carpenter. Mom was a seamstress. She died eight years ago."

"Sorry to hear that, son."

"Thank you, sir. I never thought I'd be drafted. I mean, I wanted to—show me a boy who doesn't, right?—but didn't think I was good enough. Yes, my friends call me Big Buck because I'm big and strong, but everyone says I'm a knucklehead. Which I agree I am."

He skirted the subject of his ability without a second thought. Dad warned him never to mention it to anyone, and he'd had a lot of practice concealing it.

"But somehow the Army saw it right to recruit me. And now Master Sergeant sent me to the Marketplace, so here I am."

"Yeah, strange," mumbled Master Rodriguez absentmindedly. "What did you say your mom's name was?"

"Elinor, sir. Elinor Brennan." Why the sudden change of subject? And he had not mentioned his mother's name yet.

"Ah. Right. Her."

Odd. Odder yet was the lack of further comments. Soon, the colorful chaos of the Marketplace appeared beyond the bend.

Chapter 3

Ka Yi

September 21, 41 PE (one year earlier)

Ah, the coffee.

Ka Yi leaned toward the window until his forehead met the glass. Its chill pleasantly contrasted with the enveloping warmth of the bathrobe, and the "*Ouch! Ouch! Too hot!*" screaming of his fingertips, almost scalded by the cup.

He took a tiny, careful sip.

Coffee had started growing on him. He still enjoyed the aroma more than the bitter taste, but the stimulation was worth the questionable palatability. That, and the recognition of exclusivity: no one else in New Kowloon—neither the other members of the High Council nor the Chairman himself—had ever tried the legendary drink. Coffee featured in the stories of the past, half-forgotten, shrouded in mystery. The stuff of fairy tales, along with chocolate and tropical fruit.

Until his most recent voyage. A productive expedition to cap the navigation season. New contracts signed, sensitive information collected, and artfully crafted rumors seeded. The Station's interests kept at bay. And his crowning achievement of the year, the trade deal with Cleveland. How long had he been courting the Republic of Ohio? Four years? Five? Finally, he had driven the accord to a conclusion.

Coffee was a priceless personal gift from the Ohio Republic's Consul to celebrate the treaty. How had the Ohioans come into possession of this pungent treasure? It must have changed hands at least half a dozen times on its journey from much warmer places where the plant, evidently, was still cultivated. The amount of money spent, exotic items traded, and possibly blood spilled on its way to his cup... Unimaginable.

Should he share it with a Dragon or two, to cherish their shocked expressions? Nah. The treaty had already boosted his reputation. No need to rub the insult in. Let the coffee remain his little secret. *He* knew, and that was enough.

Ka Yi glanced through the twilight haze at the ships lazily bobbing in the harbor below and singled out the *Eastern Star*. His flagship. His fleet. An ideal excuse to escape the suffocating propriety of the Great Hive and explore the world. A smile touched his lips. Goosebumps, after all these years.

Ka Yi straightened, raised the cup and toasted his reflection in the window. Here's to you, father. Couldn't have been more wrong, old man. "You'll never amount to anything, Ka Yi. Why go through the motions? Be happy with the Onyx Dragon rank our family name guarantees you." Always underestimating, never supportive. *Thanks, Father, for making me who I've become. Not owing to, but despite.*

He turned at the sounds of a commotion outside his quarters. One day to rest. Was that too much to ask?

The door opened and Wu stepped in, disheveled, red-faced, and out of breath. Completely unlike him.

"Yes?" Ka Yi tilted his head. This promised to be *interesting*.

"Golden Dragon," Wu puffed, "there's been an attempt on your life."

"Oh? Surely, I would have noticed?"

"Apologies, Golden Dragon." Wu caught his breath. "My report lacked clarity. Let me rephrase."

"Please."

"An infiltrator was identified in your wing of the Hive, Golden Dragon, before he could approach you. Alas, he died in the ensuing struggle." Wu straightened his hair.

Ka Yi controlled his face, but not his heart rate. Targeted for an assassination. His imagination obligingly rendered an image of a stranger bursting through his door with a long knife in one hand and a black gun in another. His tongue stuck to his gums in an instantly dry mouth. Ka Yi brought the cup to his lips and took a gulp, scorching his palate and throat. He gasped, but at least that cleared his head.

"Unfortunate," he lisped. His mouth burned like the Seven Hells.

Wu's eyes grew wider.

"I mean, the assassin's death before you could question him," Ka Yi hurried to clarify. Forming words without touching any part of his mouth with his tongue proved challenging.

"Yes, Golden Dragon, I take full responsibility."

"Any leads?"

"Not yet, Golden Dragon. May I proceed with the investigation?"

"By all means, Wu. Thank you."

Ka Yi returned to the window. "Traitor," he said to the coffee and put the cup down on the table. He stared dubiously at his shaking hands and shoved them into the pockets of his bathrobe.

One day after his triumphant return. No way this was random. An inside job? A collaborator in the building? The whole affair reeked of The Station. But no proof, no proof... The Chief Inquisitor wouldn't leave a sloppy breadcrumb trail.

Ka Yi shivered, and not from the cold. Had the rules of the game just changed?

September 18, 42 PE

A tiny woman in a red dress finished serving the table which now burst with steamer baskets. She topped up their teacups in two smooth, perfect motions, bowed deeply, and disappeared from the room without meeting either man's eye or making a sound.

Chiang Xi Ming took this whole traditionalist thing way too seriously, but Ka Yi didn't judge. Traditional fashion had become all the rage in New Kowloon only recently, yet Xi Ming had kept a finger on the pulse of the Metropol's ever-shifting trends. Commendable.

In the subdued, wavering light of the paper lanterns, Ka Yi glanced under lowered eyelids at the head of New Kowloon's Buffalo Mission, and found his host inconspicuously studying him in the same manner. They smiled at each other.

The ambassador chuckled. "Shall we eat?"

Over the dinner, Ka Yi and his host exchanged small talk, the latest local rumors, and the gossip Ka Yi had collected in the ports he had visited on his way.

Having finished eating first, Xi Ming waited for Ka Yi to stop chewing, burp contentedly, and sip from his wine. "On to business?"

Ka Yi inclined his head.

"First, the regular shipments," said Xi Ming. "I am sorry to say we're not in the best shape. Of the five containers of coal we requested, Buffalo supplied three. Those are being loaded onto your ships as we speak. I will put pressure on the Union but can't tell when, or if, they will come through. I am not too optimistic, but if a minor miracle happens and they deliver within a month, I'll charter a train. Hopefully, The Station won't stoop to sabotage, and you'll have enough fuel to keep the Hive warm through the winter."

"You did everything in your power, Xi Ming. I applaud your dedication. The Union acting up is old news, and we've been exploring alternative venues. Rest assured, the Hive will not freeze."

Xi Ming bowed. "Not all my news is bad. Do you like surprises, Golden Dragon?"

"Depends on their nature."

"I have a feeling you won't be disappointed with this one. I secured a large consignment of paper. And—wait for it—ten bags of nine-millimeter primers!"

"But how?" Ka Yi allowed a hint of awe to alter his intonation. Xi Ming needed to know his accomplishments were appreciated. The Hive's scientists would be ecstatic to restock on paper. As for the primers, that was beyond spectacular. A single bag would suffice not only to pay off the Locksvillers but to leave them owing, keeping the eponymous locks open for Ka Yi's flotilla for years to come. The rest would go a long way in boosting the Security Force's reloading capabilities.

"Let that remain my secret." Xi Ming afforded a modest smile. "Now, to the more delicate subject, the collectibles. Alas, procuring additional items is becoming increasingly challenging."

Ka Yi suppressed a sigh. This monkey business was getting out of hand. A ridiculous waste of money and resources. Hopefully, this Chairman's reign doesn't last much longer. More frustratingly, each minute spent deliberating this nonsense delayed the final leg of his journey home. To *her*. Leading his fleet around the lakes was great, but leaving *her* behind for so long had become insufferable.

Ka Yi pursed his lips.

Xi Ming's tone gained apologetic notes. "We have tried to keep our interest under wraps by channeling the requests via different agents. But the Union has somehow sniffed out that we are the end buyers and jacked up the prices. They purport to be subtle about this, conjuring excuses like roads washed out by heavy rains, or a sudden spike in hostilities between Finger Lakes warlords that interfere with trade. You know how these barbarians can be, convinced their plots are elegant and elaborate."

"Naturally. Let them revel in their delusions. Bite the bullet and agree to their terms. But hint, in passing, that no further orders will be forthcoming. I will, in the meantime, check other channels."

"A wonderful scheme, Golden Dragon." Xi Ming clapped twice. "My bet is, Buffalo's avarice will get the better of them. With no one else interested in the Museum of Glass, they won't find other bidders. Eventually, they may conclude that a lower commission is preferable to no commission at all."

"Indeed."

"And if they get wind of your alternative dealings?"

"Even better. That will serve as an object lesson in competition. They'll learn not to play games with New Kowloon Trade House!"

Their cups rose synchronously. "To the Trade House!"

"One question, Golden Dragon." Xi Ming sipped the tea. "Why *are* we interested in those exhibits?"

"Chairman Wong."

"Chairman Wong," echoed Ming with a slow nod. "Of course."

Ka Yi tilted his head a fraction of a degree. "You disapprove of Chairman Wong's connoisseurship of antique arts?"

"I am in no position to judge the Honorable Chairman Wong." Xi Ming's face disclosed no sign of sarcasm, but he changed the subject. "Finally, regarding the other business..."

Ka Yi leaned back, half-closing his eyes. "Yes. No word from Syracuse?" If there were, Xi Ming would've opened with that. Too bad. "We've been courting those scientists for six months. I need them, Xi Ming. Now. Yesterday. Last year. I shouldn't need to remind you this is our top priority. Offer them the Sun and the Moon! We'll give them everything and still get the better end of the deal."

Chapter 4

Marc

September 21, 41 PE (one year earlier)

"My vacation? Enjoyable, sir, I can't complain. Getting used to the idea."

Before entering, Marc had decided bravado would best conceal his discomfort. With every breath, his self-confidence seeped away. Common knowledge claimed there was no hiding anything from this man. Why try? Weinberg seemed to possess a disturbing, supernatural ability to read Marc's mind, anyway. Might as well stop pretending.

Captain Weinberg owed a solid portion of his notoriety to having a penchant for mind games. Especially with the people he wanted to make uncomfortable. Not that he needed any tricks—his very presence made the most stolid visitors twitch and fidget. If the Head of Locksville's Intelligence Service considered you a person of interest, that hardly inspired confidence.

But Marc's conscience was squeaky clean. Wasn't it? Clean-ish. Okay, not too stained. What might the unnerving captain consider a transgression? A few things in Marc's past he wasn't too proud of. To be honest, more than a few.

After losing his parents at fourteen, the responsibility of fending for Aileen and himself had fallen squarely onto his shoulders. Being a provider and a guardian for a ten-year-old sister had become a full-time job. A job he had taken seriously, but which had led him into the gray area of the law... and beyond. But since his enlistment, he'd been straight like an arrow. A mildly crooked arrow. Would his past catch up with him now, all these years later? With an exemplary service record culminating in an honorable discharge four days ago, he must have been one of the few people truly having little to hide from this uncannily omniscient bastard.

First, convince yourself... Nope. Not working.

The invitation to the agency everyone shied away from made the back of Marc's neck itch. Something to do with Aileen? What had she got herself into this time? Enough to attract Weinberg's attention?

To make the matters worse, his armchair had proved itself beyond awkward. No matter how Marc shifted around, a comfortable position eluded him. Leaning back meant sinking into the depths of the chair with his knees up—utterly impolite. Settling at the edge of the cushion, like a kid waiting to be chided by a stern adult, gnawed at Marc's resolve. The armchair offered no winning strategy.

Marc gave up on winning the battle against himself and the damn piece of furniture, and took the fight to enemy territory, as he'd been taught. He looked up and met the host's ironic eyes.

"Captain, may I get another chair?"

The host's eyebrow arched, and a tiny smirk touched his lips. "How many visitors have ever requested another chair? Guess. Throw a number."

Marc's first impulse was to respond, "I don't know, sir!" but military discipline did not bind him anymore. Besides, his brazen counter-offensive must not be allowed to lose wind. "None?"

The captain's other eyebrow joined the first. "You're the fourth, actually."

"Is that a yes, sir?"

"Most definitely is."

Under Weinberg's amused gaze, Marc struggled out of the treacherous armchair and dragged a more conventional one to the spot in front of the desk.

He tested the seat. Not as soft and enveloping, but decidedly less troublesome.

The next words out of the captain's mouth sounded as if he were continuing a conversation interrupted shortly before—which they'd never had. Had they?

"Take another week to complete the celebratory tour of the Wine Country with your friends, as befits a freshly discharged CIU officer. Finish that stash of pot you expropriated from the dead Bozos. Monday after that, I expect to find you at your desk at oh-eight-hundred. Questions?"

At least, not another one of Aileen's fine messes.

Marc hadn't considered a career in Intelligence before, but this line of business held promise. An ideal outlet for his inner trickster to be put to use without compromising integrity. An opportunity to prove himself—to himself. A chance to find his niche after years of searching.

And the casual reference to the weed he'd picked off a bandit's body, which no one was supposed to know about? Must be the captain's curve ball. Ignore.

The delay in his response was almost imperceptible. "Oh-eight-hundred next Monday, sir."

Weinberg rose from his chair and offered a hand. "I'm delighted to see I was not wrong about you, Lieutenant Novak. Welcome to the Intelligence Service!"

"Thank you, sir. It's an honor."

"Say 'Hi' to Aileen for me."

Marc did not blink. Of course, his new boss knew and, apparently, didn't care. All the better. "Sure thing. One question, after all. If I may."

"Shoot."

"Will I get such an armchair?"

September 18, 42 PE

Marc pushed himself further into the ground.

The night cooperated with the ambush: not too bright, with the thin crescent moon low above the horizon, and intermittent clouds obscuring the stars. Enough to see, not enough to be seen. He was just another heap of foliage. The Golden Lions stood no chance.

Golden Lions, my ass. Shit Jackals, more like. Fucking degenerates.

The laws of natural selection applied to bandits, too. The most brutal, careless, and arrogant gangs had long since been extinct. To a great extent, thanks to the ruthless purging by Locksville's Counter Insurgency Unit. Thus, the only gangs to survive were those sufficiently cunning to not attract Locksville's attention. Those who understood the harm such attention could cause to their health.

Still, degenerates. All bandits were. A reference to their moral qualities, not an underestimation of the enemy. The resentment, rooted in the first post-E years, ran deep. Since its establishment, Locksville had stood for law and order. The brigands personified the opposite. That's why when a new gang started making waves between Rochester and the City, the locals scuttled off to the CIU, calling it in to help deal with their pest infestation. Fat payments for these exclusive services didn't hurt either.

With Marc's sketchy past, he was not without blemish himself. But that was different, right? Right? In his teenage years, he had not been averse to skullduggery. And putting food on the table for Aileen hadn't been the only reason. No, he took pleasure in devising clever, elegant schemes. And that frightened him the most. Was he adopted? Was he not a true Locksviller? What *was* a true Locksviller? Did those exist? Or was that an abstract concept, a product of propaganda? No one he knew fit the advertised image. Everybody had their flaws, some worse than others. Yet, they all shared one understanding: violent crime was unconscionable. Difference? Difference. A huge one. Enough to call the bandits degenerates and feel good about that.

Such subtleties had never preoccupied Locksville's Defense Council. That's how Marc found himself embedded in the CIU force here, in the bush, in the no-man's-land between the Hamilton Emirate and Five Points. The Golden Lions had made one mistake too many, drawing The Station's ire with an audacious attack on a train. Banditry was banditry regardless of its target, so when the Railroad slavers proposed a cleanup contract, the Council promptly acceded. Locksvillers' antipathy toward the Stationers, whose presence in the region they barely tolerated, played no role.

CIU trackers excelled in their art. After they'd identified the trail the Golden Lions used to retreat to their hideout, all that remained was for the two platoons to set up an L-shaped ambush and wait. Marc positioned his platoon along the side of the trail. Captain Robertson's blocked the exit point.

An excruciatingly slow day had followed. A day of chewing cold, dry food and peeing into a bottle. Of judiciously considering which itch to scratch. Of allowing mosquitoes to buzz around his ears without swatting them. Of letting the thoughts run amok in his head.

Well into the second night, enemy scouts showed up, their horses cautiously stepping on the edges of the path.

A dry branch crunched under a hoof not a foot away. Danger tingled Marc's nostrils. The hunter's acute awareness spiked—of the cool ground below and the moist leaves above, of his surroundings, of the entire world. Of being alive. Marc forced his breath to slow down. Easy to forget to breathe in moments like these, and when you need to open fire, start gasping for air, throwing your aim out of whack.

As expected, the riders passed virtually on top of the ambush, noticing nothing untoward. But something wasn't right, nagging at Marc at the edge of his attention. The Lions showed the most advanced tactics and discipline he had seen in his military career. The gang fielded a small recon force, the main body with outriders to its sides, and a rearguard. Far too sophisticated for a glorified bunch of rural outlaws. Marc's instincts were screaming, and he'd learned to trust them as a sure way to increase his longevity. Something was out of place. Shit, what? Were the bandits improving, learning from the best? That didn't matter. At the end of the day, the right tactics were worth little with the wrong people. Nice try, assholes.

Marc counted breaths. Ninety-four later, the signal came. The closing fire team waited for the Lions' rearguard to pass and called the attack. Two owl hoots. The trap slammed shut.

Crossbows thrummed, eliminating the scouts and the outriders. A brief but fierce fusillade followed, mowing down the rearguard and a trailing portion of the main force, but stopping short of finishing the job. The ambush wasn't allowed to end with zero bandits standing. What a shame.

Violence. Unconscionable. Remember? Who is a degenerate now?

But this wasn't blood thirst, nor did Marc take joy in killing. In the sparsely populated world, human life held supreme value. With one caveat: that didn't apply to bandits. He was only being thorough. Not a violent crime, but a violent retribution.

After the initial shock, the gang reacted competently, despite the heavy losses. The survivors dismounted and regrouped, taking cover behind their horses in a rough semicircle.

"Locksville CIU!" Captain Robertson bellowed at the top of his lungs. "Lay down your weapons and surrender! Resist, and be shot!"

A burst of automatic fire aimed in the general direction of the captain's voice lit the night. A single, louder bark of a high caliber rifle cut it off.

"Was I not clear?" roared Robertson. "Step out with your hands up! No sudden movements!"

"Ceasefire, ceasefire!" commanded an authoritative voice on the trail. "Alright, we surrender!"

Alas, one of the core conditions of The Station's contract demanded the Lions' commanders delivered alive. For summary sentencing, or some other morally ambiguous reason. Whatever. He had his orders. But if he were in the Lions' shoes, he sure would have preferred to die, rather than end up a lifer in the slavers' labor force. For the bandits, though... A suitably cruel punishment.

Quarter of an hour later, the operation ended. The lightly injured were treated; the mortally wounded given coup de grâce; the dead dragged into the nearby ravine; the survivors tied into a chain with a rope. Weapons and equipment—collected into a sizable pile.

No celebration ensued, no conversation. This was business. Eliminate the threat, secure the package, deliver to the customer. Clean and professional. What they trained for. What they got paid for.

Amazed by the lack of attention, the gang's head honcho attempted to attract some. But instead of spewing profanities, as Marc expected, the chieftain growled to the captain a much less obvious, "Do you know who you're messing with here?"

Robertson pointedly ignored the Lions' general, ordering all prisoners gagged.

The ringleader's unusual behavior triggered something in Marc's brain and brought back the nagging sensation he had diligently suppressed for the duration of the firefight.

Something was seriously off about this bunch of miscreants.

And then it hit him.

What's the one thing all gangs have in common? Their *uncommonality*. As no two degenerates came from the same background, no two pieces of their ragtag equipment shared provenance. Bought, stolen, looted, picked off dead bodies. Guaranteed to be different.

Marc turned to the pile of the confiscated firearms. All identical. Standard issue.

Chapter 5

Rajan

September 21, 41 PE (one year earlier)

Rajan nestled in a dry spot by the fence, absorbing the last warmth of the low, toothless afternoon sun. The rough concrete slab greeted his calloused hands like a friend. The only friendly thing around.

The Masters joined their counterparts from the other train. Supervisors from both teams assembled alongside a tumbled shack for a banter. They often burst into loud laughter, and only occasionally glanced at the haulers, more out of habit than fear of what the ragtag trash might be scheming. Disinterested eyes, unworried faces. The haulers, happy to relish every minute of rest, mingled too, but in distinct groups of their own: lifers with lifers, workers with workers.

Rajan joined neither. Idle banter with the other workers? Nah. And he sure as Seven Hells had nothing to discuss with the lifer scum. He shut his eyes. Not a thing worth watching, anyway. And better not to see the Railroad Marshal connecting the two trains. His every movement brought closer the moment Rajan would have to stand up and put on the fucking harness.

It had been a long day. As usual. Rajan's half of the team had combed an industrial zone for anything useful. The Masters determined the usefulness, sniffing around and pointing at seemingly random items for the haulers to pick up and load onto the train. The other half had disassembled a dead-end railroad segment to bring the harvested materials to The Station. The two groups had met again at the switch, pulled the cars onto one track, and were preparing to head back.

The slavers would say "back home". To Rajan, The Station had not become a home, and never would. It had *not* been for three years. Three fucking years. To be precise, two years, ten months, eighteen days. Four years, one month, thirteen days left. At no time had he been good at counting and still wasn't, but these two numbers—the time spent with the slavers and the time left on his "contract"—he could recite any moment, day or night. He'd be twenty-one when it was over. If he survived, or didn't get accused of one of the myriad offences that would give the Masters the excuse to brand him a lifer. It really took little. At times, no more than crossing paths with a slaver in a foul mood. If that happened to him, he'd kill himself. Better than being associated with those lifer animals, and having nothing to look forward to.

"Yo, Rajan."

Hamid, of course. Who else? Rajan looked away, but the guy was not easily deterred.

Squatting by his side, Hamid started gibbering. Words flew out of his mouth like torrential rain hitting tin roof. "You're gonna want to hear este, amigo. A secret, sí?"

Whenever Hamid had something to say—which was pretty much every waking moment—he was convinced everyone around was eager to listen.

Rajan sighed. Why couldn't everybody just leave him alone? He didn't say that out loud. Lately, he had not been saying much out loud. That would have been a bother. Bothering brought nothing but more labor and pain. Keeping to himself promised the least hassle.

This attitude wasn't news to Hamid, but he went on as if Rajan had expressed the keenest interest. "This chica, Maria, know her? Sometimes, me and her, we do the nasty, sí?" He winked.

Rajan rolled his eyes. "*That's* your secret?"

"Espera, amigo, there's more! A slaver, Master Duerte, has his eye on her too. And he talks." Hamid stared at Rajan meaningfully, waiting for a reaction. Seeing none, he repeated, "He *talks*. You know? Talks *stuff*."

Rajan had enough. "Qué mierda you yammerin' about? This goin' anywhere?"

Hamid grinned victoriously. "He tells her things Masters tell no one! And she tells me!"

This could be interesting, for a change. Rajan motioned for Hamid to go on.

"She tells me Marshals can build a machine that hauls trains! Get it? A machine for trains, amigo. No more pulling the strap, just load stuff and lay rails, sí?"

Rajan's interest died as quickly as it had spiked. Hamid must be high on the disgusting shit the lifers had been secretly cooking in their barracks.

Supervisors' whistles announced an end to the brief respite. Rajan rose to his feet, stretched, producing a series of cracks in his spine, and trudged off to pick up the hated harness. He didn't spare Hamid another glance.

Really. Slavers and machines. Not funny.
But the thought lodged like a splinter deep under his skin.

September 19, 42 PE

"Fucking slavers!"

Shapeless blotches swam in and out of Rajan's vision. His shoulders burned, chafed raw under the dirty shirt suffused with stale sweat. His thighs and calves screamed, and his knees had turned into rusty swivels. The piercing pain shooting through his lower back with every step prevented him from concentrating on anything else.

"F-f-fucking slavers!" he mumbled again with his cracked, dry lips. For the hundredth time that day, or the thousandth, or the ten-thousandth. None of his teammates acknowledged his words. Because they'd got used to his mumbling, or because no sound came out of his parched throat. Or because the sentiment echoed their thoughts too: *fucking slavers!*

Whatever disagreements Team Five members may have had, those took a backseat behind their blinding hatred toward the Masters. The tougher the job, the hotter the hatred. And man, was this job tough! The most grueling in his accursed railroad hauler career. That ought to say something.

Coming from a wide variety of backgrounds, Rajan and his companions had a lot of choice words in different languages for their supervisors and the trader elites. They put all these words to use regularly and inventively. But when the going got difficult, and their minds got numb, all everyone could say was, "Fucking slavers!"

This numbing was coming to Rajan easier and easier. Sometimes, he could go for days on end without using his brain. Not a single thought other than "fucking slavers!"

The Masters hated to be called slavers and kept insisting they were not. Officially, they referred to the slaves as "workers". And the Masters—they simply provided the workers with an opportunity to earn a living. That this opportunity came with a strict contract was supposed to be an insignificant detail.

But seriously, how did this happen? How could someone at The Station screw up so badly? And no one noticed?

Many things could be—and were!—said about the Masters, but "stupid" was not one of those. Only the strongest, toughest slaves got assigned to hauler teams. Not a place for the feeble. Rajan, a big, sturdy boy, had not been sent on a hauling job until the first two years of his contract were up, when he turned sixteen. The Masters had figured, to an impressive level of precision, the art of calculating the number of haulers each kind of run required. Whatever the job, they knew exactly what the size of the assigned team should be. Not too big—why waste labor-power and make work too easy for the slaves?—but also not too small, because having slaves, a valuable commodity, die of overexertion was bad for business. Besides, no one wanted a car loaded with goods to become stranded, inviting bandit raids, looting by rural zombies, and whatnot.

Masters rarely screwed up. Except this time, they had. Big time.

Rajan's team was pulling two cars, not one. In itself, a common occurrence, he'd taken part in hauling monstrous four-car trains too. But this time, instead of having two full teams of thirty, only forty haulers were sent in total.

On the way there—wherever "there" might be, nobody told the slaves shit—they'd managed somehow. The outgoing cargo was grapes and wine. Two days later, at the destination, they loaded the boxcar up to its ceiling. With what? Who knew? Who cared? He wasn't sixteen anymore, way past idle curiosity. But it was fucking massive. Wooden boxes nailed shut, each heavy as all sins in the Seven Hells. Lots of them. And not nearly enough haulers. Somebody was going to get hurt.

Somebody did.

To his right, Eight Fingers misstepped, yelped, and landed awkwardly onto his ass. He clutched his foot, shrieking, "Me ankle! Bugger, me ankle! It's fucken' broke!"

A rare shitstain, even compared to his buddies, with a long and diverse career as horse thief, rapist, and murderer. The Station's guards had cut his adventures short last year, when they caught him breaking into a railroad car parked for the night. He shot one of them and injured another before they overpowered him, and for that crime had both of his index fingers chopped off to prevent him from pulling a trigger ever again. The lifer brand on his cheek still shone red. In a few years, it would fade into pink, then white. If he survived that long, which was not a given. Lifers didn't have an impressive life expectancy.

Rajan hated lifers. Most of the "workers" did. And the lifers hated them back alright. Lifers hated everyone. Traders for owning them. Supervisors for breaking in fresh convicts and enforcing discipline. Free folks for being free. "Workers" for being slated for eventual freedom—a fact that must have burned holes through the lifers' soulless hearts. Often, they hated each other, and it didn't matter why.

Divide and conquer. The fucking slavers were cunning that way.

That scum busting his ankle was the highlight of the day, his cries—music to Rajan's ears. *Oh. Wait. Fuck.* Thanks to this clumsy loser, Team Five was even shorter now, bringing the job one step closer to impossible.

On a haul, everyone tolerated the other team members as long as both groups worked their asses off equally. Neither could move the train an inch on their own. This time, it already had been crawling at the speed of a dying snail. With three lifers dropping the straps and rushing to help their pal, it came to a halt.

The supervisors peeked from under the awning on the cargo car roof. Three of the five climbed down, cursing the haulers along with their male, female, and bestial ancestors. One, Simon, came up to check on Eight Fingers' foot. The other two hung back to secure the scene. Damian leisurely twirled a baton in the air, Stefan held his across his shoulders. Simon crouched over the injured lifer's leg and tried to pry his hands off, but Eight Fingers wouldn't let him.

"Let go, you moron, show me your foot!" Simon grumbled, struggling to pull the lifer's hands apart.

Eight Fingers released his boot, outstretching his arms. The supervisor, still clutching his wrists, lost balance and dove, face down, to the ground. Stunned by the impact, he was pushing himself to his knees when Eight Fingers picked up a hefty stone and swung it, sinking it into Simon's head with a sickening wet crack. The supervisor's body convulsed and went limp.

Stefan reacted first. He raised the baton and darted toward Eight Fingers, who was still sitting on the ground with a vicious grin. Before the weapon connected, two other lifers tackled the supervisor and began pounding at him. Another of Eight Fingers' buddies intercepted Damian's baton mid-air, wrenched it out of his hand, and used it against him. Within several heartbeats, the third supervisor hit the ground, with a lifer straddling his chest and leaning on the baton to crush his windpipe.

Rajan forgot to breathe. This was wrong, all wrong. The supervisors were merciless sons of bitches, but the world had its order. And this order was crumbling before Rajan's eyes, being smashed along with Simon's skull and Damian's throat.

Shots rang from the roof of the railcar, buzzing inches above the haulers' heads. Bullets clicked and ricocheted off the gravel a dozen steps behind them, sending small stones scattering. The message to the rioters was clear: lie down and quit fooling around! Rajan dropped to the ground, mindless of the sharp stone edges biting into his knees, palms, and cheek. Around him, the haulers heeded the warning.

But a few lifers, including miraculously healed Eight Fingers and his murderous cronies, ran toward the railcar at the determined jog of experienced predators. A well-aimed shot cut down one of them, then another crumbled and rolled. But four or five more were already climbing up the sides of the car, disappearing inside the guard post. A few shots, shouts, sounds of desperate struggle... And an eerie, shellshocked silence enveloped everything. Haulers lying on the ground lifted their heads, looking around and at each other, trying to make sense of what had happened and figure out what to do next.

Rajan's neighbor gasped. Rajan followed his gaze to the train and tried to curse, but his dry and slack mouth produced no sound. Eight Fingers stood in the passenger car door, grinning victoriously. In each hand he held a severed trader's head, raised for everyone to witness. Blood dripped down his arms. Lifers' whoops and hoots welcomed the horrific tableau.

Time stopped. Rajan stared at the dark drops falling slowly, too slowly, almost hanging in the air. Something thunderous thumped in his ears. A heartbeat. Drop. A heartbeat. Drop. Then other sounds mixed in, and time resumed its rush forward. Cheers, but from another direction. The traders' heads entranced him, but something worse was coming. Rajan forced his neck to turn. A large group of armed riders had emerged from the nearby trees and were approaching the stopped train at a lazy trot.

Cobwebs of ideas, too gossamer to catch, flitted through the empty space that was Rajan's mind. That with the supervisors gone, nothing was holding the fragile balance between the lifers and the workers. That the workers didn't stand a chance if a fight were to break out between them and the lifers. That it was too much of a coincidence that Eight Fingers' unfortunate accident happened close to the forest concealing a friendly gang. That the bandits weren't likely to leave any living witnesses.

All of that mattered, and none of it did. Rajan's most primal instincts took over. If he wanted to see tomorrow, he'd better be somewhere else when those riders reached the train. He rolled over the rails and down the far side of the embankment, and sprinted to the tree line in a low crouch. Nobody noticed his escape. Or did, but didn't care to chase an escaped slave.

Chapter 6

Buck

September 19, 42 PE

Buck's eyes routinely scanned the aisles.

Look at me, just arrived—and already doing things "routinely".

But that was the truth.

He'd been to the Marketplace before, of course, accompanying his parents to the Spring and Fall Fairs, and on countless other occasions. This time was different: he wasn't visiting; he was on duty. Other people *came* to the Marketplace; he *was* here, a part of it.

When he arrived, Sergeant Gomez took him into an empty room in the Marketplace Council building and subjected him to an endless stream of instructions. Was that only an hour? Hard to believe. At first, these orders appeared confusing, contradicting each other. To make matters worse, the sergeant loved big words, and most of those flew over Buck's head without recognition. Eventually, Buck got the key idea: do nothing that may get Sergeant Gomez in trouble. The goal was to preserve the peace. Not to settle disputes, nor to determine who's right and who's wrong. Those were the Council's prerogatives.

"Prerogatives" was the sergeant's exact word. Buck had no clue what it meant, but it sounded similar to "pierogies", a dish Mom and Dad had once bought to celebrate his eighth birthday. He couldn't help but imagine the Honorable Councilors sitting around their table, eating pierogies, and deciding who's right and who's wrong. The Council's *pierogatives*. He stifled a snicker and waved the bizarre image away.

After that, the sergeant dispatched him to the post on a raised, canopied platform in the center of General Merchandise. His favorite quarter, dealing with everything that didn't belong in Food, Tools, or Clothes.

Food was, well, *food*; important, respected; routine, mostly boring—with a few exceptions like the pierogies.

Tools were no less important, but also sensitive. The Council closely monitored the trade in that quarter to ensure no overly complex items accidentally found their way onto a counter. That would be blasphemy.

Clothes were the necessary evil. In his childhood days, Buck had quietly hated the endless hours spent trying on pants, shirts, and shoes—until they'd find something that fit both his thick build and his parents' thin wallet.

General Merchandise was unlike anything else. Toy booths, his favorite as a child. Jewelry stands where Mom used to hover. The two of them had wandered the lanes and alleys of this quarter while Dad haggled over woodworking equipment in the Tools. Then the three of them would meet and have a holiday family lunch—hot corn, sweet pastries, and cider. Since Mom's passing away, the Marketplace had never been the same. Couldn't be. For a year, Dad and he skipped the Fairs, and when they'd returned, it was all about business. Besides the E Day, of course. Those had always been special, but the last one stood out. His first almost-adult one.

September 21, 41 PE (one year earlier)

The E Day. The New Year. His favorite holiday. Still. Despite everything.

In the past, time would fly so fast it had always left Buck vaguely disappointed when the celebrations ended. The precious festival atmosphere, the elation of the crowds, the tickling expectation of what the next year had in store... Not this year. The last part of the festival couldn't come too soon. Buck gladly would have skipped the rest. Was this what growing up was all about? Did every seventeen-year-old go through a similar change of heart?

As usual, the ceremony had begun with the Thanksgiving to Mother Earth, recited in chorus by the five High Priests. Buck whispered along, knowing the words by heart. They were a part of the Food Blessing, but hearing them from the stage on this solemn occasion always gave him goosebumps. The prayer was beautiful—and, thank God, short.

The Ritual of the Melting followed, an allegorical reenactment of the cleansing Enginocide. This year, the faithful had scraped up fewer machines than before, a sign that the world may be running out of dead machines. A good thing, no?

A blacksmith melted the accursed abominations with a portable foundry. The evil machines, painted in shiny black and vivid red, ominous and fascinating, succumbed to the heat of the crucible. This part of the Ritual was so beautifully mystical, Buck's impatience receded. The liquid metal flowed into casts, producing simple tools of honest labor. But then the High Priest started auctioning those off, and the magic of the moment dissipated. People who, unlike Dad, wouldn't know which way to hold these tools vied to outbid each other, proving to their neighbors how strong they were in their Faith. Two-faced liars. This was wrong, not what the Faith was all about. At last, the auction ended, and the next phase of the celebrations kicked in.

The High Priest lit the enormous, three-story tall Simplification bonfire, built the day before in a communal effort. The flame rushed with a ferocious *whoosh* into the darkening sky, to the gasps and cheers of the audience. Families affluent enough to afford actual books approached and threw those into the fire, opening the ceremony. Others followed with the straw, wood, or canvas book-shaped items, or mere scraps of paper.

This used to be Buck's favorite part. The joyful fire, fabulously attractive and scarily hot, separated the ending year from the coming one. Like all the children, Buck had enjoyed the wish-making while feeding the red beast. The louder you shouted over the deafening roar of the fire and the clamoring of the crowd, the greater were the chances the wish would be fulfilled. So said the legends. Indeed, many times Buck had received the toys he'd asked the fire for. Clearly, mysterious supernatural forces were at work.

Until the year Mom fell ill. Needless to say, on that E Day, Buck had asked the fire to heal her. Yet that one time, the only time that had truly mattered, no miracle had occurred. Maybe he hadn't yelled loudly enough.

Since then, he had never come close to the Simplification fire again. The heartache of the loss, which had dulled with the passing years, spiked on special occasions like this. How nice it would've been to be a regular kid again, without a worry in the world. A kid who could enjoy the merry wish-making and jumping around with his friends—happy, laughing, frenzied.

Was he still a child? Could he still ask the fire for a wish? Seventeen, taller and wider in the shoulders than many adults, he'd look unseemly, running and cheering. That was okay. He could make a wish, anyway. Silently, in his heart. After all, the person responsible for fulfilling his childhood requests stood right next to him, glancing at Buck with barely concealed pride.

Dad had grown noticeably older in the last year. Though this process had sped up in Mom's absence, he was still a strong man. Yet, strong or not, Dad possessed no ability to help Buck with his dearest desire this time.

Buck had become numb by the time screaming trumpets announced what he'd been waiting for—the parade. His heart fluttered. *That* was where he wanted to be. *Who* he wanted to be. To march through the Main Square next year, shoulder to shoulder with other camo-clad soldiers, clutching his own rifle, a black beret sitting askew on his head. He'd be content with the last row, far behind Colonel on his black horse, as long as he was there, and not watching from the throng of rejoicing civilians.

That was his wish. His future. Or was it?

He'd been going through the weekly Militia training for years, but that carried no guarantees. Every Five Points boy trained; only a few were selected. He was plenty strong, but the Army equally valued quick wits, and he wasn't the sharpest tool in the box. No sense denying the obvious. Would he make the cut? That would open the door to so many adventures! His throat constricted. If not, then what? Helping Dad in the workshop? Being a carpenter for the rest of his life? Sure, a decent, respectable job. But to go through day after boring day, knowing it could have been so much more? A bitter taste filled his mouth.

He would know in half a year. An eternity.

Did being an adult mean having to deal with the uncertainty? What a mess. For one day, his favorite holiday, wasn't he allowed this last chance to be a kid?

September 19, 42 PE

Last year's memories sent his heart racing. He made it! Into the Army, and even to the Marketplace Duty! This E Day was going to be different.

He kept a stone face, and only an occasional grin sneaked past his guard. Particularly when a small flock of young girls passed by, looking him over and giggling.

Earlier in the day, Buck's head had been swiveling nonstop, taking in the familiar and strange colors, the tickling mixture of smells, and the cacophony of sounds. By noon, his senses were saturated. He'd become a seasoned Marketplace Guardian.

He allayed a couple of brewing conflicts—by merely coming close to the bickering parties and touching the handle of his cudgel. Combined with his imposing bulk, or his uniform, or both, that achieved the required effect, without him having to say a word. The crowd parted respectfully, the quarrelers lost interest in the subject of their dispute, and the confrontation dissipated.

After the second such occurrence, Sergeant Gomez—who, as it turned out, had been watching Buck from a distance—came by and commended him on his performance. "Keep that up for two more days, bud," he said, patting Buck on the shoulder, "and you'll go back with my favorable recommendation. I had my expectations set to a low bar, but you're doing pretty well so far. Just don't get all proud and carried away now"—he smiled crookedly—"because that's when you screw up."

Well past noon, another commotion developed in the Religious Items aisle. Buck adjusted the cudgel on his belt, formed a confident expression, and trod with solid authority through the gaggle of marketgoers.

His arrival at the scene achieved zero deterrence. Less than zero: instead of dying down, the shouts became only more enraged.

One party was a seller, a sputtering red-faced middle-aged man with a shining bald patch on his round head. His adversary was a tall and slender young woman, blushed as only fair-skinned freckled redheads can be.

Two other salesmen loomed sullenly behind the girl, blocking her escape route. An unnecessary precaution, since she was the one on the offensive.

"Ignorant fanatic!" she yelled, leaning into the bald man's face, with her fists clenched at her sides and lips curved in disgust. Buck got momentarily transfixed by those bright red lips. The girl was like a flame, with her shock of bronze hair blowing in the wind.

Snapping out of his trance, Buck deployed his deepest voice. "What's going on here?" The inquiry needed to sound confident, as if he knew what he was doing. Because, frankly, he didn't have the greenest clue. The sergeant's briefing did not cover such situations.

Both opponents cut the invectives mid-sentence to scan him over, then fervently resumed their tirades. Buck closed his eyes. Once, on a boring morning duty back at the Base, he had thrown a pebble into a tree full of chirping sparrows. The birds had shut up for a moment, only to restart their twittering with doubled intensity, indignant at the human's rudeness. Here, his words produced the same effect.

Buck raised his hand, palm forward. "One by one. Merchant, you first."

The girl pursed her lips and frowned, but complied. The merchant graced Buck with a grateful bobbing of his head.

"The name's Bentley, sir soldier, Thomas Bentley. I'm a respected, law-abiding trader, everybody knows that. I sell religious artifacts for the rituals of our beloved Faith. And this godless, unholy heretic here, this blasphemous... *creature*... wanted me to sell her"—he dramatically lowered his voice—"books!"

A murmur swept through the dense crowd surrounding the scene.

"And not just any books, sir soldier. She asked for books about the Seven Hells!"

His words were met with startled gasps all around.

"You see, sir soldier," said the merchant, ingratiatingly catching Buck's eye, "I carry a few of these, you know, *items* for the Simplification ceremony. Some pious congregants can afford a proper book for burning on that holiest of nights. I've got many substitutes, too, catering to any taste and budget. Straw, wood, canvas, you name it—I got it."

Buck knotted his brows and nodded, covering up his discomfort. His family hadn't been religious—or rich—enough to afford anything beyond the simplest straw books. He'd never held a real one. A *book* touching his hands? He shuddered at the image.

"But," continued Bentley, "only the Council or a Preacher may sanction a purchase of the genuine items. I suspected she wasn't the real deal, I did, from the moment she stopped before my stand, so I asked her for a token of approval. I am an honest merchant, sir soldier, I always follow the rules! In my sensitive trade, that is doubly important! And I caught her red-handed, for what she is—a heretic!" He pointed an accusatory finger at the girl. "A heathen! An infidel! If we aren't strong in our Faith, the likes of her will bring another E upon us, God Almighty forbid!"

The muffled muttering around rose to a hum, Signs of Faith showing all over.

Buck was decidedly out of his depth, but he couldn't walk away to call Sergeant Gomez. If he did, the conflict was guaranteed to spiral out of control. Not that Buck had got much control over it as it was... He swallowed and turned to the girl. During Bentley's speech, she opened her mouth several times, intending to interject, but met Buck's disapproving stare and remained silent.

"What is... ah... your version of the events, Miss?"

"Yes," she stared at him down her nose, "I wanted to buy his books." Emboldened by the spectators' astonishment, she raised her voice, "Yes, books!" Then shouted, "Books! Books! Here, see? I said it, and the world didn't end! You dumb, superstitious bunch, with your boring miserable lives! Books don't kill people! People kill people!"

Buck's hands folded into a Sign of Faith of their own volition. "I see," he said. This was trouble. Trouble?! This was the mother of all trouble! Sergeant Gomez would not be happy, no question about that. Buck had to pacify the conflict, and fast.

"If nobody is willing to... ah... press charges..." His desperate improvisation came out weak and high-pitched. Buck cleared his throat, restoring a measure of depth to his voice. "Everyone, disperse and go about your business. I'll make sure the young lady... ah... leaves the Marketplace."

"What?!" the girl and the merchant erupted at once.

"I am not going anywhere!" Her indignation was palpable. "Why should I?"

"Of course, I will press charges!" Bentley toned down his words. "This cannot go unpunished, sir soldier."

An opportunity for Buck to use his excellent memory for complex phrases he didn't fully understand.

"Sir," said Buck, "it takes at least three plaintiffs pressing charges for an accused to be brought before the Council." The exact rule Sergeant Gomez had mentioned in the briefing. Such words rolled nicely off the tongue and had a tendency to impress people.

Not this time. Bentley looked at his two colleagues lingering behind the girl. "Archie, Ronald, we've had our share of disagreements, I admit, but this?"—he gestured at his opponent—"This can't be tolerated. Press charges with me!"

The men exchanged sulky glances and yielded to the request.

Buck stiffened. "Come with me to the Council building."

He attempted to take the girl by the elbow, but she wriggled out of his grip and scowled. "Don't you dare touch me, oaf!" She jerked her shoulder once again, as if to get further away from Buck's reach. "Brainless martinet! I'll walk."

"As you wish, Miss." Hopefully that sounded indifferent.

"Martinet"? Never heard the word, but "brainless"... all too familiar.

Why would she call him that? He did nothing to offend her!

"I'll take it from here, Private Brennan." Sergeant Gomez appeared at the scene, effortlessly splitting the mob. He projected unperturbed confidence, but his voice had an edge to it.

"Private," he whispered, leaning close to Buck, "are you trying to involve me in some sort of trouble? Which part of 'peace' did you not understand? Never mind, I'll deal with you later."

Louder, he announced, "I'll escort Miss McPherson and the plaintiffs to the Council for a hearing."

Facing Buck again, "Return to your post, Private."

Buck saluted, squelching the urge to justify his actions. The hot mess was taken off his hands, but the sergeant's displeasure promised consequences. Real, mortifying consequences. But... But... How could anyone have handled the situation differently?

With nothing left to do, Buck woodenly marched to his canopy and looked back. The small procession made its way to the three-story building of the Council towering above the Main Square. Bystanders spewed curses at the girl and spit on the ground, but nobody attempted anything too stupid in the intimidating presence of Sergeant Gomez.

Miss McPherson, the sergeant said. She must be famous here, if he knew her name.

Buck stood at his post, turning his head this way and that as he was supposed to, but seeing nothing around. The burning gaze of the girl's impossibly green eyes took full, undivided control of his mind. Was she a witch? Did she put a spell on him?

Two hours—ages!—later, Gomez's head reappeared, bobbing above the sea of the market-goers. As he cleaved the crowd with his forceful stride, the rest of his bulky frame came into view. Miss McPherson's fiery hair was hard to miss in his wake. Her face, pale and dreary, still radiated defiance.

Buck descended from his observation platform in time to meet the sergeant and stand to attention.

"Private Brennan."

Buck searched for any hint of what might be in stock for him, but his commander's inscrutable face disclosed nothing.

"Janet McPherson faced the Marketplace Council on the charges of blasphemy and heresy. The Council cleared her of these accusations but found her guilty of repeatedly disturbing the public peace. Her penalty: banishment from the Marketplace grounds for a year starting today, and a 'half-half' fine on her family."

Buck almost winced at that, but kept a straight face. A nauseating void opened in his stomach, as if he were to blame for this harsh verdict. If it were him and Dad, they would not have survived without half their food for half a year.

"You, Brennan," the sergeant continued, "have made a mess. Deal with its aftermath. Escort Miss McPherson to Hillcrest Community House, hand her over to their representatives, and inform them of the sentence. Once done, return to your post. Clear?"

"Sir, yes, sir!" Buck didn't dare ask if he was in trouble. He'd find out soon enough. Oh, and her name was Janet.

The sergeant stepped aside. Janet gave Buck an ireful look, but followed.

He walked silently by her side, gathering courage. His darn bashfulness, especially around pretty girls... *Come on, say something!* "Miss McPherson..."

She didn't react. Not a glance in his direction. May as well take that as permission to continue. "You seem to think what's happened was somehow my fault..."

She still refused to acknowledge his presence. "I promise I had no foul intentions." Buck shot out the apologetic words before the impending stuttering began. "I was only carrying out my duty, preserving the peace—"

She swerved to him so abruptly he recoiled. "Oh, you're as bad as these obtuse hagglers, and those self-righteous councilors!" Her eyes gleamed. "Just as bad, or worse!" She didn't shout, but each word she spat landed like a slap on Buck's cheeks. His ears burned.

"And you don't have the slightest idea what's wrong, do you?" Janet's voice had lost the anger, leaving tiredness and gloom.

Buck half shrugged, half shook his head, attentively studying the toes of his dusty uniform boots.

"Yeah, that's what I thought." She resumed the walk.

"Uh, Janet?" he asked her stiff back.

She stopped but didn't turn around.

Buck closed the distance in two steps. "Please..." A thick stew of words, all wrong, clogged his skull. His stupid—martinet?—brain fruitlessly tried to string a simple sentence together. "Please tell me."

She examined him. "Maybe you are not completely lost for humanity yet. Er... Brennan, is it?"

Buck vigorously bobbed his head. She remembered his name!

Janet smirked. "Okay. What's wrong is that you allow all these evil, illiterate, power-hungry monsters to perpetuate the existing ridiculous stagnation!"

Buck blinked. Then blinked again. Those were all impossibly high-browed words, but enough was clear: in her opinion, he helped bad people do not-so-good things. How could that be? He was doing precisely what he was supposed to!

"But Janet— Pardon, Miss McPherson, if I hadn't stepped in back in the General Merchandise," he pointed over the shoulder with a thumb, for emphasis, "that mob could've lynched you!"

The tiny spark of interest in her eyes died. Her gaze turned flat and cold again. "Oh. Right." Her words rang like prickly icicles. "You're my savior now. Hilarious." Her face showed no sign of amusement. "Let's go, Private. You've got unpleasant news to deliver to my village folk. I'm sure *they* will see you for the hero you believe you are."

Buck took the hint. Arguing no further, he turned and walked. Janet paced behind, pointedly keeping a distance that said, above anything else, "I don't want to have anything to do with you." That stung far worse than her words.

Community Houses of all the Five Points surrounded the Main Square of the Marketplace, together with the Council building forming a hexagon.

Buck's entry into the reception area of the Hillcrest House triggered an interesting transformation of the clerk's face, from a polite interest toward someone breaking his boredom, through mild curiosity, all the way to concern when he realized Buck was wearing a soldier's uniform. Then, as Janet followed over the threshold, annoyance took undivided hold.

The official stood up. "I'm Peter Hansson, the Second Secretary. Welcome to our Community House, soldier. May I assume that an escapade by Miss McPherson here is what brings you visiting?"

Buck introduced himself and succinctly described the earlier events. When he reached the punishment details, the Second Secretary's face darkened.

"The McPhersons are doing well, but this won't be easy for them." A pause. "The community will assist them through this period."

"I wish I could change the outcome," Buck blurted. He wasn't supposed to sympathize with any side of the conflict, but couldn't help it. The other side wasn't present to object, was it?

"Oh, thank you, soldier, for your kind words." Hansson forced an official smile, all the while looking at Janet, and his gaze did not bode well. "The way I see it, this is entirely Miss McPherson's fault. She should have known better than to confront a religious artifacts trader. You might have heard"—he returned his attention to Buck—"that Hillcrest Point is the most liberal community in Five Points. We pride ourselves on being tolerant of any beliefs. Or disbeliefs. But our populace"—his eyes threw a sharp dart at Janet—"knows full well that what is acceptable at home may not be elsewhere."

The Secretary's words must have carried a deeper meaning, a meaning lost on Buck, but most obviously comprehended by Janet. The red splotches covering her face up to the roots of her magnificent hair attested to that. She was on the brink of breaking into tears.

Hansson noticed that too. He hurried around the counter, wrapped a hand around her shoulders, and drew her toward the door into a back room. Before leaving, he turned and said, "I'll arrange for her to be taken back home without delay. Thank you for your compassion, soldier, our community appreciates that. Enjoy the rest of your day!"

Buck stood in the empty reception area, alone and confused. Shifting from foot to foot, overwhelmed with the unfamiliar feelings tearing him apart. Then shrugged and headed back to his Marketplace post. What else was he to do? He was just a brainless martinet.

Chapter 7

Buck

September 19, 42 PE

"Sir soldier! Psst! Sir soldier!"

The man at the base of Buck's platform kept looking around, trying to appear inconspicuous and achieving the opposite result. Passersby scowled at him, further contributing to his anxiety. A conspiratorial wave of a hand invited Buck to approach.

At the time, Sergeant Gomez's instructions had seemed exhaustive, covering every imaginable and unimaginable case. Yet, here was the second encounter in a row, catching Buck completely unprepared. Might as well check. The man wouldn't have gone to this much trouble if he hadn't got something important to say. Buck stepped down the ramp.

"What is it, sir?"

"I am terribly sorry to disturb you with this, sir soldier, but there's something you should know," muttered the man in a loud agitated whisper. "I just passed by a group of the Zealots of the True Faith—you know, those with the green armbands—and couldn't help but overhear. It's clear they were outraged by today's incident with the woman trying to buy, you know, *the items*. They said her punishment was not harsh enough. They also said that her entire village, Hillcrest Point, is a bunch of rank heretics and that they should, how that man put it, 'be taught a lesson if they are so eager to learn.' His words, not mine, sir soldier. They didn't hide their intentions to ambush the party departing for Hillcrest Point later today." The informant's gibbering petered out. He wiped sweat from his brow. "I am a simple man, sir soldier, but this is wrong. Violence against our neighbors, I mean, it is plain wrong, isn't it?"

"Yes, sir, violence is wrong! Thank you for reporting this, I'll take it up the chain of command." Buck shook the man's hand.

"Well, okay, then." The man smiled apologetically. "I'd better get going now. Don't want to get into any sticky situation, if you know what I mean." He hurried away and melted into the crowd.

Buck was not supposed to leave his post. Sergeant Gomez was mad at him as it was, and piling on additional transgressions was not likely to help Buck's case. But this couldn't wait. Reporting the threat was the right thing to do, never mind the consequences, so why waste the precious time? Buck squared his shoulders and purposefully headed toward the Council building.

He found Sergeant Gomez and Lieutenant Becker in the guardroom and stood to attention with a loud click of his heels and a thump of a fist against his chest, trying to execute those to perfection.

"What is it, Private?" asked Gomez, more puzzled than upset. "Why did you abandon your post?"

Buck faced the officer for a permission to speak. "Go ahead, Private," Becker said.

"Sir, a citizen approached me with information that may be important." Buck retold what he'd learned about the Zealots' supposed plot.

The lieutenant scratched his square chin and looked at the sergeant. "How credible do you think this report is?"

"Sounds plausible." Gomez shrugged. "Who would cook up something like that? The mystery informer, or Private Brennan?"

The sergeant cocked his head and inspected Buck with a mischievous eye. "And you're sure, Private, that your interest has nothing to do with a certain young lady?" He winked. "I admit, she's pretty special, but this is not the first time she's run into trouble at the Marketplace. Far from that. One could say she's a regular."

Still standing at attention, Buck barked, "Sir, no, sir! My concern is for the safety of innocent people, sir!" He diligently looked above the sergeant's head, but his insides turned into cold jelly at the thought of Janet being in harm's way. Somehow, *that* hadn't crossed his mind.

Becker grunted. "Between Hillcresters and these fanatics, this may develop into a serious event. I've got reports of the Zealots coming after supposed heretics—on their own, without involving the Council. People were beaten, with broken bones and such. But nobody was willing to complain."

Gomez returned his attention to Buck. "Where did you say this is going to happen?"

"Sir, the man said they were planning to ambush a group departing from the Marketplace. Must be the Hillcrest Road, sir."

Lieutenant Becker glanced at him. "Our Private got more than air between his ears, eh?"

The sergeant winced. "The road, that's beyond the Marketplace limits. Technically, not our jurisdiction. Sir, are you sure you want to get involved in this mess?"

The lieutenant's expression grew harder. Muscles rolled over his cheekbones as he clenched his teeth. "Sergeant, take Brennan and one other soldier, and go observe the road."

"Yes, sir." The sergeant rose and sketched a salute.

Becker looked him in the eye. "I repeat, observe the situation."

Sergeant Gomez acknowledged the officer's stare with a stern nod.

An hour later, Buck and Private First Class Pollack sat on a knoll overlooking Hillcrest Road and its surroundings. Sergeant Gomez lounged between them, leaning on an elbow and chewing on a dry straw. Dust devils swooped up the yellow and red foliage and blew it off the empty road. Enough time had passed to get bored, before the Hillcrest Gate finally spewed out a small group of people. Buck tracked the travelers' unhurried progress, counting off seconds and tapping his foot. Would there be an ambush or not? If all this was for nothing, his standing with the sergeant would suffer another blow. On the other hand, it would be great to be proven wrong if that meant Janet's safe passage home.

"See, Brennan? Everything's fine." Sergeant Gomez stretched like a lazy cat. "False alarm."

As if on cue, several figures detached from the small grove abutting the road. Three... five... eight of them, all carrying travelers' staves, and wearing prominent green armbands.

The sergeant shifted, pulling his limbs in and spitting the straw, but didn't move from his place.

Buck was already on his feet. "Sir?" he asked.

"We stay and observe, Private." Gomez's voice gritted like gravel. "These are our orders." He squinted and brought a hand to his forehead as a sun shield.

The group that had emerged from the tree line spread across the road. The travelers stopped at a safe distance. A short verbal exchange followed. Buck strained his hearing, but the range was too great to make out the words. The ambushers closed in. The defenders rallied tighter, bristling with their own staves, but their odds didn't look too promising.

"*Sir?*" Buck was too wound up to hide his edginess.

"Stay—and—observe." The sergeant's reply rang with steel.

And then it happened. The world lost its vibrant fall colors, shifting into shades of gray, and a quick succession of images rolled through Buck's head.

The first time he had experienced a vision, he was about five. He hadn't known what to make of it and paid little attention. He'd thought it was simply a daydream. A normal thing everybody had, no?

By the age of seven, having had similar experiences half a dozen times, he'd figured out what they were, more or less.

He went to Mom. She tightly pursed her lips and believed him. He hadn't been sure she would, but Mom always had known when his words were true, and when he was only fantasizing. She grabbed his hand and led him to Dad's workshop.

Dad listened to his story too, looked at Mom—who nodded—and the three of them sat silently for a long, long time.

Eventually, Dad said, "Son." Not *Buck*, not *Baxter*, not even *Baxter Brennan*, which was reserved for when Buck was in trouble. *Son.* The conversation was about to get serious. "You were right to come to us first. You must never-ever-*ever* speak a word of this to anyone else. Friends, adults, the Preacher—no one, you understand?"

"Yes, Dad, but why?"

"You see, son,"—Dad rubbed his cheeks as if deathly tired—"most people can't do this. And what people cannot do and you can, they see as strange. And what they see as strange, they consider dangerous, or bad, or blasphemous. And for that, they may hurt you or our family. And we don't want that, now do we?" He smiled, but his eyes stayed grave.

Buck vehemently shook his head, yet his stubbornness didn't let him shut up. "But if I see the bad things that are going to happen, I can help people fix them, no? How could I not tell Sam he was about to fall into the well?"

"Wait, you told him that?" Dad asked, with his eyebrows pinched into a knot.

"Yeah." Buck accepted the dare. "But he didn't listen and fell. Remember when all the neighbors came running to the well to pull him out? That was it!"

"Oh." Dad hunched over. "You're right, son, I can't ask you not to warn your friends or other people. Okay, let's turn this into a game: try doing it so they won't suspect you've got this... gift. Make them think you're simply a very cautious kid, alright?"

Seeing Buck's pouting expression, Dad added, "Trust me, son, I know what I'm talking about. Your mother"—he exchanged quick looks with Mom—"had a similar ability when she was young. Nothing good came of it. She had quite a reputation. People whispered she was a witch." He couldn't help but smile, this time genuinely.

"But I learned to keep it to myself." Mom's tone made clear this wasn't a laughing matter.

Since then, many things had changed. Larry and Sam had gotten used to trusting Buck's warnings without questioning them and saw nothing strange about that. Other people... Buck had become proficient in judging who would heed his advice and who was likely to take him for a nut job. Those latter ones he rarely bothered to warn.

Sharp pictures. His prediction was going to be accurate.

He saw the groups exchanging probing staff blows and falling back. Attackers' faces distorted by a rictus of hatred. On the opposite side, faces showing fear and determination. Mute shouts—only images, never sounds in his daydreams—but it didn't take a genius to understand nothing good was being said.

Then the assailants closed the ring around their prey, and one Hillcrester fell like a sack of potatoes, his skull caved in by a savage blow.

A big defender wove loops with his weapon, sending two, then three attackers to the ground, to writhe and clutch at their limbs.

And then... A Zealot with a bushy beard and a fire of madness in his eyes produced a knife and slid it into the heart of a tall, slender girl.

Buck didn't wait to see what was about to happen next.

Years ago, he'd learned to snap out of his visions at will. Without waiting for his eyesight to fully return to the colored *now*, he stomped head-first down the hill with an unintelligible roar of an angry beast.

"Private Brennan, stop right now!" yelled Sergeant Gomez into his back. "Ah, Seven bloody Hells! Pollack, come lend a hand!"

Buck, all two-hundred-odd pounds of him, slammed into the skirmish still at the probing staff blows stage. The sheer force of his body's impact sent two attackers flying, the ends of their staves sweeping two more along with them.

Buck searched around and zeroed in on the bearded man. He tackled the murderer-to-be, smashing him into the ground with a loud thud, and grabbed his neck. Two or three staff blows landed on his back, but barely registered. His attention was on the bulging eyes of the Zealot. He channeled all his strength into squeezing the life out of the man's throat.

Gomez and Pollack reached the battleground. The brawlers—those of them still standing—ebbed away, deferentially putting their weapons down and letting the two soldiers approach. The bearded fanatic meekly twitched underneath Buck.

"Let go of him," the sergeant said. "Brennan."

Buck ignored him.

"Private Baxter Brennan, that is a direct order!" Gomez raised his voice.

Buck squeezed the prostrate figure's neck one last time and climbed to his feet, avoiding eye contact with the sergeant.

"Sir."

Pollack looked at him in awe, the sergeant—with a complex, undecipherable expression. At that moment, Buck couldn't care less.

A Hillcrester approached. Second Secretary Hansson! His face sported fresh abrasions and a swelling eye, but he seemed happy to see the Army representatives. Buck didn't know the other two travelers, and the fourth was Janet. Furious, not at all shaken. Most importantly, unharmed.

Gomez faced the Zealots and the Hillcresters. "You people are coming with me. All of you. I'll need your full testimonies to account for what transpired here. Hand over your weapons."

Nobody dared to object. In a minute, a pile of assorted staves and cudgels rose at his feet. Downcast detainees turned to trail back to the Marketplace when Buck exclaimed, "Wait!" He briskly approached his bearded adversary, who could hardly stand and had his right arm slung around another Zealot's shoulders. The man's face twisted in horror and he recoiled, but Buck firmly grabbed his left hand, jerked the sleeve up, and exposed a long knife attached to the forearm.

Buck pulled the knife from its sheath. In the silence that followed his discovery, the rasping sound was deafening. He studied the narrow blade and looked at the Zealot over its edge. Equal measures of panic and hatred glared back at him with an animalistic snarl.

Buck turned around, showing his find. Gomez stared back with his jaw dropped. What a sight! Once in a lifetime. The sergeant regained control over his face, but not his voice. "How in the name of Ever Graceful Mother Earth?" he asked in a hoarse whisper.

"Saw the hilt bulging under his sleeve," Buck lied without batting an eye. "That's why I ran here so fast—I feared he was going to use it. Sir."

"The hilt? Under his sleeve? You saw it all the way from the hilltop?" Gomez pointed, articulating his disbelief. Then shrugged off any remaining doubts, satisfied with the version of the events he could report to Lieutenant Becker. "Hm. That would explain why you went berserk on our pal here."

"Grant Green," he aimed a finger at the owner of the knife, "You are under arrest for possession of an illegal weapon. Pollack, tie him up."

The motley procession trudged back to the gate. The sergeant urged Green on with not-so-gentle punches of his cudgel in the back. The other Zealots dejectedly led the column.

Pollack followed with the brawlers' weapons tied into a hefty bunch.

Buck closed the line along with the four Hillcresters. He fell into step with Janet.

Secretary Hansson turned to him with a wide grin on his battered face. "Thank you again, Private Brennan! We found ourselves in quite a sticky situation. I'm afraid we were in danger of grievous bodily harm, if not for you and your comrades!"

"You've got no idea..." Shit. No taking his words back. All four, including Janet, stared at him. If he didn't tell them, he'd look like a fool. If he did, they'd think he's crazy. Easy choice. "This man"—a nod at a Hillcrester—"would've had his skull broken with a staff. And Green was about to stab Miss McPherson with that knife."

A tense silence met his statement. "How can you know?" Hansson asked in a dumbfounded whisper.

Why couldn't he keep his mouth shut? Buck shrugged. "I just do."

Another hundred silent paces later, Janet burst with an angry, "This is all because of you! You, Brennan, and your Army!"

"Janet," Hansson clasped her shoulder, "you cannot possibly mean that. These brave men have saved us from serious danger."

The girl shrugged his hand off. "Why didn't they intervene sooner? Look at your eye, Uncle Pete! It's the Army that creates the atmosphere encouraging such mobs in the first place! You told me yourself, there have been four Zealot attacks on Hillcresters! Four! Has anyone been arrested? No! Because the Army is a bunch of sycophants to the religious fanatics!"

"Janet. Louise. McPherson. Please. Shut. Up. Now." The quiet, level voice in which he delivered this command underscored the affable Second Secretary's transformation.

Janet stumbled as if on an invisible stone and sunk into sullen silence. Even her fiery hair seemed to have lost its luster.

"I am awfully sorry for her outburst, Private Brennan," Hansson said. "Her words do not represent the official position of Hillcrest Point, and I am sure Miss McPherson meant nothing of what she said about the Army. She is obviously in shock and isn't thinking straight. I would sincerely appreciate it if you choose not to report her inappropriate remarks to your superiors."

"It's okay, sir, I am not telling anyone. You may count on that."

"Much obliged, Private, much obliged."

Janet's words seeded a doubt. The Army, Colonel, the Council—they couldn't all be wrong, could they?

"And what am I to do with you, gentlemen?"

Colonel was irritated. Buck was horrified.

This was the first time he saw Colonel up close.

Buck had seen him leading the parades dozens of times before, but as a symbol. Legendary, revered, shrouded in myth and mystery. Almost not a real person, but a walking and talking statue. Never mentioned by the name. Did Colonel even have a name? A gulf of veneration separated insignificant little Buck from the colossal figure. Had that been a child's perception? Or had the awe surrounding the leader of Five Points served as a magnifying glass?

In proximity, Colonel did not appear to be a giant. He was, in fact, of average height, and not at all what one might call a big man. But the power he exuded more than compensated for his size, and his posture left no doubt about his willingness to wield that power.

Colonel's face, split by deep lines, remained unreadable. His dark eyes shaded by massive brows—impenetrable.

The only outward manifestation of the man's emotion was the rhythmical tapping of his fingers on the desk.

Ta-ta-ta-tap. Ta-ta-ta-tap.

Enough for everyone else in the room to succumb to various degrees of panic. Colonel was famous for his just and balanced judgment, but when an unfortunate soul drew his ire... Buck cringed and tried to push himself further away. The wall behind him resisted.

When the detachment with its prisoners and the four Hillcresters had passed through the Marketplace gates, the crowd met them with surprised exclamations. The rumors spread more swiftly than a brushfire, and by the time the ragtag group had reached the Main Square, the throng of gawkers was so tight that people were unable to step back, even if they were willing to.

Once inside, the procession headed toward the Council Chamber, but Lieutenant Becker intercepted it in the hallway and, after a hushed discussion with Sergeant Gomez, led it in a different direction.

And there they were, in front of Colonel.

He listened impassively to the sergeant's report and declared the entire ordeal a security issue falling under his jurisdiction.

The Zealots were shaking. Their ringleader, Grant Green, was in an anxious stupor.

Hillcresters, though the aggrieved party, appeared uncomfortable too, shifting, sighing, and staring into the floor.

As for Buck, his situation continued to be unclear. Disobeying the sergeant's order, on top of failing to maintain the peace, did not earn him any favors.

Ta-ta-ta-tap. Ta-ta-ta-tap.

Ta-ta-ta-tap. Ta-ta-ta-tap.

"Preserving the sacred tenets of our Faith is everyone's paramount responsibility. But using the Faith to justify violence is blasphemy!" Underscoring the last word, Colonel's fist smashed into the table, a clap of thunder in the unnaturally quiet room. Buck twitched.

"The E and the years that followed claimed too many lives," continued the supreme commander, "making every soul precious. *That* is what our Faith teaches us!" He paused briefly, then announced in a different timbre, "In the name of the God Almighty, He who in His infinite mercy saved our souls with the blessed Enginocide, here is my judgment. Green's followers will be publicly lashed and pilloried for three days in the Main Square. Green will have his sinful hand chopped off and his sacrilegious tongue cut out with his own blade. He'll be branded and ousted from Five Points forever!"

A collective gasp acknowledged the unprecedented sentence. Criminals could be fined, pilloried, sometimes lashed... But normally, the crime didn't involve an attempt on someone's life.

"We did this for the Faith, you bloody apostate!" yelled Green. "You'll burn in—"

Gomez's cudgel landed on the Zealot's mouth in a short arc.

"Nobody dares talk that way to Colonel, you filthy louse!" The sergeant grabbed the fanatic's unkempt hair and tugged.

Green gurgled incoherently through the repulsive pink froth of blood, saliva, and broken teeth.

Colonel seemed unperturbed. "I am the Protector of the Faith. Five Points has seen no banditry for over a decade. I will not allow vigilantism on my watch. Any lost sheep in our communities? We will talk to them, like the civilized people we are. I will not. Tolerate. Mob. Law. In. This. Land!" He enunciated each word, gradually raising his voice until it reverberated between the lacquered wood walls. He lifted himself from the chair, towering above everyone on his high dais, with fists pushed against the desktop. The golden-red dusk light passing through the window behind Colonel outlined his figure, projecting his giant shadow onto the far wall.

"This hearing is over. The sentence will be carried out tomorrow morning." His flat tone was the last straw. Buck shifted from foot to foot, as if standing on red-hot coals, awaiting his turn to escape this purgatory.

The lieutenant opened the door and disappeared first. Sergeant Gomez escorted the trembling Green out. Pollack followed, holding the end of the rope that bound the other Zealots. Buck hurried to close the procession.

"Miss McPherson, please stay," Colonel said.

With a sinking feeling in his stomach, Buck slowed down in the doorway to glance back. He could not see Janet's face, only the fiery aura of her hair glowing in the sunset.

A solid, roughly hewn hardwood table between Sergeant Gomez and Buck held a thick candle and a tall glass bottle of cloudy moonshine. The candle supplied scarce light, illuminating only the center of the table. Enough to see that the bottle was half-empty, but leaving the rest of the guardroom shrouded in shadows. Pollack's snores rattled the door to the sleeping quarters. The other two soldiers of the Detachment were on the night patrol.

"Yeah, yeah," grumbled the sergeant for the fourth time, "everybody loves a winner. I'll be damned if I have the slightest idea, Brennan, how you pulled that trick today. Beginner's luck, or Seven Hells know what... Tell me. No, shut up. You saw that knife from two hundred meters away? Don't lie to me! That's a steaming pile of crap. Whatever, you saved those buggers' asses, that's for damn sure. Made me look good too, and for that I'm gonna let it slide. But don't you ever dare to disobey my order again! Or I'll take my cudgel and screw you in all your holes! Unless, of course, you're gonna do something stupid that will make me look good again..."

An hour earlier, when Gomez dragged Buck to the table and produced the bottle, it had been full. Most of its missing contents rested comfortably in the depths of the sergeant's gut. Buck had barely touched his glass. His hands shook without the help of alcohol. What a day.

Gomez had no such qualms. His speech grew slurred, and he started repeating himself. Losing lucidity by a minute, he could be expected to stop making any sense altogether soon.

Buck was off the sergeant's hook for the events of the day. Moreover, Gomez had developed an unexpected sentiment toward him. Equally obvious was the potential reversal of the sergeant's good graces if Buck did anything detrimental to his commander's reputation.

The sergeant seized the bottle and generously topped up their glasses, splashing the precious liquid on the table.

The door flew open. Lieutenant Becker stopped on the threshold. "Private Brennan."

Buck rose from the bench and stood to attention, almost without quivering.

"Colonel wants to see you. Move."

Gomez straightened up, looking practically sober, and sent the officer a quizzical look. Becker shrugged.

"Yes, sir!" Buck saluted and rushed through the door, nearly tripping over his chair. One doesn't make Colonel wait.

His delicate knock on the chamber entrance was barely a scratch.

"Come in," came an authoritative command from the other side.

Buck stepped in and found several people in the room, besides Colonel: two veteran soldiers whom he'd seen before, Colonel's aide-de-camp Lieutenant Kossowsky, and... Janet!

Buck took a breath in to report formally but Colonel interrupted him, "At ease, Private."

Startled, Buck slammed his mouth shut. He caught evaluating glances from everyone present—other than Colonel, who sauntered before the deferential semicircle. "You must wonder why I have assembled this peculiar group." Was there a trace of excitement in his business-like quiet voice? "Here's the deal. Until further notice, you are a Special Task Force. You may find its goals unusual, and will be right. Your mission is to retrieve an important artifact. Important enough that I am personally interested in it. And Miss McPherson"—a gesture in Janet's direction—"has knowledge of its whereabouts."

What? Buck's jaw went slack. How was she a part of this? How was *he*?

"Bring this artifact safely back to the Base. Your orders are to accompany Miss McPherson in her travels and assist to the best of your abilities with filling in the blanks in her knowledge. Never let her out of your sight. Protect her life and wellbeing. The mission is strictly confidential. Lieutenant, as the Commanding Officer of this Task Force, you'll get a credential letter carrying my personal seal and demanding full and immediate assistance from anyone presented with it. Invent whatever cover story you deem credible. Upon successful completion of this mission, you all may expect to be promoted. Return to the Base tomorrow morning to pack and make arrangements. Until then, Jackson and Lundy, you are still my personal detail. Questions?"

Dead silence was the answer.

Buck had hundreds—no, thousands of questions, but didn't dare ask one.

"Good," approved Colonel. "Lieutenant, take care of Miss McPherson's accommodation for tonight. Make sure she's safe."

A hint too transparent to be misunderstood. Kossowsky curtly nodded.

"Dismissed. Brennan, stay."

Buck, stricken with panic on the inside but using all his willpower to keep a neutral expression, stood to attention once more.

"Well, well, well. Baxter Brennan, in the flesh." Colonel's amusement sent fresh waves of shivers down Buck's spine. Events kept unfolding too fast, leaving no time to catch up. First, being awarded the Marketplace duty. Then the altercations involving Janet. As if all that weren't enough, the nomination for this mysterious Task Force. And finally, Colonel singling him out. More than sufficient to turn Buck's guts into soup. Droplets of cold sweat under his shirt streaked to the small of his back.

Colonel paced unhurriedly, hands locked behind his back, peering into the floor. "You show up, and single-handedly tip the fragile balance of power between the Faith and the Educationalists. The balance I've worked hard to maintain."

If I drop dead with a heart attack, would that be high treason?

"At the same time," Colonel continued, "if you hadn't intervened, people would likely have died. And that would have broken this balance, anyway."

Was Colonel thinking aloud, ignoring his presence?

The next words refuted that theory. "You are a curious character, Baxter, you know?"

"No, sir!" blurted Buck, dutifully staring above Colonel's head. That didn't help. The portraits of the previous Colonels glared back from the wall, stern and not in the least sympathetic.

"No? Hm. Don't underestimate yourself." Colonel definitely had something greater than small talk in mind. He stopped, cocked his head in an oddly birdlike manner, and examined Buck with mock suspicion. "Pray tell, you wouldn't hide anything from me, would you?"

"No, sir!" Did that strange hoarse voice, low and weak, come out of Buck's mouth?

Colonel swiftly stepped closer. It was all Buck could do not to flinch. Or to puke all over the highest authority in Five Points.

Colonel scrutinized Buck's face for a few awfully long seconds. Sweat permeated Buck's uniform, and it clung to his back.

"Alright, Baxter. Before you faint... I *know*."

Buck's helpless expression must have been hilarious because Colonel chuckled. "Why do you think the Army recruited you, Baxter? You understand you aren't a typical A-list candidate, don't you?"

Buck tried to swallow, but his mouth refused to produce a drop of saliva. He just bobbed his head.

"And what do you suppose earned you the Marketplace duty? I bet you don't stand out that much among your fellow rookies, do you?"

The room shook and spun around Buck. Colonel knew he was an impostor!

"Yes, Baxter, I know about your curious superpower, or whatever you call it. I have since you were ten. That's why I wanted you in my Army, and that's why I brought you here. I suspected the Marketplace might provide opportunities for you to show it, and wasn't wrong."

He stared point blank into Buck's eyes. "That's the reason you're on this Task Force. If there's a one in a million chance your ability helps save this unique mission, I'll take that. I don't understand how it works, or if you can invoke it at will. But whatever it is, I want... no, I *order* you to use it when you can. I spoke to your father, and I know you've been concealing your gift. Keep it that way. You are *my* asset, no one else should get any ideas about you. Serve me well, and you won't regret it. Cross me..."

The threat did not need to be finished. The suggestion made Buck's knees shake.

Colonel stepped back with a satisfied smile. "You must have many questions. Permission to speak freely granted."

Buck failed to herd the scattered threads of his thoughts. "Sir, how did you know?"

"Ah, Baxter, don't forget I am a Creekpointer too. Occasionally, I come home to spend time with my extended family. People talk, I listen. And put two and two together."

Buck bowed his head, flabbergasted.

"Any more questions?"

"Janet... I mean, Miss McPherson... Is she in trouble, sir?" Buck blushed. Not what he intended to ask, not at all. The question slipped his tongue.

"Janet, huh?" An understanding smile made Colonel a tiny bit less scary. "No. Not as long as she accomplishes the mission. And if you care about her, help her do that, and keep her safe. You should be comfortable with these tasks."

Then his face hardened, and Buck, who had started relaxing, froze again.

"But don't get any stupid ideas, you hear me? Like, I don't know, running away with her? Saving the poor princess from the cruel villain? She may present the situation in such a way. Don't buy into that. Help her locate and bring that artifact to me. Because if, God forbid, she runs away, I will find her, and I will find you, and—"

"I understand, sir. I'll do all I can, I promise!"

That came out childishly, but Buck's last defenses had crumbled. A naughty eight-year-old being dressed down by a Preacher would have greater control over himself.

Colonel's bottomless eyes released Buck from their hypnotic hold. "I know you will, Baxter. I know you will."

Chapter 8

Yun-mi

September 20, 42 PE

Two steps, turn. Two steps, turn.

Yun-mi paced her small partition of the darkness.

Two steps, turn.

She wasn't trying to wear an escape tunnel through the floor. She simply couldn't bring herself to sit. As if sitting equated to admitting defeat, which she'd never do. Not her.

Rats do not get defeated.

Rats do not get captured.

Rats do not get betrayed.

But she'd got betrayed. And she'd got captured. All she had left was her refusal to admit defeat.

Think. Think, goddammit!

She'd been on her feet since evening, when the squeaky hinges of the cell door and the screech of the key turning in the lock heralded the next stage of her misadventures. She couldn't sleep, she couldn't sit, she couldn't rest. She had to come up with a plan. A Rat that failed to escape a trap was a dead Rat.

Soreness spread through her thighs, calves, and the small of her back.

Not good.

She stopped.

She sat on the cold floor.

Not a defeat. A strategy. She must be well-rested and ready to strike if—no, when!—she finds a way out. Yun-mi forced her muscles to relax and went through two rounds of breathing exercises.

Think.

Joon-woo died.

Grief made a tentative attempt to pinch her heart. She intercepted and squashed it. Not now.

Yun-mi was on her own. Not a trainee anymore.

Be honest, a year or two too early.

She had been convincing herself she was ready. She had tried to convince Joon-woo too, repeatedly, but her temerity had always shattered against his mild, understanding smile. Followed by subtle lessons showing how much she had yet to learn. And now her mentor was no more. This was her graduation ceremony. Time to step up. *Ready or not, girl, you're playing on the adults' playground, by their rules.* She straightened up and squared her shoulders. Even in the darkness, where no one could see.

Big boys, here I come! You don't know me yet—but you will. Oh, you will! Think.

It was well past midnight.

The previous day could have been Yun-mi's last. Parker had made that clear.

"I don't need you." He serenely wiped his bloody knife on her dead mentor's jacket. "A smarter move would be to off you now and leave no loose ends."

His blade pricked the skin under her chin, forcing her to tilt her head back and meet his eyes.

"But I like you. Wanna hear what I like more? The money I can fetch for you from the slavers. I'll take the risk. But if you give me trouble—and I mean any trouble at all—you're as good as dead. Comprenez-vous, my little Ratty?"

Yun-mi glared back.

Her abductor did not insist on a verbal answer. "Now, I can carry you, but that'll make me unhappy. Or I can untie your legs and you'll walk. What's it gonna be?"

As if he had to ask. As if the threat was necessary. Of course she'd walk! She wouldn't enter the legendary Dixie Mall trussed like a coyote. Besides, she might come up with a plan along the way.

"Don't even dream of outsmarting me," said Parker, as if reading her mind, loosening the knots around her ankles. "Try something stupid, and that too will make me unhappy."

They walked through the lifeless West End landscape, Yun-mi in front, Parker behind. Burdened with three bags, two rifles, and her bow, he nevertheless paced lithely with the grace of a wild animal.

Yun-mi didn't doubt the seriousness of Parker's threats, but kept looking for an opportunity. Which had so far consistently refused to present itself. She searched for a sewer hole in the ground, or a broken basement window... Something. Any opening she'd be able to dive into like a spooked lizard, leaving Parker empty-handed. Twice she saw promising escape routes, and twice Parker's lazy "Uh-uh" preempted her action.

The third time she eyed one, he grabbed her by the scruff of her jacket and dragged her into a side courtyard. Startled, she yelped, but with her hands tied and off balance, could do little to resist.

In a defunct loading area, Parker released her. Yun-mi straightened. Her heart was racing.

"What did I say about trying something stupid?" he asked, circling her like a vulture. "I warned you, right?"

She did not respond.

Parker stopped behind her. Unable to see the threat, Yun-mi braced, preparing for what was to come, but refused to give in to the fear. She did not look back.

"Disobedience brings punishment," said Parker. "Now, what shall I do with you?"

Bring it on, scumbag. Having trained in martial arts since early childhood, she could take a beating.

A footstep, another one. No kicks, no punches. Instead, Parker's hand slid up her thigh. His other hand groped her chest. A flood of icy rage burst through her, sweeping away the knot of horror in her gut.

Fuck, no! Not gonna happen!

Yun-mi arched back, putting the strength of her entire body into a headbutt, to smash the asshole's face.

Yun-mi's head met only air. Parker had not been lying, he really was quick. He stepped in again, locking her exposed neck in a chokehold. His other hand insistently found its way under Yun-mi's jacket and squeezed a breast through her shirt.

"Let go of me, you fucking pig!" she growled, furiously stomping her heels, aiming for his toes.

And Parker did. His arm retracted, and he pushed her stumbling away. This time, she spun around, preparing for whatever new abuse he planned to unleash upon her next.

"You aren't my type," he said, in a half-assed imitation of indifference. "I prefer women with more meat on them."

Yun-mi stepped forward and kicked him in the balls. Once again, Parker reacted fast, blocking the kick with his thigh and countering with a vicious punch into her solar plexus. It drew the air out of her lungs and left her bent over, seeing stars and unable to breathe.

"Will this lesson suffice?" Parker's voice came from afar, through the mad heartbeat in her ears. "The slavers don't like damaged goods, but believe me, I can teach you plenty more without leaving a mark."

As before, Yun-mi refused to answer, but did not resist when he led her out of the courtyard. She needed this to be over. The reckoning would come.

That day, Parker, will be your last.

First time at the Dixie Mall. Not how Yun-mi had planned to discover this far-famed place. Duh. But at least on her own feet, if not on her own terms.

She had envisioned the moment since she was a tiny girl. The stories spoke of an enchanted place where traders and visitors from all around came together to sell their goods and purchase exotic wares. Later, she had dreamed how she, a famous City Rat, would bring her loot there, to be accosted by eager buyers fighting to outbid each other. Most recently, she'd expected to be led to the Mall by Joon-woo and learn the intricacies of this aspect of their business. Fate, as usual, had different plans for her.

The Mall itself turned out to be impressive and disappointing at the same time. Dixie was known far and wide as the biggest, liveliest, most diverse trading market west of the City. That was a fact. Yun-mi had imagined an enormous building, lovingly maintained, in better shape than any of the pre-E structures she'd seen. *This* wasn't it.

Instead, she was greeted with more of the familiar same. Crumbling pieces patched haphazardly. Sections rebuilt with improvised materials. Add-ons slapped to the main building's sides and even on the roof. Faded old paint, interrupted by clashing spots of new. Gaggles of kiosks and tents all around, with no obvious system. Piles of unidentifiable garbage. All told, a disturbing cacophony of colors, textures, materials, smells, and sounds. Same as everywhere, but bigger and concentrated. Just another shithole.

Its only impressive quality was the uncomfortable number of people milling around.

She'd never experienced being among so many people at once. If being a Rat had a job description, it would start with "loner". Crowds were unproductive, counterintuitive, and outright dangerous. Joon-woo had taught Yun-mi the ancient adage: be polite, be professional, but have a plan to kill everybody you meet. Yun-mi had wholeheartedly adopted the approach. But in this crowd...

She couldn't conceivably have a plan to kill all these people! Seven Hells, she couldn't even kill one particular motherfucker.

Parker clasped her arm and confidently weaved through the chaotic maze to an austere tent, lacking any adornments but a simple handwritten sign: *Emancipation Through Labor*. This one was given a wide berth by the dense patchwork of surrounding stands and booths, as if it were contagious.

Inside, two men met them. One, dark-skinned and silver-haired, well dressed and undoubtedly in charge. The other, big and imposing, with tiny eyes, hung behind the first. Clearly a guard.

The boss-man welcomed the visitors with a wide but patently fake smile.

"Ah, mister Parker, how nice to see you again!" he fawned in a prepossessing baritone, opening his arms as if to embrace the dear guest. "What brings you to The Station's outpost on this marvelous day?"

"Master DeGrasse." The traitorous Rat tipped his hat with one hand, prodding Yun-mi forward with the other. "I would love for you to consider a contract on this young woman. Quiet, as you may observe. Strong, agile, healthy, and reasonably well-fed."

"Hm." DeGrasse folded his arms and tapped a finger on his chin, playacting contemplation. "Will she cause much hassle?"

"Only if you allow her to!" Parker guffawed.

The slaver approached and squeezed Yun-mi's cheeks, forcing her mouth open. Caught unprepared, she didn't resist. "Good teeth." He walked around, looking her up and down. "Too skinny!"

The two continued to haggle, but Yun-mi filtered out their conversation as noise.

People are not merchandise! Rats are not for sale!

Her body began shaking, and she couldn't bring it back under control.

Derail the deal. Need a plan. A plan... A plan... Yes. Damaged goods!

She started talking. Incomplete phrases, songs, all in different voices, as if multiple versions of herself were holding conversations at once. Back home, one such super-weird boy made people uncomfortable around him. Yun-mi put her best acting abilities into portraying him.

The trader grew quiet amid the bargaining. His eyebrows skeptically crept up. "Is she unwell in the head? Are you trying to swindle me, mister Parker?"

Parker cuffed Yun-mi on the ear, sending her rolling on the floor. "What did I say about making trouble, little bitch?" he hissed, bending to Yun-mi. Straightening up, he plastered a wide smile on his face again. "Not at all, Master DeGrasse! She's totally normal, I wouldn't lie to you! She's trying to be difficult. Nothing a little educational flogging can't fix. No biggie."

"Difficult?" The Stationer grimaced. "Difficult means more breaking in, more expenses for me. And, truth be told, she doesn't strike me as a farmer's daughter. I suspect she's what you City people call a Rat. I've had experience with your kind of urban zombies in the past, mister Parker. Not my fondest memories. Way too much trouble. Not worth the effort. I'm afraid I must respectfully decline your offer. Better luck next time. Goodbye, mister Parker."

The guard moved in between DeGrasse and Parker, ushering the visitor out of the tent. Advancing one step at a time, he forced the smaller man to backtrack.

This was it. With all the commotion, distracted and outmatched, her captor lost control of the situation. Plus, the guard's bulk obstructed Parker's view of her. Not perfect, but good enough. *Don't let perfect be the enemy of good. See, Joon-woo? I remember. Go! Go, go, go!*

Yun-mi leaped to her feet and bolted out. She crossed the exclusion zone around the slavers' tent at a mad dash and entered the labyrinth of the sur-rounding kiosks. Left turn, right, left, right. Break the pattern. Make it random. Right again. Her hands still tied behind the back didn't make it any easier, but Yun-mi kept running, crouching as low as she could. She spotted an opening and dove under a pumpkin stand. The seller, engaged in a passionate negotia-tion with a customer, noticed nothing. Yun-mi, her chest heaving from stress and exertion, concentrated on breathing.

Get into Parker's head. How long would he scour the Mall before giving up? What if he stuck around to see if she eventually showed herself? And if she won this contest of wits, then what? Where should she go once she judged it safe to leave her provisionary concealment?

She needed an ally. A powerful one. Yes, Rats and allies weren't normally mentioned in one sentence, but these were unusual circumstances, calling for extraordinary measures.

What was that gibberish Parker had uttered? Some player expanding influ-ence... External rulership... Who might that be? A clan? Unlikely. Not Bloor clans—because they were the target. Not the Raccoons, because someone else hired them. Sauga clans? Nah. Neither they nor the northerners had any interest in the Bloor Corridor. So, not a clan. Must be a strong, ambitious player. The Station, New Kowloon, Locksville. The only three forces capable of pulling off something at this level. Locksvillers had many chances to expand their influence and had consistently shown no desire to do that. The slavers? Possible. The City would provide an untapped source of lifers for them and a goldmine of goods to harvest. The Chinese? Plausible. New areas to control. Mainly through trade, but who said it had to always stay that way? And they were the closest to the City.

The Station or New Kowloon? Easy. Not going back to the slavers. No bloody way.

She waited for the merchant to seal the deal and collect the payment, then rolled from under the stand into the shadowed insides of the kiosk. The owner jumped but promptly collected himself and grabbed a long knife.

To avoid escalation, Yun-mi made herself look pitiful. Tied up, on her knees, that didn't take much. "Please help me, kind sir!" Sufficiently pathetic?

That got the vendor to slow down. "Who are you? What are you doing in my shop?" He still squeezed his knife, but its tip turned a few degrees away from Yun-mi's face. "What do you want?"

"My name is Yun-mi, I was abducted to be sold to The Station, but escaped."

"Fucking slavers, abducting kids now," grumbled the trader, moving his knife a few additional inches away.

"Please untie me, kind sir."

The shopkeeper sighed, bent down, and started sawing through the ropes. He released Yun-mi's elbows and proceeded to her wrists, when a sickeningly familiar suave voice suggested from the other side of the counter, "I wouldn't do this if I were you."

Fuck. Son of a whore.

"Why not?" asked the merchant, straightening up. Yun-mi feverishly tugged against the rope, discovering a new slack.

"Because this sneaky Rat will backstab and steal from you," explained Parker as if to a slow-witted child.

"That's a lie!" cried Yun-mi. "Sir, he's the one who abducted me and wanted to sell me to the slavers!"

"Is this true?" The merchant stepped forward, raising the knife again to point it accusingly at Parker. Who, without batting an eye, hopped over the counter and slid his tanto into the man's abdomen, right through the leather apron. Leaning closer to his rapidly paling victim and twisting the blade, he said, "I warned you. I told you I wouldn't do this if I were you, did I not?"

The trader grabbed at his gut with both hands. His pumpkin knife rang on the pavement. Yun-mi gave the rope one last yank, putting all her strength and desperation into the effort, and it snapped. Yes! She rolled, grabbing the hapless merchant's knife, and sliced through her nemesis's hamstrings.

Parker had proved he was faster than her. Yun-mi was prepared for her last-ditch attack to fail, and for a lethal retribution to follow.

Miracles happen. Parker's legs were precisely where she'd hoped they'd be. He gave out a high-pitched cry and dropped like a brick.

Yun-mi was there, on the ground, waiting for him. She slammed the ten-inch knife into the side of Parker's neck. It snagged on something—the spine?—but she kept pushing until it jerked forward and its tip broke the skin on the other side, spraying blood all over the counter. There. Through and through. Parker's cry cut abruptly. His uncomprehending gaze found Yun-mi. Some panicked gurgling, and it was all over. Yun-mi closely watched the life seeping away from her enemy's eyes until they turned glassy. She drank the experience to the last drop, savoring the warm sensation of justice served. Justice for Joon-woo. Justice for this kind-hearted pumpkin dealer. Justice for Parker's other victims, whose list, without a doubt, was way too long. Justice for herself. The reckoning came much sooner than she had any right to hope.

When strong hands lifted and dragged her away from the two corpses, she did not resist. When angry armed people asked her a thousand questions, she did not respond. When they threw her into a dark cell and locked the door, she did not object. At the time, she was empty inside. A shell. A husk...

No! Once a Rat, always a Rat. The best damn Rat the City had ever known. She'd prove that. She just had to think now.

And think she did.

Parker was dead. Whoever had contracted him needed a new agent. Someone who knew the City inside out. Someone who spoke the clans' language. Someone like Yun-mi.

She stood up.

Yun-mi knocked on the door for a long time. Either she wasn't considered an important detainee, or no detainee was, thus meriting no full-time guards.

Perseverance was a virtue. She kept banging on the damned door until dull pain spread through the butt of her fist. Was stubbornness a virtue too?

Time was hard to tell in the windowless room buried somewhere in the bowels of the Mall, but the silence outside suggested the small hours of the night. Yun-mi sat on the floor, performed another breathing exercise, and unexpectedly relaxed so well that the tiredness, until then kept at bay, took over her. She laid down, wrapped herself tighter in the jacket, closed her eyes, and allowed her mind to drift away.

Sometime later—impossible to tell how long—Yun-mi woke up. Not startled, not confused, not disoriented. Opened her eyes into the darkness, instantly knowing where she was, why she was there, and what she was about to do. She rose from the floor, stretched, went through a quick calisthenic routine to get the blood running, and knocked on the door once again.

This time, she didn't have to wait long. Clanking of keys accompanied heavy approaching steps. The door screeched, and a monumental guard appeared between the jambs, filling the passage and obstructing the corridor. He shone a lamp at Yun-mi and looked her up and down, holding a hand on a cudgel suspended from his belt.

Yun-mi assumed a non-threatening posture, shielding her eyes against the light and waiting for the guard to open the conversation.

The man's eyes narrowed. "You ain't gonna make a fuss, lady, are you?"

Lately, more and more people had been asking her that question. Did she look like a troublemaker?

"No, sir. No fuss. I want to talk to whoever's in charge here. Would that be you?"

"Me?" The guard barked a laugh. "Good one. No, that'd be the Magistrate."

"Will you be so kind as to take me to him?"

"Ready to talk now, huh? Wasn't as talky the other day!"

"Yes, sir." Yun-mi had resolved to abide by any reasonable demands. She hadn't had a promising start with the people running the Mall, and further alienating them wouldn't help her case.

"Move it then, chop-chop." The guard turned sideways, leaving a narrow opening for Yun-mi to squeeze through.

He guided her with "Left" and "Right" through the hallways until they reached a massive door. Another guard, of comparable size, greeted her with a crooked smile. "Ah, Ratty-Rat grew a tongue?"

He bumped fists with the first guard and opened the door. The jailer nudged Yun-mi into the room and stepped in behind her.

The interior was minimalistic. Well-maintained, but not lavish. Smooth hardwood floor. Clean, freshly painted walls. A massive antique desk. Behind it, shelving units holding scores of tomes. Wow, that's a lot of books. Or book-keeping journals?

The owner of the desk finished scribbling in a notebook and raised his eyes. Graying hair framed a strong-willed face of someone who deserved this desk, and with it, caution, if not respect.

The initial look of annoyance slipped away. He leaned back in his armchair and cocked his head.

"Ah," he said, "you." He didn't smile, but neither did he scowl. A positive sign, wasn't it? Yun-mi assumed a similarly neutral expression and adjusted her breathing to match the host's—a technique Joon-woo had taught her to help subconsciously endear people. The Magistrate noticed and smirked.

"I was about to comment that there's nothing like a night in a small dark cell to loosen a tongue, but I see that may not be the case. Still, you're here. Must be ready to talk. Talk."

One of the most important skills she'd learned from Joon-woo—and among the hardest for her to master—was to not blurt her mind without thinking. While waiting in her cell, Yun-mi had evaluated possible responses to the inevitable questioning. Be arrogant and defiant? Stall, hoping to glean a clue about her situation? Pretend to be a simple, dimwitted hick? She had decided to play it by ear. Now, having met this Magistrate, she discarded all these ruses. Truth, and nothing but the truth. Just not all the truth.

"My name is Park Yun-mi, Magistrate," she said. "I live in Little Korea. My mentor Kim Joon-woo and I were heading to Dixie Mall to trade goods. Jim Parker of the Humber Bay Raccoons Clan ambushed us, killed Kim, and captured me to sell to the slavers here. They didn't want me. I escaped. He found me and killed the man who tried to help me. I killed Parker. And here I am."

She finished, but the Magistrate continued piercing her with his dark eyes, tapping the end of his pen on a finger.

"Alright," he finally said. "You don't play games. I appreciate that. You don't question my authority, and I appreciate that even more. Many do, and that doesn't end well for them. By the way, I am Magistrate Khachaturian, and the Dixie Trade Conclave had entrusted me with the thankless task of maintaining law and order in this rancid place."

"Nice to meet you, Magistrate." Yun-mi sketched a bow.

The man grunted, a smile curving the corners of his mouth up. "Honest, polite. Are you a real Rat, Park Yun-mi? Or a Kowloonese agent?"

Not yet. "No, Sir, I—"

"That wasn't a question. Anyhow. You aren't trying to weasel your way out, and your story checks. It matches our investigation and witness statements. I am reasonably convinced you are not a danger to the Conclave's interests. Moreover, you've done us a service by eliminating a murderer. I've got no further questions. You're free to go."

Yun-mi did not move. She'd expected to have to clear her name through a long, excruciating interrogation, not being released five minutes after stepping in.

"Samvel?"

"Yes, Magistrate." The jail guard gently pulled Yun-mi out of the room.

They marched down more corridors, but this time Samvel was in the lead. Yun-mi followed, mechanically putting one foot in front of the other, staring into the cracked floor tiles, trying to digest the bizarre experience. Was this a plot? Or was she really out of the woods? She had killed a man, and they were letting her go?

The massive guard stopped by a metal door. Distracted, she bumped into him. He regarded her with an understanding grin, unlocked the door, and waved Yun-mi in. Inside, heavy-duty shelves full of large storage bins lined the walls. The guard trudged along one side, tracing the labels with a finger and moving his lips as he read. He pulled one off the shelf and put it down before Yun-mi.

She regarded the long, squat bin, then returned her gaze to the guard with a mute question.

"Your belongings, young lady."

"My—" She kneeled by the bin, removed the lid with shaking hands, and sharply inhaled. Inside lay three loot bags, two rifles, a bow and a quiver, knives, all the other gear—hers, Joon-woo's, and Parker's. Her throat constricted. Her tongue betrayed her. She looked up at Samvel.

"What, you didn't know? Kill a criminal, get his stuff, that's the law."

The guard didn't rush her, observing with unconcealed interest as Yun-mi sorted through everything.

First, her good old knife. She strapped it on her thigh, closed her eyes, threw her head back, and savored the moment. *This* was the real freedom. Unarmed, she'd been exposed, half-naked.

Then came the stiletto's turn. It slid smoothly into its sheath on her forearm, locking in place with a satisfying click. The handle pleasantly chilled her skin.

She put a hand on Parker's kukri and froze. Her neck still remembered the touch of its blade. Fuck that. Poetic justice, bitch! She attached it to the back of her belt, the same way the renegade had carried it.

His tanto... No. It must still have had Joon-woo's blood on it. And the pumpkin dealer's. She carefully picked the murder weapon with the tips of two fingers, like a sleeping venomous animal, and dropped it into the bag. Later. She'd deal with it later.

Now, the rifles. Yun-mi had never learned to use those. With the ammo prohibitively expensive, Joon-woo had postponed these lessons, waiting for her to first become proficient with empty-handed skills and bladed weapons. She had a basic understanding of the general principles, but zero practice. Walking around with two rifles, each costing a not-so-small fortune, was an invitation for unwanted attention. Yun-mi struggled with Parker's rifle, but with the help of brute force and a few choice words disassembled it into two smaller parts and stuffed them in a bag, along with the remaining pieces of equipment from the bin. The three bags, tied together and slung across her shoulder, had a comforting heft. The other rifle went behind her back, followed by the quiver and, finally, her bow. She caressed its polished wood.

Don't worry, old friend. Didn't abandon you.

"You look like a pack mule, little lady." Samvel laughed. "A very rich, very scary pack mule!"

A compliment, and a cause for concern. Yun-mi frowned. The guard had a point. Looking scary was great. Looking rich—not so much, if the scary failed to outweigh the rich.

"Thank you for the help, Mister Samvel. Could you take me to New Kowloon's Quarter?"

"Ah, so you are their agent?" He raised a hand, quelling Yun-mi's objections. "Nah, don't care if you are. None of ma' business, lady. I'll show you the way, can't see why not."

More corridors, more hallways, filled with people at this time of day. Rich mule and all, nobody spared her a second glance. She wasn't the most extravagant character around.

New Kowloon's Quarter occupied an entire wing of the Mall's main building. An autonomous wing. No fence separated it, not as much as a line on the floor to mark its limits, yet the boundary was obvious. Yun-mi's guide, who'd been strolling with the self-importance of a top dog, making crowds part before him, halted. He saluted a man sauntering across the invisible divide. "Wong, brought you a visitor."

"Samvel." The man called Wong inclined his head.

A sense of gross inadequacy in this big world clasped Yun-mi's chest. Everybody who mattered knew each other, to such a degree that they only needed a nod and a word or two to communicate. An outsider, a stranger from the City, she knew no one at all.

She did matter! She shook her head, expelling the anxiety. Just another obstacle. She'd manage. A Rat always finds a way. And she was on the path to become the damn best Rat ever!

She stepped forward and extended a hand, giddy with her boldness. "Mister Wong? Park Yun-mi of Little Korea. Nice to meet you. I'd like to talk to your intelligence officer."

Wong shook Yun-mi's hand noncommittally, the grip of his cool, dry palm neither too strong nor too limp. "Our intelligence officer? Would you now." He quizzically studied her face, as if trying to decide whether this was a weird prank, then looked at Samvel. The guard shrugged, waved, dismissing Yun-mi as someone else's problem now, and left. The aura of authority returned to his posture with every step he took.

"And what sort of business may a young Korean Rat have with our intelligence officer?" Wong didn't hide his amusement.

"Beg your pardon, sir, but that, I'm afraid, I can discuss only with him." Firm, but not impudent.

"Huh." Wong shrugged. "But be careful what you're asking for."

Corridors. Hallways. Again. Yet these, somehow, had a subtly distinct atmosphere. Another entrance, another guard.

"Wait here," Wong said and disappeared behind the door. A minute later, he peeked out and beckoned to Yun-mi.

This office differed drastically from the Magistrate's. Carpets everywhere, including the walls. Figurines, vases, semi-precious stones, other odds and ends covered every square inch of the abundant surfaces in a dizzying profusion of shapes and colors. Or was it an effect of the aromatic incense smoking in a burner?

In the center of the room sat a huge redwood desk. *A bureau*, a strange word floated from deep recesses of Yun-mi's memory. A tiny man of indeterminate age nestled behind the desk, so well camouflaged between a black carved stone dragon and a nephrite buddha, she didn't notice him until he said, "This better be good, Park Yun-mi."

"May I ask who I am talking to?"

The office owner clenched his jaw, stretching his lips into a thin white line. His short-cropped gray hair bristled. A hedgehog suffering from indigestion.

Wong responded in his stead. "This is Onyx Dragon Hua Tsin Lin, Acting Security Coordinator for New Kowloon's Dixie Mission. You asked for an intelligence officer. This is as close as it gets here. Now state your business."

"It's an honor." Yun-mi bowed to the Dragon, not too shallowly, not too impertinently. "No disrespect, mister Wong, but the nature of my information is extremely sensitive. I wouldn't want to cause any trouble by disclosing it to those who may not be authorized. It's best if I state my business one on one with the Onyx Dragon and let him be the judge." Yun-mi rattled off the speech in a single breath and inhaled.

Bless you, Joon-woo, may the gods be kind to your soul.

Her mentor had insisted on teaching her all kinds of unusual words and how to string those into intricate sentences. At first, she had vehemently resisted these lessons, arguing that a Rat needs to perfect physical skills, not useless blubbering.

"You are right," he had replied, "if you want to be *a* Rat. But if your ambition is to become *the* Rat, the face of your clan, one day you'll get to deal with the big shots. Those people are nothing like us. Not compelled to engage in menial labor, they indulge in various cultural pursuits. These words I just used, any idea what they mean? No? My point precisely. If you ever find yourself on their playing field, you'd better speak their language. Otherwise, you'll be dealing with them from a position of disadvantage."

In time, Yun-mi had come to enjoy this skill as much as hunting. She had become a voracious reader, scouring the City's forsaken houses for the few surviving books; a challenging quest, considering everything combustible had been used for heat and cooking by the early survivors in the first post-E winter.

"Fine," conceded the Dragon begrudgingly after an uneasy pause. Several words to Wong in Cantonese sent the man out at a brisk run. When the door softly closed behind him, Hua Tsin Lin stared squarely at Yun-mi.

"Speak."

"Onyx Dragon, does the name Jim Parker mean anything to you?"

The man squinted, but the flash of surprise in his eyes was unmistakable.

Chapter 9

Buck

September 20, 42 PE

"Really?" Sam chortled. "You? Being sent to get an old weapons cache? With Lieutenant Kossowsky and two of Colonel's guards?"

"Yeah, Buck," seconded Larry. "I mean, come on, even you could've invented a better tale! That's a pile of bullshit. Or is it *Buck*-shit?"

"Whatever." Buck kept packing his rucksack. That was the story the lieutenant had come up with. It *was* stupid, but what could he do? At least Larry and Sam hadn't heard about Janet. He'd never live *that* down.

Buck had few secrets from his best friends, but wouldn't dare disobey Colonel's confidentiality orders. Not that Buck himself understood all too well what their real mission was.

"Brennan. Briefing room. Now."

Buck and his friends started. None of them heard Jackson approaching.

"Yes, sir!" Buck saluted. He exchanged meaningful looks with Larry and Sam, shouldered the backpack, and dashed to the door.

"Good luck, bud!" shouted Sam to his back. "Take care!"

There was no briefing. Lieutenant Kossowsky glanced at Buck and gestured for him and Jackson to follow. All three wore civilian clothes. Janet was nowhere to be seen, but that made sense. The Army didn't allow women at the Base, so she must have been waiting somewhere else. Probably with Lundy, who wasn't around either.

A wagon drawn by two horses waited at the gate, moderately loaded with something hidden under a tarp. The lieutenant signaled for Buck to climb on in the back and joined Jackson at the reins.

A short ride brought them to the *Firkin and Boot*.

The lieutenant tossed a coin to the groom and hurried through the door. Buck had never been in a tavern before and gawked around, trying to keep up.

They found Janet and Lundy in a backroom. The girl had her travel cape hood up. She stared out through the small sooty window, with her back to Lundy. The soldier scowled, cleaning his fingernails with a butter knife.

The new arrivals took places around the table, and the lieutenant faced Janet. "Well? Where are we going?"

Reluctantly, she tore her gaze off the window, fiddled with her fingers, not meeting Kossowsky's eyes, and finally mumbled, "I think it's the City. What they call Downtown. Where the tallest buildings are."

Buck gulped. Lundy cussed under his breath. Jackson whistled. "You *think*? We're going to that hell hole based on something you *think*? Not something you *know*?" Jackson's tone was misleadingly sympathetic.

Janet exploded. "Don't like this? Screw it! Crawl back to your Colonel and tell him I went home because you don't want to go where I *think* we have to go. See what he has to say about that, your beloved commander!"

"Whoa, lady, calm down!" Lundy raised his palms.

If Buck's own bitter experience with Janet had taught him anything, there was no stopping her. Especially when she got angry.

"Calm down?! You think the City scares me any less? You think I asked for this? Can any of you—strong, brave men—say 'no' to him?" She didn't need to elaborate which *him* she was referring to.

Janet took in their eyes. Buck averted his. None of the other soldiers replied.

"That's what I thought," she said, quieter but firmer. "Neither could I. So here we are. I found certain..."—she carefully chose the next word—"hints. Very vague hints. And yes, I *think* they lead to the City's Downtown. I have no better ideas on how to interpret them. You want to follow your orders? Go where I tell you. You don't? You can go to the Seven Hells for all I care!"

She bit her lip, as if regretting the words. Did she find mentioning the Seven Hells too rude?

Everyone else leaned back from the table as if blown away by the onslaught of her fury. The lieutenant's face turned red. Lundy glowered. Buck held his breath, fearing what might happen next.

Only Janet's heavy breathing disrupted the charged silence of the room. She crossed her arms. Her stare invited anyone to challenge her defiance.

Jackson's soft, approving chuckle broke the tension.

"Feisty! I like this girl," he said to Kossowsky, pointing at her with a thumb. "It's gonna be fun, sir."

The officer clearly didn't share Jackson's excitement. Several uneasy seconds passed before he reined in his temper, exhaling through his teeth. "The City it is. Why didn't you say so before? Such an expedition requires different preparations than what we have in place."

Janet shrugged. "You didn't ask." She returned her attention to the window.

"Miss McPherson." Kossowsky stared at the segment of the floral tablecloth framed by his tightly squeezed fists.

Buck pulled his legs under the bench so he'd be ready to intervene if the lieutenant decided to strangle her.

"Let me establish some ground rules" The officer stared at Janet.

The girl shrunk under his brooding, unblinking gaze.

"You aren't happy about this mission. You've made that abundantly clear. I am not too excited to have you on my team, either."

Janet's cheeks turned pink as she lowered her eyes. Not a reaction Buck had expected. Not from her.

"But we're stuck together for a while," continued the lieutenant. "I have my orders, which is another way of saying 'I plan to do everything in my power for this mission to succeed.' If all of us get back in one piece, I'll consider that a bonus. For that to happen, we need to act as a team. Do you know what that means?"

His words touched some chords, because Janet only nodded, not daring to meet Kossowsky's eye.

"Honestly, I am not sure you do. Let me explain," the officer insisted. "Being a part of a team means not concealing, or not failing to share, for this matter, any relevant information. It means having each other's back—"

"Enough, Tony. Stop it." Guilt was written plainly and painfully on Janet's face. "I get it, okay?"

Tony?! Seven Hells, these two had a history! A dull spasm twisted Buck's chest. He was... jealous?

Pieces of the puzzle slid together. Colonel must have had a solid motive for putting Lieutenant Kossowsky in charge of Janet's detail. Having known her before could provide a better judgment... unless this backfired. Which it might just have.

Kossowsky broke the awkward silence. "We'll see. Let's start over. Tell us everything we need to know."

This time, the wagon was fully packed. Boxes of dried food, water kegs, tins of ammo. Many tins of ammo, comforting to have in case of need, and alarming, hinting such a need may arise.

The tarp concealed their rifles within easy reach. The lieutenant planned to pose as a merchant outside Five Points. That restricted what they could openly carry to sticks and utility blades.

Buck shuddered, as he did each time he was reminded of their destination.

The City. The name mothers used to scare unruly children into submission. "Listen to me right now, or a zombie will come in your sleep and drag you to the City!"

For many years, Fivepointers hadn't seen a single zombie; no wonder the children didn't listen.

Forty years ago, that was different. Back then, the communities had to fight them off all the time. Eventually, the Army had pushed the menace away from the Boundary, into the Wilderness.

By Buck's time, zombies were little more than a fable. They possibly still existed somewhere, but the threat had lost its edge.

The City, though... Everyone knew it was real. Some had even seen it. Not Fivepointers, naturally, they didn't venture out. Merchants, crazy enough to risk approaching the City, were the primary source of knowledge. At the Marketplace, they would make a spectacle of storytelling, charging a moderate fee for the show, and never lacking an audience. They told bizarre and frightening stories that tickled imagination, and listening to them was one of Buck's favorite sorts of amusement. Growing up, he suspected most were exaggerated, some—completely made up to entertain the public. Even so, at least a part of the tales had to be true.

The epicenter of everything unusual and dangerous happening in this neck of the woods, the City was repulsive in its strangeness, foreignness, and otherworldliness—and attractive for all the same reasons.

And then there was Downtown. The eye of the storm, the den of the monster. If one were to believe the traveling merchants, it had buildings of unimaginable height, taller than the formidable three stories of the Marketplace Council; dark and damp underground catacombs, spanning tens of kilometers; enormous gloomy warehouses filled with abominable machinery—dormant now, but waiting for its hour to rise again and eradicate the remnants of Humanity once and for all.

Thinking about Downtown gave Buck goosebumps. What would it be like to *walk* it?

But first, they had to get there. Which meant passing by foreign, hostile communities. Only merchants universally enjoyed immunity and warm reception. Trade and news were welcome everywhere. In the wilderness, though, travelers risked running into bandit gangs. This danger had diminished in recent years, but still was real enough that traders traveled in large, well-protected groups.

Buck approached Lieutenant Kossowsky. The officer's forehead wrinkled skeptically when Buck opened his mouth.

"Sir, wouldn't it be better to join a caravan? Safer, lower key?"

Kossowsky's brow smoothed. "Not a bad idea, Private. We'll pass through the Marketplace on our way out. I'll ask around, see if any caravan is heading the same way. But if not, we're leaving on our own."

"Sir, one more question, if I may?"

"Go ahead."

"We're pretending to be merchants. What's our merchandise?"

"Dry food. Be aware of the roles we'll play. I am a merchant, Miss McPherson—my wife and co-owner of the family business, you—our prentice. Jackson and Lundy—hired guards. Clear?"

The lieutenant and Janet posing as a couple? "Sir, did Miss McPherson agree to that?"

Kossowsky glanced at him. "She doesn't know yet. And you're right, she won't be thrilled with this arrangement. But she'll come around, by hook or by crook. She's agreed to be a team player, hasn't she?" He smirked.

By hook or by crook? What was that supposed to mean?

"Merchants? Like Seven Hells you are!" The giant, barrel-shaped Caravan Master laughed, stroking his impressive potbelly with a pair of shovel-like hands. "Wanna try again?"

By a lucky coincidence, a caravan was about to leave the Marketplace the next morning, going up north and then west, toward the City. The lieutenant found Joe Flanagan, the Caravan Master, having his dinner in the Chamber of Commerce at the Marketplace Council building. Janet and Buck came along to corroborate the story. Which imploded with all the grace of a soap bubble as soon as the officer made the introductions.

"Any village idiot will tell you're a soldier, not a merchant. Maybe, just maybe, you'll fool some inbred sheep herders up in the hills. In a thick fog. On a moonless night." He liberated another peal of that booming laughter.

"Can't a retired soldier become a merchant?"

Kossowsky's icy voice didn't impress the Caravan Master. "Oh, yes, he can. But he must learn to control his emotions if he's ever to negotiate successfully."

Something about Master Flanagan seemed vaguely familiar, something elusive. Was it the ingrained smell of salted fish emanating from him, Creek Point's hallmark aroma? The moment Buck had stepped into the room, he felt comfortable.

If the lieutenant blew this, they could forget about joining the caravan. Buck's heart skipped a beat. The thought of venturing into the Wilderness with a large group had helped calm his anxiety, somewhat. And not a random large group, but with this loud, eccentric man who made Buck feel at home.

The lieutenant frowned. "Alright, let's say you've got me. How about you get four trained soldiers to guard your caravan for free in exchange for playing along with us?"

The Caravan Master stroked his bushy piebald beard. "See? Now we're talking. You may have basic negotiation skills, after all. Where is it you want to go with all the secrecy?"

"That is none of your business, merchant!"

"Huh? Is this the way to talk to someone whose help you need, young man?" Flanagan crossed his legs and locked his fingers on top of his protruding belly. "Remember, you need me, not the other way."

"Fine," Kossowsky gave up, taking his arrogance down a notch. "Apologies."

"Wasn't that difficult, was it? Oh, and for Heaven's sake, grow a beard! When did you last see a beardless merchant?"

Kossowsky touched his chin. "Fair point. No more shaving. As for where we're going, we'll follow your caravan along Lake O, then split off. Simple."

"Simple, eh?" The Caravan Master chuckled. "If my business with Five Points Marketplace has taught me anything, it's that nothing is 'simple' when it involves Miss McPherson." He acknowledged the girl with a broad smile and a half-hearted bow.

Kossowsky mumbled something unintelligible under his breath.

Janet pursed her lips and glowered back at the merchant.

The Caravan Master's expression changed. Gone was the amiable old man. The pinholes of his serious eyes drilled through the lieutenant. "Alright, enough fooling around. On our way here we had an unpleasant run-in with some riffraff near Burlington Heights. Rumors circulate about the Black Beans gang getting active again in the Brampton Forest area. Our caravan can always use extra hands in its security arrangements. Especially if these hands are trained to hold something better than sticks. My only question to you is, will you cause problems?" The massive man rose from his chair and towered over the not-so-short officer.

"No, sir." Kossowsky stood his ground. "You'll barely notice our presence."

The Caravan Master studied him. "Not even Miss McPherson?" A smile lurked in the thickets of his beard.

"I vouch for her, sir."

"In that case, I'll see you at the Bald Hill Gate at sunrise tomorrow. Welcome to my caravan, *merchant* Kossowsky!" His deep laughter accompanied the newly minted traders out of the room.

"Your reputation precedes you, my dearest wifey!" hissed the lieutenant as soon as they left behind the Zealots pilloried near the building's massive doors.

"I regret the day I agreed to marry you, sleazy haggler! And don't you dare ever call me 'wifey' again!"

Buck's instinct had been spot-on. The moment Kossowsky conveyed to Janet her intended role, she responded with such an outburst that Jackson stepped forward, ready to restrain her if need be. Eventually, she calmed down, *for the team*, but from that point on, she bluntly ignored everyone on the Task Force. Except for the lieutenant. Him, she tormented with relentless acid remarks. There definitely was bad blood between those two.

This was going to be a long, grueling journey.

Chapter 10

Yun-mi

September 20, 42 PE

Fifteen minutes later, the Onyx Dragon personally escorted her out of the office. Not a common occurrence, as attested by Wong's wide eyes.

Standing, Hua hardly reached Yun-mi's shoulder, but radiated strength and authority. "Wong Min Han, arrange for Miss Park to be accompanied straight to Golden Dragon Tam Wai Lam's office with all expedience. Employ non-Kowloonese assets in the Mall's vicinity. It's bad enough she came directly to our Quarter. Understood?"

"*Hai!*"

Onyx Dragon turned to Yun-mi and cracked a lopsided smile.

"Miss Park, you appear overburdened. Wong Min Han, help Miss Park convert tradable goods in her possession into hard coin before she leaves. Make sure she's happy with the exchange rate."

"Yes, sir!" Wong bowed again.

He led Yun-mi into a room where a Kowloonese trader joined her.

Yun-mi emptied her three bags onto a wide polished table. Pelts, museum artifacts, cured meats, and items she didn't recognize. She pushed everything toward the inscrutable, well-dressed man, then stuffed the remaining gear back into a bag, leaving a single item on her side of the table. The tanto. She picked it up and slid it halfway out of its sheath. A perfect blade, with an exquisite wavy pattern of folded steel. But, forever tainted, it burned her hands. She slammed it back and sent it skidding across the surface, into the pile of goods. And *bads*.

Speaking of *bads*...

Yun-mi rummaged through the mess in her bag and pulled out the murderer's leather jacket. Her turn to assume the badass image. She'd earned it.

The grown-up man's garment fit loosely on her slim frame. There was a metaphor in this, big shoes and all that crap. Fuck metaphors. No matter the size, she was as badass as it gets!

Her counterpart did not haggle. His lips moved while he evaluated, calculated, and added up, jotting characters on a square of paper.

Yun-mi followed his pencil's strokes with awe. Succumbing to Joon-woo's insistence, she'd learned to read English and Korean, but writing... Writing was a whole different level. Only a few Rats possessed that talent in the godless City. And wherever the Faith was prevalent, rumor had it, its adherents considered writing borderline heresy, one step short of engine idolization. What Yun-mi beheld was a masterful skill executed with thoughtless proficiency. The trader's pencil flew over the paper with an astonishing speed, producing straight columns of neat characters—not as a work of art, but simply to calculate how much she was owed.

He read out the bottom line. Yun-mi had no clue about the proper value of the goods, but trusted the fear instilled by the Onyx Dragon in his subordinates. The colossal amount by far surpassed anything Yun-mi had ever held in her hands. She accepted the offer without hesitation. The trader opened a lacquered lockbox he'd brought with him, counted out six heavy, tightly wrapped bags and moved them across the table to Yun-mi with a bow.

Yun-mi said, "*M goi!*" using up half of her Cantonese vocabulary, and slid the bags into her purse belt. The coins in the swollen belt pressed into her hips heavier than expected. Must have been the burden of responsibility.

With that sorted out, Wong led her to another room where several men waited. Turbans, bushy beards, kirpans. Yun-mi had known *of* Sikhs, but had never met one, let alone five. Whether they were merchants, hired guards, or bandits, Yun-mi couldn't begin to guess. A bit of all those trades, likely.

Wong made the introductions. "Miss Park, these are the Singh brothers of the West Sauga Clan. They will ensure your safe passage to New Kowloon."

The men greeted her with much flamboyance, shaking her hand, patting her on the shoulders, hugging her, as though she were their long-lost sister, miraculously found again.

Wong waited for the festivities to subside and nodded. "I'll rejoin you at the halfway point."

Yun-mi responded with a ceremonious bow. "Thank you, Wong Min Han. I look forward to seeing you soon."

With the direct access she had established to the higher level of Kowloonese hierarchy, Yun-mi didn't have to acknowledge Wong explicitly. But he wasn't a foot soldier in the local power structure, and if she was to build her own connections, showing him respect was the appropriate thing to do. They may have started their acquaintance on the wrong foot. Why not mend the relationship if it cost her nothing but a bow?

Wong's eyes gleamed with appreciation. "Park Yun-mi," he bowed in return, "I will see you shortly."

Yun-mi glanced back at the Mall for the last time, before other features of the unfamiliar cityscape swallowed it.

New Kowloon, another famous place, awaited with the promise of yet another battle of wits. Its inexorable pull contended against the crushing events of the previous day, a stone that had settled behind her sternum. The loss of Joon-woo, and with it the end of the life she'd known. The almost rape. Being sold like livestock. Her first kill.

Head in the game, girl! Head in the game!

She let the excited butterflies in her stomach lift the weight and carry the stone away. New day. New page. Moving on.

The trip proved safe, yet anything but quiet. The Singh brothers chatted incessantly. Too much talking for comfort. At first, they'd attempted to involve Yun-mi, but failed to extract anything beyond polite, perfunctory replies, and relented.

They weren't useless chatterers, though. Beyond the gregarious façade, their trained eyes scanned the surroundings, and their hands periodically gravitated toward the handles of their weapons. An entirely different mode of operation from what Yun-mi was used to, but the approach had its merits. The City Rats worked mostly individually, and that called for stealthy crawling. This Sauga Clan had adopted the opposite technique. Five heavily armed and well-trained fighters presented a force to be reckoned with. They didn't need to hide. On the contrary, like poisonous animals whose bright colors scream, "I don't do camouflage! Touch me at your own risk!" they boldly announced their presence.

If only Joon-woo were here with her... To listen to her musings, to approve or disapprove of her decisions, to advise her on what to do next. To admit, with that begrudging grin of his, that she did well.

Yun-mi's eyesight blurred. For a moment, she released the little girl in her. Helpless, clueless, alone against the hostile world. Joon-woo, her mentor of three years, her older brother by mutual choice if not by birth, gone. His body lay somewhere, being picked by insects, birds, and small animals—an appropriate burial for a Rat. But Yun-mi would always carry a bit of his soul wherever she went.

With a deep breath, she pushed the angst away. No place for weakness. A strong, determined Rat once again. One of the best. Marching through unfamiliar territory as if it were her home turf, on the way to change the world. And if the stubborn world resisted, to bend it the fuck over!

In an hour, Wong joined the company, as promised, with two silent associates. Yun-mi and Wong nodded to each other, executing the nonverbal understanding they now had. A warm, sweet satisfaction washed over her heart. There. Connected now. She knew people, too.

After a time, the group turned a corner and saw... *what?*

No words existed that could do the Great Hive justice. The stories of fabulous New Kowloon, the impressions of those who had visited it—none of that prepared her for the real thing.

Colossal, alien, it exceeded everything she had drawn in the eye of her imagination. The megastructure loomed over the last rows of houses. New Kowloon's main compound dwarfed its surroundings in both height and width. Scaffolding clung to one corner, the people moving on it smaller than ants. The Kowloonese did not subscribe to the machine-loathing Faith: Two enormous cranes turned lazily, delivering shipping containers and rails to the top. The lower levels shone with uniformly painted bright red, and only the unfinished parts showed the original faded walls. The complex emanated power. Not the menacing sort, but solid, stubborn, profound composure.

It was a statement.

In a world where "construction" meant haphazardly slapping together salvaged scraps...

In a world content with its state of barely mitigated misery and borderline savagery...

In a world where the ignorant, zealous majority saw machines as an abomination...

In a world living off the scraps of the fallen civilization's glory...

In this world, the Great Hive of New Kowloon unapologetically announced to its onlookers, "We are building the future!"

That first glimpse of the Great Hive was going to be etched in her memory. She'd lost track of time, standing on the corner of the street dominated by the enormous structure ahead.

She was a City girl, not a rural hick. And not just any City girl but a Rat, blood of the City's blood. She'd seen plenty of buildings, including some that calling them "tall" would be a gross understatement. She could, occasionally, be impressed by an outstanding tower, but wouldn't be caught gawking at one. What made the difference? The Hive was *being built*. Not inherited from the ancients, like everything around. Being built, present tense. A subtle but profound distinction.

A hand touched Yun-mi's shoulder.

Parker?!

She consciously suppressed the instinct to bat it off. Parker was dead. *Knife through the throat, glassy eyes, remember?*

Wong saw her face and his eyes widened. He jerked his hand away. "Sorry," he whispered hoarsely, then cleared his throat and looked at New Kowloon. "You've been watching the Hive for ten minutes. It has such an effect on people. Now that you've savored your moment, we should get going."

The countless layers of containers above dwarfed the maw of the compound. Their immense weight over Yun-mi's head exerted almost physical pressure.

The gate guards were armed to the teeth with automatic weapons and handguns, their combat vests bristling with spare magazines. It took all her willpower not to cringe under their examining eyes.

A thought shot through Yun-mi's head like a lightning bolt. Outside several Kowloonese officials, she was the only person exposed to whatever errands Parker had been running for the Hive. The son of a bitch had made a fatal mistake of leaving Yun-mi alive, letting his greed prevail over common sense. The highest-ranking Hive officer was unlikely to show such indiscretion. There was a strong possibility she'd never walk through this gate in the opposite direction.

Oh, shit.

Yun-mi stumbled. She would have to work extra hard to convince the Golden Dragon she was a valuable asset, as if her life were hanging by this thread. Because it was.

"Is everything okay, Miss Park?" The concern in Wong's voice sounded genuine, but that was his job. The man was tasked with ensuring her safety *outside* the Hive. If he were ordered to eliminate the unwanted witness, he'd pull the trigger without a moment's hesitation, showing similar equanimity.

With a weak smile, Yun-mi regained a semblance of composure and strode on. She'd manage. She was a Rat.

"You are a Rat." Very much a statement, not a question.

Golden Dragon Tam Wai Lam was not a pleasant man. Golden Dragon Tam Wai Lam was an unpleasant woman.

That was hard to anticipate. Not the unpleasant part, Yun-mi had no expectations in this regard. But finding a woman occupying the Dragon's quarters threw a wrench into her preparations. The elaborate opening sentence she'd planned out while waiting in the antechamber crumbled into a verbal mess.

Yun-mi collected her wits, yet not quickly enough.

"Golden Dragon." She bowed deeper than she'd originally intended, concealing her embarrassment at the expense of losing a point. The Golden Dragon surely saw right through her ruse.

Yun-mi stood in the center of a large room with a spotlight on her. Green screens of heavy fabric, arranged into an artful maze, draped the dimly lit periphery. These complex folds could easily hide half a dozen armed men. The sucking emptiness in the pit of her stomach was hard to ignore, but these invisible threats had to be accepted as a given. Otherwise, the preoccupation was guaranteed to distract her from the interview—the only thing that mattered. The only thing that might keep her alive.

Yun-mi returned her attention to the Dragon. The shadows made the hostess's features difficult to discern. With the austere expression on her smooth face, the woman appeared to be old, maybe forty. She leaned onto one of those heavy wooden pieces of furniture that the Kowloonese seemed fond of. Her desk held only a neat pile of paper, a few pens, and an odd, ancient-looking bronze and black machine with buttons and a cranking handle on the side. Despite her thin frame, the Golden Dragon commanded the room. Whether the deliberate lighting arrangement helped achieve that effect, or some other skillful manipulation, she inexorably drew attention to herself.

"You are a Rat," repeated the Golden Dragon, spicing up the challenge with contempt. "What can you possibly offer me?"

Yun-mi raised her head, defiantly locked eyes with the woman, and shot back. "Yes, I am a Rat"—she put all the pride she could muster in that word—"and you are a Golden Dragon. What can *you* possibly offer *me*?"

The ensuing silence stretched for ages. Enough time to resign to her fate. A sign from the Dragon—a twitch of a finger, a single-syllable command—and she'd be dead, with several crossbow bolts piercing her chest or a bullet ventilating her skull. A clammy rivulet of sweat ran down her spine, but Yun-mi preserved her bold expression. Every muscle in her face wanted to rebel, to twitch or to relax. The effort of holding them at bay demanded all her strength, physical and moral. One second longer, and she'd crumble.

A smile cracked the porcelain mask of the Dragon's face. "Alright. I can see why Hua and Wong believe you may be an asset."

Yun-mi shuddered internally and allowed herself to quietly exhale. The Dragon had been testing her. She must have passed. Not a reason to loosen up, though. Who knows what other tests this woman had in stock?

Tam Wai Lam elegantly disengaged from her monumental chair, strolled around the desk, and stopped in front of Yun-mi. She leaned back onto the tabletop and crossed her arms. Her simple, unadorned green shirt and pants were coordinated with the drapes but a shade darker. Yet, clashing audaciously—and completely out of the character Yun-mi had built in her mind—the Golden Dragon wore white running shoes. With the different lighting angle, her visage shed years. Joon-woo's age, not even thirty.

"Enough with the bullshit, Yun-mi," the woman said. "No more tests, no more tiptoeing around. You know why I am a Golden Dragon? Not because of being born into the right family, kissing a strategically important ass, or warming the Honorable Chairman's bed. No, I'm a Golden Dragon because I'm a go-getter. An overachiever. I care nothing about ceremonies, propriety, or someone's hurt feelings. All I care about are the bottom-line results. And I appreciate the people who help me achieve my objectives."

She studied Yun-mi's face. "Now, tell me what you know, how you know it, and what your offer is."

Yun-mi ran a hand through her hair. "No bullshit?" She met the Golden Dragon's eye.

"No bullshit," the woman confirmed, mischief wrinkling the corners of her eyes.

"How many crossbows are trained on me right now?" Yun-mi asked nonchalantly.

"Oh, I don't know. Three? Four? Why?" The Golden Dragon looked amused but also a bit impressed.

"Can we talk like two adults?" Yun-mi was complimenting herself, knowing Tam Wai Lam knew that, too. "With no one listening in?"

Her eyes on Yun-mi, the Golden Dragon raised and opened a fist. A soft rustle of retreating steps behind the drapes confirmed the execution of her order.

"That's it?" The relief emboldened Yun-mi. "No one left behind?"

"What a Rat!" This time, the word came out of the Dragon's mouth as a praise, not a slur. Her smile grew wider, too. She raised her fist again, opening and closing it twice. Another rustle of steps.

"No more?"

"Don't push it. Now talk." The hostess was all business again. For a second, they'd had a moment, a human connection... No, that couldn't be true. *Okay, careful now. Assess the strategies.*

Downplay her role? That was likely to render her irrelevant. Meaning, dead.

Pretend she knew more than she did? Inflate her importance to create the impression she was the only one with the chops to get the job done, whatever that job was? Promising, but if her bluff were called, she'd be out of options. And probably dead.

Or tell the truth and hope the utilitarian Dragon would find her valuable enough to retain her services. Any services, as long as she didn't get squashed like a bug.

"The truth is," Yun-mi said, stepping off a cliff, "I don't know much."

No secret trap door swung open under her feet. No spiked ball fell from the ceiling to crush her skull. The world didn't end in a storm of lightning and fire. Tam Wai Lam patiently waited for her to continue.

Yun-mi was suddenly out of air.

Breathe.

Her attempt to inhale inconspicuously failed, and a small sob-like sound escaped her throat. This one little sound must have ruined any positive impression she may have made on the Dragon up to that point.

Only a step apart, but a gulf divided them. The woman had ten years over her and commanded an immense power. Technically, Yun-mi didn't belong to the organization controlled by Tam Wai Lam, but the Dragon had the sway to control—or end—Yun-mi's life in every imaginable way.

Something touched Yun-mi's forearm. Incredulous, she stared down. No, not a hallucination. The Golden Dragon's palm really was resting on Yun-mi's arm. Her anxiety receded.

"Miss Park." Tam Wai Lam's level, quiet voice soothed Yun-mi's feverish face. "Calm down. I don't know what sort of stories you've heard about me, but they must've been exaggerated. I don't kill people for fun. I don't even kill all the people who could use some being killed. I am an administrator. A damn fine one, but just an administrator. I deal with strategic resource allocation."

None of that made sense. Yun-mi understood most of the individual words, but how did all that relate to her?

"You've already proved your mettle. For such a young age, and a girl at that, you're an exceptional Rat, based on what I hear and see. This makes you a useful resource, which is good enough for me. I only need to decide how to put you to best use. Now, the question is, am I good enough for you?"

Yun-mi's capacity for shock had been long exhausted. Or so she thought. The question helped her discover a whole new, untapped reservoir.

"H-h-h..." Her throat urgently needed clearing. "How do you mean?"

Tam Wai Lam's lighthearted laughter rang like little silver bells. "As an employer, Miss Park. Am I good enough for you as an employer? In plain words, will you work for me?"

And that was it. The never-before felt sense of being appreciated, valued, needed. Seen, by a Golden Dragon, no less! By this amazing woman, capable of combining the highest authority in the land with a simple human touch.

Yun-mi was hers. Hook, line, and sinker. Not just an expert administrator. A master manipulator.

By way of response, Yun-mi offered a hand, and the Golden Dragon shook it. Her grip was firm. A pleasant warmth spread up Yun-mi's arm. Or was that a figment of her imagination?

"We'll continue our conversation tomorrow," said the Dragon. "You've had plenty of excitement for one day."

Yun-mi's first instinct was to argue, to convince her new boss she could go on and on. But what for? Tam Wai Lam was right. The most important part was behind her. Yun-mi was alive, and the prospects of staying that way for a little longer looked promising.

Squeezing the hostess's hand one last time and meeting her eyes, Yun-mi said, "Thank you, Wai Lam."

What happened then didn't register with her.

Next thing she knew, she was kneeling awkwardly on the floor with her wrist twisted at an impossible angle, and agonizing pain shooting through her arm all the way to the shoulder. White shoes dominated her field of vision.

The Golden Dragon, about as tall as Yun-mi, didn't need to bend much to bring her face close to the back of Yun-mi's head. Her warm breath in Yun-mi's ear reminded her of Parker's. The déjà vu amplified the horror of the situation.

"Do not presume." The Dragon's whisper was barely audible, which made it all the scarier. "Do not. Mistake. My openness. For a weakness." She pushed the words into Yun-mi's ear one by one, underscoring each with an imperceptible movement of her wrist. Each twist edged Yun-mi ever closer to blacking out.

"I am New Kowloon's Golden Dragon." Twist.

"I am your boss." Twist.

"Not your girlfriend." Twist.

"I am fair"—no twist?—"but ruthless." A vicious jerk squeezed tears from Yun-mi's eyes, tightly shut in pain.

"Is that understood?" An unseen sharp movement sent her splayed onto the floor.

Yun-mi lay for a few seconds, nauseated, waiting for the white splotches in her eyes to swim away. She finally pushed herself off the floor with one arm and sat on her knees, nursing the tortured hand in her lap. She sullenly glanced at the

Dragon and then surprised herself with a broad smile. "Just an administrator, eh?"

Tam Wai Lam extended a hand first and helped Yun-mi onto her feet. Yun-mi suppressed a vengeful urge to return the favor by putting the Dragon's arm in a lock. That would've been an insanely bad idea.

Instead, she stepped back and bowed formally. "Thank you for the lesson, Golden Dragon."

"I hope you're a quick learner, Miss Park. Until tomorrow."

"Until tomorrow, Golden Dragon." Turning to leave, Yun-mi muttered under her breath, "Nice shoes, by the way!" Never to be outdone. The last word was hers.

The Golden Dragon shook her head.

A silent man met Yun-mi outside the Golden Dragon's office and gestured for her to follow him. A servant? A guard? Was she a guest or a prisoner?

The guide led her through endless corridors and down a few flights of stairs. Strictly utilitarian passageways, where their steps echoed hollowly on metal grates, contrasted with upscale areas decorated with murals and lined with carpets. Potted plants adorned intersections. A pair of intricately carved human-sized dragon statues marked an entrance to an undoubtedly important room.

Eventually, they stopped at a door that did not differ from the dozens they'd passed on the way. The servant-guard pushed it open and gestured again, inviting Yun-mi to step in.

She hesitated, then shrugged off her doubts and entered the room. Given how well her conversation with Tam Wai Lam had gone, it was reasonable to assume she wasn't in immediate danger.

Went well? The dull ache in her wrist brought a smile to her lips. She could see how this woman had achieved the highest position in the Hive's notoriously patriarchal society. Take no shit, give no fucks, a perfect motto for the Golden Dragon. Seven Hells, Yun-mi was totally going to mention this to Wai Lam next time they talked!

Wai Lam, yes. Out of pure contrariness, nothing else. A dangerous game, one slip and Yun-mi would be in deep trouble, deeper than a twisted arm, for sure. But the danger was titillating.

The room, not too big, as far as rooms go, was way bigger than anything Yun-mi had ever had at her disposal. Her puny Christie Station partition would fit four times into this space. Not to speak of the Dixie Mall cell. The suite was outfitted with a bed, a small round table with two chairs, a sofa, and a closet with double mirror doors. A washroom behind a wooden divider completed the interior, with a bath, a toilet, and a basin. Two oil lamps under the ceiling gave enough warm light for comfort.

Luxury accommodations, by Yun-mi's standards. Roaming the City, she sometimes had ventured to the top floors of high-rise buildings. The size of those units and their contents had defied her imagination. But all that was long dead and useless. Who in their right mind would want to live on a thirtieth floor? Yes, the view was breathtaking, but dragging yourself, your food, your water, and everything else you might need up thirty flights of stairs? Bat shit crazy. Not counting those apartments, her current room was pretty darn swell.

Having finished the initial survey, Yun-mi turned to thank her guide, and didn't find him. She peeked into the deserted corridor. Unlocked and unguarded. Not a prisoner, then. Free to roam the Hive. Which she fully intended to do, after resting a little on that mattress, indecently appealing after the last night's concrete floor. Yun-mi shut the door and dove onto the bed. Only to stretch...

A gentle touch on the shoulder woke her up. She spun explosively out of the bed, drawing her knife before her eyes adjusted to the light. A different man, not the servant from before, stood in the room, patiently waiting for her to come to her senses. Not Parker either. She straightened, eying him suspiciously.

"Miss Park," the visitor said, "I am doctor Chen, here to check up on your wrist." He put his arm on a sizable leather bag sitting on the table.

Yun-mi blinked. "My wrist?"

"Yes, Miss, your right wrist."

She looked down at her hand, still holding the knife.

Oh! Wow. The Golden Dragon took care of her assets, didn't she? Even if she had inflicted the damage herself. That sprain? It was nothing, Yun-mi had far worse. Her body boasted a rich collection of scars and a fair number of once-broken bones. Sending a doctor to check on her was a goodwill gesture. A peace offering, but also a demonstration of who called the shots.

Following a thorough examination that involved bending Yun-mi's arms this way and that, the doctor left her with a bandaged wrist, an ice pack, and a vague recommendation not to overexert the injured limb. His implacable expression provided no hint of what the doctor thought about the practical necessity of his visit.

Yun-mi placed the canvas bag filled with shaved ice on top of the bandage, just for fun. Why not?

Minutes later, a delicate knock announced the next visit. Two young girls came in and meekly apologized for the intrusion. In a whirlwind of flying hands, they swiftly set the table with a dozen different sized dishes—seafood, noodles, salads. A teapot and two cups completed the setup. Before Yun-mi, slack-jawed, could react in any meaningful way, the girls collected their empty trays, bowed again, and disappeared into the corridor, softly closing the door.

This was beyond Yun-mi's wildest expectations. She had never been pampered like this. Definitely not a prisoner!

The tension receded from her limbs, her stomach, her chest. She had been running on grit and determination for two days. Fear, hatred, and hope had kept her going but were too exhausting to maintain. An inevitable crash was coming and being in a safe, comfortable environment when that happened could not hurt.

The excessive salivation in her mouth prevented further reflection. Her stomach, baited by the onslaught of smells wafting from the table, insistently rumbled. Damn! She hadn't eaten since the day before. Devouring the exquisite dishes was a sacrilege, but Yun-mi couldn't stop. She burped and slowed down to pour the tea, wondering about the purpose of the second cup, when yet another knock caught her mid-sip.

"Come in!" What next?

The servant—not a guard!—entered, bowed, and inquired with a perfectly neutral expression, "Would Miss like the company of a young man or a young woman for the night?"

Yun-mi snorted, sending the tea up her nose. Flustered, she prepared to blush at the first sign of the servant's scoffing, but not a muscle moved in his face.

Yun-mi had heard legends, whispered in disbelief, about the Kowloonese treatment of select VIP guests, but had never dreamed of finding herself in that role.

Her imagination began conjuring racy images, but an unbidden recollection of Parker's hands on her body shattered the mood and made her skin crawl. She flinched. The vision dissipated, leaving her unclean. She'd need to spend hours scrubbing in a bath before she'd be ready to allow a man to touch her again. And women? No, not her thing.

"Thank you, that won't be necessary," she managed crisply. "Some other time. I'll sleep alone tonight."

"Very well. Some other time, then. Good night, Miss." The servant retreated.

Yun-mi finished her meal and plodded to the bath, undressing on the way. Relax, unwind. So nice to not have to watch her back and fetch an arrow with every suspicious rustle. To feel at home.

Home?

Yun-mi's reflection in the mirror greeted her with a goofy, lopsided smile. Sure. Why in the Seven Hells not?

Chapter 11

Marc

September 21, 42 PE

Trepidation, defiance, hope. Could the three overlap? The proof was sitting in front of Marc.

Thick neck with protruding veins. Round shoulders. Muscular arms. The physique of a man doing hard labor all day, every day. Yet, something under the layers of muscle hinted at youthfulness.

Dusky skin. Eyes with irises so dark they appeared black. Long hair of a similar shade, collected into a frayed ponytail. A short curly beard hiding half the face.

Dirty, well-worn, faded shirt with old sweat stains, hanging loosely on his burly frame. Threadbare, baggy pants of an indeterminate color. And almost new military-style boots. The slavers cared about their workers' feet more than their overall hygiene, which made perverse sense strictly from a hauling efficiency point of view. That smell, though...

The guest wolfed down a plate of food, wiped it to a shiny gloss with the bread crust, and downed the fourth glass of water. Then the silence stretched, and stretched, and stretched some more, leading the young man to expose a gamut of emotions. Grim, to timid, to expectant, and back.

Captain Weinberg maintained an amicable smile through the man's meal and its silent aftermath, artfully judging the length of the suspense to achieve the most unsettling result. Finally, when their guest showed first signs of fidgeting, Weinberg cleared his throat. The man interrupted him, blurting, "The name is Rajan, sir, Rajan Gupta."

Marc's boss remained unperturbed by this outburst. He'd been steering the fugitive toward it all along. "Nice to meet you, Rajan. I am Captain Weinberg.

This is Lieutenant Novak." He left out their responsibilities. "I understand you've got an interesting story. But first, tell us a bit about yourself."

Rajan clutched his hands, "Master, no mucho to tell, vero."

Marc cringed. The haulers' lingo, a weird mix of English, Spanish and Italian with a sprinkle of Tamil, took an effort to decipher.

"I am not a Master, Rajan," the captain corrected with a mild smile. "No Masters here. That said, not much is better than nothing, am I right?"

Rajan considered the captain's suggestion. "Bene, sir." He nodded several times, as much to himself as to his interviewers. "Born in New Hope Colony. Mis padres tended sheep. I got two older hermanas y un hermano. Two younger hermanas, raiders stole them. Mi familia was well off, had cans for all of us. Mi time came, they called la ceremonia. Only it turned malo..." Rajan fell silent.

Marc frowned. "What? What's he talking about?"

"You've never heard of canned food divination? Quite a bizarre tradition. A few communities practice it. Next time you visit New Hope, look for can openers hanging above the doors. 'For luck and abundance,' they say."

"Uh, okay. But what's la ceremonia?"

"Simple. When a child is born, the happy parents buy a can of food, if they can afford one. They hide it until the child reaches the age of majority. Fourteen, yes, Rajan?"

"Yes, Mas— Sir. For boys. For girls, thirteen."

"Right. On that birthday, the can is retrieved and opened, with all the relatives, friends, and neighbors in attendance. If the food is still unspoiled, that's a good omen, a promise of a long and prosperous life. But if it has turned bad... May all the deities in the world help the kid."

Marc returned his attention to Rajan. Poor guy.

Rajan collected himself and continued, "Yeah, from that day, Rajan the Rotten Can was nobody's amigo anymore. Mis padres let me stay in la casa, but no one else would talk to me. Feared to catch my bad luck, or something. That what people do where I'm from. To think I treated other kids the same, before, you know. What a fool." He sunk into sullen silence again.

Weinberg didn't egg him on.

Marc grabbed the pitcher and poured more water into Rajan's glass.

The guest started, then smiled gratefully, made a few gulps, and went on. "Later that year, a drought came. And then a plague killed all the sheep. Bad, very bad year. Hungry year. So mis padres sold the Rotten Can to the Masters. Don't blame them. I'd do the same in their place. One less vay to feed, and mucho denaro to put food on the table for la familia. Hope they got good price and survived the winter." Rajan dwelled more on the memories. "That was four years ago. Three to go 'til mi contract ends." His face contorted into a sour smile. "Was until yesterday. Now they brand me as lifer, for escape before mi term end."

Marc's guess was correct. This burly man was a teenager with years of hard physical labor under his belt.

"No one's branding you, Rajan," Weinberg said. "You are your own man now, under the protection of the Free City of Locksville."

Rajan's jaw dropped. "Que? How?"

A thin smile split Captain Weinberg's face. "I bet the Masters don't want you to know, but we have an agreement. Any 'worker', as they call you, who reaches Locksville or contacts our representative and asks for asylum, is released from the contract without repercussions. If they've got blood on their hands, it's more complicated. But otherwise—yes, all you need to do is formally ask. Do you? Or would you rather return to The Station?"

"No! Not goin' back to the fucking slavers!" Rajan's short flareup died down, followed by a subdued, "Beg your pardon, sirs. Yes, I ask for a-sy-lum!"

As rewarding as delivering such news was, Marc's and the captain's interest in this man-boy went beyond strictly humanitarian. Marc hoped to prove to Weinberg that his hunch was based on more than a random, one-off occurrence. That there was an emerging pattern.

"Great!" said his boss. "With that out of the way, tell us about yesterday."

Chapter 12

Ka Yi

September 21, 42 PE

It wouldn't be much of an exaggeration to say that by the age of thirty-one, Shang Ka Yi, the Golden Dragon of New Kowloon's Trade Fleet, had seen a lot. Far more than what a dozen of his contemporaries put together would see in their entire lives. And yet, this one spectacle he'd never gotten used to. Leaning on the cold railing of the immense metal gates, ignoring the spray thrown at him by the wind gusts, Ka Yi watched the hypnotizing turbulence of the water filling the lock chamber.

Any other wonder of the lost civilization he'd encountered was static. Buildings in the City whose height defied imagination, enormous bridges spanning serious rivers. All these relics were magnificent—but dead. Not the locks. The locks functioned. Oh, the ancients, you'd had such unimaginable levels of technology, and screwed up so badly, losing everything. And then came the Faith, spreading like a plague, burning books, tearing down libraries, and smearing any trace of progress as apostasy. Rebuilding was bound to take forever. If only his secretly fostered group of scientists could pick up pace... Their meager advances were too few and excruciatingly slow. A meaningful breakthrough in Ka Yi's lifetime was utterly improbable. His efforts to scrounge every scientifically minded individual within reach meant little without the body of knowledge. Even with the smartest brains in the realm, rediscovering every bit of science and tech would take eons.

Locksville was lucky to inherit one of the few surviving marvels of prehistoric engineering in working condition, strong enough to stand as an island in the sea of the Faith's encroachment, and wise not to squander its main treasure.

Certain functionaries in New Kowloon's top echelons considered anyone of non-Chinese lineage lesser humans, incapable of ever reaching the same levels of greatness as the descendants of the Celestial Empire. What a dangerous, arrogant folly. The founding fathers of Locksville, the city owing its very name to these magnificent structures, deserved great respect. They had made the right call in those uncertain times, having enough foresight to realize that after the initial anarchy had run its course and the dust of the subsequent military campaigns had settled, trade connections would become the key to redevelopment. And whoever controlled the most convenient, high-throughput arteries would exert a tremendous amount of influence. Clearly, no one needed the locks to drive a wagon drawn by a scrawny mare from one village to another, or a fisherman's dinghy from a creek to a pond. But that wasn't civilization, that was eking out a miserable existence. No, moving forward required something scalable. Something that would connect the towns and communities along the shores of the Great Inland Seas. New Kowloon understood that, sending its trade fleets further and further, to the ends of today's small world and beyond, making it bigger again. The Station understood that, jealously protecting and rebuilding the railroad infrastructure. And Locksville understood that, too, sitting on a crucial intersection of these two most commercially viable means of transportation.

Knowing one's power meant being aware of its limitations. Abuse it once too often, and your domain would crumble, burying you underneath the wreckage. Locksville's top brass was not too vain to disregard this rule. That's why, when Ka Yi entered the office of the Trade Secretary and silently placed a bag of primers on his desk, Noor Alizadeh, his counterpart of many years, did not bargain. He stood up and shook Ka Yi's hand. No words were necessary, no agreements had to be signed. They'd collaborated long enough to establish a sufficient level of trust. Ka Yi did not worry about being shortchanged.

With that taken care of, he allowed himself to enjoy one of his favorite attractions, watching New Kowloon's flotilla descending through the series of locks.

The angry roar of rushing water masked the other man's steps. One moment Ka Yi was alone, the next—someone was mirroring his posture, leaning on the railing to his right. Ka Yi spared the new company a sidelong glimpse before the bubbling whirlpools beneath drew him back.

"Golden Dragon," the man shouted over the noise.

"Captain Weinberg," Ka Yi returned the courtesy. "One person whose attention I'd rather not attract."

Locksville's Head of Intelligence Service accepted the compliment with a lopsided grin.

Neither spoke. Ka Yi didn't want to be the first to talk business, cherishing the opportunity to steal a few more precious moments of quiet meditation.

Finally, the water level stabilized, and the air quieted.

"You're a smart man, Golden Dragon," said the local. "I fancy myself being not too shallow, either. Can we talk freely?"

Ka Yi squinted. "Nice try, dear Captain. I've got my secrets, as you've got yours. We'll never talk freely, will we? With that caveat, I accept your offer. No games. Ask away."

Weinberg's eyes darted to Ka Yi's. "What's going on?"

Ka Yi turned to face the host squarely. "What's going on? How do you mean?"

Captain Weinberg studied Ka Yi's face for a few seconds before relenting. "The attacks on The Station's trains?"

"Oh? Is this supposed to mean anything to me?"

A shadow of annoyance briefly manifested on the captain's face. Or was deliberately allowed to slip. "Shang Ka Yi, my friend, how long have we known each other?"

Ka Yi ran a quick calculation. "Seven years, give or take."

"I count the same. And here I was, convinced we had an understanding. That perturbations are bad for trade. That both our sides are interested in maintaining peace in the region. That if some developments threaten to disrupt the status quo, we'll work together to restore it. Am I missing anything?"

"I wouldn't endeavor to word it any better myself, dear Captain."

"Charming. With that, when we agree to not play games, may I count on your cooperation?"

"You most certainly may, Captain. Alas, I assure you I am unaware of any attacks on The Station's interests. In turn, I am incredibly curious to learn what led you to conclude I may possess any such knowledge."

"Hm." Weinberg stroked his cheek. "Alright. But first, Golden Dragon, an inconvenient question. Is it possible you are not a hundred percent aware of everything going on behind the Great Hive's closed doors?"

"Dear Captain, since we are both in the business of asking questions, allow me one of my own: what can you tell me about my standing in the Hive?"

"Let's see. The five of you, Golden Dragons of the High Council, are supposed to be equal. Informally, some Dragons are more equal than others, so to speak. You exert greater power than your fellow councilors. It's possible your influence is on par with Tam Wai Lam's, but that's hard to judge quantitatively. Shall I go on?"

"No, dear Captain, that is quite enough. I have to admit, begrudgingly, I find your knowledge of the Hive's internal workings deeply unsettling. But

I'll extend you the professional courtesy of not asking how you've come to be so intimately informed. The point is, knowing what you know, you should understand how little of any significance happens in New Kowloon without my express or indirect involvement."

"But you've been sailing for—how long? Two months?"

"Very little happens without my knowledge," Ka Yi enunciated every word. "*Very* little, Captain."

"I see." Weinberg gazed into the distance, rearranging the pieces on a mental chessboard.

"I'm going to take a leap of faith," he said after a while, "and trust your words at their face value. Which makes the situation, admittedly, all the more intriguing. What you claim not to know is that two attacks on The Station's trains have occurred in as many weeks. A couple of low-ranking traders and a dozen supervisors killed, some cargo plundered. Each raid, in and of itself, could've been written off as an aberration, if these events hadn't shared strange commonalities. Both appear to be exceedingly well planned and executed to perfection. Both were conducted by run of the mill rural gangs. Supposedly. Only they were too well trained and equipped with identical, centrally supplied weaponry. How many parties in the region can pull off such a feat?"

"I understand the implications, Captain. I'm sure you've got more than you're letting on, and it all conveniently points to New Kowloon."

"Indeed, I have, and indeed, it does. A bit too conveniently. Somebody is eager to nudge us to the conclusion that all the evidence points to you. Whoever is betting on this game is overplaying their hand. By a small margin, but enough to make me suspicious."

"To sum it up, what have we got? This trouble is not of our doing and, I'm reasonably convinced, it isn't of yours. That leaves the Railroad people. Why would they stage attacks on their own trains? And frame us?"

"I hoped you'd tell me, Golden Dragon."

Ka Yi sighed. He faced the water and leaned on the railing again, more heavily than earlier. "I may have an idea."

Chapter 13

Rajan

September 21, 42 PE

"So, Rajan..." The scarily nice officer, Captain Weinberg was his name, smiled.

A superior—an officer, and not the last one in the local command—being nice to him, a lousy worker? Suspicious.

Rajan obligingly smiled back, trying to appear glad to meet again. He must've failed because the officer frowned and raised a pacifying hand.

"No need to worry, Rajan, you are in no trouble."

The shift from a smile to a frown put him at ease. Rajan didn't know how to handle nice. Shouts he could deal with. Humiliation, beatings. His years of being a slavers' "worker" had taught him to obediently take abuse while growing an ever-thicker skin. But nice? No one had ever been nice to him. Maybe his padres, a lifetime ago. He couldn't even remember their faces. A few fond memories from early childhood—touches, smells—were preserved in the depths of his mind. On rare occasions, he brought those forth, like fireflies lighting up a tiny portion of the endless night. And those occasions grew rarer and rarer.

Now, when the officer turned unhappy about something Rajan did—well, that was familiar! Enough to relax a bit, un poco.

"Bene," said the captain, showing his familiarity with the lingo, "much better. Now that you are a free man, un hombre libre, what are your plans? Go back to New Hope? Settle somewhere else?"

Ah, this was it, the eviction. Not that the thoughts about what's next hadn't crossed Rajan's mind since their previous conversation, but he carelessly chose to enjoy the moment. To be unburdened. To savor the unfamiliar taste of independence. He had pushed the concerns away and strolled along the Canal for hours, observing the locks in their overwhelming action. Most of all, he enjoyed *not having to*: not having to follow anyone's orders; not having to do anything in particular; not having *to have to*. He still wasn't ready to make his own decisions, but was absolutely done with others making them for him.

Until an armed man in a uniform approached and politely invited him to a meeting with Captain Weinberg. Drunk on his newly gained freedom, Rajan had almost unleashed his rich stock of swearwords on the messenger, but had enough sense to follow. Free people had to heed soldiers, too.

Decision time.

"New Hope?" Rajan cautiously tested the name. It sounded awkward. Foreign. A bucket of random sounds that evoked no images. Nothing remotely close to "home". What awaited him there? Would he recognize his relatives? His parents? Would they recognize him? His sisters were married into other families by now, for sure, and had children of their own. His brother must be the head of the family, and the last thing he'd need was a male sibling undermining his authority. And the way the community had treated him after la ceremonia... "No, sir. The sold-out Rotten Can come back? Nah. Ain't got no familia there, no mas. Why ask?"

"Because I've got an offer for you," the captain said.

"Que?"

Rajan listened quietly while the officer described the idea, but clenched his teeth so hard his jaw muscles spasmed. He pushed his mouth open, like a fish on a riverbank, and forcefully exhaled. The sound that came out of his throat could be a sob or a laugh.

"What if I say 'no'?" he asked, frightened by his newborn audacity, but also encouraged by it.

Captain Weinberg shrugged one shoulder. "Niente. Nothing. You'll be free to do whatever you want. Todo lo que."

Stupefied, Rajan wasn't sure how to react. He was ready to be threatened with punishments, and depending on these threats' severity, to either cave or keep resisting. This polite indifference threw him off.

Weinberg cracked a mirthless smile. "Let me help you decide."

Rajan met the captain's eyes.

"What do you have anywhere else?" Weinberg asked. "Nothing. Who do you have anywhere else? No one. What skills can you offer a potential employer? None. What separates you from the competition? Little, if anything at all. And I am not talking about the odd religious practices of the few places that might consider taking you in."

It was all true. Rajan hung his head. "Can I stay here?"

"Stay—you may. But what will you do? We don't run a charity house here. You'll have to earn a living."

"Can I join your army?"

Weinberg's eyebrow crept up. "We don't recruit outsiders. Questionable allegiances, incompatible values. But what I'm offering you will eventually open the door for you to join my organization."

"Your organization? You're not the army?"

The captain smiled again. "Technically, yes. Practically, as you may have guessed, I'm with Locksville's Intelligence Service. In this capacity, I possess a certain latitude in decision making. Want to work for me?"

"And for that, I must go back to The Station and pretend I'm still their 'worker'? Like before? You ain't leaving me mucho choice."

"Do that and send me occasional reports on subjects of interest. My people will be in touch with you."

"Yeah, and how I gonna learn anything interesting? Come to a Master, like, 'Yo, Master, what's that train taking to Locksville?'—and he'll be, like, 'Thanks for asking, dear Rajan, we're sending them a ton of rotten tomatoes. And somebody flog this son of a bitch worker, so he doesn't ask stupid questions no more.' Right? 'Cause that's how it'll go down."

Weinberg didn't take the bait. "I'm sure you can see and overhear enough if you keep your eyes and ears open. I am not asking you to befriend any Masters or bribe supervisors. Be yourself, but your more observant self. Can you do that?"

"I s'pose... Do I have a choice?"

"Not really." Captain Weinberg smiled dryly and stood up.

Chapter 14

Buck

September 21, 42 PE

With the sun halfway through its evening descent, and the chilly breeze probing its way under Buck's shirt, the Boundary finally appeared on the horizon.

By then, the lieutenant had come dangerously close to exploding. He squeezed the driver's bench until his knuckles went white. The inch-thick oaken board all but crunched. For a change, that wasn't Janet's fault. She'd spent the day quietly curled up in the back of the wagon, immersed in the thoughts she chose not to share with her entourage.

Lundy and Jackson strolled lazily on the sides of the road. Guards weren't needed inside the Boundary, but this was an opportunity to rehearse their roles.

Jackson engaged in non-committal conversations with the caravan's genuine guards and merchants, attracted by his inviting smile and the florid harmonica tunes he skillfully extracted from the exotic instrument.

In stark contrast, Lundy's grumpy face advertised his contempt toward everything and everyone within sight. If that was his trick to keep people away, it worked wonderfully well.

Buck stayed quieter than a mouse.

Thus, the reasons for the lieutenant's anxiety lay outside the Task Force. It was the lethargic rate of the caravan's movement.

As instructed, the lieutenant had driven the wagon up to the Marketplace's Bald Hill Gate in the predawn haze. The Fivepointers' would-be travel companions had shown no surprise. Master Flanagan pointed out the slot at the tail of the caravan, and without further ado, off they... crawled.

The train of fourteen wagons trailed so sluggishly, the lieutenant must have regretted his promise to make no fuss a hundred times over, and then a thousand times more. The Task Force had its orders, and Colonel's orders tended to be carried out with the utmost swiftness.

But the pace had been determined by Master Flanagan, and on the road he was the supreme ruler, second only to God.

The possibility of unfriendly encounters on the high roads was the only reason Buck's team still hadn't taken off, leaving the trudging caravan in a cloud of dust.

At first, Buck rode by the lieutenant's side, feigning invisibility to avoid Kossowsky's ire. To fill the time, he observed the goings-on of the other caravanners, learning to act the part.

Most teams traveled with prentices and hands, but only two other women were present, both older. Janet wore plain clothes and hid her distinctive hair under a knit hat, yet there was no disguising her being the youngest and prettiest. Naturally, she received a healthy share of sideways glances from the male audience, but nothing inappropriate, even by Buck's jealous standards. Were the caravan folk too virtuous to make advances on a married woman? Doubtful. More likely, their restraint had to do with her husband's cold eyes and broad shoulders.

Buck got bored on the bench and slid off, joining Jackson.

The bits of conversation he caught revolved around the weather forecast, the outlook for the winter, and the impressions from the week spent trading at Five Points Marketplace. The Zealots' ambush inspired animated discussion, but the caravanners had only a second-hand, vague idea of what had transpired. None suspected that only a few meters separated them from the central figure of those events.

Jackson magically maintained friendly chats with everyone at once and no one in particular, divulging nothing meaningful from his side. Before the day's end, two-thirds of the caravanners would consider him a pal.

Buck didn't interfere, building his own impressions based on the soldier's probing remarks and the responses he received.

At one point, they were left alone. Jackson tucked his harmonica into one of the many pockets in his bulky, form-concealing attire, and sharply glanced at Buck. "Your thoughts, kid?"

"About what, sir... er... Master Jackson?"

"Let's say this lad I talked to, Stevie. And call me Tim, alright?"

"Alright, Master Tim."

"No," Jackson chuckled, "just Tim."

"Tim." Calling the grizzled soldier, a member of Colonel's inner circle, by his first name didn't come easy. Buck chewed on his lip. "Stevie, he's a simpleton.

Really. Unlike, say, Limping Doug, who wants us to think he is, but is shrewd and clever."

"Like you," said Jackson noncommittally.

Buck choked on the words ready to leave his mouth and regarded Jackson with a questioning look. The veteran grinned. "No need to be shy. That was a compliment."

"Uh, thank you?"

"Don't mention it. Back to Stevie?"

"Ah. Yes. Stevie. He does what his older brother tells him. They own the business together, but Mitch calls the shots. What else... Ah, yes. I suspect Stevie is fond of Mitch's wife."

"Like you are of Master Kossowsky's," Tim murmured.

Buck's cheeks burned.

Jackson laughed. "It's okay, kid. She'll come around to see your worth. You're handsome, and not too dull. A word of advice? Stop gazing at her with those dreamy ox's eyes." He punched Buck in the shoulder. "And yeah, you hit the nail on the head. With Stevie, and with that sneaky bastard Limping Doug too. You're pretty good at this. But try to better control your face. Our overly literate hostess may say you're an open book to anyone who cares to read it. Pardon the comparison."

Buck frowned. "Tim, you shouldn't be joking about, you know, books," he finished in a low, conspiratorial voice.

Jackson's brows rose. "Didn't take you for such a pious type. You won't declare me a blasphemous heretic, will you?"

"N-no, sir. I mean, Tim."

"That's a relief. Then, if you don't mind a piece of wisdom from an ungodly, profane miscreant like myself..."

Buck adamantly shook his head.

"Stop being such a pain in the arse about books. Because your not-so-secret sweetheart sure isn't."

The thought was like a chunk of greasy food, sitting uncomfortably in the stomach. An attempt to digest it met limited success. It held undeniable merit, but went against his grain.

"Thank you for the advice, Tim," Buck forced out, if only because that was the polite thing to do.

"No problem, kid, any time." Jackson smiled blithely, signaling his willingness to turn a blind eye to Buck's insincerity. "Now I'd love to hear your story."

Buck choked for the second time in as many minutes. "There's no story, Tim," he mumbled, looking the other way.

"Alrighty. No story." Jackson accepted Buck's claim with suspicious ease.

Toward sundown, the long snake of diversely sized and shaped wagons cleared the Wainfleet Bend. Once it sprawled along the stretch ending at the Boundary gate tower, Flanagan's plan became clear: to spend the night under the auspices of the Army contingent, in Five Points territory. The last safe and quiet camp before exposing the caravan to the mysteries and dangers of the Wilderness.

Remembering Jackson's advice, Buck did his best not to gawk.

The Boundary was overwhelming.

Earthworks taller than a grown man supported a three-meter-high wall. Wooden catwalks on the inside and barbed wire on the outside crowned it. Guard towers twice as tall protruded every kilometer. It wasn't so much a *wall* as a *barrier*. Built of a crazy patchwork of the most unusual construction materials Buck had ever seen: hundreds and thousands of pre-E horseless cars. Rusted and still colorful; squished into twisted metal pancakes or keeping their original shape; small to huge, mind-bogglingly long wheeled boxes large enough to swallow their entire caravan, with space left to spare. These boxes formed the foundation of the barrier. Dirt, sand, stone, and gravel filled the insides of the cars.

The gate, a monumental double fortification, straddled the road connecting Five Points to the outside world—from which the Boundary disconnected it.

This was Buck's second visit to the Boundary. He first encountered it at the tender age of eight when he started asking too many questions about the world, the E, and how life was before, and how it was after, and the City, and the zombies... An awful lot of questions. Dad took him to see the Boundary where it passed close to Creek Point.

Bored to death, the soldiers manning the tower welcomed the distraction. Incredibly, the father-son duo was allowed to climb up to the observation platform. The soldiers called it a "pillbox", a strange word that must have had its roots in the misty pre-E past. The views from the top through the narrow slits stole Buck's breath away. The Boundary was... a *boundary*, dividing the world into two: home on one side, the rest of the realm on the other. A stern, unyielding line curving like a drawn longbow for as far as the eye could see. On the outside, the obstacle bristled with three inhospitable rows of barbed wire on iron rods, followed by a moat. It was comforting to be on the inside. On the *right* side.

Since that visit, the Boundary had changed. Or maybe it was Buck who grew up and learned to notice the less attractive details. Dirty smudges of cement and wood planks in various stages of decomposition patched the crumbling sections of the barrier. Enemy raids? The elements? Its old age? It still held the distinction of being the most impressive engineering feat Five Points had ever achieved. It just didn't look as perfect as it had years ago.

The word on the street was that these days the Boundary fulfilled mainly symbolic purposes: to mark the limits of Five Points' territory, and to boost the state's reputation. But according to malicious tongues, in the absence of real threats, the fortification served only to keep the soldiers busy and justify the Army's outrageous upkeep.

Buck cared little for the naysayers. As a kid, he had slept better knowing the Boundary separated his home from the world beyond, with trained armed men making sure nothing slipped in undetected. Rumors or not, he still did.

Of course, to live in such peaceful times was a blessing. Outside the Boundary, it was a different story... And that was where they were headed. A shiver jerked Buck's shoulders.

The gate had no space for a guesthouse. The caravan camped for the night in a waste-ground marked for that purpose. At least it was leveled and had a row of latrines nearby, downwind from the gate. Practically a luxury.

Kossowsky had disappeared as soon as the Task Force had finished its supper. "Went to have a private word with the gatehouse sergeant," Jackson whispered to Buck. "To get the latest intel on the situation on the road ahead. At least that's what I would've done if I were him."

Lundy lit a campfire, and sadness filled Buck. He was going to miss the E Day celebrations at the Marketplace, Simplification and all. This year, being a green recruit, he would not have marched in the parade, even if he'd stayed. Still, among other firsts, this was going to be the first time he didn't attend the festival.

He lay on a blanket, hands behind the head. Soft music from Tim's harmonica seduced his mind to drift away, up into the limitless dome above. The stars shone as brightly as they only can in the chilly fall air, with the summer haze and dust gone, but before the skies became overcast more often than not. Two-three constellations looked familiar in the sea of white sparks on a velvety black backdrop. He pointed up at something he'd seen before, but had never had a chance to ask anyone. "See that star? It's moving! What's the meaning of that?"

"Too much we don't know about what's going on up there," Jackson said. "Don't clog your brains with this rubbish."

"It's called a satellite," Janet interjected absentmindedly, gazing into the fire without as much as peeking up. "A manmade machine that circles the Earth in space."

Buck swiftly sat up and made a Sign of Faith.

"When it reflects the Sun's light," she continued, ignoring the three men staring at her, "it looks like a moving star."

"Is it watching us?" Lundy asked with uncharacteristic doubtfulness. "Should we hide under the tent?"

Janet snorted. "It's ridiculous how ignorant you are. No, it doesn't 'watch us'," she mocked his intonations in a fake basso. "It doesn't care about us. It doesn't care about anything. It can't care. It's an 'it', not a 'he' or a 'she'. Only a stupid machine, cogs and bolts. It isn't good or evil. It just... is. Useless. Forgotten." She fell silent, hypnotizing the flames, or hypnotized by them. The fire glinted on her hair, two relatives having a mute conversation.

Buck broke the awkward silence. "What was it there for?"

Janet shrugged. "No clue. I've seen drawings in the books, but haven't found an explanation yet. People used to launch machines into space before the E, is all I know. I've heard that many fell and burned in the first years PE, but some remain in their orbits. I wish I could fly up there to live in one of those machines. Leave all this hopelessness behind."

"Circles around the Earth, eh?" Jackson closely controlled his voice.

Janet sneered. "You know the Earth is a sphere, yes?" Meeting blank stares, she sighed. "A ball, a giant ball. Or do you barbarians think it's flat?"

Why did she have to be so nasty? "My Dad told me it isn't perfectly round," Buck said. "It's a giant egg."

"Miss Mc... er, Mistress Kossowsky," Jackson murmured, "you know a great deal more than the three of us. Some yokels may think it's blasphemous. I, for one, find this impressive and sexy, if you'll excuse an old soldier for being blunt. But when it comes to your social skills, a spoiled ten-year-old would do better than you."

Janet heatedly threw her head up, met Jackson's calm and unyielding gaze, and deflated, looking ashamed.

"We're in the same boat, young lady. It's gonna be us against the world out there. Let us try not to lash out at each other. Think you can go along with this?"

The girl nodded.

"Besides," the soldier continued with a cunning smile, "we're willing to learn from the fountain of your wisdom, at least some of us, aren't we?" He glanced invitingly at Buck, who enthusiastically bobbed his head. Lundy pretended not to care. Or really didn't.

"I'm sorry, Tim," Janet whispered. "You're right, I shouldn't have... I'm used to it being *me* against the world. And, as you military men say, the best defense is a good offense. All these uneducated, arrogant, pious people mocking me, hating me, denouncing knowledge. Nobody, besides my friends and family, has ever accepted me for who I am." She let her guard down, and the words gushed like a stream through a burst dam. This girl with a spine of steel and the skin of cast iron was on the verge of tears.

Buck was torn between awe and pity. Awe at the personal Boundary she had built around her inner self, and pity at how lonely and helpless she must have felt inside that enclosure. As always, words betrayed him. Encouraged by Tim's subtle gesture, he rose from the ground to comfort her, but froze when Kossowsky's shape entered the bonfire's circle of light.

"Howdy, gents! Keeping my dear wife entertained?"

Janet sprang up, threw "Son of a bitch!" at him in her regular crusty voice, and rushed into the tent.

"Whoa!" The lieutenant helplessly spread his arms. "What was that about? What'd I do?"

"I'm afraid you've ruined the moment, sir," Jackson said melancholically.

This was nothing short of betrayal. Kossowsky's appearance deprived Buck of something wonderful and important that was about to happen. He glared at the officer ... What was that grimace contorting the lieutenant's face? Pain? Sorrow?

September 22, 42 PE

In the morning, the wake-up call came well before dawn. Master Flanagan wanted to hit the road early, to make good time and meet the next night at Pelham, under the protection of its palisade.

Buck had had the oddest dream, and its vivid impressions refused to let go of him. He clung to the quickly dissolving images, trying to memorize them.

"Have I lived a good life? I suppose. Could it have been better? Of course. Could it have been worse? For sure. Infinitely better—or indescribably worse. I have seen the small world and helped make it bigger again. I lived in the ruins of dead cities and saw them bustle again."

The old man paused. A wry smile shattered his somber expression. "And now I sound like a pompous old fart from fabulous ancient legends. Knights, elves, dragons, all that. How low I have fallen." Small wrinkles in the corners of the eyes. Soft laughter.

"Have I achieved everything I wanted?" The stranger grew serious again. "Seven Hells, no! Am I proud of anything I have achieved? Seven Hells, yes! Am I ashamed of things I've done? You bet. Am I missing someone?"

The old man sank into silence. Heavy eyelids drooped as he plunged into his memories, but eyes still glimmered through the thin slits, scanning the surroundings. A light breeze played with the strands of his white hair, picking them from his parchment-like forehead before letting them settle back. And the wiry hands with dark pigmentation spots and fingers disfigured by swollen joints, casually holding the rifle in his lap, did not relax for an instant.

A hint of a sad smile touched his weather-beaten, pale lips. "But I have brought you here, albeit indirectly, haven't I? What you've done makes me proud. And my heart breaks at the thought of those you've lost."

Yes, the oddest dream, by far. Like one of his visions, but in his sleep and with words.

Buck stood up and kicked the cold gray ashes of yesterday's campfire.

Nobody said a word about last night. Janet acted her usual self, remote and self-possessed. She did not avoid eye contact, as Buck suspected she might. Her pretend-husband was the only person whose presence she completely ignored.

The soldiers lowered the drawbridge, and a small contingent moved out to secure the nearest stretch of the road ahead. At their *all clear* signal, the remaining guards raised the portcullis. As the gate spit out one wagon after another, the soldiers waved and wished them Godspeed.

Once the last wagon had rolled, clattering and shaking, over the drawbridge, Master Flanagan set a much faster pace than the day before.

The recon force waited for the caravan's tail to pass by and leisurely withdrew into the maw of the gate. With a strange yearning, Buck observed as the drawbridge chains retracted into the towers, cutting him off from everything he had ever known. He wanted to discover the big world, to have real adventures. And to fulfill Colonel's orders, of course! But the little-boy-from-a-small-village part of him apprehensively shrank away from the inhospitable lands outside Five Points. He was crossing more than the Boundary. He was crossing into adult life, leaving childhood behind.

With the Boundary receding, Buck turned his attention to his surroundings. His head swiveled left and right, eyes darting and scanning, searching for threats. He tried to will his ability into action, to find what awaited behind the bend. As always, in vain. The visions came when they came, refusing to be coaxed.

A year back, Buck had resolved to discover their limits and patterns. Cursed with a strange gift? Why not put it to good use? Turned out, only immediate danger to him or someone nearby triggered the visions. And that danger had to be very, very real. The risk of losing a card game, for example, did not count. Unless he cheated so badly, he was about to have his ass handed to him on a platter. That took getting rich fast off the table. The job of a village weatherman was not an option either. When a tornado is around the corner, it's a bit too late to announce. Also, sometimes his visions had a dark side... No. Wasn't gonna think about that.

The lack of visions, thus, was encouraging. He wasn't in jeopardy.

A sharp pain from the bitten lip woke Buck from his transfixion. His entire body vibrated like a taut string. His fists were so tight his fingernails dug into his palms, leaving angry red marks when he forced them to unclench. Soreness spread through his muscles.

Buck examined his shaking hands and took a deep breath. He met Jackson's mischievous gaze and scowled. The veteran walked on the side of the road with the carelessness of a rich merchant on a promenade after a Sunday sermon. He gestured invitingly. Buck responded with a *why not?* shrug and jumped off the wagon.

"First time outside the Boundary, eh?" asked Jackson.

Buck, trying to appear unfazed, pushed his hands deep into the pockets of his jacket.

"It's okay, kid," the man said. "I've seen my share of people venturing outside for the first time. Let me tell you, you're handling it way better than many."

"You aren't saying that just to make me feel better?"

"Not at all!" A short laugh and a dismissive wave of a hand. Not entirely convincing. "I saw a strong, grown-up soldier hiding under a pile of hay, quivering like a feverish mouse. I saw a young trader who, five minutes after crossing the bridge, ran back shrieking, banged on the gates, and they couldn't let him in one moment too soon. Seven Hells and the Prophet's skinny butt, I myself clung to my rifle so hard my hands went numb for half a day!"

Jackson's casual blasphemy did not prove he wasn't inventing these stories on the go, but Buck welcomed any reassurance he could get.

"Look, Buck." The soldier's tone lost its cordiality. Paradoxically, that made him sound more genuine. "I know what it's like. Everybody does. You've grown inside the Five Points bubble, listening to the stories of the Great and Horrible Wilderness. Bandits and zombies, mutants and monsters, what not. Only the fact is, most of that is fairy tales, or ancient history, at best. Nowadays, it's pretty quiet and safe out here. Granted, an occasional roving gang may lay waste to what their grabby hands can reach, and that's why caravans hire guards. But as a rule, everybody prefers to get along peacefully. More or less."

Jackson glanced at Buck to gauge his reaction. Buck had plenty to show.

First, the shame. Shame for letting everyone see him for a scared little kid. Shame for not questioning the stories he'd been told as that scared little kid—stories he'd used to love listening to, with a mix of tingling fear and hunger for more.

Then, the doubt. Doubt in the veracity of Jackson's words. Doubt in the alleged safety of the surroundings. This was the Wilderness. The World Beyond. The lawless land lacking rules and structure. The land where they could cross paths with anyone, without the impregnable Boundary and the unshakable might of the Army to protect the innocent. The caravan—and Buck with it—were on their own.

Finally, the fear. Self-respect? What self-respect? He was scared shitless. Was the fear understandable? Yes. Reasonable? Yes. People who fear nothing die first. Who said that? Never mind. Someone smart. And alive. Jackson's words, even if not true, helped too.

"I see you're getting there. Now, avoid the other extreme."

"Which is?"

"Don't get into your head this is a walk in the park, and everyone we meet is going to become your next best pal. Keep your eyes peeled. I hear you've got an enviable sight. My old peepers wouldn't have noticed a dagger in a sleeve from a hilltop. Anyhow, remember we aren't here to entertain your curiosity."

Buck chewed on that. "Hey, Tim?"

"Uh-oh. Why do I have the feeling I'm not gonna like your next question?"

"How come you know so much about the world outside? I thought the Army doesn't leave the Boundary."

"Well..." Jackson scratched his neck. "I've accompanied Colonel on a few diplomatic missions to the neighbors."

"And that's all?"

"And that's all you need to know." Jackson's tone remained playful, but the hint was unmistakable.

Tilting his head to the side, Buck asked slyly, "What happened to being a part of the team? Not concealing any relevant information?"

"Ha! Not bad, kid, not bad!" Jackson delightedly rubbed his hands. "Alright. This information isn't relevant, but what the heck. Tell me, does Colonel need to keep informed on what's going on outside Five Points?"

"I suppose."

"You 'suppose'. Oh well. And how do you think Colonel gets this information? From the traveling traders' hearsay?"

"I've never thought about that. How, then?"

Jackson didn't answer, expectantly looking straight back at Buck.

"Oh! Oh. I see."

"No, you don't. This was a hypothetical conversation. Nothing to do with anyone you've met. Got it?"

"Got it."

"Good. Now go check on Mistress Kossowsky. I bet it's her first time outside, too. I wonder how she's faring."

Buck didn't need to be asked twice.

He found Janet coping with the Wilderness much better than he had. She sat quietly in the wagon, looking around, but not in fear or anxiety. Buck failed to come up with a conversation starter. He climbed to the driver's bench by Kossowsky's side, projecting confidence. The officer—no, the merchant—gave Buck a curious sidelong glance. "Got a serving of Jackson medicine?"

Buck half-nodded, half-shrugged. A day earlier, he would have barked, "Sir, yes, sir!" Apparently, he had come to grips with the role of a merchant's prentice, enough to exhibit mild insubordination.

The target of his insubordination spared him more than the usual brief look. "Okay," Kossowsky said and returned his attention to the road.

Buck waited, but nothing else came from the "merchant", neither praise nor rebuke.

Fall colors surrounded the caravan, ranging from green through yellow to scarlet. Leaves shone in the low sun as if each had an internal source of light. Fall, Buck's favorite time of the year. It meant the E Day celebrations, the wish-making, the Fair, and all the fun. But the fall he'd loved and everything related to it were a part of Five Points. Should he feel differently about the outside fall? Buck searched for any omens, symbols—anything—to confirm that this Wilderness fall was foreign and did not deserve his love, but nothing sinister stood out in the landscape. Yellows were the same yellows, scarlets—the same scarlets. Did this mean that the world beyond the Boundary wasn't that dissimilar to what he'd known his entire life? Maybe. Until proven wrong, he might as well enjoy the beauty.

Soon, the caravan started passing abandoned cars on the road. Someone had pushed the smaller ones to the sides a long time ago to clear the passage. Their rusted carcasses were overgrown by vegetation and appropriated by birds and small animals. They sagged into the ground, barely identifiable, local natural features rather than manmade artifacts.

At one stage, the caravan came upon a monstrous vehicle, similar to those forming the Boundary's foundation. It occupied the center of the pavement where the E had caught it. Here, by the looks of it, no one had enough resources to move it off the road, so the road had to move instead. A gravel bypass widened the shoulder. While their wagon cautiously navigated this slapdash arrangement, Buck had enough time to peek inside the enormous box. The opening in the back of the car was ajar, with one door hanging from a single hinge and the other having fallen off altogether. The once white panels forming the box's sides had peeled off. Dry leaves, broken branches, and animal refuse filled its interior, along with unsavory looking leftovers no one had found interesting through the years. Buck started tallying the gigantic wheels, but lost count after twelve.

The rest of the morning passed uneventfully. No, even that description was too generous. Traveling, as it turned out, was boring. What a stark contrast to the day before, when he'd been antsy about seeing the outside. He'd witnessed it now, and it didn't live up to the hype. He sunk into a strange, semi-meditative state in which the reality, while being seen and heard, didn't register.

In the afternoon, the guards up ahead straightened, their gait lost its laziness, shoulders tensed, and arms found weapons. Their reaction drew Buck out of his trance. Something in the scenery must have changed. Then Kossowsky's wagon crested a small hill.

Rows and rows of houses stood along the road.

Buck wasn't raised in a dugout. Fivepointers lived in houses too. Only theirs were smaller and newer, built after the E with reclaimed materials. As such, they looked... makeshift? Maybe. After all, they really were.

The ones here were proper. Hard to imagine what kind of engines the ancients had used to build them, but even the most run-down among the houses here looked more solid than Creek Point's best. And they were huge! Not Downtown huge, scraping the sky, if he were to trust the stories, but bigger than anything he'd ever seen. Worst of all, there were so many of them! Empty windows, caved-in roofs, and front yards overgrown with shrubbery failed to spoil Buck's awe.

"Pelham," a voice announced nearby. Buck flinched. He hadn't noticed Jackson approaching the wagon. The veteran's face bore the typical unbothered expression, but he now held a staff, using it as a walking stick. Lundy moved closer too, on Kossowsky's side of the wagon.

"Pelham?" asked Buck. "Doesn't it have a palisade?"

"Pelham Village does," Jackson said. "This is Old Pelham. We must cross to its north end."

Deeper into the built-up area, more and more streets, all with similarly impressive houses, stretched in both directions. How many people had lived here before the E? At least as many as in all of Five Points. Within Pelham, scores of cars lined the pavement and the houses' front yards. Did everyone have a car before the E? Wow.

"Nobody lives here?" Buck asked. "All these houses, and—no one?" The sheer scale of this wastefulness was flabbergasting.

"Can never say 'no one' for sure." Jackson cracked a smile. "That's why you must keep your eyes open. But no, no one lives here permanently. Only in the Village, behind the palisade, as you said."

"Don't lose your shit, boy," grumbled Lundy from the other side. "It's not too bad here."

"Yeah," agreed Jackson, "this close to Locksville, we're pretty safe. They do a decent job of keeping the boneheads of all stripes at bay. All this"—he shook his staff—"is for show. If some busybodies spot our caravan, they won't mistake us for a soft, tempting target."

"Locksville?" Buck's attention instantly switched. "We're visiting Locksville?"

"Well, duh! Would a trade caravan skip Locksville?"

"Cool! Will we see the Falls?" Buck couldn't curb his enthusiasm.

"Don't get too excited." The veteran chuckled. "*See* the Falls? We won't even hear them."

"They don't teach them maps for shit these days, eh?" he asked Kossowsky, who only grunted in response. Whether the lieutenant aimed his resentment at Buck's ignorance, at Creek Point education system's failures, or at Jackson for asking rhetorical questions remained unclear.

"Niagara, with its falls, is a different river, kid," Jackson explained. "Locksville stands on the Welland Canal."

"Oh." How embarrassing. Hopefully, Janet hadn't overheard this part of the conversation. Buck stole a furtive glance over the shoulder.

A furrowed brow. A downward crescent of the mouth. She sure did. Luckily, something else caught his attention, enough to eclipse the awkwardness. He seized the opportunity to change the topic. "What is that? Some sort of fortification?"

The caravan was passing through an intersection. An enormous structure occupied one of its corners. Single-story, but so long and wide it defied Buck's imagination. Blind, windowless walls of cracked concrete. A faded green sign along the top edge, completely illegible. And an entrance made of glass, shattered a long time ago. Who would build an entrance out of glass? Entries, the weakest points of any defensive position, had to be hardened first. Buck's limited understanding of military tactics suggested that much. Glass? Ridiculous!

"Used to be a store," Jackson responded, a bottomless well of knowledge about the Wilderness. "Like our Marketplace, but all under one roof."

"They were called 'supermarkets.'" After remaining silent for hours, Janet saw it right to say something. Buck waited for her to go on. She didn't.

"But why the glass entrance?" The question still gnawed at him. "Wouldn't that make the weakest point weaker?"

"That's because the ancients weren't as obsessed with fortifying everything as we are," Janet said levelly.

Was she avoiding an argument? That would be a first.

"I wonder what that says about the state of our society, compared to theirs."

Ah, there.

The question hung in the air. No one volunteered a response.

A few intersections down the road, the ghost settlement ended. Could it be called a *city*? Not *the* City, but at least *a* city? The label didn't matter. What mattered was that a very different structure towered ahead, separated from Old Pelham by a wide, well-maintained clearing. Pelham Village's palisade.

Buck had never seen one, but he'd heard enough to form a vague image of a wall of sharpened sticks, or tree trunks, standing on their ends. Similar in purpose to Five Points' Boundary, but on a smaller scale.

Pelham's palisade did not meet those expectations. It exceeded them, by far. It was made of H-beams, as his memory obligingly offered. Hundreds and hundreds of rusty H-beams. Their lower ends were buried in a berm. A dense comb of sharp lances protruded from the top. Buck's stomach clenched. Wouldn't want to try scaling those.

The road continued through the clearing, to be swallowed by an opening in the wall. Wide enough to allow a wagon through, but barely. The gate, a crisscrossed lattice of the same rusty beams, had been lifted to let the caravan in. Passing underneath, Buck ducked, succumbing to the irrational fear that the chains holding the massive door up may snap and it would squash him like a bug.

On the inside, a tall earthen embankment topped by boardwalks backed up the palisade. From there, instead of watching the perimeter through the embrasures, the sentries gawked at the caravan, grossly neglecting their responsibilities.

"Don't they have a Master Sergeant?" Buck muttered.

That earned him a cackle from Jackson. "Pelham hasn't seen serious action in decades," he said. "They started building their palisade early on, soon after the E, but a few years later, Locksville came to prominence right around the corner, and it's been crushing into thin pulp any buggers stirring shit in the area ever since. The Pelhamites never finished the construction. They'd been lucky to find a warehouse full of these beams, but that wouldn't have covered half the perimeter. What you see is the front entrance intended to impress passersby and project strength. Go around and check the other side. You won't be as thrilled, I promise. What you'll find is a pile of dirt and a glorified picket fence. Which seems to be okay by these fine folks." The veteran's broad gesture encompassed the soldiers up on the ramparts and the villagers lining the periphery of what must pass for the main square here.

Once, it had been the parking lot of another one of those *supermarkets* which occupied one side. Old but neatly groomed houses made the other. Pre-E houses people lived in. A window into the past. Would Buck be able to get a glimpse of the ancients' lifestyle if he peeked inside?

A loud rattling noise drowned out people's voices, horses' neighing, and every other sound contributing to the din of the improvised market. The conversations died down, and all heads turned in that direction.

The source of the noise entered the square, and a nauseating wave rose in Buck's stomach, filling his throat with a vile taste.

A car rolled out of the side street.

On its own.

The machine had two small wheels in the front, and a pair of giant ones under the cab. A crooked pipe spewed thick clouds of dark smoke. A fluted box hid a very obvious engine. A *working* engine.

Buck made a Sign of Faith. And another one, because one might not suffice. The Faith didn't prescribe what to do in such situations—because such situations did not occur. Engines could not work. Should not work. Not after the E. Was he supposed to pray? Beg God to strike the abomination and cleanse the Earth once more?

Jackson materialized by Buck's side. "Better not do that here, kid," he said in a low voice, but with an undeniable urgency.

"Do what?" Buck's head, stuffed with ringing emptiness, refused to solve Tim's riddles.

"The Sign of Faith," whispered the soldier, furtively checking if anyone around had noticed Buck's behavior. "They strongly dislike it here."

"Dislike what?"

"The Faith, you idiot!" growled Jackson under his breath. "They don't like the freakin' Faith! And don't look kindly on its signs!"

"Are... are they all Satanists here?"

"No!" Jackson's eyes bulged. "They are not Satanists! They are regular people! Don't have to be a fucking cultist to be normal!" Jackson's voice kept rising, and the last sentence came out the loudest. The moment the words left his lips, the soldier snapped his mouth shut, but the entire team stared at him with expressions ranging from puzzlement to horror.

Jackson raised both hands in surrender and turned away. "Stupid! Stupid! Stupid!" A jerk of his head emphasized each exclamation.

Kossowsky looked from Jackson to Buck and back. "You really got under his skin, didn't you?"

Ignoring the question, Buck asked his own. "What did he mean, si—er, Master? And why is there a working engine?"

Jackson reined in his emotions in an amazing display of self-control. "Forget my words," he said in a level voice that only the team could hear above the deafening rumble of the engine. "What's important for you all to know is that the people of Pelham have had their share of violent run-ins with militant adherents of the Faith. They harbor no warm feelings toward it, to put it mildly. So, no Symbols of Faith. No talking about the Faith, the Prophet, and all that. If you mention Enginocide, I don't know you and you don't know me, it's your funeral. Understood?"

Everybody, including the lieutenant, nodded.

"But Tim?" squeaked Buck. "The engine?"

"Yes," the veteran responded harshly, "the engine. It's there. It's working. Fucking deal with it!" Then, dialing it down a notch, he pointed at the machine sputtering in the distance. "You see it doing any harm?"

The team obediently looked across the square. The panting and puffing contraption had come to a stop by a caravan wagon. Merchants and locals were transferring boxes into a flatbed trailer hitched to the self-propelled car. They talked and laughed, as if there was absolutely nothing wrong with this situation. As if there was no rumbling engine spitting its toxic fumes not a few steps from them. Jackson had a point. As hard as it was to believe, no visible harm was coming to any of these heathens, nor to anyone around.

"But it's corrupting their souls!" Buck could hear the Preacher say. He shook the image off.

Buck had always had somewhat of a mixed attitude toward the Preacher and his teachings. Buck considered himself a Believer. How could he not? He was raised into the Faith, and the Preacher was its face. The one who taught it, explained its intricacies, rectified doubts. The focal point of the congregation. The master of ceremonies for Sunday sermons. In short, the Preacher!

But deep inside—so deep he hadn't dared to admit this even to himself, even alone, even in the dead of the night in a dark room—Buck had had his reservations for a long time.

Even as a little child, Buck had developed a keen sense for when adults lied to him, told half-truths, or omitted important details. He also often knew, intuitively, what was expected of them. He understood these must be the rules of the game and played along.

With the Preacher, Buck got the feeling that his teachings had more to them, something he'd omitted to tell. That the man didn't fully believe what he was preaching. That a barely tangible duplicity came through the Preacher's words. Something, at the edge of perception, didn't ring true.

That had been the source of Buck's greatest conflict, the one he couldn't bring himself to face, diligently burying it for years. And now it was all coming to a head. Suppurating, eating at the resolve of his belief. The cracks in the dam. Master Rodriguez with the asphalt. Janet and her books. Jackson's outburst. And the engine, the goddamn working engine in this community, thriving despite their complete rejection of the Faith.

Was he wrong all along?

What if... No! Disgusting. But the temptation returned, more insistent than ever. What if he tried to understand how this engine worked? Tried to *see*, the same way he now knew the inner workings of a firearm?

Kossowsky's wagon was among the last to pull into the square, but the locals eventually reached it, sparing Buck the need to fight his demons... for the time being.

"Heads up," Lundy muttered.

The residents accosted the caravan as much for the latest news and distraction from their daily grind as for a chance to purchase something. Commerce was commerce, even if Pelham did not represent as great a trading opportunity as, say, Locksville, and merchants weren't about to turn down a deal.

"Remember your roles," whispered Kossowsky, frowning.

"No engine talk," Jackson growled through his teeth.

"Hey, folks!" A tall, broad-shouldered man flashed a toothy smile. "Whatcha sellin'?" He juggled a small leather bag, which clinked every time it landed in his palm. Two wide-eyed children, a boy and a girl, accompanied him.

"Good evening to you and yours," responded Kossowsky with the dignity of someone who knows his value, and an unexpected drawl. "I've got salted fish, beef jerky, dried fruit. Would you like some?"

"What dried fruit?" the customer asked.

Kossowsky counted on his fingers. "I've got apples, I've got peaches, I've got apricots. I've got raisins and prunes. Will give you a good price! Got hazelnuts and pecans too, but those'll cost extra." The performance looked and sounded authentic enough. The officer had been hiding impressive acting skills.

The man looked questioningly at his children. Both enthusiastically nodded.

Buck could relate. Dried fruit! The best snack ever! Had he remembered what he'd been sitting on all along, he may have swept a handful for himself. No merchant should expect anything less from a proper prentice!

The buyer made a show of surrendering to his kids, weighed the purse in his hand, and came to a decision. "Two pounds of mixed fruit and a pound of nuts. How much will that set me off?"

Buck almost applauded when the lieutenant moved his lips, running the "complex" calculation. "That'd be twelve coins for the fruit, and ten for the nuts. A special price for the sweets for your sweet kids, sir."

Unmoved by the cheesy compliment, the buyer scratched the stubble under his jaw. "Twenty even, all in?"

Kossowsky gave out an exaggerated moan, as if it pained him to accept this price. "You've got it. Janet, sweetie, be a darling, prepare this man's order."

Janet lowered her eyes. A stranger could mistake that for a sign of docile consent, but the gesture concealed a spark of fury. She turned to the wagon and froze with a blank expression. She had no clue how to fulfill the request.

Neither did Buck, but he rushed to rescue her from this pickle. "Master," he exclaimed, "may I?"

The lieutenant's brows crept up a smidge. With an ironic smile, he responded, "Can't see why not. Ain't that what I'm keeping you for?"

For a minute he observed as Janet and Buck, equally nonplussed, fumbled their way through the boxes in the wagon. Both blushed and avoided meeting each other's eyes. Having had his share of gratification, Kossowsky explained to the buyer in a loud conspiratorial whisper, "New wife, new prentice. See what I'm forced to deal with, day in, day out? How's a man to conduct his business with two extra mouths to feed and no help?"

The local nodded, sympathizing.

Kossowsky issued a long, percussive sigh. "Sorry 'bout these no-gooders, sir! Don't wanna keep you waiting. Tell you what. Go on with your rounds, and when you come back, we'll have your order all packed and ready. Or send over your young ones with the coin."

Not too happy, the buyer accepted the suggestion and moved on. His kids looked back every few seconds to make sure the wagon didn't disappear into the thin air with the promised treasures.

When they left, Kossowsky joined his clueless helpers at the tailgate. "Gotta teach you two yokels everything, ain't I?"

Buck bit his lip. Posing as traders was the lieutenant's idea, and he should have planned this all better. Buck wasn't the brain of the outfit; being made the butt of the joke was simply unfair. And Janet? She was probably too proud to ask.

Soon, they both learned which crate held what, where to find the wraps, and how to use the scale.

More people came by. Kossowsky haggled heatedly, as if the success of their mission depended on his commercial acumen. Buck and Janet did their best to conform to their roles, with varying degrees of dexterity. Jackson and Lundy zealously supervised the commotion, projecting their guardian authority. The first buyer's kids ran up. The boy warily dropped the coins clutched in his small fist into Kossowsky's palm, and the girl joyously grabbed the treats.

The fundamental questions and crises weren't going away, but trading provided a welcome distraction.

And then the sun began setting down, bringing one of the longest days in Buck's life to an end. Almost—but not quite.

The crowd of locals had gradually dispersed. Caravans come and go, but another day of work awaited in the morning.

Lundy and Jackson laid out their bedrolls on the ground, bracing the wagon. Buck curled up in the driver's seat. Kossowsky and Janet made their beds in the wagon.

Beds, or a single bed? No. Knowing Janet, highly improbable. Buck didn't dare check.

Debilitating fatigue weighed on him. Not from physical activity, he didn't engage in any throughout the day. The blame lay squarely on mental overload. It filled his head with cast iron, pulling it to the ground. Too many overwhelming impressions, topped off by the rude affront to his religious beliefs. Too much to process. Would he ever get used to the sheer amount of fresh information this big world had to throw at him?

The last of the caravanners settled down. Buck was getting drowsy too when a muted but distinct—and now recognizable—noise made him rise with a spring. Another engine? And then came the music. His weariness vanished. No way he'd be able to fall asleep fighting the curiosity.

He slid off the wagon, tiptoed a dozen steps away, and then raced toward the sounds. The music led him to the supermarket. He sneaked through the wide entrance. Hm. That was unexpected. He'd imagined an open space with a bunch of stands and kiosks, same as in the Marketplace—but under one giant roof. Instead, he discovered a long corridor with entryways on both sides, lit by ceiling lamps.

Buck skulked halfway down the hallway, then abandoned the caution. No reason for that. He wasn't doing anything wrong. This looked like a public place, with no signs of access restrictions. He squared his shoulders and sauntered on, peeking left and right into the dark and lifeless side entrances. And then he reached the fourth one to the left. Loud voices spilled into the hallway from that door, along with the sounds of music and... spots of colorful lights. Buck's breath caught. Colorful lights? How was that possible?

Overcoming hesitation, he entered and stopped dead in his tracks. The space was a pub, with a bar, tall stools, tables... and a *machine*. Lights in a variety of colors ran around its rim, and it was the source of the music. Mesmerized, Buck traced the lights, listening to the melody. Odd and beautiful, it resembled nothing he'd ever heard. Energetic, enticing, it made his foot stomp to the rhythm. No instruments he knew produced such an unnatural sound.

A hand wrapped around Buck's shoulders. He flinched, awakening from the daydream, but still not a hundred percent present. Ah, the man who'd bought the treats for his children earlier.

"First time here? Lemme buy you a drink!" The cheerful local led Buck to the bar.

Buck climbed onto a stool next to his benefactor. "Thank you... sir?"

"Norman's the name." The man extended his shovel of a hand and firmly shook Buck's. "Call me Norm."

Buck mimicked the introduction. "Baxter. Call me Buck."

"Sean!" Norman yelled over the machine's music and hailed the barman. "Make us two Milton ales, would ya?"

Sean, not bothering with a verbal response, gave him a thumbs up and went about filling two mugs from a cask.

Buck's eyes stayed glued to the gleaming box, enchanting and frightening. His entire upbringing weighed in, insisting he hate the machine, but the Faith shattered against the admiration. The machine, an embodiment of magic, represented the impossible. It made music! How could it be evil?

Norm patted Buck on the shoulder. "Our pride and joy! The genny guzzles a crap ton of fuel, and the music gets old after a while. But hey, nobody's complaining. A miracle it still works! Once it's gone, it's gone. Could be the last jukebox in the world."

"Juke... box? What's inside it? How does it make music? And the lights?"

Their beers arrived. Norm downed half his mug in hungry gulps. He licked the foam off his mustache and chuckled. "Hey, slow down! What's with the questioning?"

"I've seen nothing like this..." How could Buck explain why he needed the answers, if he wasn't sure himself?

"Aha." Norm rubbed the back of his neck. "I see. Man, must be some real boondocks where you're from. Bet you were happy to escape!"

Several responses popped into Buck's mind, one after another. Indignant. Uncertain. Glum. In the end, he only shrugged.

"Lemme guess." Norm ignored Buck's obvious discomfort. "Saint George? New Hope? No, don't tell me... Caledonia!" He smiled triumphantly, proud of his sleuthing skills.

"No, sir. I'm from Creek Point."

"Creek Point?" Norm creased his brow. "Where's that?"

It was Buck's turn to stare back. The first person he'd met who hadn't heard his native village's name.

"Um... One of the Five Points?" He let the answer end in a question mark, unsure if this reference would suffice.

It did.

All benevolence disappeared from Norman's face, along with the first signs of inebriation. The corners of his mouth slid down, and his eyes turned harder.

"Ah. There." He glanced around, checking if anyone had witnessed their exchange. Leaning closer to Buck, he whispered, "You better leave now."

Buck recoiled from his hot, pungent breath. "Why?!"

The local shook his head and shooed the guest away with both hands. Buck stood up. Uncomprehending, resentful, clutching the mug with his untouched drink.

"Leave the beer," said Norman, painstakingly avoiding Buck's eyes.

Withdrawing hospitality was the last straw. Unheard of. Buck slammed the mug on the bar top, spilling half the contents. He considered spitting on the floor under Norman's feet, like he'd seen enraged men do in such situations, but thought the better of it. Offended as he was, he sought no confrontation. He glared at Norman, then turned and stomped out of that fine establishment.

Buck left the supermarket in a haze, walking wherever his feet took him. With no lights outside and overcast skies, landmarks were difficult to discern, but he didn't try. He only watched his step to not tumble.

"Trouble, Brennan?" The Caravan Master's unmistakable salted fish aroma surrounded Buck.

Straining his sight, he distinguished the bushy beard and the whites of the eyes. "Honestly, Master Flanagan, I don't know."

The dark shape cocked its head to a side, puzzled or alerted. "Do tell."

Buck haltingly retold his bizarre encounter at the pub. "Why?" he asked, to fill the pause that followed. Unable to see the Caravan Master's face, he was left to guess the reasons for the continuing silence. Angry? Or as baffled as Buck himself? "What can he possibly have against Five Points?"

"You really don't know, eh?" The big man scratched his beard, the rustling unexpectedly loud in the quiet night.

In the last two days, Buck had been repeatedly reminded how little he knew, compared to everyone else. A disheartening position to be in. That had to stop. "Can you please tell me already?" Hysterical notes seeped into Buck's voice.

Flanagan pulled Buck by the shoulder further away from the nearest houses. "Have you heard of the Crusades?" His tone left little doubt he didn't expect a positive answer.

Buck didn't disappoint. "Cru... what?"

"Yup, what I thought." Flanagan sighed. "Early on after the E, what later came to be known as Five Points had been a major outpost of the spreading Faith. And, boy, were you guys violent about that! You were prepared—no, eager!—to go to war with anyone unwilling to accept your creed. Your most fanatical folks had split away and founded the Dark Island—because the rest of you weren't ardent enough to their dogmatic tastes. But, let me tell you, those not ardent enough were plenty ardent for everyone else!"

He paused, allowing Buck to absorb the information and react. Thoroughly confused, Buck remained quiet. The Caravan Master mistook this for acceptance and went on. "Pelham was the worst offender for the true believers. Because the people of Pelham saw nothing wrong with using machines. And use them they did."

"How?" breathed out Buck.

Flanagan chucked. "Some machines had survived the E. Very few. One percent, maybe less. Their insides didn't burn out, and they only needed fuel or power."

"Power?" The word meant force, political or military, or physical strength. What could it have to do with machines?

The big man quietly whistled. "Never ceases to amaze me how uninformed you people are. Anyhow, Pelham looked for functioning tractors, generators— No!" he brought up a hand. "I can't explain everything to you. Just listen. Bringing those back, restoring them to working condition was a grueling task, but Pelhamites persisted. They had found a way to produce biodiesel, a kind of fuel. And they weren't reluctant to use all this, not in the slightest. You can imagine how abominable that looked to your Faith devotees."

He paused again. Buck nodded. Until as recently as today, that had looked abominable to him, too. Remembering Jackson's earlier admonition, he kept his mouth shut.

"Five Points had sent one military expedition after another to eradicate this heresy. They called those the Crusades. Why do you think Pelham constructed its famous palisade?"

"What?!" The implication stung. *He* was the bad guy? People needed walls for protection from *him*?!

"Yeah," continued Master Flanagan, "a lot to wrap your brain around. Your Army had attracted Locksville's ire and got its nose bloodied more than once. Your Council decided—wisely, in retrospect—to stop trying to fix the world and mind its own affairs. Five Points fenced itself off with its Boundary and became a textbook example of isolation. Not that you'd know what a textbook is. Bottom line, here we are. Apparently, where you're from, they're too ashamed of the past to teach it to the youth. But Pelham has never forgotten."

Individually, each of Flanagan's statements could be discarded as an outrageous lie. Taken together, they made a weird sort of sense, like the pieces of a wooden puzzle he had as a kid. Who would bother to forge such an elaborate myth?

He'd ask Janet in the morning. And Jackson. How much did they know? He had an awful lot of questions, but one was the most burning. "Now you tell me, Master Flanagan, am I in trouble?"

Chapter 15

Yun-mi

September 22, 42 PE

The Singh brothers kept babbling on, and on, and on. How was it possible to find so many subjects to talk about? Yun-mi had never been a big talker. Was that the side effect of her way of life, or had she chosen to become a Rat because of being a silent loner? Impossible to tell. Nor did she care.

She tried to listen in, to check if she could pick up another skill. Never know if one day the ability to talk someone into bored loss of vigilance may come in handy.

Useless. No way she'd ever be able to replicate *that*. The brothers chatted about a common acquaintance's chain of misfortunes, then jumped with no obvious segue to a piquant situation in which a relative had found himself with a wife of another relative, only to switch abruptly to the prices extorted this season by their clan's blacksmith.

No. You either have this, or you don't. Yun-mi clearly didn't. But that was fine, she had enough to offer as it was. The last forty-eight hours' events had proved that.

These two days had been the most... what? *The most* in too many aspects to list. One thing they were not: boring.

She'd survived, which hadn't been a given, and came out on the other side. With a new set of goals, and a different understanding of the world she lived in. With new connections and new dangers. The tightrope she'd been walking throughout her life was still taut and thin, but instead of bridging single-story roofs, it now spanned a chasm between the top floors of skyscrapers. And a storm was looming, threatening to knock her down. She was playing by the adults' rules now, and the stakes had become infinitely higher. Well, she had it coming. Quoting Wong, "Be careful what you're asking for."

Though Yun-mi had concluded she'd never be able to invoke the same talkative mode as the Singh brothers, she kept listening in. At the most basic level, their conversations provided entertainment, something to add a flourish to the monotone hike through the abandoned neighborhoods. But her interest had another, deeper motive. Precious nuggets of useful information hid in the flood of verbosity. Having never visited West Sauga, she was given a glimpse into their way of life, customs, social structure. Without ever meeting the Singh brothers' family, she'd learned more about their kids and kin than she knew about her neighbors at Christie Station. Enough to develop a degree of affinity for the West Sauga Clan. Being dressed like one of them contributed too.

This had been Wong's idea. In the face of Yun-mi's skepticism, he'd insisted she should receive the same armed escort she'd had on her way to New Kowloon. He swore that a lot of heads, including his, would roll if something happened to Yun-mi before she reached her designated area of operations. The fearsome Golden Dragon had made that abundantly clear. When Yun-mi succumbed to his arguments, Wong asked her to dress the part, wearing a white turban, a yellow scarf, a gold-embroidered vest, and a wide green sash. "Bladed weapons," he observed dryly, "you've got enough of your own."

At first, Yun-mi had found the suggestion ridiculous. Nobody might mistake a Korean Rat, even wrapped head to toe in all the right attire, for a Sikh warrior. Having given the masquerade additional consideration, she admitted the idea may have its merit. How did she distinguish clan affiliations when she crossed paths with strangers in the streets of the City? By the way they dressed. The colors, the fashion, the accessories. Clans had always been conservative in their self-identification, and the dress codes were among the most jealously preserved traditions. On top of that, people of the City were naturally averse to short-distance interactions and obsessively protective of their inflated personal space—unless they sought confrontation. A legacy of the old times, when any uninvited encounter was likely to end in one party's premature demise.

A complex system of nonverbal communication—gestures, hand signs, particular ways of wearing certain items—had developed over the years. This made it possible to signal a universally understood request for help, an offer of trade, or an intention to parlay without coming too close to trigger a defensive reaction. At such distances, facial features were hardly discernible.

If she saw someone wearing a black leather jacket in the City, she didn't need to think twice. She'd know she was looking at an Islington Russian. Similarly, if someone were to see Yun-mi, wrapped in the same unique garb as the Singh brothers accompanying her, they'd have to have a compelling reason to check closer—close enough to discover that Yun-mi's face bore no similarities to her retinue.

A shrill whistle behind their group distracted her from these thoughts. In an instant, the brothers formed a protective ring around her, bristling with weapons. Yun-mi crouched in the middle, bow drawn, scanning for hostiles.

Why not a rifle? She had two now.

Yun-mi swatted the thought away. Without months, if not years, of intensive training, she'd never reach the same level of proficiency with firearms as she had with her bow.

The whistle repeated. An intricate three-note tune. The brothers relaxed, slung their rifles, sheathed their blades, and started explaining to Yun-mi, all at once, that everything was alright.

Yun-mi rose to her feet but held onto her bow—until she had her own assessment of the tactical situation. Once, not long ago, she had trusted someone already. Where did *that* get her?

Two figures came around the corner of the street that Yun-mi and her bodyguards had just crossed.

A dark-skinned man hobbled in the front with hands tied behind his back and leg movement constrained by a short length of rope. The enormous bruise covering half his face was turning darker with every passing second. His affiliation was impossible to determine. The prisoner either belonged to a clan Yun-mi wasn't familiar with, or concealed his true identity.

His captor presented an entirely different puzzle. One look at his face identified him as the Singh brothers' close relative. Yet his garments were anything but West Sauga Clan's. He wore the most nondescript pants and jacket Yun-mi had ever seen. Deliberately so, bringing to mind the tales of urban camouflage that soldiers of yore used to have: a mix of gray, white, and black spots. The eye slid off the random pattern, having nothing to focus on. A drab green combat vest, a shemagh of the same shade wrapped around his neck, and a turban too washed out to determine its color matched the outfit. Even the kirpan at his belt sat in a dull, unadorned scabbard. A scoped rifle in his hands, enveloped in brown rags, completed the picture.

Coming up, he kicked the prisoner under the knee, sending him to the ground. He shook hands with Yun-mi's guards, clapped their shoulders, and went through the same genial ritual as the other brothers. Finally, he faced Yun-mi. "Ajinder Singh. Nice to meet you in person!"

Yun-mi took the offered hand and answered the man's hug, fascinated and ashamed. How shallow her impression of their clan had been! When she thought she'd gotten the measure of its people, they proved how much more complex and multifaceted they were than the mental image she'd created.

"Your senses were on the money, Jihan," Ajinder said. "This sad piece of crap trailed you all the way from New Kowloon. He didn't know what hit him when I put an end to his stalking."

Jihan, the older of the brothers, halfheartedly nudged the prisoner in the ribs with the boot, extracting a muffled grunt. "Who are you, carrion? Why were you following us? Who are you working for?"

The kneeling man did not respond. His face showed the grim resignation of someone who knew he was going to die, and soon.

"Oh." Jihan's disinterested intonation conveyed how little he cared. "You think we're going to torture and kill you? Ha! We've got better things to do and places to be. We'll send you back to the Hive and let them take care of you." He spat on the road.

The prisoner's face went ashen. He started shaking.

Preet, another brother, approached from behind, drew a knife, and ripped open the collar of the spy's shirt. He yanked the flap sideways, exposing a strange tattoo on the captive's shoulder: two narrow horizontal lines crossing half a dozen wider but shorter vertical bars.

"Knew it!" Preet returned the blade to its sheath.

"What's that tattoo?" Yun-mi asked, humbled by being the only one not in the know.

"That, my friend," Jihan said, "is a railroad. This man here is an officer of The Station."

Yun-mi swallowed something thick suddenly blocking her throat, the memories of helplessly waiting to be sold momentarily flooding her.

"I'm sure Master Wu will find this exciting," Jihan continued, looking through the Stationer with a strange combination of mockery and disgust. "He *will* want you to answer a few questions." He barked a laugh. "My, does he know how to be persuasive!"

The prisoner sagged, as if his spine were yanked out, but stayed silent.

"Okay," Jihan said in a different tone, a commander giving orders now. "Preet, take this maggot back to New Kowloon. Eyes open. Ajinder, cover him, in case Mister Slaver has got friends in the area. You know the drill."

"You've got it, brother," Ajinder confirmed with a wicked smile. "No one will come close to them." He pulled the bolt back and chambered a round in a sleek, predatory movement. Then clicked the safety on and winked at Yun-mi.

Jihan slapped his shoulder. "We'll see you there."

There. Such a simple word, meaning such different things to different people.

To the captured slaver, pain, followed by a certain death.

To the Singh brothers, a place to pick up occasional jobs for a powerful patron, lucrative due to their discretion.

To Yun-mi... What *did* it mean to her? Until two days ago—nothing in particular. She'd known New Kowloon existed. Who didn't? But the Pacific Ocean existed too. These two pieces of knowledge bore about the same level of abstraction. It had been another place on the map. And now... Home. It was home. Little Korea, her birthplace, had commanded her loyalty for no real reason. She hadn't been close with anyone other than Joon-woo, blessed be his memory. It used to be her home, but only for lack of a better option. The Golden Dragon had offered her a new one.

The four remaining brothers walked in a tighter formation around Yun-mi, gravitating to the sidewalks and overtly scouting the surroundings. Gone was the chattering intended to spook chance passersby, replaced with quiet professionalism of fighters expecting trouble—and ready to meet it with deadly force. An unnerving side effect of this change was the absence of the background noise Yun-mi had quickly gotten used to.

A distant gunshot echoed through the empty streets. Yun-mi pulled her head into her shoulders. Another shot followed.

Jihan met her mute question with a reassuring smile. "Ajinder is taking care of business."

Thank gods these people were on her side. Had it been the other way, she would have been dead many times over. Then again, with what she'd signed up for, she'd have plenty of opportunities to fulfill the death wish she didn't have. Nothing ever came free. The strings, oh, they were most definitely attached.

The tunnels beckoned, but that meant parting ways with the brothers, the prospect less alluring than it should have been. A different person was returning to the City. Not the inexperienced but overly confident student that had accompanied Joon-woo, excited to see the great Dixie Mall. Not yet a seasoned Rat either, not by a long shot, but a thoroughly disillusioned one, for damn sure. With first-hand practical experience in fighting for her life. *And in killing. Let's not forget the killing.*

The habit of operating alone would not be easy to overcome, but she came to appreciate the luxury of being surrounded by trusted people. Here's to the hope this wasn't the last time.

Her companions started showing unease after crossing Etobicoke Creek, and especially following an energetic dash over Highway 427. This was, possibly, as far east as the brothers had ever ventured. Still, none of them complained.

Almost there. Kipling, the terminal subway station, showed in the distance. The first step of the home run for her. The point where she'd thank her guardians and say her goodbyes.

A third party preempted her perfect plan. As usual.

Two figures rose from a concrete barricade thirty meters ahead. Black leather jackets, blue jeans, black boots, and bandanas of the same unoriginal color.

So much for sneaking home undetected.

One man walked toward the travelers but stopped in response to a flurry of gun safeties clicked off all around Yun-mi. His face bore a sardonic expression, not a bit scared.

Yun-mi raised her hands, palms down, and shouted, "Calm down, everybody, these are friends!" as much to her escort as to the unexpected greeting party. Friends? Should be. Or not. Who could tell what was on this guy's mind today?

His clan recognized no half-tones, accepted no middle ground. If they considered you a friend, they'd smother you with hospitality. But if they thought you'd offended them somehow—say, by bringing foreigners to trespass on their land... The gods themselves would weep for you.

No one was freaking out. Whew. A haphazard shot, and all Seven Hells would break loose with her in the middle. That would be a shame. Yun-mi advanced, keeping her hands where everyone could see them.

At five steps away, the man tipped his hat. "You keep odd company, Park Yun-mi."

The cloud of uncertainty lifted, and her tentative smile grew broader. "Good to see you too, Kostya!"

They closed the remaining distance and embraced, patting each other on the back, as the local ritual prescribed. Yun-mi glanced behind her. The Singh brothers lowered their weapons. She waved, inviting them to join her.

"Just to make sure: they aren't holding you hostage or something? Do you need my boys to mow them down?" asked Kostya in a low voice, eyeing the approaching Sikhs. With him, it was impossible to tell whether he was joking or deadly serious.

"No, not today!" Did her laughter sound too strained? "Let me make the introductions. The Singh Brothers of the West Sauga Clan. Jihan, Kulvir, Mankaran, and Ranbir," she said, pointing at each. "Meet Kostya Malyshev of the Islington Clan."

Kostya whistled. "West Sauga, eh? Are you lost, brothers?"

"No, we love traveling," Jihan laughed.

Kostya finished shaking everyone's hands when his face grew puzzled. "Hey, where's Joon-woo? Since when does a little Rat like you scurry around without adult supervision?"

"Joon-woo is dead," said Yun-mi. That flat tone cost her a lot.

"He's what?! How— Who?!"

"Doesn't matter. I have avenged his death, and that's that."

Kostya put a hand on Yun-mi's shoulder. "Really sorry to hear that. He was a great guy. I'll miss him. There's a story which you will tell me someday."

"Someday. Promise." She wasn't here to tell stories. She was here to... Huh. What a grotesque idea. Yun-mi bit her lip. *Don't overthink it. Trust your instincts.* See, Joon-woo, wherever you are? She was paying attention. "Different subject," she announced in an all-business tone, as if discussing the purchase of a head of lettuce from a neighbor. "Kostya, Jihan, I request a formal alliance between Islington and West Sauga. I vouch for both sides."

Their "You what?" and "Come again?" overlapped. The two men exchanged comically similar looks.

Formal alliances were not a trifle. They crowned lengthy brokering and negotiations between parties that had already worked with each other informally.

"In Joon-woo's memory," Yun-mi added to keep the momentum. "Do this to honor him."

A deliberate choice of word. Honor, a cornerstone of Islington Clan's ethical system. Their understanding of honor might sometimes appear strange to an outsider, but transgressing it was among the worst conceivable sins.

Spot on. Kostya squared his shoulders. "*Ilyukha, davay syuda!*"

His companion approached.

"Ilya," said the boss, "you, and everyone here, bear witness and spread the word that I, Konstantin Malyshev, on my authority as Islington Clan's Chief of Operations, unaware of any outstanding disputes or blood feuds between us, declare a formal alliance with the West Sauga Clan, represented by these fine men."

"I witness," said Ilya. His face showed nothing. Keeping an unreadable expression, yes. Another of his clan's virtues.

"This is all highly unusual, but I see no grounds to object," the oldest Singh said, perplexed. "It is my honor to partake."

He recited his side of the pledge, and added, "I did not get to know this Joon-woo, but he sounds like an exceptional fellow."

This was too easy. Nothing in life was supposed to be so easy. But... Maybe she deserved an occasional break? For something *not* to be a struggle once in a while?

Kostya faced Yun-mi. "Happy?"

"Thank you." She had every reason to be. On a whim, without thinking it through, she had achieved the unimaginable. This was how legends were born. And she hadn't been on her new mission one full day yet! Why wasn't she happy?

Joon-woo. Wherever you are, I hope you're watching. Did I make you proud? My greatest achievement, and you aren't here to witness it.

Yun-mi sighed. "I've got another favor to ask."

The Chief laughed. "Of course you have! Any more alliances?"

"In time." *Do not smile.*

"O-o-okay..." Kostya drew the word over three syllables. "We really should talk."

"We will. Soon."

"*Khorosho.* I'll take that. What's that other favor you need?"

"Send men to accompany the brothers on their way back. I must be sure they encounter no surprises this side of the Creek. Once they cross, they'll take care of themselves."

"Park Yun-mi of Little Korea, are you trying to insult me as a host?"

"Huh?" Did she just squander all her accomplishments?

"Were you not present when we swore the alliance? They're in my territory! Their safety is my responsibility. Everything else goes without saying. But!" he lifted a finger to punctuate the sentence. "No agreement is valid without a proper feast! Brothers, share a meal with us to celebrate! I refuse to let you go anywhere without that!"

He sternly pointed the same finger at Yun-mi. "You too. Don't even think about slinking away before you're fed and drunk! I'd take that as a personal offense!"

Chapter 16

Buck

September 23, 42 PE

Buck drew his knees closer to his chest and pulled the worn blanket tighter. That did nothing to prevent sneaky drafts from chilling his bones.

He had spent most of the night tossing, drained of energy but unable to fall asleep. Heavy thoughts had burdened him, running in circles, stirring, jarring, throwing his emotions off-balance.

At last, after dawn had already painted the sky above the palisade in lighter shades of gray, he'd blacked out.

The bench was hard, the morning—crispy cold, Buck's body—stiff. Sitting up? What a ridiculously outlandish idea. But someone persistent kept shaking his shoulder and calling his name. With difficulty, Buck lifted one eyelid. A human shape vaguely resembling Kossowsky jerked him into an upright position. Buck hunched and snuggled in the blanket, but the lieutenant yanked it off his back.

"Hey!" Indignant at such treatment, Buck finally opened both eyes.

Kossowsky growled, "Rise and shine, moron!" and smacked him upside the head.

Buck looked around, bleary-eyed. The caravan was getting ready to move, horses brought out from the stables and harnessed, merchants milling near their wagons with professional efficiency. He was the last to wake up.

Deathly tired, still groggy, and having lost the last bits of the blanket's warmth, Buck hugged himself and slid into a half-conscious trance again. Another slap from Kossowsky rudely restored his grip on reality.

"What was that for?" Such heavy-handedness, in a very literal sense, did not fit the lieutenant.

"Be thankful I don't bury you in a pile of horse dung behind the stables!" hissed the officer.

Nauseating anger twisted Buck's guts. The threat sounded disproportionately harsh for the relatively insignificant misdeed of sleeping in. He was sick and tired of people berating him for not meeting their expectations. Especially if no one had bothered to inform him what those were. He leaned toward Kossowsky until foreheads nearly touched, and hissed back, "What the fuck?!" Then added, as an afterthought, "Master?"

The lieutenant, momentarily taken aback by Buck's audacious reaction, turned purple. Fists clenched, he opened his mouth, but a hand on his bicep prevented the looming explosion. Jackson, having appeared out of thin air as was his wont, whispered into Kossowsky's ear loudly enough for Buck to overhear. "Sir, let us not make a scene here? We've already attracted more than enough attention. I advise against aggravating the situation any further."

The officer noisily exhaled through his teeth. "You're right. I apologize for my outburst." He jumped off the wagon and went to check on the horses.

Still seething, Buck asked the lingering veteran, "What's gotten into him?"

Jackson smiled mirthlessly. "Master Kossowsky's morning began with an unpleasant conversation with Master Flanagan."

"You little fucker," muttered Lundy from Buck's other side. With anger-induced tunnel vision, Buck hadn't noticed him coming close. "Going around wagging your tongue. 'Blah-blah-blah, I am from Five Points! Blah-blah-blah, my people killed your people and burned your machines!'"

Jackson frowned. "But seriously, what were you thinking?"

Buck exploded. "How the fuck was I supposed to know?! No one tells me shit! You cautioned us not to talk about the fucking machines or the Faith—and I fucking didn't! That motherfucking asshole asked me where I'm from, for fuck's sake, and I fucking told him. Did any of you smug fucks warn me not to?"

A thin smile curved Jackson's lips halfway through Buck's tirade, growing wider with each word. Buck took a breath and finally surveyed the surroundings.

The lieutenant glared at him over the horse's back, brooding rather than angry. Lundy gawked. Jackson flipped a dried prune into his mouth, chewed, spit the stone, narrowly missing Lundy's head, and said, "You may want to ease up on the 'fucks', kid. Your impassioned speech was well-articulated, but consider the lady traveling with us." The bastard relished every moment.

Buck twitched and swerved around. Shit! How could he forget?!

Janet, amused, had been sitting right behind his back all this time! Buck lowered his eyes. His face flushed. Jackson patted him on the shoulder and jumped off, ostensibly to do some useful thing or another, leaving the two alone in the wagon.

"I... I'm sorry, Miss... Mistress Kossowsky," Buck mumbled, twisting his hands, unsure what to do with them. "I was out of line."

"At ease, Private!" Janet said in a poor imitation of a deep male basso, and giggled. "That was perfect!"

Buck's eyes darted up in surprise.

She continued, "Do you really think you said anything I haven't heard? Or, for that matter, anything that hasn't been said to me? Relax, Brennan, I am not offended. To be sure, that vocabulary doesn't suit you, but I was glad to see you stand up to bigotry."

She had raised her voice, ensuring her last sentence carried outside the wagon.

"You may yet grow a spine, *prentice.*" Janet was mocking him, but Buck didn't mind. "Now, shoo. Off you go." She waved him away with an exaggerated ladylike mannerism. "It's inappropriate for a prentice to be alone with his master's wife!" Another giggle. "And the caravan is already on the move."

Half an hour out of Pelham, the skies rapidly darkened, and the first drops hit the wagon. In less than a minute, torrential rain produced a deafening drumbeat. The two veterans marching on either side of the wagon didn't seem to care, squinting through the water mist. Buck retreated to the protection of the tent, leaving Kossowsky alone in the driver's seat. The miserable officer pulled his raincoat hood as low as it allowed.

Served him well for the stunt with Buck's blanket! Buck almost stuck out his tongue at the lieutenant's back, but met Janet's cheeky gaze and shrugged instead. She rewarded him with a thumbs up.

Eventually, the wagons stopped. Locksville greeted the real and fake merchants with a continued downpour. The wall of water made sightseeing impossible. Jackson and Lundy climbed aboard, removed their capes, and shook the water off like a pair of dogs.

"We've arrived," Jackson said, stating the obvious, and wiped water off his face with a sleeve. "Our guard services are no longer needed."

After excruciatingly long minutes of boredom, occasional sighs, and the snoring of Lundy, who'd fallen asleep the moment his head touched the hay, Buck took the initiative. "Anything I shouldn't be talking about in Locksville?"

"Ah, the kid learns from his mistakes!" Jackson didn't miss the opportunity to rub in Buck's missteps. "Let's see." He spent a moment in contemplation, then perked up. "I say, knock yourself out. Blather away." He caught Buck's suspicious eye and grinned.

"Never say you like slavers," Lundy said without opening his eyes. "They really, really don't like slavers," he added, as if that was supposed to explain everything.

"Ah..." The revelation left Buck wordless. "Uh," he tried again, "why would I say I like slavers?"

"Dunno, don't care." Lundy turned to the other side, gave out a thunderous snore, and liberated a fart.

Buck helplessly directed his attention at Jackson.

"What?" Tim spread his arms. "It's true. They really, really don't like slavers."

Buck gasped in exasperation. "Will you people stop speaking in fu—" He glanced at Janet. "In riddles?! Who in the Seven Hells are slavers? And why should I be talking about them at all?"

"Slavers are people who own slaves," explained Jackson, patiently articulating every word, as if talking to a four-year-old. "And that is precisely the point, you shouldn't be talking about them, at all."

"Gah!" Buck squeezed his eyes shut, clutched his head, and buried it between his knees. He was being pushed dangerously close to poking holes in some people with a knife.

"Have you two clowns had enough entertainment for one day?" Janet's frosty tone chilled the air in the wagon. "Lundy... well, he's Lundy, and that's that. But you, Jackson? I expected you to be better than this."

"Why? Do I not strike you as a fun-loving guy?" Under her heavy stare, he relented and raised his hands. "Alright, alright, you win. See, Buck, slavery is universally frowned upon. With one exception: The Station. They call their slaves 'workers', but for all intents and purposes, those are slaves. Everybody knows that, and hates The Station for that, but Locksvillers hate them the most. Thus, the first rule of dealing with Locksville is, don't mention the slavers."

"Then why doesn't Locksville fight them?" asked Buck. "To free the slaves?"

"Why, indeed?" Jackson snorted. "Politics, my friend. Politics, and reluctance to shed more blood than is absolutely needed. The Railroad is too strong to be easily toppled. And an important trade partner for many in the region. Everybody looks the other way and maintains the status quo."

"The what?"

"Never you mind, boy."

A heavy silence hung in the wagon. Silence? The rain was over!

Everyone arrived at the same conclusion simultaneously. Except Lundy, who kept snoring.

Buck peeked outside. The wet and muddy world inspired no desire to leave the warm comfort of the wagon. But then locals appeared and showed the caravan to their stalls inside a vast warehouse. After the horses were unhitched, cleaned, and fed, a new person attracted Buck's attention.

A solidly built man, dressed in something that could pass for military fatigues but with no insignia, waved goodbye to another wagon's crew and approached Kossowsky's team. He glanced around, sizing up the Fivepointers, and a smile touched his long, narrow face. "Well, well, well. I'll be damned if these aren't Jackson and Lundy. Well met, gentlemen, well met!"

"Captain Weinberg," Tim acknowledged. "I'd be lying if I said the pleasure is all mine."

"Oh, Mister Jackson, your words cut worse than a knife!" The visitor regarded the Fivepointers with renewed interest. Inexplicable anguish filled Buck while Weinberg's eyes stayed on him. He'd been stripped of his fake persona, dissected, and cataloged. But before Buck squirmed, the captain's gaze moved on to Janet.

Having finished this second survey, Captain Weinberg turned back to Tim with a quizzically creased eyebrow. "Mister Jackson, may I assume you would honestly warn me if your arrival brought any trouble? For the sake of good old times?"

"You'll see no trouble from us, Captain."

"Great!" Weinberg clapped. "Now, kindly introduce me to the rest of your peculiar little party."

"Everyone," Jackson mumbled, exasperated, "meet Captain Weinberg, the Head of Locksville's Intelligence Service. Captain, meet everyone." Under Weinberg's disapproving stare, he yielded a detailed introduction. "These days, Lundy and I serve as armed guards for this here merchant Kossowsky, his wife, and prentice."

Weinberg's eyes compliantly followed, then returned to Jackson. "*Pah*-lease, mister Jackson. This is insulting to both your intelligence and mine. 'Intelligence'," he barked a laugh and pointed his index fingers at the veteran. "See what I did there?" A deadly serious expression wiped off his almost-not-fake smile.

Buck recoiled half a step.

"Gentlemen. Lady," the captain acknowledged each one on the team, in a voice of someone used to having his tentatively expressed wishes treated as strict orders. Of someone like Colonel. "Enough with this charade. I sense a conversation is in order. Please follow me to a place where such a conversation may be had without unwanted interruptions."

No one questioned the captain's directive. The Fivepointers obediently trailed after him through courtyards, passages, and stairwells.

Buck had expected their journey to end in a dank interrogation chamber, with walls covered in dried blood. Instead, he found himself in a sizable room, brightly lit by the after-storm midday sun. He stole a glance through the large window at what must have been the Canal and the famous locks.

The host gestured for the guests to sit down. Kossowsky and Janet claimed the leather couch, side by side as befitted a supposedly married couple. Lundy sunk into a deep armchair, leaving Buck and Jackson to climb onto a pair of tall stools. The captain dropped into his seat behind the desk.

A man came in with a tray, distributed steaming mugs of herbal tea, and left without uttering a word.

"Welcome to my office, travelers," Weinberg said. "Hope this is enough to show my goodwill and put you at ease. Now, would someone please explain to me the nature of your business here? How about"—he scanned the room and fixed his gaze on Kossowsky—"you?"

"I am—" started the fake merchant.

"No," interrupted the host, rather rudely, "wait. Let me try. You are with the Five Points Army, naturally. A captain? No, a lieutenant. Am I in the ballpark?"

Something in Kossowsky's face and posture changed. An arrogant merchant vacated the scene for a career officer. "You are, sir. Lieutenant Kossowsky, Colonel's aide-de-camp."

"Thank you, Lieutenant. And as for your mission..." The captain left the half-formed sentence hanging.

"Not at liberty to discuss it, Captain, sir." Kossowsky kept an impressively straight face. That couldn't be very easy. The host's gravitas, combined with the fearsome title, supplied a wealth of intimidation. "I assure you, though, that our mission doesn't affect Locksville or its interests. We are passing through with the caravan."

"Hm." Weinberg reclined with his chair, balancing on its rear legs and rocking back and forth. "I'll take that. As a side note, I'd advise you against making assumptions about Locksville's interests. Sometimes, their extent surprises even me. But otherwise, I find your assurances satisfactory. That, and Tim's presence, of course."

Um, what?

Both men, Jackson and Weinberg, stood up at the same time.

"Was this necessary?" Jackson asked grumpily.

"Come here, you old sleazy snake!"

They embraced and patted each other on the backs. Lundy, as usual, grunted something unintelligible, most likely obscene. Buck, Janet, and Kossowsky gawked in disbelief.

The host sat back in his chair. Jackson brazenly perched on top of the captain's desk, childishly dangling one foot. "Their faces," he said. "Look at their faces, Dave. This is precious!"

Weinberg's smile widened.

"Jackson?" said the lieutenant. "An explanation?"

Captain Weinberg looked from one man to another and shook his head. "You're incorrigible, Tim. Though I'm curious to watch you squirming your way out of this pickle, I'm going to excuse myself. But before I leave you to your fun, I've got a favor to ask, Lieutenant."

Kossowsky's face grew somber. "What is it, Captain?"

Weinberg waved off the concerns. "Oh, nothing much. Give a ride to two people. Not too far, to The Station. Your caravan will pass it on its way, no?"

"I believe it will, sir."

"It's settled." The captain cheerfully clapped his knees and stood.

"Ah, Captain, sir?" Kossowsky remained seated, looking confused.

Buck, too, had a hard time following the pace of the conversation. The captain had skipped a few steps that were kind of needed to secure the other party's agreement.

"I need more information before I can agree to this request." Kossowsky's face hardened.

"No, Lieutenant, you do not," Jackson replied for the captain. "The less you know, the better you'll sleep."

The Locksviller shrugged. "Okay then. I trust you'll find your way back to the warehouse? Stay here," he encompassed the room with a broad gesture, "for as long as you please." With that, he left, not waiting for a response.

Lieutenant Kossowsky stared blankly at the closed door, appearing to be out of words. Or maybe trying to pick the right words. The right words that weren't expletives.

Buck and Janet exchanged puzzled looks. "What just happened?" she asked.

"God Almighty and the Prophet's beat-up shoe on a stick, aren't you people dull as ditchwater!" Lundy's ability to string together such a long and coherent phrase was as shocking as its blasphemous content. More words in a single serving than his average daily allowance.

Every head in the room turned in his direction. The day kept giving...

Two men showed up at the Fivepointers' stall a couple of hours after commerce had concluded for the day. They could hardly be any more different.

One, in his mid-twenties, tall, of medium build, with closely cropped blond hair and a neatly trimmed beard, brought a large, heavy-looking duffle bag.

The other, younger, possibly Buck's age, not as tall as his companion but wider in the shoulders, had long black hair, a shaggy beard, and a dusky skin tone. He carried a canvas drawstring rucksack slung over one shoulder. But his eyes, dull and indifferent, stood out the most. The eyes of a much older person.

The first man addressed the lieutenant. "Master Kossowsky? I hear we may hitch a ride with you."

"I was told as much," the lieutenant replied dryly.

The blond man smiled. "I wonder who may be spreading those rumors. I'm Marc, this is Rajan. But you haven't met us, didn't give us a ride, and none of this has ever happened. We'll spend all our time inside the wagon and get out of your hair before you notice. Two clicks east of The Station. I'll show you the location."

"I don't suppose"—Jackson joined the conversation—"you'd be willing to tell us what interest a Locksville officer might have around The Station?"

Marc sized him up amicably. "You'd be right not to suppose that, Master Jackson."

Master Jackson. Colonel's Weinberg, Five Points' second most powerful man. The second scariest, by virtue of his *real* job. And Buck had called him Tim. Unbelievable.

Locksville provided the caravan with fine facilities.

Cooking the food in a proper kitchen, and eating while seated at an actual table, was not a given anymore. Buck came to appreciate this after the roadside meals he'd enjoyed since embarking on this voyage. And "enjoy" was not the most accurate term to describe those underwhelming experiences.

He'd never considered himself particularly spoiled. Growing up, he'd had a warm house, food in his stomach, and clothes on his back. A comfortable life—many people couldn't always account for that much—but not something to brag about. His parents had worked hard to ensure he would not want for necessities, and Buck appreciated that. He didn't take his lifestyle for granted. But Five Points had far richer families, which put everything in perspective. He had seen his quality of life as a baseline, with only one way from there: up.

The recent days' experience had proved him wrong.

Only when deprived of these small comforts of life did he realize how big a role they'd played in forming that baseline.

Buck's recipe for a rude awakening:
Take one small but cozy home, replace with a windswept wagon.
Take one creaky but familiar bed, replace with a thin lumpy bedroll.
Take one old but solid dining table, replace with an unclean cloth on the ground.

Throw in one Buck.
Shake well.
Add a pinch of engines and serve.

The conversation over supper, strangely, took a turn in the same direction.

Buck ended up sitting near Marc. In the shifting yellow light of the oil lamps, Rajan's face across the table looked older than in the daytime. The young—or was he?—man ate with determination, concentrating on his plate and never as much as meeting anyone's eye or joining a conversation, let alone striking one himself.

Buck leaned toward Marc and whispered, "What's his story?"

"Story?" repeated Marc, with a sideways glance at Buck. "An interesting choice of word. Story." He cocked his head as if tasting it. "Positively."

"Tell me, Baxter," he said, seemingly without connection to the prior conversation, "you're in the service, aren't you? A soldier?"

The guy knew Kossowsky and Jackson. No sense pretending. Buck opted for, "Um-hum."

"And tell me, soldier," Marc continued with an odd expression, "have you seen combat?"

The tips of Buck's ears started burning, even though he had nothing to be ashamed of. "No," he mumbled under his breath.

"Maybe you have experienced war or a natural disaster?"

"No." Buck's reply was almost inaudible.

"And you've lived all your life in the safety of Five Points." A statement.

Buck nodded, unable to squeeze out a word.

"Hey, it's all good, Baxter. No need to apologize," Marc said with unexpected cheerfulness. "Many people would kill to have a peaceful life like yours. Uh, that came out wrong." He smirked. "Anyhow. See, Rajan there"—he lowered his voice so only Buck would hear him and tilted his head toward the subject of their conversation—"had a dramatically different sort of life. The settlement he'd lived in never had a wall or a powerful military. No military at all, in fact. Imagine that. He knows first-hand what famine is. What a bandit raid is. What being a pariah is. And his parents sold him into slavery at the ripe age of fourteen."

Buck choked on the water he was gulping to cover his discomfort and descended into an agonizing bout of coughing.

Marc patted him on the back. Which could be an attempt to help clear Buck's airways, or as a nonverbal way of saying, *See? I told you, you have it good!*

Everyone around the table, even Rajan, paused their chewing and talking to stare up at Buck. He raised a reassuring hand, signaling he was okay.

But he wasn't okay. How could he be? In a world where hungry four-teen-year-old kids were sold into slavery, how could he long for a stupid table?

Marc was right: the last time the Five Points' Army had engaged in fighting had been long before Buck's birth. All he'd known was a quiet, peaceful life. And the wild stories about zombies, bandits, wars—those were great to tickle young children's imagination, but surely did not reflect reality? Turned out, they did.

Outside the Boundary, people raided, raped and pillaged, killed and enslaved. And Buck had known nothing of this. He'd been a wide-eyed kid on an extend-ed version of a Fall Fair, treating this trip as an adventure. A bigger-than-life, thrill-filled, educational adventure.

Educational? Ha! He had gotten more than what he'd bargained for. His eyes were forced open.

Machines still worked, and maybe—at least some, like the magical music box—weren't evil. But they were dying. As Norm had said, once they were gone, they'd be gone. No one knew how to build them again. Maybe Janet could find more books with those drawings she'd mentioned? Could that help? Yeah, fat chance. The world was running out of books. Because people—his people!—burned them. People—his people!—had launched Crusades to de-stroy the last surviving machines. To destroy that jukebox. His people were a part of the problem, not the solution. They had robbed him, and everyone else, of beautiful music; of colorful lights; of who knew what other miracles that could have been around.

This trip had turned educational, alright. If not for it, Buck would have still praised the Enginocide, burned books, and thanked God Almighty for his wonderful deeds.

How could he be so naïve?!

He was going to be sick.

Buck lurched to his feet, toppling the heavy chair, and rushed outside, gasp-ing for fresh air.

An indeterminate time later, he leaned into a link fence, painfully clenching its cells, peering into the black water of the Canal and seeing nothing. A strange keening sound rang in his ears. He was unable to place it until tracing it back to his own throat, sore from making it. He made it stop.

At the periphery of his vision, a quiet figure moved.

"That, Baxter," Marc said in the abrupt silence, underscored by quiet splash-es of water below, "was the sound of a burst bubble. Sorry to be the one who pierced it. But it's probably for the best, here and now. Imagine this happening out in the wild. In Rajan's world."

Chapter 17

Ka Yi

September 23, 42 PE

One doesn't rise to the Golden Dragon's stature without achieving proficiency in a basic skill of keeping one's face. Shang Ka Yi's mastery had come close to perfection. Inscrutability represented the normal state of his mimic muscles. It was expressing emotions outwardly that required a conscious effort.

Thus, even the people closest to Ka Yi—in terms of both long-standing relationships and physical proximity—would never have caught a whiff of the anxiety rising in him as the ship approached New Kowloon.

Multiple subjects had fed his impatience. The salient matter that had come up in the conversation with Weinberg, for one. The information he'd collected over two months of circumnavigating the Great Lakes had the strategic potential to influence the Hive's policies for the years to come. He missed the game of intrigues and backroom maneuvering; the fluid, ever-shifting alliances and counter-alliances—everything forming the day-to-day routine of the Great Hive's top echelon. And... someone special waited in New Kowloon, for whom he yearned the most.

But he kept his face.

He kept it when the flotilla hit a windless calm after clearing Welland Canal and lost an entire day. His *Eastern Star* had been recently retrofitted with a diesel engine, thanks to the Science Lab's advances. Had he ordered the captain to start it, they'd have arrived home in under three hours. That wouldn't have put his other ships in any danger. The few sneaky pirate companies remaining on Lake Ontario knew better than to approach them with hostile intent. Yet, abandoning his flotilla would have been unseemly. He kept his face.

He kept his face while the *Eastern Star* approached the pier, steering with excruciating slowness, executing the docking with smart perfection, as befitted the Golden Dragon's flagship.

He kept his face through the mooring, patiently waiting for the shore crew to lower the gangway, ignoring the urge to leap overboard. He descended with dignity, acknowledging the sailors bowing on either side. He meticulously measured out the obligatory pleasantries to the solemn welcoming party. He dispensed the appropriate affability to his household staff while changing out of his travel clothes, bathing, and dressing up for the Council meeting.

Lowering himself into his chair in the High Council Hall, Ka Yi finally afforded himself a minor indulgence. No, not to lose his face. Only a genuine smile.

Home. He was home.

"Councilor Shang Ka Yi, it pleases us to see you safely returned home," Chairman Wong said with a benevolent mien after all the High Council members took their seats. "We cannot wait to listen to your report on what you have seen and heard, and how you have advanced our trade interests. And, of course, what you have achieved in expanding our collection."

The other councilors had perfected their face-keeping skills too, but inwardly rolled their eyes. Ka Yi's years of practice in discerning the minute shifts in their facial expressions made that obvious.

For the entire world outside the High Council Hall, Chairman Wong occupied the apex of the Great Hive's hierarchy. The all-powerful ruler of a magnificent trade empire. Except he was not. The Chairman served as a figurehead. That was one of New Kowloon's best-kept secrets. The five Golden Dragons of the High Council wielded the actual power. When the time came for a new Chairman to ascend, they chose a middling member of the nomenclature. The perfect candidate would be sufficiently self-aggrandizing to concentrate on the outward symbols of the rulership, while not interfering with the Council's affairs that truly mattered. Such an arrangement allowed the Golden Dragons to stay in relative obscurity and operate with flexibility unavailable to a nominal head of state. But since the Chairman's word was to be the last in the Council's decisions, the selection process involved a nontrivial amount of jockeying. The Dragons competed to install the candidate whose ear would be infinitesimally more open to them than to their competition. Currying favors went a long way to solicit the Chairman's goodwill.

Ka Yi's smile widened. "Beloved Chairman, countless faithful people in your employ toil relentlessly every day. On their behalf, allow me to present you with this humble gift." He approached the Chairman's podium and handed a black lacquered box to Wong with a deep bow.

Chairman Wong had developed a penchant for glass art. A relatively harmless hobby, especially when compared to some vile predilections of certain of his predecessors. Those were better left buried in the past—the predecessors and their predilections alike.

The Chairman eagerly snatched the box and flung its lid open. Inside lay eight exquisite glass figurines of marine creatures. Wong squealed delightedly and pulled them out one by one for a closer examination. His preoccupation guaranteed he'd pay zero attention to any discussion happening in the meantime. Probably for the best. Apparently, the man's self-control, eroded by delusions of power, had significantly deteriorated since Ka Yi's departure. The Chairman would need to be replaced with someone better balanced and well-adjusted, and soon—before the subtle act descended into a travesty.

With the Chairman engrossed by his new toys, Ka Yi delivered a succinct summary of his travels. Nothing to be shy about.

Tam Wai Lam greeted him with a snide smile. "Essentially, Golden Dragon, what you're saying is that your mission to the Western Erie was a grandiose fiasco."

"Thank you, Golden Dragon, for so expertly taking my words entirely out of their context." Ka Yi reciprocated with a similar grin. "Essentially," he mockingly emphasized her word, "I am saying that my mission was an overwhelming success, achieving all its primary objectives. Michigan Nation's continuous refusal of our advances—consistent with their stance in the last six years—can hardly reflect on the otherwise exceptionally fruitful expedition. The Station had been dumping prices of their overland delivery in exchange for exclusivity."

"So you say, Golden Dragon." Tam Wai Lam, undeterred, crossed her arms.

"So I say, Golden Dragon." Ka Yi performed an insultingly shallow bow.

"Golden Dragon," Siu Ho Fai joined the interrogation, "the new deal you signed in Cleveland remains full of question marks..."

And it dragged on, and on, and on; the traditional way the High Council conducted its sessions. As much a competition in one-upmanship as an exercise in mind-sharpening verbal jousting. The fun part of being a Golden Dragon. This time, the attacks posed no challenge. He did undeniably well.

Ka Yi leaned into the chair's back and lowered his eyelids.

Tam Wai Lam, ramping up yet another attempt to cast doubt on his achievements, cut herself mid-phrase. "Is my inquiry boring you, Golden Dragon?"

"Not in the least, Golden Dragon, not in the least. I am savoring every moment. Please go on, I beg you."

His tormentor took full lungs of air for a caustic response, but the Chairman returned to the land of the living from his personal illusionary world. "That will be enough, my delightful councilors. I find Golden Dragon Shang Ka Yi's service to the great Trade House of New Kowloon exemplary, and am thrilled with the news he brought home." The Chairman's hand caressed the lacquered box resting in his lap. "Let us conclude this session and allow the esteemed Golden Dragon to rest and enjoy the comforts of the Great Hive, which he undoubtedly had missed on his lengthy voyage while advancing our interests among the savages."

Punctuating the end of his long-winded and rather pointless speech, the Chairman snapped the box lid closed and stood up.

The five Golden Dragons rose to their feet too, balancing the requisite haste with dignity.

Chairman Wong stepped off the podium and left the chamber through a back door leading into his quarters.

The Councilors courteously nodded to each other and went their ways.

Ka Yi was relaxing on a loveseat, sipping splendid red wine, when his manservant entered the room. "Golden Dragon Tam Wai Lam is here to see you, your excellency."

"Thank you, Tsang. Show her in. You may leave after that; your services won't be needed today. Inform Soong Bao we'll be discussing delicate matters."

The head of his personal security would ensure the privacy of their conversation.

Tam Wai Lam's quick steps tapped lightly in the hallway. He rose to his feet in time to embrace her when she threw herself at him. A head shorter than Ka Yi, she buried her face in his chest and fiercely squeezed him. Something cracked in his spine. His hand tenderly brushed her hair, tracing the contour of the earlobe. She tilted her head back without releasing the hug. Their eyes met. "Did you miss me?"

A rhetorical question. But if she wanted to play a shallow, capricious mistress, he was delighted to oblige.

"Golden Dragon." Ka Yi's mischievous tone turned the honorific into a serenade. "You've got no idea! It took all my willpower not to grab you right in the Council chamber and drag you to my rooms."

"Why didn't you?" Another fake frown.

"Well, you know, unlike you, a young upstart, a respected councilor such as myself has to pretend to be proper and stately. Besides, you cannot honestly tell me you didn't enjoy badgering me a single bit!"

"Oh, I relished every moment of demolishing you in front of these pompous farts! While imagining an altogether different way of destroying your reputation." Her playful wink snipped something in Ka Yi's soul. He pulled her closer in and whispered into her ear, "If you could hold off causing further damage to my reputation, I have plenty of business to discuss with you..."

Wai Lam put her hands on his chest and, with a predatory smile, shoved him onto the bed.

Wai Lam stretched with a satisfied grunt of a lazy cat in a warm sunspot. The blanket slid off, but she didn't pull it back, letting Ka Yi enjoy the exquisite view.

He did. Thoroughly.

Lying on his side, propping his head with a hand, he traced and retraced every inch of her body. Intimately familiar, yet still demanding close study.

Long bangs covered half her face. He caught her surreptitiously peeking through, reached out, and pushed them off her forehead. With an impish grin, she shook her head, restoring the artful disarray of her hair.

A rebel. His favorite rebel in the world.

"You should go away more often, Golden Dragon," Wai Lam purred.

"Oh? Am I too much for you, Golden Dragon?"

"Don't flatter yourself. You're..."

While she searched for the right word, Ka Yi's heart skipped a beat. He was an accomplished man, a Golden Dragon who in his thirty-eight years had had more women than he cared to count—not a young boy fawning over his first love interest. And yet, this woman's one word outweighed the world's opinion of him—though she was guaranteed to turn this into a jest.

"You are adequate."

"Adequate? Adequate?!" She was teasing him, but Ka Yi sketched indignation, anyway.

In one fluid motion, she toppled him onto his back, straddled him, and sealed his lips with a kiss. Then pulled away, as if savoring wine aftertaste, and delivered the final verdict. "Yes, definitely adequate."

Ka Yi couldn't help but laugh, pulling her into a hug.

"You should go away more often, Golden Dragon," she repeated into his neck. "This makes your homecoming delightfully sweet." She peeked up at him. Through the veil of her mischievous hair, naturally. "Just don't leave for too long."

After a while of enjoying the quiet proximity, the tenderness of hands, and the softness of lips, Wai Lam delicately disentangled from Ka Yi's embrace and plodded to the shower. He followed her, and it took substantially longer than strictly necessary for hygienic purposes. The Golden Dragon status came with many unique perks, including a limitless supply of hot water.

When they finally emerged, flushed from heat and exertion, both wrapped in Ka Yi's thick fuzzy bathrobes, he stepped out and promptly returned with a tray of food. Soong Bao, his indispensable confidant, never failed to take care of Ka Yi's most sensitive and unusual business. Among others, serving a private supper for two and not batting an eye at the sight of his patron emerging from a meeting with another Golden Dragon with wet hair and a bathrobe.

"We've got a problem." The playful tone of Wai Lam's statement didn't match her words. Two golden pendants dangled, clinking, from her hand. Each featured a dragon in a massive circle attached to a thick chain. Their rank markers. "How will we know which is mine?"

"I yield to your fine taste, Golden Dragon. Pick the nicer one." His turn to tease her. The five Golden Dragon pendants had been crafted by the same jeweler, specifically tasked with making them indistinguishable. All to prevent any claim of superiority by one of their bearers.

Without looking, Wai Lam chose one and slid it over the table.

"So, Golden Dragon." Wai Lam picked up the chopsticks and dug into the meal. Even with a mouthful of food, she remained classy. "I seem to recall you wished to discuss business? Serious enough to keep your woman waiting?"

Ka Yi stopped chewing. The reference to business met a deaf ear. It was the last part that struck him.

Your woman.

They'd been secretly close for quite some time. With their mutual affection abundantly obvious to both, he'd never paused to think about what kind of relationship they had, how to label it, and where it was headed.

Wai Lam noticed his confusion, fastidiously put the chopsticks down, and took his hands into hers. He couldn't peel his eyes away from the pale, elegant palms enveloping his weather-beaten fingers.

"Men! You may be the brilliant strategists, intricate schemers, and most devious machinators, but when it comes to matters of the heart, you instantly turn into blubbering idiots."

Ka Yi looked up. She locked eyes with him. "Yes, Golden Dragon, I said 'your woman', and I meant that. Deal with it."

She was spot on. None of his past relationships had prepared him for this moment. Raised by a stern, demanding father and an indifferent, remote mother, he didn't have the right words because he'd never heard the right words. This unchartered territory presented a stiff challenge. What would be the right thing to do? Flip the table and grab her into a bearhug? Too melodramatic. Macho hero was someone else's role. Walk around the table, hug and kiss her? They'd already done so much hugging and kissing in the last few hours, more wouldn't be special enough. Say something? His superb rhetorical skills took a leave of absence when they counted the most. Anything that wouldn't be cheesy, or cocky, or flat. Anything that would be him. In the end, he squeezed his woman's wrists, thin but strong and deadly. Squeezed, mindfully measuring out the force. Gently enough not to hurt, strongly enough to convey everything he needed to. And saw the cautious expectation hiding deep in her bottomless eyes melting away.

They sat, and sat, and sat. Eventually, he knew, one of them would have to break the magic of the moment. With a sigh, he took the plunge to spare his woman the awkwardness.

"About that business…"

Wai Lam laughed. An easy, unencumbered laughter. "Thank you," she said. "My man. My knight in shining armor."

Ka Yi shook his head. "Am I an open book for you?"

"Sometimes. Like now. Other times, you are so unreadable, I am not entirely sure you're even a book." She caressed his cheek, and he melted under her touch.

"How about we get to that business at last?" Her words traveled from far, far away, pulling Ka Yi out of his reverie.

"It can wait till the morning."

Chapter 18

Buck

September 24, 42 PE

Who had been that wide-eyed, excitable boy? Two days out, and he'd lost all interest in the surrounding scenery. Another field overgrown with weeds and brush. Another abandoned car, half-digested by ruthless time and stubborn nature. Another corpse of a township. Just more dead stuff. Nothing new, nothing romantic. Meh.

The bright morning did nothing to improve his mood.

That apathetic state was wrong. The world still brimmed with discoveries—places, cultures, people—well worth his attention.

But his barren soul, covered with the cold ashes of burned illusions, remained unresponsive. He'd get over it. Eventually. Maybe. For the moment, the landscape rolling lazily by the sides of the road failed to arouse his interest.

Buck slid into the back of the wagon and cozied up in a corner, hugging his knees. Being miserable offered perverse pleasure.

Janet touched his shoulder. "Are you okay?"

Her concern, this physical contact... Wasn't he supposed to be happy about that? A remote thought, as if someone else's. Buck flicked it away and stayed quiet. He kept staring in front of himself, seeing nothing, basking in self-pity, without acknowledging the one person he adored.

Janet helplessly looked across the wagon at Marc. The Locksviller shook his head, mouthing, "Leave him be." She abided, but moved closer to Buck and put a hand on his arm. The gesture warmed his heart. A bit. Maybe more than a bit. But he didn't move, engrossed in his brooding.

When the vision swept him, it was short, but its violence almost turned Buck inside out. No details, just bullets flying everywhere, wreaking havoc. People shot, wounded, dead.

Buck uncoiled with the force of a released spring, grabbing Janet by the arm and hurling her out of the wagon's back. He yelled, "Contact! Out! Out! Take cover!" at the top of his lungs.

With enough presence of mind, he grabbed everyone's rifles and combat vests from under the tarp and threw those outside before following his own advice. Marc and Rajan jumped out on his heels, clutching their bags.

Janet was too stunned to resist when Buck dragged her under the stopped wagon. Shortly, the other teammates joined them, shrugging into their vests and loading their guns. Marc opened his duffle bag, took out two parts of a heavy scoped rifle, snapped them together, pushed a magazine up the well, unfolded the bipod, and waited.

Seconds creeped on. Nothing happened. Buck's ragged breathing was the loudest sound. Eventually, all the eyes turned to him.

The events in the vision were imminent, had to be. He trembled, both scared of what he knew was about to occur and embarrassed by this ridiculous situation.

"Hey!" hollered the driver of the caravan's last wagon. It had been trailing theirs and was forced to halt. "What's going on there? Why did we stop?"

"Yes, Brennan, why did we stop?" asked Kossowsky in a pointedly neutral tone. Buck better have had a convincing answer.

"You threw me out of the wagon!" added Janet, caressing her shoulder. "Seriously?! I understand you are angry, or sad, or whatever's going over you—but that is un—"

"Hey!" the closing driver called again. "What the—"

His head exploded. Automatic fire tore his wagon's walls into shreds.

"Heads down!" Marc commanded urgently, before the unseen assailants shifted their aim and splinters rained down around the team.

Time lost its continuity, turning into a series of brief episodes with nothing in between.

... Buck crawls to shield Janet from the shots, hugging her back and covering her head with his upper body...

... Marc, calm and collected, observes the attackers through his scope. "Count sixteen, eighty meters north east, one machine gun." He pulls the trigger. The machine gun chokes up and goes silent. "Fifteen," says Marc in the same business-like tone...

... "Lundy," yells Kossowsky, "evacuate Janet and Jackson to the other side!"

"Please take Rajan with you," adds Marc...

... Seeing the four crawling to the safety of the ditch, Buck finds his Garand and joins Kossowsky behind the wagon's wheel. The officer takes well-aimed shots. Marc keeps counting down for both. "Twelve. Ten..."

... Buck tries to align the sights. His rifle wavers wildly until he forces himself to breathe and concentrate on the task. He aims again, this time with greater success. He sees figures rushing across the field toward the caravan, running several steps at a time and going prone again. He finds one, waits for it to climb to its feet, and fires. A miss. He fires again, but the figure had already dropped behind cover. He curses himself. Tries to recall the fundamentals of marksmanship. Breath. Grip. Sights. Squeeze.

The figure crumbles and doesn't come up.

"Seven," counts Marc...

... The rest of the caravan finally awakes to action. Rifles and shotguns blast at the attackers.

"Five, four, three," says Marc in quick succession, and takes another shot. "Two..."

... The rate of fire slows down, then ceases. In the ensuing silence, cries and moans of pain become audible through the ringing in Buck's ears...

... The two remaining attackers are kneeling with their hands behind their heads. Master Flanagan is towering above them. Half of his face is slick with blood. His right hand is hanging limply. With his left, he awkwardly pulls a handgun from behind his back and shoots a prisoner in the head. The other one screams and cowers. The Caravan Master asks him something, and the man eagerly responds. Flanagan then pistol-whips him, and signals to the accompanying guards to tie the man up and drag him away.

"Smart," comments Marc. "At least someone left to ask a few questions of..."

Finally, with a whoosh, the time regains its normal flow.

Buck and his two companions emerged from under the wagon. Janet rushed toward them, scanning for injuries. "Tony! Thank God, you're okay!" She squeezed Kossowsky in a hug. Buck blinked. Such affection? And God's name? But he was too groggy for jealousy.

Janet released a similarly baffled Kossowsky, came over to Buck and hugged him too. "Thank you."

What exactly had earned him the gratitude? "Thank God I'm okay too!" he said, opting for dark sarcasm to cover the awkwardness.

Janet, returning to her usual self, grinned. "Yeah, that. You thank him. Come on, it's only a figure of speech."

"Do I get a hug?" Marc asked innocently.

"I'd better go talk to the Caravan Master," said Kossowsky. "To see where we stand, and how to proceed. Also, one of our horses is dead, we'll need a replacement." He peered straight at Buck. "But before I go, I have to ask. How did you know?"

Buck had accepted that he wouldn't be able to lie his way out of this one. He stubbornly shook his head. "Can't tell."

"I expected that much." The lieutenant turned and left toward the head of the caravan.

Jackson laid a hand across Buck's shoulders and pried him away from the others. Buck meekly followed.

Jackson turned Buck toward himself, grabbed the back of his neck, and pulled until their foreheads touched.

"You did well, kid," he said, peering into Buck's eyes from centimeters away.

Buck nodded, as much as this awkward position allowed him.

"I mean it," said Jackson. "You did really, really well. You've saved our bacon today. And many in the caravan owe their lives to you, too. Also, you didn't freeze under fire. How many kills?"

"One."

"Your first kill? Congrats!"

As if that was something to be congratulated on. Buck did not respond.

"Was it the same as with that dagger you 'saw' on Grant Green?"

There. The real reason Jackson wanted to have a conversation. Buck remained silent.

"Alright," the veteran relented. "Don't want to talk about this? Fine. I'll make sure no one else does, including our hitchhikers. But know this: if someone—someone hostile—learns about this ability of yours, that will paint a big fat target on your back. Everyone will want to use you. And if they can't have you, they'll kill you, so no one else can. Do you understand?"

Buck nodded again.

"Good." Jackson let go of Buck's neck and shoved him back toward their wagon.

Shouts and commotion at the head of the column turned their heads. A large group of riders milled around Master Flanagan. Two dozen of them moved along the road, hugging the caravan on both sides. Buck started raising his rifle, but Jackson's hand on his forearm stopped him.

"The Station people. Stay calm, we've got no beef with them."

While they waited for the riders to approach, Marc joined them. "Master Jackson," he said. "May I ask you to tell these people you picked up Rajan along the way, not far from here?" He showed no outward signs of distress, but the moment he opened his mouth, his tone made clear this was a question of life and death. "Captain Weinberg and I would greatly appreciate it."

Buck and Jackson looked back. The stocky young man stood with Janet and Lundy. He had changed into dirty rags, which he probably had stashed in his bag all along. Streaks of dust and mud smeared his face and hands.

"Of course, Marc." Jackson showed no surprise. "And you're a Fivepointer traveling with us. Say, another former lieutenant, a co-owner of the Kossowsky business?"

Marc bowed his head. "Working with you is an honor, Master Jackson. This will go a long way in preserving my hide intact," he added with a wry smile.

The horsemen reached the last wagon and stopped a few meters away. They held their rifles at a ready, not aiming at anyone but prepared to use them at a short notice.

"You there," barked the leading rider. "Drop your weapons, now!"

Buck glanced at Jackson for guidance. The veteran obediently put his rifle on the ground. Buck and Marc followed suit.

"What if there is another attack?" asked Jackson.

"You are under The Station's protection now. Won't be needing those."

"Happy to hear that. Now what?"

"Now we collect your weapons while you return to your wagon and await further instructions."

"Not too friendly, eh?" observed Buck.

"No, they are not." Jackson frowned. "It's easy to despise them. But imagine how friendly you would be if you knew everyone in the world hates you."

"You sound sympathetic to the slave-owning bastards, Master Jackson." Marc's tone bordered on impolite.

The fake sergeant studied the Locksviller. "Of course not. But an intelligence officer would do well to understand how his opponent thinks."

"Ouch. I deserved that."

"You did."

The day promised to be long, and could not be expected to improve Buck's perception of the world.

"I don't understand, Sir." Kossowsky maintained control of his face, but barely. "What's with the interrogation? Are you accusing us of something?"

"That remains to be seen." The Chief Inquisitor, as the man had introduced himself, did not hide his disdain.

Buck had been questioned, first alone and then together with his companions, for the better part of the afternoon. He had little to keep secret, besides the hitchhikers' true identity and his part in warning the team. While waiting with the shot-up caravan, the Task Force had coordinated a version of the events to stick to, and Marc's alleged role in their trade expedition. Buck did not doubt the others would echo his words.

Rajan was a different story. He'd been taken away early on and had not been seen since.

Buck had learned the final toll of the ambush from the interrogators: four caravanners killed, twelve injured. Eight horses had been lost, dead or badly wounded. Three wagons had suffered irreparable damage. The attackers had had a solid plan that involved disabling the first and the last wagons, blocking the caravan on the road, and then leisurely mowing down everything in between like fish in a barrel.

Overall, considering the brutality of the surprise attack, the caravan got out of it in not the worst possible shape. Not unscathed, what with all the dead and injured... Buck shuddered at the recollection. It was the first time he'd seen people die in combat. On both sides. And he had a hand in this. Had it not been for his warning and for Marc's quick silencing of the machine gun early on, the outcome would have been dramatically worse.

Yet, the Chief Inquisitor kept asking the same questions over and over. Those could be boiled down to: *how come your intervention was so successful?* As if the Stationer regretted the low body count on the ambushed side. Did he?

Buck had actively disliked the Inquisitor from the first sight. The impression worsened once the man had opened his mouth. Buck tried, earnestly, to follow Jackson's advice to Marc and put himself in the Inquisitor's shoes. Tried—and failed. Not a single line of arguing brought him to justify higher casualties, however he looked at it. The inevitable conclusion was, he wouldn't make a decent intelligence officer. Not that he'd ever entertained this sort of career.

"I'll ask you again." The Chief Inquisitor's dull voice made the room stuffy. "How can you explain such proficiency with firearms? Why do you have such advanced weapons?"

"Chief Inquisitor!" The edge in Kossowsky's voice was becoming sharper by a minute. "We are the aggrieved party here. We were attacked and helped repel the bandits. Why are you treating us as suspects?"

"You are forgetting yourself, merchant!" Irritation seeped into the Inquisitor's tone. "I am the one asking questions here."

The two had gone through several variations of the exchange, getting nowhere. The Inquisitor kept rephrasing the same questions, and Kossowsky kept pushing back without giving him anything.

"Merchant Kossowsky, if you do not start collaborating with the investigation immediately, I will lock up your entire crew. Indefinitely. Until you do. How does that sound?"

"On what charges?"

"Charges? I am the Chief Inquisitor. I don't need charges. I can do with you whatever I want. I can brand you as a lifer. I can send your pretty wife to the workers' brothel." A salacious smile curved his lips. "Or"—the Chief Inquisitor held a dramatic pause—"I can pay you handsomely if you give me something useful."

"Or"—Kossowsky started rising from the chair—"I can—"

Janet's hand on his forearm chilled the lieutenant's rage. He deflated and flopped back.

"Tell us about the payment option, Chief Inquisitor," Janet said.

"Hucksters." The Stationer sneered. "Teach your woman not to speak out of turn, merchant. But that's your problem, not mine. Answer me this, and I'll cover the cost of a replacement horse for you. Were you trained by the Chinese? Did New Kowloon send you?"

"Huh?" Kossowsky shook his head, as if unsure he'd heard right. "What?"

"Chi-nese," the Inquisitor enunciated and reflexively touched a long purple scar on the side of his neck. "Did they send you?"

"No!" The indignation was written plain on Kossowsky's scowling face. "Is this some kind of joke?"

"I see. You are unwilling to cooperate."

"I am!" cried Kossowsky in exasperation, losing the last remnants of his temper. "How do you expect me to prove it?!"

Jackson, seated behind the lieutenant, leaned forward and whispered, "The letter. Show him the letter from Colonel and let's be done with this farce already."

Kossowsky turned his head. "You sure?"

"Why in the Seven Hells not?"

"What is it?" The Chief Inquisitor raised his voice. "Order! Quiet in the room!"

Kossowsky stood up, reached into the inside pocket of his jacket, and stepped forward.

The two silent guards flanking the Inquisitor shifted and aimed their guns at the lieutenant.

He raised his arms, showing a piece of paper he retrieved, and handed it to the Inquisitor.

Suspiciously frowning, the Inquisitor unfolded the letter and scanned it. Then read it again, more attentively, and cleared his throat. "Five Points, eh?"

His fingernail pushed the paper back across the desk, gingerly, as if it were poisonous. He finally looked up at Kossowsky. "Why didn't you say so?"

The lieutenant met his gaze and said nothing.

"Just wasted my time." The Chief Inquisitor's once menacing tone turned cantankerous. "You're free to go." He waved them away, in the general direction of the door in the back of the room.

"What about our horse?" Janet asked boldly. "We answered your question, didn't we? A deal is a deal."

Chief Inquisitor pursed his lips but refrained from inflammatory comments. "You'll get your horse," he conceded and signaled to a guard. "Jonah, see to it."

Once outside, Buck shook his head in disbelief. "What a dick! Were his threats real?"

"Very," Marc nodded. He didn't look like he was planning to elaborate, but seeing Buck's questioning face changed his mind. "The Station isn't exactly a bastion of civil rights, you know. Once you've stepped on their turf, you're at their mercy. Of which they rarely have much to spare." He stared meaningfully at Buck, who got instant goosebumps.

"Yeah," added the Locksviller, "and this Chief Inquisitor guy? He's a notoriously sadistic asshole."

"Can we please get out of here?" Buck asked in a small voice. "Like, now?"

"As soon as we can, Brennan," said Lieutenant Kossowsky. "Not a second later."

Buck perked up. "Hey, what about Ra—"

"Sh-sh." Marc's urgent whisper cut him short. "He's where he needs to be. And he'll be better off if you never mention his name again."

"Uh... okay."

Astonishingly, trade activity went on at the beaten-up caravan's overnight parking. Most of the teams were busy caring for their injured, patching up wagons, checking the goods for damage, and otherwise licking their wounds, but a few enterprising merchants engaged in trading their stock with the locals. Shaken or not, they made it this far, and there was money to be earned. What a resilient bunch.

Their own wagon showed signs of having been combed, but nothing appeared to be missing. Bullets had left holes dotting the wooden boards and the canvas, but caused no structural damage. From now on, no eating the dry fruit from their cargo without looking out for lead fragments.

Flanagan stopped by. He had his right bicep wrapped in a red-suffused rag and resting in a cravat bandage. Another dressing adorned the Caravan Master's forehead. Traces of coagulated blood on his cheek painted the gray bristle rusty, underscoring the signs of age.

"Your team starts growing upon me, Master Kossowsky." Flanagan winked and winced at the pain, touching his bandaged temple. "That was a close call. An inch to the left, and I wouldn't be talking to you. Anyhow. Maybe I won't regret letting you into my caravan, after all. That's all I had to share."

"I say, that's as sentimental as I've ever seen the man!" Jackson said when the Caravan Master left. "Marc, something I wanted to ask you. The Inquisitor kept grilling us about the Chinese. Any idea what that's all about?"

Buck pricked his ears.

The Locksviller hesitated with an answer. He furtively examined the surroundings. "I'd rather not discuss this here. Let's revisit the subject once we're on the road."

Chapter 19

Yun-mi

September 24, 42 PE

Stupid pieces of shit! Yun-mi kicked the door of her tiny partition. The hapless door, guilty of no offense, swung in and hit the wall, shaking the whole ramshackle structure.

"Hey!" someone bellowed down the train, surprise and indignation merged into a single exclamation. "Knock it off!"

Yun-mi blew the air through her teeth with a hiss.

Until a week ago, she had been content with her way of life. It may not have been perfect, but she hadn't known things might be different. The minor, and even not-so-minor inconveniences had been an integral part of her world. Whatever she couldn't change, she disregarded. If everything was the way it was meant to be, why dwell on that? Annoyances making her life less than ideal became tolerable once she'd learned to ignore them as background noise.

The plywood dividers pretending to serve as room walls are so thin you can hear a couple arguing on the other end of the subway train? Be thankful you've got a compartment to call your own. Ignore.

No running water? Come on, who *has* running water? Wash up in the communal bathhouse and ignore.

Latrines up in the street? Too bad you've got the shits in the winter night. You'd better hold it while you skip the stairs two steps at a time. Everyone has to put up with this, ignore.

People not willing to listen to a young girl—because she's young, and especially because she's a girl? What gave you an idea you may expect anything different? Ignore.

No! No, damn it to Seven Hells!

She was not that person anymore. She'd seen how different everything could be. *Should* be. Private rooms, plumbing, and an ensuite bathroom could wait. But these self-important wrinkled Elders—they'd listen to her! She'd make them!

Her coming home the other day was supposed to be triumphant: as an emissary of a superpower, a mediator who had brokered an alliance out of thin air. If nothing else, as a distinguished Rat who had survived her mentor, avenged his death, and came back with bucketfuls of money, having sold the clan's loot at a rate beyond anyone's wildest dreams.

In reality, her return had remained largely ignored, proving anticlimactic.

Yes, the news of Joon-woo's untimely demise had shocked the community. He'd been the clan's top Rat. But then, Rats came and went. Sometimes they went and didn't return, and, more often than not, their bodies would never be found. An occupational hazard.

Yun-mi's story of slaying her mentor's murderer had been met with soft skepticism. No one had openly called her a liar, but she had seen the disbelief plainly written on their faces. All she had got was paternalistic patting on the shoulder. *If you did, good for you,* their eyes said. *And if you didn't, we'll let your tall story slide as a traumatized young girl's fantasies.*

Her other business had proven even trickier. She couldn't barge into the Elders' Hall and say, "Hey, folks, what's up? Cool, cool. Listen, I promised New Kowloon to do this and that. Consider yourselves informed and be sure to fall in line." The issue demanded a smarter approach. She'd have to subtly lead them to the desired conclusions, leaving them convinced these had been their own decisions all along. There was only one hiccup. For that plan to come to fruition, she had to get their attention. And therein lay the key problem: she was denied an audience.

Stupid pieces of shit!

Being a Rat was a calling, not a profession. Clansfolk were free to go hunt and scavenge at their leisure. Some did. Few proved successful. Those proudly identifying as Rats tried to make a living off this. They trained, and trained, and then trained some more. They learned how to venture out and come back in one piece. And not just come back, but bring something of value. Otherwise, what was the point? You could be good at this, or you could suck. No Rats' Guild existed to certify you. No official Rat designation by the clan. You could appropriate the title all you wanted, but you'd be judged by your achievements.

Everyone in Little Korea knew Kim Joon-woo. His contribution to the clan vastly exceeded that of other self-proclaimed Rats. His name rang far and wide, well beyond the clan's lands. And he had invested significant efforts into bolstering his brand. "When people know and respect you, that's beneficial for business," he had used to say. "Makes travel safer too."

Oh, the bitter irony…

He miscalculated. The awful, world-shattering phrase she'd happily forget, but never would.

Paradoxically, being Joon-woo's trainee had earned Yun-mi greater recognition outside Christie Station than at home. Elsewhere in the City, she'd been seen as Joon-woo's protégé, basking in his glory and awarded a fraction of his fame by extension. To the Little Korea Clan, her personal net contribution had been negative, because tutoring her had distracted the clan's best Rat from his primary job. Nobody had questioned Joon-woo's choice to his face, but she'd heard as much muttered not too kindly behind her back. Until she proved herself tangibly, on her own merit, she was no one. These old farts, the Elders, wouldn't deign to lend her their half-deaf ears.

Screw them.

She had planned to start the mission at her birthplace. Evidently, a mistake.

She'd have to work with other clans first. After they all had joined forces, she'd come back, and the Elders would have no choice but to listen to her.

Oh, Joon-woo, if only you were here…

Her shoulders sagged. Had Joon-woo still been alive, neither of them would have learned about New Kowloon's initiative until it had been well underway, spearheaded by someone else. Maybe Parker.

Parker. His sharp blade against her neck. His disgusting voice in her ear. His sleazy hands on her body. An ice-cold illusory draft stirred her soul. Yun-mi shivered.

Stop it. The asshole is dead. By your hand! The thought carried a bittersweet taste of triumph and vindication. She probably shouldn't have felt so good about killing a man. *And what? Be ashamed? Sad? No fucking way!* How had the Golden Dragon put it? "There are people who could really use some being killed." Jim Parker of the Humber Bay Raccoons Clan had topped Yun-mi's list.

The memory of Wai Lam, by contrast, warmed her heart. Someone she was looking forward to coming back to.

Little Korea had nothing and no one to offer Yun-mi. Her few childhood friends had taken conventional paths in life. As a teen, she had been a black sheep, too different to have common ground with anyone her age. All that notwithstanding, she had considered the place her home. But had it ever truly been? Would it ever be again? Unlikely. New Kowloon had replaced this abandoned nest. She looked around her room. Foreign, in a span of a week.

A plan had formed in her head. She would leave again, like a true Rat. Head out in the morning, back to Islington. Kostya had offered his help, and she'd take him up on that careless promise. Besides, Yun-mi owed the man a conversation, and she intended to become widely known as a woman of her word.

Yun-mi delicately closed the door, miraculously still attached to its hinges after meeting the wrath of her boot. Then laid out all her belongings on the narrow bed, and started packing everything she had unpacked such a short time ago.

Chapter 20

Ka Yi

September 24, 42 PE

Ka Yi woke up first.

He needed less sleep than most. One of his success's secret components: he had more productive hours in a day, plain and simple. When the competition checked out, he continued for three or four hours longer, well into the night, and still woke up in the morning fresh and rested. Or he could go to sleep at a "normal" time, to wake up at the crack of dawn and plow through his day, bristling with energy. Chances were, the sleep deficit would catch up with him eventually, but he'd seen no signs of that thus far.

This morning, he had something infinitely more important than digging into overdue paperwork or rousing his miserable subordinates for a meeting. He dedicated the time to the observation of his woman sleeping.

Their affair had begun nine months earlier, on the Lunar New Year. The top tier of the Hive's functionaries and selected ambassadors, all with their families, took part in a lavish celebration. New Kowloon had been doing better than ever, and the coming year's outlook held even greater promise. Throwing extra money at the festival had been called for and boosted morale.

Fanciful foods rivaled exotic drinks. Toasts followed in a quick succession, praising the Chairman's impeccable guidance, his councilors' wisdom, and the hard work of their loyal servants.

Boring. The protocol left no space for fun deviations, and Ka Yi's status obliged him to go through the motions.

With the mandatory part of the program over, having had a tad too much food and a few too many drinks, he started looking for an inconspicuous way to skip the remainder of the party. His salvation came from the least expected direction.

Golden Dragon Tam Wai Lam, the youngest, the brightest, the most tenacious—and by far the most annoying—among his Council peers, approached Ka Yi's table. She gestured at the chair by his side and mouthed a question, inaudible in the ambient din.

Every Golden Dragon had a spot reserved at the party for a "plus one". Ka Yi had been suffering—or enjoying?—a bout of acute seasonal misanthropy, and the chair to his left stayed notably empty.

Until that moment.

Without waiting for his response, Tam Wai Lam claimed it and lounged. "Thank you for the invitation, Golden Dragon," she said. "A charming speech tonight! You managed not to skip a single cliché!"

"Why, thank you, Golden Dragon! Coming from such a talented speechwriter, this means a lot! And I am honored to concede, if retroactively, to your self-invitation!"

A woman of action, Tam Wai Lam despised officious speeches, according to Ka Yi's sources. While perfectly capable of maintaining verbal wit contests, she outsourced speechwriting to dedicated personnel.

Her thin smile and a fake frown acknowledged the touché. She leaned toward his ear and whispered, "I couldn't help but notice, Golden Dragon, that you'd rather be somewhere else. One might conclude you don't enjoy this pretentious gathering of pompous fools."

Ka Yi turned to check her face, unsure if he'd heard correctly. Her sardonic expression left no doubt he did not mishear. He lent her his ear again.

She didn't miss a chance to sting him once more. "This may surprise you, Golden Dragon, because I have a superior faculty of my face, but I too am bored out of my mind here. What would you say about going somewhere and doing something meaningful? I know it's an unorthodox way to celebrate the New Year, but my brain is going numb."

Ka Yi considered the offer. Entirely unorthodox, indeed, but he didn't care. His mind threatened to vacate his skull if he'd stayed.

One last hurdle left to clear before agreeing to this unexpectedly alluring proposal. "What about your guest?" He bobbed his head toward the young man occupying Tam's "plus one" chair. Her companion appeared content to concentrate on the beverages, neglecting the food—and oblivious to Tam Wai Lam's absence.

Of course, Ka Yi knew who it was. He knew everything there was to be known about anyone who was someone in the Hive. The drunk guest was Tam Wai Lam's distant relative, an insignificant nobody parasitizing on her eminence. And she knew that he knew, but openly disclosing such knowledge would have been unbecoming. The game had its rules.

"Ah, never mind him." A dismissive wave of a hand. "The only thing my second cousin excels at is holding his liquor. You can't tell by looking at him, but I promise you he's already drunk as a skunk."

"In such case, Golden Dragon, lead the way."

Ka Yi had never been in Tam Wai Lam's reception chambers. An enormous desk dominated the center of the room. Behind it towered one chair—hers. A monumental contraption matching the desk in scale and severity, intended to instill fear and respect in the audience.

"Please wait here," the hostess said, and disappeared behind the drapes, leaving Ka Yi to gawk around. A minute later, she dragged in another heavy chair with a painfully high-pitched screech. "Have a seat, Golden Dragon."

Taking her own "throne", she folded her hands in her lap and gazed at him amiably. He stared back, not quite sure what to do.

"Well," she said, "what do you want to work on, Golden Dragon?"

"Ah, doing something meaningful wasn't a figure of speech?"

"Did you think I brought you here to sit idly by and enjoy each other's company? That's what we have the Council sessions for!"

She shuffled a stack of papers on her desk and fished one out.

"If I recall correctly, this subject must be of particular interest to you, Golden Dragon." She dangled the sheet before him and read its title with an exaggerated excitement. "*Prioritized schedule of retrofitting the trade fleet*—your trade fleet, Golden Dragon!—*with restored diesel engines.*"

She neatly put the paper back on the desktop and gazed up at him. "You look decidedly disinterested, Golden Dragon. I hoped you'd be more engaged."

Ka Yi leaned over and kissed her. With his eyes closed. She was going to mutilate him, for sure.

As expected of every Hive officer, Ka Yi practiced martial arts for the prescribed hour two times a week. He had not deluded himself: he was barely passable, far from an accomplished fighter. Tam Wai Lam, rumor had it, trained two to three hours a day, every day, with the best Jiu-Jitsu and Wushu instructors New Kowloon had on the roster. When Ka Yi took the plunge, he was prepared to be punched in the throat or kicked in the crotch. At the very minimum, to have his arm broken. He'd let her surprise him.

She did. By kissing him back.

When they let go of each other, her eyes twinkled mischievously. "I was beginning to fear you'd never gather the courage, Golden Dragon," she said, struggling with the buttons of his shirt.

"You are too intimidating, Golden Dragon," he replied, trying to find his way into her intricate dress.

Sometime later, they lay on her desk, catching their breaths. The perfect stack of the papers had scattered all over the room.

"Look what you've done, Golden Dragon!" Wai Lam exclaimed in mock horror, pointing at the floor. "I regret to inform you, your diesel retrofitting project may now be delayed. Due to circumstances beyond my control."

"Maybe... if you'd learned... to exercise... better control... Golden Dragon," Ka Yi huffed. "Regardless... of the circumstances..."

"You'd want that, wouldn't you?"

"Over my dead body!"

"That can be arranged." She gave him a long kiss. "Asphyxiation through oxygen deprivation, a definite possibility."

"Please asphyxiate me more."

Later yet, they helped each other dress. Not a trivial task, considering the complexity of their holiday attire. Ka Yi gentlemanly collected the papers from the floor.

Wai Lam halted with a hand on the doorknob, locking eyes with him. "This never happened."

"Absolutely, Golden Dragon." Ka Yi bowed with a straight face. "When may this *not* happen again?"

At first, Ka Yi didn't read much into the encounter. As exciting and sublimely enjoyable as it was, he wrote it off as a one-night stand between two moderately inebriated adventurous peers, fed up with a tedious party and seeking a piquant way to enliven the night. An extrapolation of their regular verbal sparring onto a different plane—the plane of her desk, as it were.

Over the years, Ka Yi had seen a variety of partners. Neither handsome nor athletic, rather on the chubby side, he didn't consider himself physically attractive. Nevertheless, as a scion to one of the Hive's most influential families, he had never lacked female attention. Precious few had been capable of maintaining a conversation, and none at all had come close to stimulating his mind the way Tam Wai Lam had.

Ka Yi had sought nothing beyond casual pleasures and undemanding companionship, with undemanding being the key. Interested in his name, title, and the associated luxury, a few of his paramours had crossed the line, scheming to become something more. With those, he'd cut ties immediately.

Such a bright, powerful woman as Tam Wai Lam must've had a lineup of aspiring suitors to choose from, too. Without a doubt, when she'd still been climbing up the ranks. Ascension to the Golden Dragon status had put her in a delicate situation. She could not date someone prominent yet below her rank. Her options had narrowed to low-ranking pawns who'd never dare utter a word of such indiscretion... or an equal. Of which a vanishingly small pool was available, and it flattered Ka Yi to be the chosen one.

Not that he'd never seen her as a woman. Most of the time, he had perceived her as a fellow councilor and Golden Dragon, extraordinarily astute and superbly irritating. But, being a mature male specimen, every so often he couldn't help but appreciate her for the exceptional woman she was. Yet, he had never considered a "what if" scenario involving the two of them.

Until that fateful New Year's night.

In short order and with a great measure of surprise, Ka Yi discovered he was unable to get her out of his head. She ruled his thoughts most of the waking time, venturing into an occasional dream, too. In her presence, his concentration went out of the window. Several times he was called out on that at the Council meetings and failed to produce appropriately caustic retorts. That was unheard of.

A long-overdue honest analysis yielded a verdict as obvious as it was shocking: Councilor Shang Ka Yi, Golden Dragon of New Kowloon's Trade Fleet, intelligence and counterintelligence supervisor, one of the Great Hive's sharpest minds—that very man was in love, head over heels, smitten like a pimply teenager.

Love? The word had not existed in his vocabulary. Affection, he'd had plenty. Toward his job, his fleet, his Science Lab. But not people, never. His austere upbringing had made sure of that.

Ka Yi sought another private audience with Tam Wai Lam and confessed. True to her style, she subjected him to a rap sheet of stinging quips for being unable to control his hormonally driven behavior. The tirade ended with a kiss which led to another paper-scattering tryst on her resilient desk. This time, for a change, they were sober.

They had been keeping their relationship secret. Not for fear of scandalizing the establishment. Not because his family would have disapproved; he couldn't care less. The secrecy granted them a unique competitive edge in the Council. Playing their usual roles of bitter antagonists allowed corralling the unsuspecting councilors into the corner of their choosing.

But the time has come to go public. Enough with the games, with sneaking around. Secrets of this sort would always trickle to the surface. Better to stay ahead of the news and make the announcement on their own terms.

The soft light of the early morning made Wai Lam's skin glow. Another perk of being a Golden Dragon: a suite with windows overlooking the lake.

"How much longer are you planning to stare at me?" she asked without opening her eyes. "It's creepy."

"Your fault. You're too beautiful."

A breakfast was arranged through Soong Bao's invaluably discreet services.

Wai Lam rushed to the table, ravenously devouring the food with her eyes, but waiting for Ka Yi to join. She collected her hair into a bun and fixed it in place with a chopstick. "Did you know," she said, "how close your Science Lab project had come to being shut down in your absence?"

"What?" Blood left Ka Yi's face.

"Siu brought up the subject at a Council session. Said it's a waste of the Hive's resources. That you're abusing your position to appropriate and divert the budget into this sinkhole. That nothing useful would ever come of this pet project of yours."

Ka Yi frowned. His heart picked up speed. "And? What happened?"

"*I* happened, dear." The happy little bells of Wai Lam's laugh instantly repaired his mood. "I advised them to let you dig yourself deeper into this hole, making it easier to sack you later."

"What would I do without you, Golden Dragon? How exquisitely devious!"

"Thank you, Golden Dragon. Now, can we please, please, eat? I'm starving!" She dug into the omelet without giving Ka Yi a chance to respond. "And let's talk about the business already. The suspense is killing me! I'm getting the sense you're trying to hold off this conversation by any means possible."

Intended as a joke, her words resonated. "I guess I am." That came out glum.

Wai Lam's playful expression grew serious.

"Remember that discussion," asked Ka Yi, "you and I had before I sailed, about our potential expansion into the City?"

"Ye-e-s?" Wai Lam dragged her tentative response. "What about it?"

"Have you acted?"

"Here and there, preliminary probing. Why?"

"Seen any pushback?"

"Nothing to lose your sleep over. Haven't kicked any hornets' nests yet, if that's what you're asking."

"I see." Ka Yi sat, quiet, tapping his fingers against the tabletop.

Wai Lam waited for him to continue.

"The problem is, something has triggered The Station's anxiety. Could be the fallout from our reciprocal assassination attempts. Or they've planned this all along and are in a hurry to execute before any consequential activity grinds to a halt for the winter. The reasons are less important. What's important is that they've been scheming to frame us for something outrageous."

"Really? How?"

"Crudely. But subtly enough by their standards, and there's a risk our partners may fall into this trap."

"What are you talking about?"

"The Station will present us as untrustworthy, backstabbing bullies. Pretty much what they are."

"Aha." It was Wai Lam's fingers' turn to drum a beat on the table. "Now it starts making sense."

"What does?"

"Some strange activity lately. Wu is interrogating a Stationer who tried to spy after one of my assets."

"Tried?"

"He didn't account for the Singh brothers."

"Ooh. I see. Anything useful from Wu?"

"Nothing of importance yet. He's working on it. But tell me, how did you come to know about this plot?"

"Weinberg."

"Weinberg." Wai Lam's skepticism could curdle milk.

"Yes, Weinberg." An edge of annoyance crept into Ka Yi's voice. Their first family quarrel? He purposefully toned down his next words. "I acknowledge your misgivings about the man, but trust him on this one. Our interests are aligned."

"If you say so. And how did Weinberg learn about this?"

"Come on, it's Weinberg. He knows everything. He even knows that your influence in the Council rivals mine."

"Really."

"Yes, really. He told me so himself."

"Oh, I wasn't doubting that. Here I was, convinced that my influence far surpasses yours..."

"You forgot to add, 'Golden Dragon'."

"Golden Dragon," she conceded with a matching grin. It would appear they'd successfully navigated their first squabble.

"Now, seriously, Wai Lam. No matter how, Weinberg had got ahead of the curve on this one. And shared this information with me. The Station doesn't know that we know. For whatever reason, they haven't triggered the trap yet. Maybe they're setting up something big. Something we'll have a hard time counteracting."

Wai Lam knitted her brows. "Tell me everything. We need a plan. By the sound of it, we may already be late."

"I hope you don't regret postponing this conversation till the morning?"

"Not for a second!"

"Alright. And then you'll tell me what you've done in the City."

Two hours later, having exchanged all the pertinent information, they were none the wiser. Something was afoot, but how to neutralize the threat? Where to begin? A nagging idea tried to break through the surface tension of Ka Yi's subconscious, but kept eluding him. He retraced his chain of thoughts. There. The point when he sensed it last time...

"Huh."

"*Huh?*" Wai Lam threw her head up. She'd come to appreciate those *huh* of his.

"The head honchos in the two attacks. Weinberg said they both had been genuinely convinced that their forces had been trained and armed by the Kowloonese. This isn't true because, well, we didn't, right?"

"Right. Go on."

"If we find who impersonated us..."

"That's a good *huh*. Finally, something actionable. Now we're talking."

"We don't have a clue *who* trained the Golden Lions and the Fat Bastards, but they said *where* their training took place. Send Wu to investigate. Even if he finds no one, activities on such a scale going on for months on end can never be fully concealed. Someone must have seen something, heard something. Locals, neighbors, passersby, you know."

"Sounds like a plan. Better than—"

A delicate knock on the door interrupted her. They exchanged surprised looks. Disturbing a Golden Dragon's privacy? Highly unusual.

"Expecting someone? Another woman, perhaps?"

Ka Yi shook his head earnestly, disregarding the joke. "For Soong Bao to allow this... Must be something serious."

He rose and went to get the door.

A glimpse of Soong Bao's body lying across the hallway was all Ka Yi caught before the dull glint of a blade forced him to retreat on pure instinct.

A human shape, wrapped in black from head to toe, materialized in front of him, moving faster than his brain registered. A flurry of attacks and feints followed, demanding all of Ka Yi's lackluster training to block and evade. He stood no chance.

The knife disappeared. The attacker, empty-handed now, turned all attention to Wai Lam, who burst into Ka Yi's narrowing field of vision. Ka Yi watched her unleash a jaw-dropping level of violence, accompanied by furious *hi-yah* cries. She was stark naked, having discarded the bathrobe that limited her mobility. The chopstick she pulled from her hair looked more formidable in her hand than any blade. Inexplicably, Ka Yi's horizon shifted, and the fight scene continued playing out above him. What a peculiar effect. The deadliness of the combat had somehow retreated to the back of his mind. Instead, he marveled at his woman's lethal grace, beauty, and the efficiency of her movements. He could observe this forever if his vision weren't blurring with each deafening heartbeat.

The black figure's knee buckled unnaturally when Wai Lam's foot connected with its side. She threw herself into the air, caught the attacker's head in a scissors lock, and dropped to the floor. Following their movements, Ka Yi looked over his own chest. Something obscured the struggle. Was that... a hilt?

Two glassy eyes stared at him lifelessly through the holes in the mask as Ka Yi drifted away into the cozy darkness.

Chapter 21

Yun-mi

September 25, 42 PE

"Yun-mi!" Kostya greeted her with open arms. "What a pleasant surprise! Didn't expect to see you again so soon. Hoped—yes, but did not expect."

She had made no attempt to sneak around, letting Islington scouts pick her out the moment she had emerged from the subway tunnel. Kostya was waiting for her at the terminal with a wide smile.

"What's with the outfit?" he asked, showing her into the building.

Yun-mi had deliberately dressed to provoke such questions. She wore her hakama pants, not as a tribute to any clan's dress code, but because she loved their convenience, how they concealed her leg movements while not restricting them. Her upper body was clad in the faded brown leather jacket, formerly Parker's, her proud trophy. Badass, yeah? A bright yellow scarf wrapped around her neck, part of the West Sauga's garment set; during their emotional farewell two days ago, the Singh brothers had insisted she kept it. The black bandana, a souvenir Kostya himself had given her on the same occasion, completed the wardrobe.

Neither of these gestures had been a mere feel-good gift. They bore a deeper meaning. The Singhs and Malyshev had thus invited her to become an honorary member of their clans. By choosing to wear these items, Yun-mi signaled her acceptance.

"I hoped you'd appreciate it."

"Oh, I do! That scarf clashes with your skin tone, but the bandana suits you exceptionally well!"

Kostya's office occupied the top floor of the high-rise towering above the station. Being invited there represented, without a doubt, a rare honor few were granted. But climbing all those countless stories up? Not for the faint of heart. Literally. Despite being in top shape, by the time they cleared the last flight of stairs, Yun-mi was panting heavily. Her pulse manically fluttered in her throat.

Kostya, to the contrary, looked fresh, breathed easily, and didn't seem to notice the weight of Yun-mi's bag he'd volunteered to carry like a true gentleman. He'd offered to take her bow and Joon-woo's rifle too, but she refused. The host winked. "Suit yourself."

While the good old bow felt like a part of her body, Yun-mi struggled to find a comfortable position for the rifle—a position where it wouldn't kick one limb or another with every step. After observing her trying to work her way around this nuisance, Kostya nodded at the firearm. "Do you even know how to use it?"

"I will... after... you teach me..." she gasped, taking three breaths to finish the sentence.

"O-o-kay," Kostya responded in his typical manner.

His suite occupied an extensive area, overlooking the City through miraculously intact panoramic windows.

Kostya escorted Yun-mi to a cozy armchair and brought her a glass of water. She emptied it in three gulps and flashed him a grateful smile. Then took off her armaments, stowed them by the chair, and collapsed into its comfortable embrace. Stretching her burning calves induced a long sigh of relief. Another minute to catch her breath. All the while, the host patiently waited.

"You torture all your guests like this? Or those you hate the most?"

Kostya grinned. "Only the strongest ones. Or the most stubborn."

"Which category am I? The strongest or the stubborn?"

"The best category: both. Those that I know won't drop dead on me halfway to the top."

"Is this a metaphor?" Shrewd. "With you, all the way to the top?"

Uncharacteristically, Kostya did not supply a quirky response. He turned, opened a cabinet, and put two heavy crystal glasses on the desk. "Scotch?" he asked. "Gin? Vodka?"

"Oh, Hells, no!" Yun-mi shook her head in abject horror, with the memories of the celebratory feast—and its disastrous aftermath—still too vivid.

At the celebration three days earlier, she had been seated between Kostya and Jihan as a guest of honor. Both had seen it as their sacred duty to top up her glass.

She'd always been averse to alcohol. Consuming a substance that would dull her senses and inhibit her reaction? What Rat would agree to that? Yet, in this clan, refusing an offered drink or skipping a toast would be considered rude—or a personal insult. Yun-mi had forced herself to take minute sips each time she had to, but the pledges had followed in such a quick and seemingly endless succession that those tiniest amounts had accumulated. She urgently needed to rest her head on the table, unable to hold an upright position.

She had only a vague recollection of what had followed. At Kostya's signal, two women came up and helped Yun-mi—or carried her between them—to a private guest room. They took her clothes off and laid her on a bed. One woman placed a pitcher of water on the nightstand. The other poured a glass of unidentified liquid and put it on the table along with a plate of pickles and some kind of pale kimchi.

"You'll want these in the morning," she explained. "The hair of the dog."

Too dazed to inquire about the meaning of such an odd expression, Yun-mi blacked out.

During the night, she woke up a few times, fighting off the urge to puke her stomach out—and losing. Luckily, she found a bucket strategically placed right where she bent over the bed's side.

In the morning, she rose with a parched mouth and a monstrous headache. Recalling the cryptic instructions, she bravely downed half the mystery glass, chomped on the pickles, and flushed it all with water. That did improve her condition, but the horrifying experience made her swear to never have a drop of booze again.

Kostya chuckled and poured amber liquid into one glass. He raised it and solemnly announced, "*Shtob sdokhli vraghi!*"

Meeting Yun-mi's blank stare, he translated, "May our enemies croak!"

What an odd toast. Definitely something to drink to. She raised her glass of water, mirroring his gesture. Toasting with water broke the protocol, but the host let her transgression slide.

Kostya puffed his cheeks, sploshing the drink in his mouth, savoring the taste. Then swallowed and looked askance at her. "Did you come here to accept my marriage proposal?"

Shit. He remembered!

At the feast, Kostya, expectedly, had taken an opposite approach to drinking. For each of Yun-mi's reluctant sips, Kostya had dashingly upended one glass after another. Eventually, he'd gotten buzzed. Not full-on drunk, but reaching that state when tongues loosen, gestures become exaggerated, and toasts turn from ceremonial into extravagant. At one point, he leaned closer to her and said, in a whisper loud enough to carry over the tumult of the party, "Yun-mi, you're an amazing young woman. If you ever consider marriage, I demand to be at the top of your suitors' list!"

Jihan had frowned, voluntarily assuming the role of an overprotective chaperone. "Mister Malyshev, I hope your intentions are honorable!"

Kostya had raised his hands in mock surrender. "Mister Singh, I wouldn't dare disrespect Miss Park with anything less! Cross my heart!" An enigmatic smile had floated on his lips.

Ilya, Kostya's second-in-command sitting to his right, had bent toward the boss and uttered something into his ear. The disapproving grimace made his opinion of the announcement clear. Kostya had waved him off.

Yun-mi had held a neutral expression through the exchange, discarding the antic as a wacky shenanigan of a man in his cups. She'd hoped he wouldn't remember any of that when he sobered up. Was she wrong...

She looked away and touched her ear. Same as then, the awkwardness made her itch. What to make of this charade? She wasn't prepared to seriously entertain the notion of marriage. Maybe in a distant future, but not yet, for sure.

For sure?

A nagging doubt raised its head. Kostya's attention was flattering. He was a complex, grown up man, a clan leader no less; not a teenage jerk, the sort she grew up with and whom she came to resent. Most importantly, he saw her for what she was—for *who* she was!—and accepted it.

"*But he is not Korean!*" she could hear the apoplectic Elders wail, indignantly shaking their wrinkled heads. Maybe she should go for it, if only to see them have a cow. She almost giggled. But... no.

The right words eluded her. Did the right words for this exist? Her face twisted into an apologetic expression.

"Just what I thought," concluded Kostya lightly, taking her refusal in stride. His voice carried none of the expected bitterness. "Hoped—but did not expect." This gave the phrase he'd used to greet Yun-mi downstairs a whole new meaning.

"Kostya—"

"Please." He raised a stopping hand. "Yun-mi, dear, do not degrade our conversation with banal apologies. Forget everything I said. I'm sorry for putting you in this embarrassing position. You're here on business—let's get to it."

The connection Yun-mi had hoped they'd established was crumbling before her eyes. Panic raised its ugly head.

What would Wai Lam do? How would the strong, mature, self-confident woman Yun-mi wanted to become resolve this situation?

Yun-mi stood and walked up to Kostya. He swiveled in his chair, staring up with a mute question. She put both hands on his shoulders and looked squarely into his eyes.

"Shut up and listen, okay? I'm a Rat. Settling down, having babies, all that... This is not the Rat's way. But if I ever change my mind, I promise you'll be the first to know. Deal?"

She offered a hand. Kostya shook it. "Deal."

"Are we still friends?"

"Best friends ever!"

Yun-mi squeezed out a forced smile, but her heart was still racing. She'd almost lost the man whom she counted among her very few friends, and whose help she desperately needed.

Discarding her resolutions, she grabbed the bottle from his desk and threw the drink straight down her throat. No taste, only the burning sensation in her chest.

Kostya's eyes went wide and round. "Whoa, tigress! Slow down!" He rose from his chair and wrapped her in a chaste, enormously comforting hug. "Slow down," he whispered, stroking her head. "We're good, *Yunmishka*. It's all good."

She pulled away, relieved but bewildered. "What did you just call me?"

Kostya wore the guilty look of a dog caught chewing its owner's boot. "Sorry, I direly needed a diminutive name. Did I offend you?"

"No!" She convulsed in a relieved laughter. "But that's the weirdest thing anyone has ever called me."

Kostya gently pushed her into his chair, perching on the desk nearby, and looked at the City through the windows. After a brief pause, he glanced at Yun-mi sideways and asked wryly, "May I still call you that, from time to time? When no one else hears?"

"Please do."

They sat in silence, taking in the cityscape. The high clouds moved fast, their shadows crawling over the terrain below. Yun-mi could never have enough of this view.

"You know..." Kostya started, trailed off, then gathered his thoughts and continued. "You don't have to be strong all the time, Park Yun-mi."

They locked eyes. She waited.

"It might seem like you're completely on your own. One little girl against the entire hostile world. Especially now, with Joon-woo gone." Kostya raised his glass toward the City in a silent *in memoriam* toast and gulped its contents. He didn't offer to pour Yun-mi another one, for which she was grateful.

"You're not alone. You've got friends. And allies." He winked, then grew serious again. "What I'm trying to say is, you can afford to be weak sometimes, when you are among friends, like now. Let your guard down. Unstring your bow, so to say. On my honor, no harm will come to you here." Half-turning around and pointing back at the arsenal by her armchair, he said, "I mean, look at that. The bow, the gun, all the blades you're carrying. You refused to let go of those, even when I invited you to my office. *My* office!"

"I'm sorry—"

"Don't apologize, I understand. I am not insulted, just sad. For you."

Yun-mi sighed.

"I'll tell you what we're gonna do," Kostya said, shaking off the melancholy. "I'll call a few big, strong Russian women. They'll take you to the *banya*—a real sauna, not that joke you Koreans have—and show you how it's properly done. They'll take care of you, the way they see fit. And you will let them, you hear me? Your arsenal will wait for you. Then, and only then, you may rearm yourself to the teeth if you feel the need, and we'll talk business. How does that sound?"

"*Khorosho*," Yun-mi whispered, exhausting her knowledge of Russian to Kostya's absolute delight.

She turned away in his chair and stared out of the window again, not wanting him to see the tears in her eyes. That would be a secret, between her and her City.

Kostya did not lie. This *banya* thing had worked miracles, expelling her tension and anxiety.

It had taken all of Yun-mi's perseverance to get, without fainting or begging for mercy, through the sophisticated torture unleashed upon her. She'd been stripped naked, pulled into a wooden steam room, forced to sustain the impossible combination of heat and humidity, beaten with a bunch of birch twigs, and doused with ice-cold water, cycle after cycle.

In between, she had a mug of an odd fermented drink that tasted like beer but didn't have the bite.

An indeterminate time later, the procedure had ended. She'd been given a clean set of clothes and guided to another room for lunch.

The food proved as foreign and bizarre as every other part of the experience: a bowl of red-brown stew with pieces of beef, beets, tomatoes, and—oddly—cabbage. It tasted sweet and sour, but Yun-mi could see how it might grow on her.

She ate, amazedly analyzing the sensation in her body. Floating on air, filled with soft down, relaxed beyond her wildest imagination. Above the physical comfort and the culinary delights, she was at peace. Finally. For the first time since Joon-woo's death, and possibly since much earlier. The unexpectedly profound luxury of not having to care about the mundane, such as physical needs or personal security, of allowing someone trustful to do that for her...

An appearance of a man pulled her out of the meditative state.

Yun-mi didn't know Ilya, Kostya's sidekick, too well, but disliked him. His expression had almost always been implacable, occasionally glum. Every time Yun-mi was around, he'd had something unflattering to whisper into his boss's ear. To be fair, Ilya had never as much as looked funny at her, let alone said anything rude or offensive. Most likely, the guy saw her as a threat, with all the attention she'd been garnering from Kostya. A risk to his own standing, a distraction from Malyshev's clan-running responsibilities. Understandable, but didn't mean she had to like him.

At Ilya's dismissive gesture, the women hurriedly vacated the room, softly closing the door. Yun-mi was not alarmed. Kostya had promised her safety. She put the spoon down and expectantly looked at Ilya across the table. He shifted, gathering the courage.

"Miss Park, I've always been loyal to Konstantin, but I cannot stand by anymore. I know I will regret doing this, but I've got to warn you. Stay away from this man."

Made sense. With Yun-mi's unexpected return, Ilya would try to spook her away. Would he open his cards? "Why?"

"He is not what he wants you to believe he is."

Uh. Way off the script she'd had in her head. "What's that supposed to mean?"

Before Ilya could respond, a rowdy disturbance erupted outside the room. Something heavy fell and rolled on the floor. The shouts became louder. "Where is she?!"

The door flew open and a tall, angry woman burst in. She zeroed in on Yun-mi and stomped toward her. "You!"—she pointed an accusatory finger—"Stay away from my husband, filthy whore!"

Yun-mi was feverishly assessing the possible weak points of the much larger opponent when Ilya intervened. He stood in the woman's way, shielding Yun-mi behind his back. "Svetlana, stop," he said in a low, harsh voice. "She is not your enemy."

The woman glared at both for a second longer and seemed to deflate. Not angry anymore, but miserable.

New voices clamored outside, and Kostya stepped into the room. He momentarily took the scene in, and his face distorted into a grimace Yun-mi had never seen on him. Wrinkled nose, downward curve of the mouth... Hatred? She winced when his back-hand blow landed on Svetlana's cheek, sending the woman tumbling to the floor. "You stupid, stupid bitch!" he growled. "*Suka*, you always have to ruin everything!"

Who was this man?! The honorable, considerate Kostya she knew wouldn't raise a hand on a woman! And then the pieces of the puzzle started coming together. Yun-mi desperately wanted to push them back apart, but they relentlessly clicked into an ugly picture.

"He is not what he wants you to believe he is."

"Stay away from my husband."

Mother. Fucker.

"Kostya?" She tried—and failed—to keep her growl not too threatening.

"What?!" he snapped back. "Yes, Park Yun-mi of whatever goddamn clan, this whining piece of miserable shit is my wife!" He kicked the woman. Not too hard, but enough to elicit a yelp.

His expression shifted from fury to a sly smile. "But it was a wonderful game while it lasted. Admit it, I almost had you!"

Yun-mi played back in her mind their interactions of the last three days, viewing them through the newly discovered lens. All that... everything... had been a pretense?

Joon-woo had always been leery around this man—a memory that she had subconsciously pushed away under Kostya's charm offensive.

"All this noble gentleman act..."

"I'm good, ha?"

"You... You're—"

"The words you're looking for are 'manipulative psychopath'," said Kostya with smug pride. "I've been called that. I've been called many things, but that's my favorite."

Yun-mi counted to ten, letting all the expletives boiling in her head settle down. Calling him names would not change a thing. The sick bastard may yet get off on that.

Her world was rapidly falling apart. Again. When she thought she'd found a fragile equilibrium. When, convinced by this two-faced scumbag, she let her guard down and allowed herself to relax. To be weak, for once, to trust another person with taking care of her.

Never making this mistake again. Come, misery, the Rat's way.

She headed for the door. On her way out, she bent to the woman quietly whimpering in the corner. "I'm sorry," Yun-mi whispered, "I had no idea."

Svetlana flinched when Yun-mi touched her shoulder. On the spur of the moment, Yun-mi hissed, "Leave him! Leave the abusive fucker and come with me!"

The woman stared back in horror. Kostya sneered.

Oh, how wonderful it would feel to kick and punch him, to make him hurt. To make him bleed. Yun-mi straightened up and stepped forward to leave.

Kostya blocked her way, frowning. "Where do you think you're going, little girl?"

She ought to have been terrified. Especially after taking a mental inventory of any force multipliers and finding only a wooden spoon. The fear peeped into her soul—and recoiled. She was walking out of this room, no matter what. She'd claw her way out if need be. She would tear out the throat of anybody who'd dare stand in her way. With her teeth, if she had to. She was a cornered Rat, the most dangerous creature in the world. Cornered, wronged, and betrayed.

She came to a stop inches from Kostya, slowly raising her head until their eyes met. He was a half-foot taller, yet she stared down at him, and he saw something in her face. Something like a promise of his death that meant nothing to her. A flash-forward to his twisted body, feebly wheezing and gurgling blood on the floor, with her indifferently stepping over.

Animalistic terror flickered in Kostya's eyes, and he moved aside. "I'm only letting you go because of the people who sent you!"

Weak. Whatever he needed to tell himself to save face. She'd let him.

Yun-mi walked out of the room without looking back.

Frightened, distressed women waited outside, not knowing what to do.

"My things, please," Yun-mi said into space, to no one in particular. One woman swiftly brought a bale of her clothes, bag, and kit. Yun-mi untied it and absentmindedly checked for anything missing. Nobody here could be trusted. To her mild surprise, everything was in place.

Ilya followed Yun-mi. "See her out!" yelled Kostya into his back, and shut the door from the inside. Poor Svetlana.

Ilya frowned at the unnecessary command, but said nothing.

Without a second thought, Yun-mi took off the borrowed clothes and started dressing in her own. Ilya hastily turned away. Such virtue.

She finished strapping her gear. "Ready. Let's go."

What now? Where to? She had counted on Kostya's assistance, but that was off the table, painfully and obviously. How could she be so foolish?

Back at square one. Shall she return to the Hive, with the tail between her legs, and admit she had failed? No way. West Sauga? The Singhs would be happy to help, wouldn't they? Had they developed any personal loyalty to her? Would the yellow scarf be enough to commandeer their time and resources, or were they in it for New Kowloon's hefty purse? Could she be sure of *anyone's* true nature anymore? Ever?

She was on her own. Well, she'd have to manage, like the Rat she was. Next? Why not High Park? As good—or bad—an option as any.

Ilya silently accompanied her to the tunnel. She turned and handed over a black bandana. He cringed. "I'm sorry. About everything. I tried to talk him out of this madness. I came to warn you, but it was too late. I'm so sorry."

"You weren't too late. Too late would have been if I'd fallen into his trap. And I wouldn't have believed you anyway, before seeing it with my own eyes." She fell silent, listening to herself.

No emotions. No anger, no self-pity, no remorse. Absolutely nothing. She was burned out on the inside. Old. Not adult—old.

One more question needed to be answered before she closed this chapter of her life. "How can you stand him? Be his second? Haven't you got any self-respect?"

Ilya twitched. "This isn't how it works in our clan."

"No? Then how does it work? A sick, twisted asshole tells you to look the other way—and you obey? Don't you see this brings shame and dishonor onto your clan? Can't you take him out and assume his place?"

"This isn't how it works," Ilya repeated stubbornly, not meeting her eyes. "Again, I am very sorry."

"Yeah. Tell that to Svetlana."

She turned and walked into the darkness, leaving Ilya to stare helplessly into her back.

Chapter 22

Rajan

September 25, 42 PE

Supervisor Ghassan loved cats. People—not so much, but cats were his passion. He named each of the twelve cats employed by The Station to safeguard its granary from rodents. He could describe their personality traits and quirks with a disturbing amount of detail.

Rajan had discovered this by accident.

Under Ghassan's watchful eye, he had been carrying a slop bucket to the latrine across the prison block's courtyard when his path crossed with that of Alice, a long-hair tabby. Rajan put the buckets on the ground and squatted to pet the cat. The friendly animal purred, turning this side and that, and brushing against his knee.

Supervisors never allowed workers idle time. So, even though this job did not imply any urgency, Rajan had expected Ghassan to curse his laziness and promise punishments in various degrees of harshness.

Instead, the supervisor came over and joined Rajan. The cat went ecstatic, dropped to the ground, and let them rub her belly.

And that was how Rajan had learned about Ghassan's weakness.

All the man's empathy was used up on felines, with nothing left for bipeds. Rajan's attention to the cat had promoted him to an advanced category in Ghassan's world, of not-completely-subhuman. That didn't earn him any special privileges, other than not being watched as closely, and not being shouted at as often. The price he had to pay was being forced to listen to the endless cat-talk, but he didn't mind. He was used to much worse.

After the ambush, he'd spent what was left of the previous day being questioned. By one Inquisitor, then another, then two together, and finally by the Chief Inquisitor himself.

Rajan stuck to his story. The simplest truth was the easiest to not mess up. The made-up parts were those he'd been worried about.

They'd been hauling the train when the lifers rioted.

Then the armed riders showed up.

Then he ran away because he feared for his life.

He strayed through forests and fields for days before stumbling into the caravan, and the kind merchants gave him a ride back to The Station.

No, he had known nothing about the lifers' plans.

No, he did not recognize any of the riders.

No, he hadn't heard of Fat Bastards.

No, he had never met a Chinese in his life.

No, he did not run away.

Yes, all he wants is to labor through the rest of his contract, like the disciplined worker he is, and earn his freedom in due time.

No, he does not want any trouble.

In the end, his story must have been found convincing, because the Inquisitors had relented. As a reward for his good behavior, he was immediately put back to work, and not even punished.

All the hauling teams were out, in a race against the looming cold spells. For the time being, he had to settle for cleaning the toilet buckets in The Station's prison.

Whatever. Work was work, and this job wasn't particularly back-breaking. The important part was, they'd bought into his story. Captain Weinberg could be proud of him.

The Station never trusted workers to do anything on their own. A supervisor, Ghassan, was assigned to follow his every step. And follow he did, though not too closely, given the associated smells. He also didn't bother entering prison cells with Rajan, content with unlocking the doors and waiting outside.

In some cells, he was greeted by fellow workers, locked up for minor infractions. In others, lifers tolerated his entry but showed no desire to chat. A few occupants he couldn't place, as they didn't fall into any identifiable category.

About halfway through the block, Rajan found one such lying on a cot. The inmate's face was so badly beaten and disfigured, it took Rajan a few moments—and a shocked second look—to recognize Marc. He saw a spark of acknowledgement in the one eye the Locksviller could open.

"How?!" Rajan mouthed.

Marc's quick whisper forced Rajan to lean closer. "They caught me in the forest. Pure chance." The words didn't come out quite right through his broken, crusted lips. "Brought me here. Were about to release me back to Five Points... The Golden Lions' General recognized me in the yard."

This made little sense, but at least provided an explanation that didn't involve Rajan.

Marc threw a furtive glance at the door. Rajan turned his head, too. Ghassan was not around, shooting the breeze with the prison guards.

"Rajan, leave everything and run back to Locksville. Tell Weinberg... Tell him the Chief Inquisitor is behind the attacks. He's planning something big, and soon."

"What about you?"

"I'm done for. This time I am not getting out. They're gonna break me. I can't allow that. Got a knife? Something? Anything sharp?"

Rajan's heart sank to his stomach. This could not be happening. Not to Marc.

"Please, Rajan. Look at me. You'll do me a favor."

Rajan checked the door again, reached into his boot and pulled a shiv he always carried, just in case.

Marc snatched the blade and hid it under the mattress. "Thank you!"

They looked at each other. This was a goodbye.

Rajan picked up the bucket and walked out of the cell.

Don't look back. Don't look back.

He emptied the load into the latrine, his eyes aimlessly wandering around. Alice the cat came, rubbed against his shin, and went on. A second later, she appeared on the other side of the fence. Huh? Rajan peeked behind the corner of the wooden cabin. There it was, a hole in the ground dug under the chicken wire. Large enough to squeeze through, if he lifted the bottom of the fence... This could work.

Rajan turned and asked Ghassan if they could take a lunch break. The supervisor, lulled by the uneventful day filled with cats, raised no objections.

In the canteen, Rajan hurriedly downed the bland meal. On his way out, he slowed down behind Horseradish, a leader of a lifers' faction, and whispered into his ear, "I heard Mendoza call you 'goatfucker'..."

He'd heard nothing of the sort, but the claim was entirely believable and too serious to ignore. Horseradish, a thin but sinewy guy with a shaved, tattooed head, who'd earned his nickname for his hot temper that had caused lots of tears, wasted no time. He jumped to his feet with an angry growl and charged across the mess hall at the table occupied by the rival gang. His followers scurried after him without questioning his actions. Within moments, a furious scuffle erupted with chairs and people thrown around.

Supervisors, yelling for reinforcements, rushed into the fracas to break the fight.

With everyone busy, including the kitchen staff, who had abandoned their duties to enjoy free entertainment, Rajan slipped through the back and out of the building. He knew the drill. In case of a large-scale riot, the Masters locked themselves in their reinforced luxury cars while the supervisors put the brawl down.

He headed to the hole in the fence behind the latrines. Half-way through, he froze.

He could not leave.

In Rajan's experience, kindness did not exist. It was a myth. People were bad, without exception. Some worse, others not as terrible, but still bad. Good people were a myth too, and Rajan had outgrown myths a long, long time ago. Before his family had sold him to The Station. Before becoming a Rotten Can, or right around that time. Good did not survive. Kill or be killed. Dog eat dog.

Rajan was bad too. Not bad to the bone, like the lifers, but not good either. Don't have to be a predator, but at least have teeth and claws sharp enough to discourage others from seeing you as prey.

He had no feelings other than hate. Some people he actively despised. To most, he was indifferent. Love? No such thing, just procreation, animal instincts. Family? A sham. Friendship? Worse. Why would people pretend they needed nothing from each other and still care? Ridiculous. People always wanted something from you. Like Weinberg.

Then why couldn't he leave?

Marc was one of the few people to ever take an interest in Rajan. To ever help him. Even if Locksville was using him. Leave Marc to the fucking slavers? No way. No matter why.

In the grand scheme of things, delivering the message to Weinberg was a higher priority. If Rajan did not leave right away, the window of opportunity would close. And Marc could have already taken his life. But...

His legs were already carrying him back before he finished a heavy sigh. Stupid. Screw it.

The single guard left in the prison block appeared mildly surprised that someone may still carry out such menial duties amid the chaos, but showed no signs of alarm.

Walking with two empty buckets down the corridor, Rajan held his breath. Would he find Marc's body in a pool of blood?

His friend—friend? Yes, mierda, friend!—was sitting on the cot behind the bars. His battered face concealed the surprise.

Rajan inhaled. Bene.

The guard unlocked the cell and let Rajan in. He walked to the corner and dropped the bucket in its place. On his way back, he stopped in front of Marc and asked, "Qué carajo you lookin' at, cabrón?"

Marc, quick to pick up on the game, stood on shaky legs and sketched a half-hearted roundhouse punch. Rajan easily ducked it and pushed Marc onto the cot, falling on top and pummeling him with what he hoped looked like real blows.

"Hey, hey! Waddafuck's goin' on!" The guard rushed into the cell and dragged Rajan off the prisoner, turning his back to Marc. With a speed hardly expected from a man in such an awful shape, Marc fetched Rajan's shiv and buried it in the guard's neck. A fountain of blood from the severed artery sprayed the wall, and the guard collapsed.

With Rajan supporting Marc at the waist, they half-ran, half-limped out.

He prayed to all the gods there were and, for good measure, to those there weren't, that all the Stationers would still be busy at the canteen. Either the gods listened, or by sheer luck, the fugitives met no one.

They made it through the hole in the fence and were painfully slowly closing the distance to the nearby forest when the wail of a siren rose to the skies, spooking a murder of crows from the trees up ahead. Somebody must have found the dead guard.

Rajan cursed. At this pace, they would not make it. He grabbed Marc's leg and arm, heaved him onto his shoulders, ignoring the man's weak protests, and ran.

If he could haul trains about which he didn't give a flying fuck, he sure as Seven Hells was up to hauling the man he was determined to save.

Chapter 23

Buck

September 25, 42 PE

The caravan trundled west, leaving The Station behind.

Not fast enough. Marc's stories prompted irrational dread that defied logical arguments. Buck resolved to be extra vigilant until they cleared The Station's lands, in case the Chief Inquisitor changed his mind.

Some of Marc's accounts sounded too far out there. Could the Locksviller's descriptions be *slightly* exaggerated? His visceral rejection of everything Stationer would explain that. But even the most believable parts were bad enough to make Buck's skin crawl.

He had woken up countless times throughout the night, listening to the sounds outside the wagon. Humans snoring; horses neighing; wind howling; the wounded moaning... While not comforting, none of these had spelled troubles. He'd strained his eyes, ensuring every member of the team was where he'd last seen them. Janet. Marc. Jackson. The lieutenant. Lundy. All had been accounted for, not quietly abducted and dragged to a brothel.

In the morning, shortly before departure, the caravan received its weapons back. Marc skillfully field-stripped his rifle and checked the parts, paying special attention to the striker. Then reassembled it and cycled the action a few times, leaning with his ear to the gun. Satisfied, he put it aside and met Buck's inquisitive stare. "Making sure they didn't sabotage it. Filing off the tip of the striker is all it takes to turn a gun into an unwieldy melee weapon."

Buck hurried to check his. It looked perfectly fine, as far as he could tell.

Lieutenant Kossowsky surprised everyone, demanding their machine gun. His request led to a commotion involving a confused Stationer soldier, a gloomy Stationer officer, and a patient explanation by the lieutenant that the members of his team had taken out the operators of said weapon and that, by rights, made it his trophy. The net result of these negotiations was a bulky firearm with two tins of ammo, now resting comfortably on the wagon's tail-gate.

Once on the road, Marc had provided the promised explanation. Which ended up exceeding everyone's expectations—not just Buck's, but even Jackson, judging by his long face. Under the crushing burden of one of the best kept, darkest secrets in the realm, Buck wished he *hadn't* known something, for the first time in his life.

Until three days ago, Buck had not heard of The Station. It would have been a monument to human resilience, had it not been run by gruesome slavers. Its history had begun with a passenger train stranded by the E in the middle of nowhere. Not even *a* station had existed, never mind *The* Station. Nothing but endless vineyards and orchards. Like everyone else, the survivors had lacked self-propelled transport. *Unlike* everyone else, they had a railroad. The original train had grown into an entire city on wheels. The residents had put to work the scores of prisoners of war they'd locked up after skirmishing with roving gangs, rural zombies, and unfortunate stragglers. Using the relatively well-preserved pre-E railroad network, The Station sent trade parties as far as Michigan to the west and Rochester to the east. Lately, their fierce competition with New Kowloon for the markets slid toward a clandestine conflict.

And there was Buck, stuck with his team in the crossfire. That was way more than what he had signed up for. Accompanying Janet to the City shaped up to be a complicated and dangerous affair.

The Fivepointers' wagon now trailed the caravan. The one that had followed them had been shot up too badly. The survivors had joined another crew for the rest of the trek. That made it easy for Marc to sneak out unnoticed. In a wooded area, the Locksviller slid off the back, waved goodbye, and disappeared between the trees, heading back to Weinberg with the news of the ambush, and the first-hand impression that The Station itself had orchestrated it. Before leaving, Marc had pleaded with Kossowsky and Jackson to hurry to New Kowloon, find a Golden Dragon named Shang Ka Yi, and discreetly convey this information. Kossowsky, understandably, was not too excited. He already had one impossible mission on his hands. What helped him make peace with the new errand was Marc's assurance that in exchange for the information, the Dragon was guaranteed to provide them the assistance they wouldn't find anywhere else.

Marc's departure left a void in Buck's chest. The bonding effect of going through a firefight together, or of bursting Buck's bubble a day prior? Whatever the reason, Buck said a quick prayer for Marc's safety.

Buck kept glancing back through the machine gun's scopes.

Marc had given him a theoretical crash course. Thankfully, nobody had commented on the inadequacy of the five-minute explanation. Squeezing the handle of the fire-spewing monster provided the much needed, if unsubstantiated, reassurance. Buck had witnessed the carnage it could unleash, and cherished not being on its receiving end. Was he getting used to dishing out violence? A disturbing question, with a worse answer.

The Golden Dragon was far away; The Station—practically around the corner; the oily smell of the machine gun—soothing. But the gun could spend some time alone while Buck joined Jackson on the road. If another vision showed an impending attack, he'd jump back into the wagon.

The veteran-turned-spymaster walked along, acting the part of a hired guard. In contrast to the day before, he openly carried his kit and rifle. The similarly equipped Lundy accompanied him. Another striking—and depressing—difference was that no one came up for a chat. The mood among the caravanners was glum and subdued. Most were seasoned travelers who'd seen their share of trouble, but being attacked and losing friends was no small thing. A memory of his own nervousness on the first day outside the Boundary brought a lopsided smirk to Buck's lips. To think he'd considered *that* leg of their voyage dangerous.

Jackson's thoughts followed a similar route. He pulled his harmonica out of its pouch, fiddled with it, and put it back. "Too soon," he said. "Have you heard? Mitch was killed yesterday."

The question caught Buck by surprise. "No. Ah... who?"

"What do you know, Stevie may now have a shot at Mitch's wife, after all. Uh, sorry, maybe 'a shot' wasn't the best choice of word, considering."

It took Buck a second to fill the gaps. Yes, the merchants they had discussed on the first day of the trek. How long ago was that? It's been *ages*. A month? A week? Only four days?! No way!

How much he had changed in such a short span of time! No, not that. Rather, how different the four-days-ago-Buck's *world* had been from today's.

He used to be naïve, wide-eyed, excited and excitable.

He used to know what was good and what was bad. What was right and what was wrong.

He used to have strong convictions.

His life had been straightforward. Not without pain and tragedy, but simple.

Everything had changed. Who was he? What was he? What did he believe in? Whom did he believe? So many questions. So few answers.

He wanted to talk to somebody. He *needed* to talk to somebody. Urgently, before the pressure made his head burst at the seams.

Marc could have helped, with his uncanny ability to poke holes in other people's bubbles, but he wasn't around.

Jackson? He wasn't the same approachable Tim he'd been those four days ago. With his true role exposed, he'd turned into almost as remote a figure as Colonel himself. Wouldn't confide his qualms and insecurities in Colonel, would he? Buck giggled at the absurd image, attracting a puzzled look from the veteran.

Lundy and the lieutenant? Certainly out of the question.

That left... Buck stopped in his tracks.

He climbed into the wagon and lowered himself by Janet's side. She looked up, arching an eyebrow into a question mark.

"Can we talk?" exhaled Buck.

The worst question ever, the harbinger of a tough conversation. In response, a gamut of expressions chased each other over Janet's face: surprise; interest; annoyance; insecurity; compassion; pity. Finally, polite attention. Not what he'd expected or hoped for.

Buck sagged.

Janet noticed, and her face changed again. This time showing remorse. "Look... Buck."

She called him Buck for the first time since they'd met. Not Brennan, not Baxter. Buck. Encouraging. Or maybe it shouldn't have been. When someone who'd always called you formally used your nickname, that ought to be an alarming sign.

"I haven't been kind to you from the beginning, and I apologize for that. I've had so much on my mind..." She shook her head. "But also, enough time to rethink many things. And I want to say, I'm really sorry."

Buck did not react, trying to process what he'd heard.

Janet misinterpreted his silence and, overcoming reluctance, broached the subject she must have hoped to avoid. "Listen. I am not blind. I see the way you look at me. I... Please don't take this the wrong way, but you and I—this isn't going to happen."

Buck remained silent, strangely emotionless.

Janet searched his eyes. "Buck, did you hear what I said?"

"Yeah."

Why *was* he calm?

Was it because he came to Janet to discuss his revelations about the world—which, at this junction of his journey, felt immensely more important than the immediate matters of the heart?

Was it because he'd discovered how much was happening around him that outweighed, by and large, his petty personal wants and needs?

Was it because, as the grand total result of all their interactions to that day, he had subconsciously come to expect no reciprocity from Janet?

Did he ever actually... love her? Putting this into words, even in his mind, helped evaluate his true feelings. And the answer—it was amazing how little he was surprised—was negative. He'd been enchanted, captivated by something special that had entered his life like a bright shooting star. A radiant splotch of color against what had been a dull background of his Five Points existence. These days, the background proved anything but dull. Buck still struggled with the sheer amount of color he'd discovered. Janet remained Janet—dazzling, extraordinary, attractive; knowledgeable—yes, that mattered for Buck too. She simply didn't hold the monopoly on his sensory stimulation anymore.

He wasn't even sad. This all fitted nicely into his new picture of the world. "Yeah," he repeated. "Yeah, okay."

"You already knew this."

Buck nodded.

"And you came here to talk about something else."

Another nod.

"Stupid me..." Janet's voice trailed into a coarse whisper.

Unlike her, to be out of words. That was Buck's area of expertise. "Yeah, well. Don't be sorry." Did he want her to feel sorry? Eh... A little, but that was petulance talking. The residual sorrow for himself. He was past that, wasn't he? "What I wanted to talk about is..."

What *did* he want to talk about? The intricacies of life? The complexities of the world? Nah. Janet wasn't much older than him. Inordinately better educated, yes. Raised without the blinders he'd had, yes. But was she wise, life-smart enough to give him advice? Not necessarily. On top of that, how could he open up to her? The words were said out loud that put the last nail in the coffin of his hopes—hopes on which he had already given up, but the rejection stung nonetheless. Things were different now.

But one more subject demanded attention. "What are we looking for?" Buck finally glanced up at Janet and met a blank stare. Right. The context existed only in his head. "This mission? The City? What is this all about? We should all know."

Janet pursed her lips in her trademark stubborn grimace, but Buck did not relent. "Yesterday made me think. Any of us could've been killed in that ambush. Including you."

Janet's mouth relaxed, but the corners of her lips slid down.

"May still happen any moment," finished Buck.

"I see where you're going with this." She frowned. "Alright. At the next stop? So that everyone can hear?"

"At the next stop. Until then, out of curiosity..." Buck was well past dancing around rules and conventions. "*You and I* isn't going to happen—why?"

Janet flashed a deadbeat, hunted down glance at him. She would not pull any punches.

"You are a nice guy, Buck. Annoying at times, but mostly nice. Easy on the eyes, too. But I don't have feelings for you. It's that simple."

Yup. Not much of a punch. Not anymore. "But you do for Tony." Buck surreptitiously watched her out of the corners of his eyes. She blushed, then stole a quick peek at the driver's seat. All the confirmation Buck needed.

If the lieutenant had heard their hushed conversation, he showed no sign.

"Who told you?" Janet whispered.

"I am not blind," Buck quoted her with a wry grin. "What's the deal with you two?"

She hesitated, then exhaled decisively. "We grew up as neighbors. Our families had known each other since *they* were children. It was almost inevitable that we... You know." She made a vague circular gesture. "We were engaged."

"You *what*?" Buck's eyebrows jumped up.

"Yes. But then he volunteered for the Army."

"I see." Buck dragged the last syllable, easily filling in the rest. "You weren't ready to marry a martinet. That's the word you once used for me, right?"

"Yes..." Janet's whisper was almost imperceptible. "And yes."

"Um-hum." Buck looked at Kossowsky's back with an unclear feeling. Could be compassion, come to think about that. Poor guy. But the lieutenant sure wouldn't want his pity. "What now?"

"Now we're stuck on this ride together, thanks to Colonel's insidious cruelty."

"And?"

"And that's it!" Janet snapped in a low but edgy voice. The conversation was over.

"Got it," said Buck. "None of my goddamn business."

Getting more cynical by the hour? Keep this in check. Don't want to turn into another Lundy.

He tried to imagine these two, Janet and Kossowsky, as a family. It made sense in an odd, unorthodox way. This would never be one of those quietly blissful marriages where the husband and the wife hold hands watching the sunset and complete each other's sentences. Oh, no. Even if they bridged their differences and got together again, their union would be an endless chain of fights and arguments. Which, paradoxically, may form the basis of their happiness. The ever after.

Interesting. But none of his business.

This lake felt different.

Creek Point sat on the Lake E shores, and a huge part of its everyday life revolved around the water. Dad's carpentry shop served the fisherfolk. Mom had sewed and repaired boat sails. As a child, Buck had spent countless hours in and on the water. Lake E was family.

Lake O was blatantly foreign and did not conceal that. Buck reciprocated with visceral mistrust. He sincerely hoped they wouldn't have to tolerate each other's company for much longer.

He had Master Flanagan to thank for the unplanned introduction to this other Great Lake. Having announced a quick break, the Caravan Master visited each wagon to check on their teams. When he finally made his way to the Fivepointers, Kossowsky met him with a question. "How long before we reach New Kowloon?"

With his right arm in a sling, Flanagan clumsily brushed his beard with his left. "Three or four days, depending on the weather and road conditions. Add another day if the gang activity around Hamilton is bad enough. That'd force us to take a bypass, paying for safety with extra time. Especially after everything, you know."

The lieutenant shook his head. "Too long. We have to get there sooner. Any other way?"

Master Flanagan's beard received additional treatment. He wisely avoided asking questions. Instead, he pointed north with the healthy arm.

"There."

Buck and his teammates obediently turned in the shown direction, finding nothing interesting to see.

"Take the next right, then left, then right again. Continue till you see the lakeshore. That'll bring you to the Port of Grimsby. You should be able to hire a boat to take you to New Kowloon. I'd say, that should set you thirty coins shorter. If someone demands more, they're gouging you. If an offer is below twenty, shoot them on the spot, it's a pirate trap."

Pirates. Another childhood horror story that proved to be real. Probably not the *Argh!*-saying kind with a wooden leg and a parrot on the shoulder. A week ago, Buck would have shuddered at the thought of encountering a pirate, as much as at the idea of shooting someone on the spot. The new, outside-the-Boundary Buck shrugged and took note.

Cynicism. Need a reminder? Lundy. Poor role model.

He exchanged meaningful looks with Janet. She nodded. The overdue conversation was going to have to wait longer.

Master Flanagan said his goodbyes and warmly thanked the team for their contribution to fighting off the ambush.

At the next crossroads, Kossowsky steered the wagon to the right, as instructed. For a short time, it followed diverging courses with the caravan until a copse cut off the view of the main road.

Another farewell. Another group of people whom Buck had come to know left behind.

Buck had been surrounded by the same people his entire life. Some had passed away, like Mom; others were born. But for the most part, he hadn't met many new people, nor had he parted ways with those he knew. Crossing the Boundary had turned it all upside down. He'd been making new acquaintances and friends—only to say goodbye a day or two later. The bitter longing did not make Buck want to go home, but brought a new appreciation of what he still had. *Whom* he still had.

The port waited exactly where the Caravan Master had said it would be. Half a dozen boats of different sizes were moored at the pier.

If any of the shady local characters were pirates, they hid that well. The lieutenant's no-bullshit appearance, Jackson's frown, and Lundy's scowl possibly played a role. That, and their casually held rifles.

A brief bargaining session demonstrated the clients' awareness of the going price. With that established, Kossowsky reached an agreement with one sailor in no time. Thirty-five coins, including a surcharge for strong seasonal winds and tall waves. As a bonus, the sailor's family would watch over the wagon and the horses until the travelers' return. The gleam of avarice in the captain's eyes did not go unnoticed. Jackson insisted on extending the deal: if said wagon and horses were found in good condition and health, respectively, upon their return, more coin would exchange hands. Were that not to be the case, he promised a generous dispensation of military-grade lead. Unsurprisingly, the sailor was amenable to these terms.

Transferring the wagon's freight took a while. "Their" captain, who had introduced himself only as Farley, supervised the weight distribution under the deck. His silent teenage assistant prepared the rigging. The remaining sailors observed from a distance, neither helping nor interfering. Dry food boxes and water casks did not spike their interest, but the treasure trove of ammo tins caused their greed to trump caution. Their eyes lit up.

Let them stew a few minutes, and who knows what kind of stupid, suicidal ideas they may get.

With a huff, Buck pulled the machine gun out of the wagon, carried it halfway to the boat, and stopped in front of the idle onlookers with the muzzle pointed their way by pure accident. "Any of you a pirate?" he asked, squinting.

A discordant chorus of "No!" and "No, sir!" accompanied shocked and fearful grimaces.

Buck sighed. "Too bad. Always wanted to meet one and shoot him on the spot."

The sailors shrunk under his innocent gaze. Their shifty eyes lost their glitter. Two excused themselves, suddenly remembering urgent matters that required their immediate presence elsewhere. The rest decided it was time to attend to their own boats.

Buck shrugged and lugged the heavy weapon to the boat.

Jackson met him at the gangplank with a wink. "Well played, kid. Proud of you."

The weather did not welcome the travelers onto the lake. The wind, as promised, was strong and blew in the wrong direction, forcing the captain to tack the boat time after time. The vessel kept rising and falling on the waves, making the experience miserable for those not accustomed to maritime travels. Everyone besides the captain, his assistant, and Buck hid under the deck. Buck wasn't much of a seafarer either, but had sailed with Creek Point fishermen, lending a hand for a few coins, and wasn't afraid of open water.

The mix of the drizzling rain with the foam torn off by the wind reduced the visibility and made Buck's presence outside less than pleasant, seeping under his clothes and chilling him to the bone. He did not relent and was rewarded with a respectful glance from the captain.

And then the sun peeked out, changing everything. Even the lake shed most of its hostility. But what Buck saw ahead made him forget to breathe.

The City.

No one told him. He simply knew. Couldn't be anything else.

It spanned most of the horizon. Miles and miles, the far end disappearing in the foggy distance to the east. He traced the skyline from left to right. An enormous structure that must have been a bridge once was missing its middle section, but the scale of the standing parts was jaw-dropping. Taller buildings receded into smaller houses of the already familiar sort, then ebbed again to scrape the low clouds. And again, and again. And then—the clump of the tallest buildings, with an oddly shaped needle towering above them all.

How many had populated the City before the E? Tens of thousands? Hundreds of thousands? Buck tried to run a mental calculation. Every one of these tall buildings could house his entire community? No, that couldn't be right. His math must have been off. Buck's head spun, and not because of the waves.

Someone joined him at the bow. He didn't check who, unable to tear his eyes off the shore.

"So, that's the City." Janet.

"So it is."

They silently absorbed the view.

"Do you know how many used to live here?" The question kept nagging at Buck.

"I've seen different numbers. The most common is three million in the City itself. Twice as many if you count the surrounding areas."

"Six *million*?! As in, six thousand times a thousand?"

"Yep."

"How are we going to find *anything* there?" Buck gestured, encompassing half the horizon.

"Not all of it is the City itself. Some of that are smaller cities surrounding it."

"Smaller?" The ridiculousness of this word!

"Yes. Not small, small-*er*. But we don't need all the City, only its Downtown. See?" She pointed at the group of the tallest buildings, and that needle with a thick knob. "That must be it. But let's hope we find someone in New Kowloon to help us narrow down the search."

"Well? What is it we are looking for?" asked Buck, glued to this *Downtown*—intimidating and menacing, yet strangely attractive. In absence of response, he turned to Janet and found her staring at him with a weird expression.

"What?" he asked.

"You will not like the answer."

If that was supposed to discourage him, she could not have come up with a worse way. "Try me."

Janet pursed her lips as if to say, "I warned you." Her reply rang with the finality of a judge's verdict. "The Seven Hells."

Part 2

FOUND

Chapter 24

Yun-mi

September 25, 42 PE

Yun-mi entered Old Mills station and stopped. The two times she had passed here in as many days, it had been with mixed feelings. Parker, may he rot in the Seven Hells forever, had not represented his entire clan. They may not be all as bad. On the other hand, she'd killed one of theirs. And not just anyone, but supposedly one of their best Rats.

Had the Raccoons already learned of Parker's fate? Unlikely. But the word from Dixie Mall was guaranteed to reach them, eventually. Parker's blood was on him. The question was, would his clan see his death in the same light? Yun-mi would be safe to pass through in any case, protected by the immunity the Treaty granted to any Bloor Line traveler. But if the Raccoons decided they had a grudge against her, sooner or later they'd hunt her down.

She had to get ahead of the matter and settle any unresolved issues on her own terms.

Her plan had been to restart her mission in High Park, but why not the Raccoons? As good a clan to lobby. And in their case, Yun-mi had a unique conversation starter.

"I killed your Rat."

The Triumvirs exchanged puzzled looks. Not wary—she still failed to achieve that effect on people, as much as she'd wished to—but she surprised them alright. Whatever notions they'd had about her visit, they hadn't expected *that*. Her conversation starter worked miracles to grab their attention. The next goal was not to lose it, nor let it transform into vengefulness.

Yun-mi studied her audience.

The only thing the Triumvirs had in common was their coonskin hats. Bizarre. Raccoons wearing raccoons had a somewhat cannibalistic vibe, but... whatever tickled their fancy. She'd seen weirder traditions.

On the left sat a fat, round-faced man. His expression of polite interest was ruined by the patently fake smile plastered on his lips. Ah, *that* type. Shrewd, cunning, slippery. This man required extra care.

The one on the right struck her as a fighter type. Not huge, but with muscles rippling under his shirt with every movement. An ugly scar disfigured the left side of his face. Someone—or something—had taken off the top of his ear, closely missed the corner of his eye, and tore his cheek down to the jawline, cleaving his short beard into two uneven parts. A hardened stare evaluated her in return, pausing on the pieces of her arsenal. Dangerous, this one, but not the most dangerous.

That role belonged to the man in the middle. Not that there was anything special about him, besides the dead, expressionless eyes on an otherwise unremarkable face. This one would order her killed without batting an eye. And the muscular fighter looked capable of carrying out that order.

She had to make sure it didn't come to that.

"Parker?" asked the fighter.

"Is it the jacket?"

"And his kukri behind your back."

"He broke the Treaty." Yun-mi firmly controlled the pace of her words. She was not offering excuses. Explanations, yes. Guilt, no.

"And who may you be?" asked the fat man.

"Park Yun-mi."

"Of Little Korea, I presume?"

"Formerly. Of New Kowloon now." She jutted her chin out. Challenge *that*!

"Oh?" The fat man rubbed his cheek. "That's... unprecedented, I might say. Why are you here, Park Yun-mi, supposedly of New Kowloon?"

She ground her teeth at that *supposedly*. About time people started taking her seriously. "Two reasons," she said in a deliberately flat voice, holding the flames of her rage under the surface. "First, I wanted to personally bring you the news of your best Rat's demise. That was the right thing to do."

"*The best* may be a bit of a stretch," muttered the fat man, as if to himself, but with an obvious intention to be heard.

The fighter's grunt could pass for approval. "The right thing, huh? Brave. Stupid, but brave. And the second reason?"

The dead-eyed Triumvir broke his silence. "She killed one of ours. She must die." His unexpectedly high-pitched voice grated on Yun-mi's ears.

"She said it was a good kill, Francis." The fighter rolled his eyes. "That Parker had broken the Treaty."

"And you bought into that. She's a Rat, Laszlo. She lies for a living. You would know. But even if it's true, screw the Treaty. The clan comes first. If you've become too soft, I'll kill the little cunt myself."

"Hey, dickhead, I'll show you how soft—"

"Shut up, both, you idiots!" hissed the fat man.

Aha. That was who was really in charge here.

"I apologize, Park Yun-mi *of New Kowloon*." This time, the man on the left underscored the attribution. "My fellow Triumvirs may get easily distracted sometimes. Kindly proceed to the second reason for your visit."

Yun-mi acknowledged his welcome intervention with a curt nod. "My second reason," she said, "is to continue Parker's mission."

"Huh. That was Parker's mission, you say?" The nameless fat man furrowed his forehead, unconvinced. "How come we've heard nothing about this from him?"

"Can't speak for Parker. Maybe because he was an asshole."

Laszlo—the man on the right—chuckled and shook his head. "That he was, big time."

Conversely, Francis, the one in the middle, slammed his fist into the desk. "You don't get to talk like that about a Raccoon, you filthy little bitch!"

Yun-mi snapped. A blinding, all-consuming, liberating wave of rage washed through her. A moment earlier, she'd stood five steps away from the Triumvirs' ornate desk. In a heartbeat, she was leaning over its surface into Francis's face. The Triumvir recoiled, and for the first time his eyes showed emotion. Fear.

She didn't reach for a weapon. She didn't raise her voice. She spewed the words quietly, but with such ferocity it was mildly surprising they didn't burn holes through the paled Raccoon. "I get to talk any way I want! I get to use every fucking curse in the world, and that still won't be enough to describe the two-faced son of a whore! The motherfucker who cowardly murdered my mentor! Who tried to rape me and sell me to the slavers!"

An "Ahem!" sounded from her left, and Laszlo's vicious cussing to her right. She stared Francis down for a few more seconds, then straightened up. She may have driven the message home.

"You've made your point, Miss Park," said the fat man. "Would you mind stepping back now, or do I need to call the guards to escort you out?"

Yun-mi glanced at him sideways. "That won't be necessary." She retraced her steps.

Francis's eyes glowed with hatred now. Maybe dressing him down in front of his peers was a mistake. He won't forgive her that fear, and he'd never forget she'd seen it. She didn't make new friends, yet her list of enemies grew longer. All her safety mechanisms and self-control, trained and practiced over the years, flew out of the window. Foolish. But it felt so good!

"Miss Park," asked Laszlo, "that mentor of yours, was it Kim Joon-woo?"

She squinted at him. "How did you know?"

"Not too many Korean Rats take female apprentices. The word travels. I'm sorry to hear about his passing away. He was a fine man, and an exceptional Rat."

"Thank you. He was."

"So." Laszlo tilted his head. "You said you're going to continue Parker's mission. Does that mean you're planning to kill off more Rats?"

What?! Yun-mi jerked her head up. "I am not murdering any Rats! That was his moronic idea!"

A relief brightened the fighter's face. Ah. The man was a Rat himself. Afraid that if she were to pick up Parker's killing spree, his clan's Rats would be the logical place to start. Ha! She *could* make the Raccoon rulers wary of her, after all.

"I'll tell you what, Miss Park," said the fat man.

"You know my name," Yun-mi interjected, "but I don't believe you've introduced yourself."

The man skillfully reined in his confusion. The subsequent blip of annoyance was almost imperceptible. "Right. Triumvir Gustavo dos Santos. Now, if your curiosity is sufficiently satisfied, Miss Park, may I continue?"

Yun-mi ignored the barb and gestured forward. "By all means, Triumvir dos Santos."

"Thank you kindly. As I was saying, I have a counter-proposal for you. Obviously, we cannot commit to any of your requests. If it weren't for your, um, *convincing personality*, I would have dismissed them outright. As it is, I am leaving the door open for further discussion. Please arrange a meeting with an appropriately senior official on the Kowloonese side. We'll see where that may take us."

Noticing her frown, Gustavo hurried to explain. "I don't cast a doubt on the veracity of your claims, Miss Park. But given the sensitivity of the matter, I must insist on the involvement of—"

"Of someone with actual power," Yun-mi finished for him. "And not a self-proclaimed ex-Korean Rat. Got it. I'll see what I can do."

The Triumvir's face soured. He must have been unaccustomed to being interrupted. Much less interrupted repeatedly. Get used to it, Triumvir dos Santos. What was the motto she'd invented for Wai Lam? Take no shit, give no fucks. Hells, yeah! Not a meek clanswoman seeking an audience with the all-powerful Triumvirate to beg humbly for a favor. A Rat. A New Kowloon Rat, the first of a kind! She'd be crass, and insubordinate, and step on as many toes as she could reach. And enjoy every fucking moment of it!

Yun-mi said none of that out loud. Instead, she bobbed her head. "That concludes my business here today. Thank you for your time, Triumvirs."

"We'll look forward to hearing from you soon, Miss Park." Dos Santos forced a smile.

Outside the building, Yun-mi sat down on a warm curbstone and fetched a bag of jerky from her backpack. She needed a snack before going anywhere. And she needed to decide where that *anywhere* would be. She was hollowed out, drained of all energy. Being strong, standing up to people unwilling to take her seriously, and averting an occasional plot to kill her along the way proved to be an exhausting job.

Try her luck in High Park, as had been her original plan? Or return to New Kowloon and attempt to convince Wai Lam to send someone to talk to the Raccoons? They didn't say "no". Her first lead. Maybe it was better to hammer down this deal and use it as a reference. Besides, she was spent. Physically and morally. The VIP treatment she had received in New Kowloon came to mind and refused to leave. Enjoying it again grew more attractive by the second. Fine. The Hive it is.

"Miss Park?"

She glanced up. The fighter-Rat-Triumvir. "Mister Laszlo?"

The awkward smile made his face more asymmetric. "Just Laszlo, please."

He expected her to reciprocate by allowing him to call her by the first name. That would have been the polite thing to do. She didn't. Make him uncomfortable and see what comes out. "What is it, just Laszlo?" Crass. Toes. All the way.

"Uh. Miss Park, I see I'm interrupting your meal. Would you like to share dinner with me?"

"Are you asking me out, Laszlo? For a date?"

The tips of the Triumvir's ears reddened. "Only if you'd like me to." A clumsy attempt to turn this into a joke.

"No, thanks. Next question. Are you going to befriend and betray me? I don't do that more than once a day."

"N-n-no." Laszlo shook his head, repudiating the suggestion. "Just dinner, Miss Park. And a conversation. You'll be free to leave at any time."

Proper food for dinner? Beats gorging on dried beef and stale water. Then again, this could be a trap, to lure her somewhere and kill her quietly. Always a possibility in this line of work. But if that was the case, Laszlo had to be lousy at baiting his victims. The dinner outweighed the risks. "Alright," she agreed with a shrug, throwing Laszlo off again. He clearly had prepared to do more convincing. She packed the jerky and shouldered the bag. "Where to?"

"This way, Miss Park. Not far."

They bypassed the Food Terminal and walked to the nearest low-rise houses. Laszlo observed her from the corner of his eye. "You don't need to grip that stiletto in your sleeve, Miss Park. I truly mean you no harm."

"Would you tell me if you were?"

"Touché. And we're here. This house, Miss Park. After you."

Walking through the door, Yun-mi tensed in anticipation of an ambush, preparing to burst into action if need be. The ambush must have been postponed. Possibly until after dinner.

If this was how people lived when they could afford a house and not a partition on a subway train, she could get used to such a level of comfort and privacy. Easily.

An older woman bustled in the kitchen.

"Your wife? Or your mother?" Oh, how delightfully crass!

Laszlo gave her a strange look. "This is Clara, my part-time housekeeper. Miss Park, why are you trying so hard to embarrass me?"

Why was she? She'd been burned a few too many times and now instinctively protected her soft emotional underbelly with preemptive strikes. He didn't need to know any of that, but dialing down the level of rudeness seemed appropriate. "Apologies, Laszlo," was all she was ready to give him.

The host nodded. "Accepted. Would you like to wash up before dinner?"

Was he implying she was dirty?! No, probably being hospitable. Why did she always have to assume the worst? Could use warm water. "Yes, please. That would be great. Thank you, Laszlo."

Her sudden politeness made him search her face for signs of mockery.

The dinner—a flavorful stew, followed by baked fish—far exceeded her expectations. Yun-mi complimented the cooking and was gratified to see Clara's face light up. At least that woman wasn't there to kill her. It felt good to say something genuinely nice to someone. Wasn't so difficult, was it?

Laszlo let her finish the meal before talking shop. Between spoonfuls of food, they attempted small talk, with limited success.

"Laszlo."

"Yes?"

"What kind of name is that? Like Leslie, but different?"

"Sort of. It's after King Ladislaus of Hungary."

"Who? Of what? King of hungry?"

"Hun-*ga*-ry," Laszlo repeated patiently, evidently used to such questions. "A country in the Old World."

"So, his subjects weren't hungry."

"No. Maybe. Sometimes. Come on, it wasn't about hunger!"

"Relax, I'm pulling your leg. Do you speak this... Hungrian?"

"Hun*ga*rian. A few words. My family preserved nothing but the names. What about you? What does yours mean?"

"It's stupid. I don't want to talk about it."

"You can't do this! I told you about mine."

"Alright. Fair is fair. But promise you won't laugh! The last part means 'beautiful'. The first part, Yun, may mean 'flower', or 'brave, a hero'. I like the second meaning. But it's still ridiculous."

"I think they both suit you well."

"What was that?"

"I said—"

"I heard what you said. I'm asking what you *meant*. Were you being polite or trying to hit on me again?"

Laszlo helplessly stared back at her, unable to figure out how to navigate his way out of the bend.

Men! So dense sometimes. Yun-mi sighed, shook her head, letting him off the hook, and concentrated on the food. The small talk died down.

Clara took away the dishes and brought a teapot with steeped berries. Laszlo thanked and dismissed her. Time for the ambush?

"You must wonder why I invited you here, Miss Park."

"Ruling out the date, I thought it's out of the kindness of your heart. I imagine you couldn't stand by and watch a poor little girl pathetically stuffing her face with dry food out in the street."

"Naturally. That, and a conversation."

"And a conversation. Yes, you mentioned that. Do converse, please."

Laszlo nodded. "Miss Park, you are—"

Yun-mi's stopping hand silenced him. "If you're going to tell me I'm an amazing young woman, I will barf all over your table." She was serious. Hearing Kostya's words from this man would have been a nightmare.

The host looked more than a little irritated. His voice turned harsher. "Okay. Good to know. Wasn't planning to. I was about to say that you are obviously in pain."

Yun-mi cast her eyes down, concentrating on the intricate detail of the tablecloth pattern. Shouldn't have so blatantly presumed this man's intentions. And he was right.

Laszlo did not wait for a confirmation. "I am sorry that a member of my clan caused it." He straightened up and delivered the next sentence in a formal tone. "On behalf of the Humber Bay Raccoons Clan and its Noble Triumvirate, I extend our sincerest apologies and heartfelt condolences on the loss of your mentor, Kim Joon-woo." Then he leaned forward, elbows on the table, and continued in a gravelly whisper that sent shivers down Yun-mi's spine, "Informally, I want to add that if Parker still had been alive, I would have cut off the fucker's balls myself."

Sitting across the table from her was the dangerous man she'd seen earlier, capable of snapping her in half. She had been too arrogant, mistaking his politeness for weakness. His was born from strength, not insecurity.

"Thank you, Laszlo," she whispered. "That means a lot. Especially the last part." She lifted her eyes to meet his. "You may call me Yun-mi."

Laszlo smiled, and the ruthless fighter melted away, leaving behind the amiable host. "Are you trying to embarrass me again?"

"Trust me, you'll know when I do."

He winked. "I think I'm developing a feel for that. Now, with your permission, back to the serious conversation."

"Go for it."

"I need your assurance that you won't be harboring any hard feelings toward my clan."

"I already told you I am not going after your Rats, no?"

"There are other ways to harm a clan. Much worse ways, especially for someone with your connections. Can you promise, or not?"

"You're giving me too much credit. I am just a homeless Rat."

Laszlo tilted his head back and barked a laugh. "Yeah. Right. And I'm a Golden Dragon."

Yun-mi smiled slyly. "You sort of are. Your clan's Golden Dragon."

He grinned back, then wiped the smile off his face. "Yun-mi, you are still avoiding the answer. Am I to conclude you will not make that promise?"

This was becoming annoying. Had he not been pushing so hard, she would have agreed already. But now her stubborn essence demanded digging in her heels until the disposition was fully cleared. "And if I don't, will I walk out of this house alive?"

Laszlo's face darkened. "I promised you may walk out any time you wish."

"And Francis won't wait for me outside with his cronies?"

The host's features further hardened. "No harm will come to you in our clan's lands. I will escort you myself wherever you're going next, to ensure your safety."

No harm will come to you. The words shocked her like a lightning bolt. The very same pledge earlier that day didn't turn out quite true. Yun-mi buried her face in her hands. Her eyes stayed dry, but the little girl inside her, frightened and betrayed, wept her heart out.

She had to be strong. To hold it together long enough to get back to New Kowloon, to Wai Lam, where everything would be better. Everything.

"Yun-mi?"

Consumed by the emotional storm, she hadn't noticed Laszlo coming around the table until he touched her shoulder. What kind of Rat was she after that? A rookie mistake! One that could cost her her life. But the hand was solid and warm. And so reassuring.

"What's wrong? Is it something I said?"

She vehemently shook her head. "Sorry, Laszlo, not you." A raspy voice came out of her throat. A stranger's voice.

Survive long enough to return to New Kowloon.

She looked up at him over her fingers. "I promise, Laszlo. I promise. I promise. I promise." Something broke in her. She kept repeating the two words.

"Hey, hey, it's okay, Yun-mi, it's okay." Laszlo embraced her.

Another déjà vu. A man comforting her for the second time in a day. The first time she had found it was all an act. This was a different man, not Kostya. But Kostya had been a perfect gentleman, too... Until he wasn't. Will she ever be able to trust a man—anyone, really, but especially a man—without the fear of betrayal?

"What can I do to help?"

Yun-mi pushed away from Laszlo. A wet spot was spreading on his shirt where her face had been. She had tears left in her, after all. "I need to be alone."

"I can take you upstairs..." Seeing her eyebrows sourly curling up, Laszlo hurried to explain. "Separate room, locks from the inside. You can bar the door if you wish."

Yun-mi sniffed. "Thank you, that sounds great." She grabbed her backpack, the rifle, and the bow from the floor.

Laszlo did not offer to help. At least that differed from Islington, then. A Rat, he understood how she'd feel about parting with her gear. Instead, he picked her untouched mug of steaming berry tea from the table and carried it upstairs for her. A nice little touch. Very human. Sweet.

The room was enormous by Yun-mi's standards. It even had a bathroom. As promised, the door had a heavy latch and fittings for a bar. The windows boasted thick shutters that could be closed from the inside. A fireplace with a stack of wood, a barrel of water, and a small pantry completed the picture. A true Rat hole. Laszlo's Rat hole. He was giving her his own room.

Laszlo rolled the used bedding into a ball and left with it, returning with a pile of clean linens and a blanket.

Yun-mi wistfully watched him make the bed. Wistful not for the man, but for the soft, cozy mattress. She was tired. So, so, *so* tired. A different sort of tiredness, not the one she was used to. Normally, her body would be the limiting factor. She could subject it to such rigorous training that by the day's end it would feel like her limbs were made of cast iron. But inside the confines of that crawling sack of bones, she'd still burst at the seams with eagerness and curiosity. Today, it was the opposite. She could jog all the way to New Kowloon and not break a sweat. What she lacked now was that driving force that used to be such a central part of her. The toll taken by this last week had been too heavy. Joon-woo. Parker. Dixie Mall. Little Korea. Kostya. Death. Failure. Betrayal. Too much. She needed to crash and sleep it all off. Then it would be a new day. A new beginning. New Kowloon.

Joon-woo's murder had thrown her into the water with a simple choice: learn to swim, or sink. She swam. She made it to safety, only to find that the shores were no less treacherous. They had swamps, flash floods and brush fires. And she had to navigate these alone. Relying on no one but herself. Trusting no one. This adult thing turned out to be harder than she had foreseen. Would it always be like this? The paranoia? The precautions? Kill or be killed? Yun-mi against the world? Not very promising odds in *that* fight. She was bound to make a mistake. To fucking *miscalculate*. The world would win, as it always did.

She could not do this alone. She had to learn to trust again. Not everyone, only some people. The right people. *Her* people. People like Laszlo?

She had spaced out again and missed the moment when Laszlo had finished the preparations and came up to stand in the doorframe. She jolted when he called her name.

"Goodnight, Yun-mi. I'll wake you up for breakfast in the morning. Until then, you'll be all alone, as requested."

She did ask for that, didn't she? Then why did the thought of being left alone hurt so much?

Yun-mi clutched Laszlo's shirt, right by the wet spot of her tears, and pulled him back into the room.

Chapter 25

Buck

September 25, 42 PE

New Kowloon met the arrivals with polite antipathy. Not the overt, rude who-are-you-whatcha-want-get-outta-here sort, but a wealth of minute signs of annoyance.

Scores of armed men on and around the pier made Farley visibly uncomfortable. Clearly, not a normal state of affairs.

A port official watched indifferently and offered no help with mooring. The captain's assistant had to jump off the boat and tie the ropes himself.

The official pointedly ignored Kossowsky and his entourage until they approached. He neither greeted the visitors nor introduced himself. "Mooring fee, five coins a day. Warehouse use, fifteen. Arrival and departure count as full days. Longshoring extra." The man's monotonous mumbling discouraged discussion. His glazed eyes stared above newcomers' heads.

Kossowsky frowned. "Sir, we're here to talk to Golden Dragon Shang Ka Yi."

That changed the disposition. The Kowloonese finally paid attention to the people before him. He took measure of the lieutenant, dropped a "Wait here," and left toward the building overlooking the docks.

Ten awkward minutes later, another man emerged and approached the group at an energetic gait. This one, exquisitely dressed, showed much better manners. "Jasper Dragon Choi Cheok Bou, the Portmaster. I am told you want to talk to the Golden Dragon. May I ask what this is about?"

"Nice to meet you, Jasper Dragon. My name is Tony Kossowsky, and I'm afraid the information I have is for the Golden Dragon's ears only."

"If that's the case, Mister Kossowsky, I regret to inform you that your travel may have been in vain. The Golden Dragon does not accept visitors at this time."

"When will he be receiving visitors?"

"Once again, Mister Kossowsky, I apologize, but the Golden Dragon will not be seeing you."

The lieutenant's cheeks pinkened.

Jackson stepped forward. "Dear Jasper Dragon," he said, "I truly sympathize with the delicate situation in which you've found yourself through no fault of yours. I would hate to see a mere misunderstanding causing detrimental effects to your reputation or, God forbid, career in the Great Hive."

The polite smile did not leave the Portmaster's face, but the corners of his dark eyes pulled down. Before he could react, the Fivepointer provided him with a face-saving out.

"The Golden Dragon might consider lifting the restrictions this one time if he learned we bring him information from Captain Weinberg of Locksville. Kindly convey this to whoever is entrusted with the Golden Dragon's visiting schedule, and you may yet be surprised."

Whatever-his-name-Bou stepped into a small booth at the base of the pier, picked up a curved object, and cranked a handle. He spoke into the contraption, but the words were impossible to make out.

"A telephone!" Janet whispered. "A real, working telephone! Is this place amazing, or what?"

Buck filed the information for a future review. Neither the place nor the time for technical questions.

The Portmaster finished his one-sided conversation and returned to the pier. He studied the Fivepointers with respect. "Your assumptions proved correct, Mister..."

"Jackson. Tim Jackson."

"Thank you. Will you be unloading any goods, or is your visit entirely informational?"

"Our cargo needs to be unloaded and stored securely," said Kossowsky.

"This is New Kowloon, Mister Kossowsky. *All* our storage is secure. This will be taken care of while you conduct your business with the Golden Dragon. When you are done, I will meet you in my office to discuss further details. Please follow me."

The famous New Kowloon. The scale, the idea, the complexity. The technical capabilities required to raise it. The already familiar rattle of generators somewhere in the complex. Despite all those, the awe didn't come. Buck was impressed, mentally, if not emotionally. He *understood* how fascinating New

Kowloon was, but with everything that had happened *around* him, *to* him, and *with* him in the last week, he had exhausted his capacity for wonderment. Being impressed was going to have to suffice.

At the end of a long walk, with a heavy presence of armed guards along the way, Buck and his teammates entered a reception room. A full platoon occupied the key points and suspiciously eyed the foreigners. The team obeyed an officer's demand to disarm. Even Janet did not protest being frisked for hidden weapons.

Then a soldier led them into an office, staying behind the visitors.

The room offered no guest seats. The only chair present was occupied, presumably by the office owner. A woman! Pale and worn out, with the black bags under her eyes. Shang Ka Yi, could it be a female name?

"You... are not Shang Ka Yi, are you?" Kossowsky struggled with a similar doubt.

The probably-not-Shang-Ka-Yi behind the desk quit her feverish writing and looked up. For a second, she had difficulty focusing. "No, I am not." The woman put her hands on the desktop and reprovingly stared at them.

Buck followed her gaze to her trembling palms. How much sleep deprivation did it take to get to that state?

"Forgive my manners." She forced a wan smile but did not rise from her chair. "I am Golden Dragon Tam Wai Lam. You asked to converse with Shang Ka Yi, but I'm afraid he is... indisposed." The last word sounded carefully chosen. "Anything you were planning to tell him you can tell me."

"With all due respect, Golden Dragon—"

"Oh, spare me." The woman winced. "Don't. Just don't. I'm in no mood for these games. What message is so important Weinberg needs five people to convey it?"

Tell me now, or get the fuck outta here was not said out loud but plainly implied.

"Ma'am—" Kossowsky attempted to talk again, saw her cringing, and corrected himself. "Apologies—Golden Dragon, we are not from Locksville. We are Fivepointers." The lieutenant paused, awaiting her reaction. Seeing none, he continued. "We passed with a caravan through Locksville, and Captain Weinberg asked us to give a ride to his men. On our way to The Sta—"

The Golden Dragon cut him mid-word again, sharply raising a hand. Kossowsky fell silent and waited, puzzled.

"Sergeant, leave us," the Golden Dragon commanded.

Given her peremptory tone, the guard should have vanished right away. Instead, the sergeant shuffled his feet but did not move. "Golden Dragon, are you sure?" he asked with a sideways glance at the visitors.

"*Yes*, sergeant." She did not raise her voice an iota. "I *am* sure."

The guard smartly saluted and left.

"Was there an attempt on Shang Ka Yi's life? By The Station?" Jackson asked, out of the blue. "Is he alive?"

A shadow of an unidentifiable emotion momentarily rippled over Tam Wai Lam's face. She closed her eyes, reestablishing self-control, and responded in a perfectly level tone. "You will refer to the Golden Dragon by his formal title, Fivepointer. Your aspirations to impress me with your deductive skills are misplaced. Golden Dragon Shang Ka Yi is alive."

She did not deny the other part. The glaring omission couldn't be random.

The woman returned her attention to Kossowsky. "Continue."

The officer obliged. "We traveled in a caravan. It was ambushed halfway between Locksville and The Station. With the help of Weinberg's man, we nipped the attack in the bud, with minimal casualties to the merchants. We were then taken to The Station and questioned by the Chief Inquisitor himself."

The Golden Dragon was unable—or unwilling—to squash the spark of interest in her sunken eyes. "Your impressions?"

"He was awfully insistent on finding any connections we may have with you. Not you personally, Golden Dragon, with the Chinese in general."

"Was he? Considering you are all here and in one piece, I imagine he did not find any such connection."

"No, Golden Dragon, he did not. But I got a distinct impression he really wanted to. He seemed to be especially motivated by the fact we had averted the massacre of the merchant caravan. Marc, Weinberg's man, wanted us to tell you that, in his opinion, the Chief Inquisitor is the one behind the attack. This one, and the previous two. And that since this last attack had effectively failed, the Inquisitor will try to put together something else."

"I see. And how were you able to escape his clutches?"

"We presented him with a credentials letter from the Colonel of Five Points."

"Shall I ask how you possess such a letter?"

"No disrespect, Golden Dragon, better if you don't."

"Understood. Where is this Marc you keep mentioning?"

"He went back to report to Weinberg."

"And the Inquisitor let him go too? Just like that?"

"The Inquisitor was under the impression Marc is one of us."

"Interesting. Shall I not ask how this happened either?"

While Kossowsky struggled with an answer, Jackson came to his rescue. "The pertinent question, Golden Dragon, is what compelled us to stray from our planned route to deliver this information to you, posthaste."

Tam Wai Lam cocked her head. Her inscrutable black eyes studied Jackson. "Alright, I'll bite."

"Captain Weinberg and I have a close personal relationship. He has a similar one with Golden Dragon Shang Ka Yi. I would like to establish the same."

The woman, reinvigorated by the conversation to this point, wearily rubbed her face with both palms. "Why?"

The question, muted by her hands, was so loaded it took Jackson a moment to unpack.

"Birds of a feather," he said, "should flock together."

The Golden Dragon snickered, startling everyone. "Birds. Right." She rested her chin on the interlaced fingers. "A sparrow wants to soar with the eagles."

Buck held his breath.

If Jackson had taken offense, he hid it well. "A hawk, Golden Dragon," he corrected with a gentle smile. "A small but curious hawk wants to soar with the eagles."

Tam Wai Lam slapped her palms on the desk. "Very well," she said, rising to her feet. "So be it. Come with me."

Chapter 26

Ka Yi

September 25, 42 PE

The dreams were unsettling. Weird and unsettling.

The settings differed, the participants, the circumstances. But one common thread was ever present: his failure.

Whether he was accosted by bandits and tried to load his gun, but his sweaty palm kept sliding off, losing the grip...

Whether a group of assassins sprang an ambush and he tried to wield a knife, but it tumbled out of his clumsy fingers...

Whether something dark and nebulous threatened New Kowloon, and he was unable to block its advance because the blackness swept right through him...

...He kept failing, again and again. Periodically, his father appeared, observing with the mildly peeved satisfaction of someone whose unflattering opinion had been proven right.

Sometimes, a female figure stormed in to save the day, but most often he was left to savor his bitter downfall alone.

Occasionally, the disturbing dreams retreated, clearing the stage for steamy fantasies involving him and Wai Lam. But those were few and far between. Mostly, he was haunted by the endless chain of fiascos.

And the pain was always present, tedious, unrelenting. From time to time, it proliferated into his dreams. He could fail because of the pain, or the pain could afflict him because of his failure.

A few times he realized those were dreams and tried to wake up, coming close to breaking through the boundary separating illusion from reality... But failed, always failed.

Until one time it worked, with the help of the ubiquitous female figure. Of her voice.

"Can you hear me, Ka Yi?"

Opening his eyes took all his strength. How could eyelids be so heavy?

A round shape floated before him. He struggled to focus on it.

A face.

A human face.

A woman's face.

Wai Lam's face.

His lips stretched into a smile of their own volition.

Wai Lam hugged him, burying her face in his shoulder.

Doctor Chen, looming above her, frowned disapprovingly.

The embrace caused the dull pain in Ka Yi's chest to flare into a thousand sharp needles, but he hardened his resolve and did not squeak. Instead, he reassuringly patted her back.

Wai Lam lifted her head. Her eyes were dry. Did this woman ever cry? "I thought I lost you."

"I am not that easy to get rid of, Golden Dragon."

"Don't you dare ever test that again, Golden Dragon! Next time, I am opening the door." Was that forced, haunted grimace meant to be a smile?

"If I get to see you fighting naked again—by all means."

She slapped his wrist. "I'll arrange a private demonstration for you." Wai Lam glanced at the doctor, as if only then noticing they weren't alone in the room.

Chen's face disclosed no emotion. Arguably, when it came to discretion, no one in the Great Hive could surpass Doctor Chen. The good doctor had undoubtedly kept much juicier secrets than this.

"You must thank Doctor Chen," Wai Lam said. "He saved your life."

"After you did."

Ka Yi met Chen's eyes, and the doctor nodded his acceptance before Ka Yi could say a word. "It was my duty and my honor, Golden Dragon."

"Thank you nevertheless, Doctor."

"That was a close call, Golden Dragon. You were lucky the knife didn't nick major blood vessels. Your lung had collapsed, though. You will need time to recuperate. No strenuous physical activity for the next two weeks. No exercising. And"—a dry smile cracked his professionally inscrutable face—"no naked fighting for at least a week."

Never before had Ka Yi seen Wai Lam blushing.

Since waking up, Ka Yi had hovered between slumber and alertness, randomly venturing in either direction. When awake, he could not tell day from night in the windowless room, but his meals gave him a rough idea, arriving according to a schedule. He wasn't hungry, and all the dishes tasted the same, but Doctor Chen had insisted he must eat.

Wai Lam visited him often. Not often enough for his liking, as he would have selfishly preferred her by his side at all times. But realistically—more often than she could probably afford. She was running the shop for the two of them, and in crisis mode. With every visit, Wai Lam looked worse for wear.

"When was the last time you've slept?" he asked on one of her stopovers.

She dismissed his concerns with a wave. "Sleep is overrated."

"Wai Lam, dear, you're going to burn out and crash. *Then* who's gonna do our work?" A cheap, transparent manipulation, but in his groggy state Ka Yi failed to come up with anything more elegant. In the end, he extracted from her a promise to rest.

Next time she showed up, she peeked into the room before walking in. "Are you decent?"

"Hilarious."

"You've got visitors. Will you see them?"

"Are they going to try stabbing me?"

"Only if your jokes are as flat as this."

"Then what are you waiting for?"

A peculiar group followed her into the room.

A young man projected being in charge. A junior officer, judging by the way he bore himself.

An older man, with a touch of silver in his temples, disclosing much less of his internal workings. Seasoned, this one. A dark horse.

One more, the same age as the last, not too stocky but muscular. Could have been handsome a decade ago, if not for the scowl permanently affixed to his face. An enforcer, by the looks of it.

The next member of the delegation did not fit. Young, barely past his teenage years. Big, burly, but lacking the assessing eyes of an experienced killer. Not another enforcer. Who then?

A red-headed girl walked in last. Not a fighting type by any stretch of the imagination, but with that determined expression stubborn young people have when they're often forced to prove their mettle. Even odder.

Wai Lam stopped by Ka Yi's bed. "Fivepointers, meet Golden Dragon Shang Ka Yi."

Fivepointers? How peculiar.

"Weinberg's man had urged these fine gentlemen—and a lady—to bring you important information about The Station."

"Oh? Do tell."

"In a nutshell, there's been another attack, this time on a merchant caravan. The attack failed to achieve the intended level of devastation, thanks to this team's skillful defense. During their short and not too indulgent stay at The Station, they came to realize the Chief Inquisitor himself stood behind the attack. In addition, they conveyed Weinberg's man's assessment that another attack is imminent."

The news fit into the bigger picture. Snugly.

"Thank you, Fivepointers. That Weinberg's man, would his name be Marc, by any chance?"

"Yes, Golden Dragon," responded the young officer.

"Aha. I am inclined to trust this assessment. May I ask who you are?"

"Lieutenant Kossowsky. This here is Jackson, this—"

"Jackson?" Ka Yi perked up. "As in, Timmerman Jackson?"

"Beg your pardon, Golden Dragon?" The man presented as Jackson wasn't proficient in keeping a straight face. "How do you know me?"

"I know *of* you, Mister Jackson. It is my job to know about anyone who matters in every place that matters. Nice to put a face to the name."

"Color me impressed, Golden Dragon. I was hoping we could have a private conversation—"

"Mister Jackson, I have no secrets from my wife." Ka Yi squeezed Wai Lam's hand. Not a muscle moved in her face. "As for your companions' presence, I'll leave that up to you. Unfortunately, a longer conversation will have to wait. As you may see, I am not at my best, courtesy of our mutual friend, Moctar Khalifa."

Jackson nodded, while the rest of Fivepointers blankly stared back. "Ah," Ka Yi said, "the Inquisitor still prefers the formidable title over his actual name. I presume it's late in the evening now? With your permission, let us reconvene tomorrow morning."

"Not a problem, Golden Dragon. Good night." Jackson tactfully refrained from well-wishing.

"Just one question, Mister Dragon..." The redheaded girl's face plainly showed her struggle between the impropriety of her imposition and the engrossing curiosity.

How could he be mad at her? "Yes, young lady?"

Jackson rolled his eyes.

"Golden Dragon," Wai Lam corrected, peevishly.

"Golden Dragon, I saw the Portmaster using a telephone. I'm... Wow! That's amazing! What else do you have?"

Finally! Finally, someone appreciating his efforts! A Fivepointer at that, the least likely of all. Ka Yi's heart melted. "Wai Lam, dear, would you take this lovely lady on a tour of the Science Lab? Please?"

Wai Lam stoically refrained from commenting and led the visitors out of the room.

Later, she returned, switched the lights off, and crawled under the sheets on his good side. "Your wife, eh?" She nuzzled his neck.

Before Ka Yi could come up with a suitable response, her tickling breath calmed down and her arm on his stomach grew limp and heavy. She had finally checked out. Stifling a grunt, Ka Yi moved aside to give her space, and slid a pillow under her head.

The news from The Station deserved his undivided attention, but his thoughts kept sticking together, like a clump of overcooked noodles. Ka Yi gave up and let the consciousness slip away.

His wife!

He fell asleep with a happy smile.

Chapter 27

Buck

September 25, 42 PE

They were going to exclude him from the conversation, for sure. Mom and Dad had always sent him to his room when they'd had "grown up stuff" to discuss.

Did he want to be let in? That was a resounding *yes*. Why? Curiosity. Worry. But most of all, the spine. As Janet had said, he may yet grow one. There he was, doing exactly that. Not a pushover anymore, for everyone to kick around. His own man. Kind of. Staying for an adult conversation... if they allowed him. Tim would, wouldn't he?

Tim? No, Timmerman. What kind of name was that? Buck had been sure Tim was short for Timothy, never giving it a second thought.

Even stranger than Tim's name was the local kitchen.

Buck had discovered the Hive's cantina over an hour ago, and had no plans of leaving it anytime soon. With the free food and no questions asked, he was determined to taste as many dishes as his stomach would take. So far, he was finishing the seconds, and hasn't seen a sign of trouble. What should he get for the next round? Tough choice. Should save space for sweets...

"There you are!" Janet, flushed and brimming with energy, took a seat across the table. Practically glowing, she was magnificent. Buck forgot to chew, caught in admiration. He was over her. No, really, he *was*. But damn...

"Buck, you won't believe it! *I* can't believe it! This lab they've got—it's... It's amazing! Everything I could dream up, and more. They're working on power generation, and antibiotics, and communications. They're installing engines on ships, Buck! Buck?"

He shook himself, swallowed, and grinned.

"What?" Janet tilted her head.

"Nothing." Buck swerved his fork in the plate, trying to collect a bunch of noodles. "It's nice to see you so..." He looked up, searching for the right word. "So happy."

"Thank you." The red on her cheeks deepened. She averted her eyes. *You and I—this isn't going to happen.* Janet must have remembered that, too. Awkward.

"Tell me more about the lab," Buck said, to change the subject.

Janet sighed, picked her fork, and dug into her plate. "They've got scientists," she said between bites.

"What's that?"

Her hands dropped to the table, and she stopped chewing, staring at Buck. "Come on. For real?"

Buck apologetically spread his arms, then followed her gaze, tracing the meatball that flew off his fork. They smiled at each other.

"A scientist," Janet explained, "is someone who deals with, well, science. Tries to understand how things work."

Could it be? Was he not the only one with the visions? "Then I'm a scientist too."

Janet chortled, but grew sober under his stare.

Buck sucked on his lip. Janet had already seen him experiencing visions twice. Seven Hells, she was in both. No sense pretending nothing had happened. "I see things," he divulged in a low voice, not to be overheard. "Sometimes, it's what's going to happen. And sometimes—it's like you said, I *understand* how things work."

Janet creased her brow. "That is not how science works. You have to know something to understand it."

"Okay," Buck easily agreed. "Then I'm not a scientist." He returned to his food under Janet's puzzled examination. "Those scientists," he mumbled with his mouth full, "you said they *try* to understand how things work. How's it going for them?" Buck innocently glanced up, munching.

Janet waggled her hand. "With limited success, I gather. They haven't got much knowledge yet, but are working on it. Taking apart the old tech, trying to reverse-engineer it."

"Um-hum."

"Sorry, to figure out how stuff is supposed to work, so they can build it again. If only they had the books, the drawings, that would've—"

"Drawings? Like pictures?"

"Uh, yes and no. Not just any pictures. There used to be a special sort, schematics, showing all the parts, and how they fit together—"

"That's exactly what I see."

Janet fell silent. Her lips parted to say something, but pressed into a thin line instead. "Baxter." She took a deep breath. "If it's a joke, it's a poor one. Cruel, even."

Buck threw his head back, rolling his eyes to the ceiling in exasperation.

"Janet Louise—" he started, mimicking Secretary Hansson to get back at her, but the ceiling reminded him where they were. "Mistress Kossowsky, I am serious."

Janet's cheeks reddened again. "I apologize, Buck. It's hard to believe. No one can do that."

Aha. He *was* the only one. "No one can see a knife up a Zealot's sleeve, or a machine gun in the bushes, yet here we are."

"I'd never properly thanked you." Janet covered Buck's hand with hers.

Buck shuddered as if zapped by a static discharge from a woolen sweater. He *was* past her. Was he? He pulled his arm back awkwardly, looking away. "That's not why I brought this up."

"I know. Still, thank you for saving my life. Twice."

Buck's ears burned.

"Uh, okay." Janet sounded uncomfortable, too. "So, you can see how things work? All the things?"

"No. Only a few. Have to take them apart too, and put them back together, many times. And most often, nothing happens. But sometimes, I get a vision of all these parts moving, working, and... I can't describe this. It's beautiful."

"Huh. What have you seen so far?"

"Not much to *understand* in Five Points, you know. A rifle, that's the trickiest." Buck was bursting with pride and excitement. "Did you realize it's like a small engine?" He trailed to a whisper, out of habit.

Janet shook her head. "Is it?"

"Yeah. And then I really wanted to *understand* the jukebox at Pelham, but—"

"The what?"

"A machine that plays music."

"They had a music machine? And you didn't tell me?!"

A few heads in the cantina turned, and Janet hunched over.

"I was busy being lectured by Master Flannagan," Buck said. "And then almost had my head bitten off by... by your husband!" There, a small revenge.

Janet put a hand over her eyes. "Next time, show me such things. Please. If it isn't too much hassle."

"I'll try to remember." Buck let the residual vindictiveness sip out. "If you promise me one thing."

Janet peeked through the fingers. "Should I ask?"

"Promise you'll help me become a scientist one day."

Janet rose, grabbed Buck's wrist, and pulled him from the table. "Come with me."

"But—" Buck resisted. "The sweets! I haven't tried the sweets yet!"

Janet leaned her head to a side. "Really?" Her brows slid closer together. "Really?"

Buck stood up with a guilty, meek smile.

He lost his bearings after three or four turns, but Janet strode confidently through corridors, gantries, and stairs. She paused only twice, orientating at busy intersections, and decisively picking the direction. Buck obediently followed, asking no questions, until they reached a large metal door with two surly guards.

"No entry," snapped one, staring the foreigners down.

Another Kowloonese appeared out of nowhere and whispered into the guard's ear. The security man's stare lost its prickliness. He nodded and pulled the door open.

"We're being followed." Buck risked a furtive glance over his shoulder, but their mysterious minder had stayed outside.

"Are you surprised?" Janet had a point, but Buck's attention already wandered.

"What is this place?"

More than anything, the space resembled a workshop. Workbenches all around, hosting a few familiar tools—and a whole lot of items whose purpose Buck wouldn't guess. Several people sat or stood, busy doing... something. Try as he might, it was impossible to figure out what. Wires, tubes, and mechanisms cluttered every surface. Things vibrated, whined, and moved on their own.

"The science lab." Nice of Janet to let him arrive to the conclusion.

She winked, beaming as if the lab were hers.

One labbie—labster? scientist?—turned and smiled. "Ah, Janet! Back already?" Not a Chinese. Eh?

Janet waved back. "Hey, Marv. Brought a friend. Meet Buck."

Buck approached Marv's bench, eyes glued to what was sitting on it. A machine. And it was *alive*. It purred, rocking mildly, and turned a small wheel attached to it. Buck's hand woke to life and reached for the metal casing.

"Don't—"

Buck jerked the wayward limb back.

"—touch the wires," Marv finished with less urgency. "Unless you like electric shocks."

Buck finally acknowledged the man's presence. "Sorry. I should've asked."

"It's all good. Touch it, just not the wires."

Emboldened, Buck tried again. With a tip of a finger first; when nothing happened, pressing his palm against it. The vibration spread up his arm, and it was not unpleasant.

Abandoning the Faith was one thing. Actively breaking its commandments—the next level of apostasy. He was touching an abomination. Not with the mind to destroy it, but offering it a hand of friendship. Fear fought curiosity—and lost.

Janet came closer, grinning from ear to ear. And why wouldn't she? This was her victory, too.

Would he be able to *understand* the machine?

"Marv? Is it possible to look inside?"

The man fetched a screwdriver, undid four fasteners, and lifted the casing. "Here you go, pal. Stay clear of the moving parts, okay?"

Buck leaned closer, keeping his hands to himself this time.

It hit him, the vision superimposed over the machine. Buck marveled at the view, holding his breath. Such an elegant solution. A work of genius. "It's..." He needed air—and words. "Amazing!"

"Right?" Marv basked in pride.

"But..."

"But?"

"That thingy there, that closes this part—" This wasn't working. He didn't have the right names, and Marv's wrinkled forehead proved Buck wasn't making much sense.

Buck sighed, searched around, and grabbed a notepad and a pencil. Bending over the desk, with Marv breathing into his one ear and Janet into another, he feverishly drew what he'd seen.

With Buck's lackluster skills, the drawing refused to form into anything remotely as impressive as his vision, but at least it made more sense than his worthless words.

"Aha," said Marv, "This goes there, yes."

"So, this"—Buck pointed at a mushroom-shaped object in the drawing—"plugs this hole."

Marv touched his chin. "Yeah."

"But some stuff from inside here leaks. Seal it, and the whole thing would work better." Buck's words were utterly inadequate, but hopefully the drawing helped clarify them.

"Hm." Marv scratched the back of his head, and understanding lit up his face. "Damn! You may be onto something. How could you know this?"

Buck glanced at Janet and found a spark of new appreciation in her green eyes.

He shrugged. "Maybe I am a bit of a scientist, too."

Chapter 28

Marc

September 25, 42 PE

The leaves smelled of rot. This early in the season, the recently shed top layers were still dry and clean. It was the bottom of the pile, the yesteryear's brown-black garbage that stunk so bad.

All the better. If the pursuers had dogs, the stench of the forest floor could throw them off. With that in mind, Marc had smeared himself with the pungent mud and made Rajan do the same. Someone else might have objected, but Rajan proved to not be a squeamish type. Stained head to toe, they dug into the leaves under an ancient maple and waited.

Not moving had a downside. Limping on had demanded full mobilization of Marc's resources. He had to detach himself from the pain. The bruised hip, beaten with a stick; the right-hand fingers, broken with a hammer, then placed in a haphazard twig-and-rag splint by Rajan, and throbbing angrily; the crusted lips, cracking and bleeding into his mouth when he opened it; his ribs, making him cringe and creak with every careless movement. The bouts of dizziness, though, presented the greatest challenge, coming dangerously close to swiping him off his feet. While in motion, he had a goal that helped subdue his body's signals of how badly broken it was. Stationary, this became much more difficult.

Rajan surprised him again. Marc was afraid a civilian, untrained for long ambushes, would get antsy and pester him, demanding to know how much longer they had to wait. And yet, the guy lay calmly nearby, showing no sign of anxiety.

The group of pursuers whose voices they had heard earlier entered the clearing. Marc studied them through a thin slit between the leaves.

Four. Too many. Bad. Rifles. Bad. No dogs. Good. Keep waiting.

After escaping the perimeter, Marc had guided Rajan west, in the direction opposite from Locksville. Then they turned north, intending to eventually head east and circumvent The Station on their way home. Search parties being sent even here? Way to kick a hornets' nest.

The voices disappeared into the forest. Marc counted three hundred heartbeats before judging it safe to leave their lair. He touched Rajan to attract his attention and climbed out of the leaves...

... to find himself face to face with two more soldiers.

All three froze. Marc's better-trained reflexes kicked in faster. The soldier to his left started raising the rifle. Marc sidestepped, putting the enemy between himself and the other Stationer, and closed the distance. In a lightning-fast series of circular motions, Rajan's shiv in Marc's left hand sliced the soldier's forearm, the bicep, and finally his throat. Marc turned to the other foe, but he had already been taken care of. Rajan had knocked the second Stationer down with the truncheon expropriated from the prison guard.

He continued whacking the body, long after the prone man's wheezing had ceased. Marc did not interrupt. If Rajan needed to get the rage out of his system, what better opportunity could there be? After a while, the ex-hauler stopped, breathing noisily through the mouth. His arms hung limply by his sides. The bloodied truncheon fell to the ground. Tears rolled down Rajan's wet cheeks, and a string of saliva drooped from the corner of his mouth. Marc cautiously hugged his rescuer and let him weep.

The sobbing subsided. "I can't go back. No mas. You know what they do to me?"

"Nothing pleasant, I expect." On cue, Marc's body went through a muster of its own grievances.

"Yeah. A year ago, they caught a worker, Hamid, snooping where he shouldn't. Made an example of his execution. So no one else gets such ideas, nunca. It was bad. So bad, two lifers puked and one fainted. Lifers, Marc!"

"I hear you. You are not going back, Rajan. You'll be fine."

"Marc, you owe me, sí?"

"Of course."

"Promise, if they get us, you kill me first. Promise!"

The hysterical notes in Rajan's voice were alarming, but Marc was in no position to do anything about that.

"I promise. On the plus side, we've got guns now." He bent down and picked a rifle. "Know how to use it?"

"What's to know? Point, shoot."

"It's not quite as— Never mind, you're right. Don't forget to take the safety off first." He clicked the selector, showing Rajan how it's done. "And this here is the magazine release. Don't mix them up."

They picked everything useful off the two dead soldiers. Marc replaced his prison slippers with a pair of military boots. Rajan's work boots were fine; besides, his feet were too big to fit into the spoils.

Rajan hefted the rifle. "Let's catch up with the first bunch and shoot 'em!"

"That's a no. The sounds of shooting carry far away. If we don't want The Station's entire army on our asses, I'd prefer keeping a low profile."

"As you say. But if we see more of them, we kill them."

"If there is no other option." Rajan's eagerness to rush into battle could become a problem.

They followed a course perpendicular to the first pursuing force, cut right an hour later, and came upon a creek. That was when the dizziness got the better of Marc, not taking no for an answer, and the world dissolved.

He came to, tentatively. Bright lights blinded him through the blurriness in his eyes, and he allowed himself to drift back into the blissful comfort of the darkness.

Later yet, he opened his eyes again.

"Hey, buddy!" a familiar jovial voice greeted him from above. "Welcome back!"

Weinberg? What was he doing in the forest?

Weinberg really was there. The forest wasn't. It was Locksville's infirmary, where Marc had spent his share of time during his military service.

Marc looked around. Rajan was present too. Marc raised an unpleasantly weak right hand and found it tightly wrapped in a thick bandage. He let it drop back onto the bed and lifted an equally feeble left hand for a fist bump. Rajan met it with a wide grin.

"We made it," Marc said. "*You* made it."

"You've got no idea!" his boss interjected. "Your resourceful friend stole a canoe and paddled downstream and through the lake, all the way from Jordan Harbour!"

Marc tried to produce an impressed whistle, but with his lips' condition it came out as a *pft*. Everyone, including Marc himself, laughed.

Weinberg grew serious. "You did well, Marc. It's unfortunate that you got caught, and I'm sorry for what you've had to endure." He planted his palm on Marc's shoulder. "But! If there's any silver lining, it's that our hands are untied now. By torturing you, The Station had violated the formal neutrality of our relations. The Defense Council has unanimously accepted my motion to apply a full range of countermeasures, including an embargo on all trade with The Station and their trains' transit through our bridges. Effectively, they're cut off from the eastern half of their markets. We will work with New Kowloon to bring forth the change in The Station's rulership. Marc, your misfortune cleared the road to all these changes. I hope this gives you some consolation."

"Sir, if it helps take down the slavers, I'll go back and take more beatings."

"No need, buddy, no need. But tell me, are you up for another field trip?"

"You tell me, sir, am I? You must be better appraised of my condition than I am."

"Um, let's see. Mutilated fingers, bruises all over, but nothing else broken. The worst part is your concussion, but you'll be fine. We're taking the express route."

"How so? Have you rediscovered the secret of flying, sir?"

"Close, and almost as fun. We'll travel in my motorboat."

Marc swallowed the *Your what, now?* question, and let Weinberg triumphantly enjoy the dumbfounding effect of his words.

"Oh, and Marc? Please congratulate your fellow intelligence officer, Rajan Gupta, on joining the service."

September 26, 42 PE

"Sir, are you sure?"

The boat did not inspire confidence. In the absence of a sail, or even a mast, there was something woefully incomplete about it. At least a pair of oars was stashed under the seats, but Marc did not look forward to paddling across the lake in his banged-up state.

"Didn't take you for such a scaredy cat!" Weinberg laughed Marc's concerns off.

"Not scared, sir. Apprehensive. Not the same."

Boarding ships for inspection in the safe and quiet Canal waters was one thing. Sailing on the lake? Ugh. If it was going to be like that amphibious assault exercise... Heavens forbid. Alas, this time Marc did not get a say. At least the breeze helped chill down his feverish forehead.

Weinberg climbed to the stern, lowered the engine into the water, squeezed a pump, and pulled the cord. The engine wasn't in the mood. Possibly, having spent most of its life on land, it was as reluctant as Marc to cross the lake. The second failure offered a glimmer of hope, brutally quashed by the guttural rumble of the motor on the third try.

Marc let out an anguished sigh and shifted closer to the boat's side, strategically positioning himself to vomit overboard.

Lake O exceeded his worst expectations. The damn cockleshell of the boat rose and fell with the waves, ensuring its crew was sprayed head to toe.

On particularly deep dives, Weinberg hooted and laughed maniacally. Marc gave up on any aspiration to keep a small portion of his breakfast inside and switched to worrying about his commander's sanity.

Weinberg firmly steered the boat until a furious gust of wind turned it sideways. The next wave didn't wait for another chance and capsized the vessel, spilling its crew.

These dire circumstances revealed several fun facts.

Fact one: the water was wet and cold. Much wetter and colder when it was all around, compared to merely being splashed.

Fact two: the faded, uncomfortable vests Weinberg had made them wear worked. Marc was floating on the surface, carried up and down by the waves, miraculously avoiding sinking like a stone. That led to the discovery of facts three and four.

Rajan, a land creature, did not know how to swim and panicked, shouting and thrashing. Weinberg did not know how to swim either, but the mad smile on his lips only grew wider.

Marc pulled Rajan closer by the loop on the back of his vest. Without the isolating effect of the boat, the deafening noise of the wind and the waves became much louder. Marc shouted words of reassurance, convincing the big guy to stop flapping his arms and conserve his energy.

He turned to Weinberg. "Now what, sir?"

"Now we swim to the shore! It isn't far, we've made it three-quarters of the way!"

Marc's limbs were already going numb. How long did they have before hypothermia took hold?

An unfamiliar voice posed a more interesting question. "Yo, there! Wanna come aboard, or are you good where you are?"

Marc turned in the water, searching for the source of this absurd question, and was relieved to find a man holding a rope and preparing to throw it. Even more heartening was that the man came as a package deal with a large sailboat.

The rescue took a while, with the boat drifting and dragging them behind before all three finally lay on the deck, panting and dripping water.

"Can you tow our boat?" Weinberg asked the rescuer—the captain, considering that the other person on board was a quiet teenager. The captain didn't deign to answer, but his dubious expression matched everything Marc thought about the question.

"Where were you lot headed when the Lake got the upper hand?"

"New Kowloon," Weinberg responded, gauging the captain's reaction.

"You've gotta be fecking shitting me!"

"Why?"

"We were jus' comin' from there! Not goin' back."

"We'll pay you."

"You ain't got enough. Them Chinese gone crazy! Guns, guns everywhere, like there's a fecking war comin', and so rude! The folks I brought, took 'em hours to talk their way in. No, not goin' there."

"Then what's the closest you can take us?"

The captain scratched his temple. Then tacked the boat. Then scratched his temple some more. "Bronte. How's that sound? Will drop you there for free."

"Bronte? It will take us half a day to hike to the Hive!"

"I dunno... Oakville? Twice as close, but that'll cost you."

"Let's stop playing games, captain..."

"Farley. Call me Farley."

"Captain Farley, we're profoundly thankful for saving our wet souls. But we've got an important business that cannot wait."

"Looks to me like you're ungrateful sons of bitches. Beggars can't be choosers. I'll drop you where I say. End of story."

"Or we can commandeer your boat."

"Or I can throw you back into the water."

A wicked smile stretched Weinberg's lips. "Dear captain, from one captain to another... Oh, I'm sorry. Where are my manners! I haven't introduced myself. Captain Weinberg, Locksville. A pleasure to make your acquaintance."

Farley's face went paler than his sail. "Why didn't you begin with that, Captain? You'll be in New Kowloon in no time at all!"

Farley didn't lie. In an impressive demonstration of top-notch seamanship, an hour later he was docking in New Kowloon's port.

"Captain Weinberg, we'll wait here 'til tomorrow noon, if you decide to go back," shouted Farley into Weinberg's back.

Weinberg turned around and waved. "Thank you, captain Farley, that'd be swell. I'll let you know if we require your services."

The sailor eagerly saluted.

Marc could never get used to this. "Your name has a peculiar effect on most unexpected people, boss."

"Let's see how well it works here. Farley wasn't lying, something's really off with the Hive."

An important-looking civilian waited on the pier, accompanied by two heavily armed guards. "Greetings," he said. "I couldn't help but overhear that sailor calling you Captain Weinberg."

"That's me."

"Welcome, sir. I am Jasper Dragon Choi Cheok Bou, the Portmaster. Please follow me. I'll let the Golden Dragon know you're here."

Marc knew Weinberg well enough to see when his boss was surprised. Not a common occurrence.

"Are we expected, Portmaster?"

"Not as such, sir. I'm executing my judgment. Visitors arrived yesterday and were cleared for a meeting with the Golden Dragon after mentioning your name. Curiously, the same boat brought them here."

Weinberg exchanged meaningful glances with Marc.

"A solid judgment, Jasper Dragon. I will mention this to the Golden Dragon. Out of curiosity, who were these visitors?"

"I'm afraid I only caught two of the names, sir. One Kossowsky and one Jackson. Accompanied by three others, including a young woman."

Marc high-fived the captain. "The bastards made it here before us."

"A resourceful bunch. Jasper Dragon, what's with all the extra security?"

"Apologies, Captain, I am not at liberty to say. Maybe the Golden Dragon will shed some light for you."

So, this was the famous Great Hive. Marc's nausea and the pain in his battered body retreated. Neither his dripping clothes nor his boots, pathetically squishing with each step, could distract him. With his head on a swivel, he was only worried he'd miss too many things that ought to be noticed.

Their journey ended in a large hall.

"You'll find a change of clean and dry clothes here, along with all the basic comforts," said the Portmaster. "Hot meal will be served shortly. In the meantime, I'll arrange for you to see Golden Dragon Tam Wai Lam."

Weinberg stopped mid-stride. "Jasper Dragon? I thought we were going to see—"

"Golden Dragon Shang Ka Yi? Yes, everybody wants to see him. But I'm afraid Golden Dragon Tam Wai Lam is who you will have to meet instead." The Portmaster bowed and left. His two silent guards took positions outside the hall's door.

Weinberg shook his head. "I don't like this. I don't like this at all. Something's seriously wrong."

"I agree, sir. I counted more guards along our way than we've got in the entire CIU! Didn't you say New Kowloon has no army?"

"Theirs is a *security force*, not a field army."

"Aha."

Marc clumsily undressed, dried himself with a towel, and put fresh clothes on, groaning and wincing. He barely finished before someone insistently knocked on the door.

"Come in!" Weinberg raised his voice.

The promised food? Marc's empty stomach gurgled impatiently. But the woman entering the room carried nothing in her hands. Two guards stepped in and took positions at her sides, with fingers on their guns' triggers.

The captain met this unconcealed threat with arched eyebrows. The woman waved the armed men away like annoying flies, and they promptly vacated the room.

"Weinberg." She nodded.

"Golden Dragon." Weinberg bobbed his head in response. "You look like crap. Tough times?"

"Thank you, Captain, kind of you to ask. Did you take swimming lessons on your way here?"

"In fact, we did."

"How's the water?"

"A tad warmer than you, Golden Dragon."

Marc wasn't much of a diplomat himself, but *that* exchange was too bizarre. Not a way for two senior officials to talk to each other.

The Golden Dragon's gaze flickered over Rajan and stopped on Marc. "I'm guessing this one is the infamous Marc?"

A knot tightened in Marc's stomach, and not because of hunger. How could she know him? And... *Infamous?* He had to respond because his commander didn't. "Yes, Ma'am."

Both Weinberg and the Golden Dragon cringed.

"The proper honorific is Golden Dragon, Marc," the captain corrected him. "That is, if you value the integrity of your bones. Am I right, Golden Dragon?"

"Yes, my dear Captain. Although, presently, I cannot guarantee the integrity of anyone's bones."

"Okay," said Weinberg, "let's cut the protocol crap. What's the matter? Where's Ka Yi?"

Chapter 29

Yun-mi

September 26, 42 PE

Laszlo focused on methodically eliminating his scrambled eggs. Yun-mi, in marked difference, was absentmindedly mutilating the food on her plate with the fork.

She'd had her share of bizarre ways to spend a night.

Once, about two years ago, she spent a night on the CN Tower's observation deck. The place was haunted by the souls of the people who died on the day of the E, a popular superstition claimed. Supposed to slide up the needle all the way to heaven, some got stuck before reaching the tip, blocking the tower's veins and causing the ugly bulge that deformed the slim and elegant spire.

Her then-boyfriend had succumbed to his stupid friends' peer pressure and dared her to a sleepover halfway into the sky. The little assholes had been making fun of her career aspirations, intent on exposing her as a fraud. Yun-mi didn't believe the ghost stories and accepted the challenge with a shrug. At the time, before she'd given up on the boys her age, she had still felt the need to prove herself to those infantile jerks. She had been keen to show she was more than a walking womb and a cook.

She snatched a half-empty bottle of murky moonshine from one of the snickering shitheads and proudly strode into the building at the needle's base. It took her a while to climb up, but when she did, the gorgeous sunset over the City stole away what was left of her breath. She forgot everything and lingered by the windows, mesmerized. In the end, remembering what brought her there, she leaned over the guardrail, waved to the tiny figures below, doused them from the bottle, and went to find a place to sleep where she'd be protected from the ubiquitous vicious drafts. And maybe the ghosts, just in case.

If any wayward souls were stuck in the tower, they must have accepted her as one of their own. She slept like a baby.

Next morning, Yun-mi woke the clump of the boys dozing off down below by throwing the bottle at them. It exploded into a myriad of shards that almost reached the spectators. Their frightened and angry shouts carried to her perch. She laughed, descended to the ground, broke up with the gullible moron, and left without looking back. Without ever looking back.

Another time, last year, she got stuck in an air duct.

Joon-woo had been instructing her in high-rise exploration. Whether the lesson was intended or impromptu, it was utterly humiliating. She still blushed at the recollection.

The room she was tasked with getting into awaited on the other end of that duct. She was convinced she'd be able to squeeze through the tight clearance. Turned out, she was not as slim as she thought. She had gained muscle mass, and her damned thighs grew wider. Plus, something in her gear snagged.

Joon-woo chuckled in his usual soft way, wished her goodnight, and left her, speechless with incredulity, to contemplate her plight. At first, she was angry—at him for abandoning her like that, at herself for making such a foolish mistake. She pushed and pulled, but only got ensnared worse. Eventually, she gave up and resigned to patiently wait for the morning. She was visited by a family of raccoons—real raccoons, not Humber Bay clansmen—who were not too happy to make her acquaintance, but ultimately ruled her out as a threat. She even managed to catch some sleep.

Joon-woo returned late, hours after dawn, leaving her with enough time to start doubting he was ever coming back. The embarrassment took her weeks to live down.

Last night's weirdness easily eclipsed these experiences.

Yun-mi stole a glance at Laszlo's inscrutable face. "I'm sorry," she breathed out, to break the unbearable silence.

"What for?"

"For torturing you like that."

He didn't answer for a long time. What responses was he weighing in his head? His next words were, "Feel better now?"

"Can't you tell?"

"I don't want to presume."

"Yes, Laszlo, I feel much, much better! Better than I have in ages!"

"Then the torture was worth it."

This time, *she* didn't know how to respond.

Last night, when she had pulled him into the room, he firmly stopped her. "What are you doing?"

What kind of silly question was that? Was he daft? Didn't he know what men and women did behind closed bedroom doors? Yun-mi wasn't going to explain. She made another attempt to pull him toward the bed, but he stood his ground like a solid, unmovable rock, crossing his arms and repeating the dumb question.

She found the courage to meet his eyes. "You don't like me? Is that it?"

"You know I do, but that's beside the point."

"What point?" Misery and confusion tangled the elusive thread of the conversation.

"The point that you're distraught, and not thinking straight, and that I will not take advantage of that."

She shook her head, sending her hair flying from side to side. "But I can't be alone tonight."

"Then you won't be. I'll stay with you. But I will not sleep with you."

At that stage, anything was better than spending the night alone. Laszlo diligently looked away while Yun-mi undressed down to her briefs and undershirt and dove under the sheets. He then perched on the edge of the bed and held her hand. Between the softness of the mattress and the warm weight of the blanket, the last remnants of her strength seeped away. She sunk into a heavy slumber.

Several times through the night she woke up, startled by dreams she couldn't recall. Every time her eyes found a dark figure sitting nearby. He gently squeezed her hand, and she slid back into the vast blackness. Another time, she awakened in tears, remembering a nightmare she would rather forget. She pulled Laszlo closer and wrapped his arms around herself, curling up like an embryo inside the comforting shell of his protection.

In the morning, Yun-mi rose unusually rested. Outside the window, the world had regained its colors, with the sun shining and the birds chirping. She cautiously tested her feelings.

Relaxed. Complete. Not-alone.

Behind her, Laszlo was fast asleep, snoring softly. Yun-mi gingerly extricated herself from his embrace and sat up. The snoring stopped.

She turned and found him staring back. Roles reversed, she took and squeezed his hand with a grin. "Morning, sunshine."

With a disapproving look, Laszlo wrapped her in the blanket, in a nonverbal reminder of how scant her clothing was. Still fully dressed himself, he climbed out of the bed and left the room. Soon, the pot rattling downstairs announced the coming breakfast.

And here they were.

"Laszlo..."

The man in front of her looked up from his plate and quizzically arched one eyebrow.

"I don't know how to thank you."

"Then don't."

"But you don't understand how much this night meant to me!"

"I may."

"I was selfish!"

"Yes, you were."

Was he teasing her? Was he now trying to embarrass her? "Are you mad at me?"

"What gave that away?"

"But why? I already said I'm sorry!"

"Yes, but for the wrong reasons."

Her great mood was dissipating by the second. Who was torturing whom now? She slammed a fist into the table. The plates clinked plaintively. "Talk to me, Laszlo, please! More than three words at a time!"

He put down his fork. "Yun-mi, I am not mad because you 'tortured' me. I'm a grown-up man who can keep it in his pants. Even when a pretty girl presses herself against me in bed. I am mad about your recklessness."

He could as well have slapped her. Even the *pretty girl* reference didn't make his words less painful.

"What?" Her voice came out low and hoarse.

"You threw yourself at the first man who showed you kindness. What if that man had turned out to be another sleazy monster, like Parker? How would you live with yourself after that?"

Yun-mi took Laszlo's words in. Then stood up, came over, and poked him in the shoulder. "Are you real? Or am I imagining you?"

The muscle under the shirt sure felt real enough.

She swept his plate aside, perched on the table in front of him, and cupped his face in her hands. "I had no idea men like you existed."

She planted a kiss on his cheek.

"Are you sure?" he mumbled.

"Shut up." She moved to his lips.

"Won't your Triumvirate pals miss you?"

"I'm a Rat. I come and go when I please. They'll manage."

Laszlo insisted on accompanying Yun-mi to New Kowloon. Her attempts to convince him she knew the way and would be perfectly safe shattered against his unyielding resolve. More stubborn than her. Imagine that. It was easier to agree. In truth, the little arguing she did was perfunctory, only because her independence had to be reasserted after everything that happened between them. *Especially* after that.

The recent events had proved that her safety along the route was not at all as assured as she tried to project. Having Laszlo alongside was a vast relief. As a bonus, bringing a Triumvir to the Hive gave weight to her request for negotiations.

Half a dozen people they encountered in the Raccoons' lands greeted her companion with smiles, without exception. Hearing "*Good day, Mister Gabor!*" the first time made her look around in search of another person. Until she put two and two together—and blushed. The man she'd spent the night with, even if not in the most conventional way... And then spent the morning with, in a *very* conventional way... She hadn't even known his full name! Well, she did now. "Mister Gabor."

"Yes, Miss Park?"

"Nothing. Just testing the sound of it."

"And?"

"It's ridiculous." She liked it. Rolled nicely off the tongue.

Laszlo stopped and delicately lifted her chin for a kiss. After he let her go, she stood with her eyes closed; head upturned, lips parted, savoring the sensation. "I can get used to this."

"Don't get too used."

Yun-mi straightened. Her eyes opened wide; her heart fluttered helplessly at the pit of her stomach. Shit. Not again. Should've known better. "Why?"

He touched her cheek, and the affectionate warmth of his fingertips pulled her entire body to his palm. She relaxed as instantly as she had tensed a second earlier. His words came from far away. "You're still a Rat. I don't want you to get too comfortable. Bad for the long-term... everything."

"Good point. But you've got my six, yes?"

"Of course. When I'm there."

And when he wasn't? No. Not now.

They walked on. "Did you just mention long-term relationships?"

"Did I? Must've been a slip of the tongue."

Yun-mi grabbed Laszlo's hand and forcefully turned him to herself. What he saw in her face wiped the smile off his lips. He hunched over to bring their eyes to the same level. "A stupid attempt at a joke, I swear!"

Yun-mi was still clasping his arm with all her strength. She let go of it. He rubbed the place.

She sternly waggled a finger at him. "Don't you dare joke about this!"

"Yes, Ma'am! You've made that perfectly clear."

"Befriend and betray, we talked about this, remember?" Yun-mi's fake smile was a desperate attempt to conceal the pain in her eyes.

"Yun-mi, I'd never—"

"I'll kill you." That was a promise. If this scared him away, better now, before she grew used to... *this*. Him. To having someone in her corner in that bareknuckle fight against the world.

He stayed. "I believe you." A corner of Laszlo's lip twitched, betraying a suppressed smile.

"Stop."

"What?"

"Stop looking at me with those adoring eyes."

"Uh, no. If I stop, kill me."

Shit. Yun-mi turned and marched on, mainly to hide the warmth in her cheeks. She failed to deter him and had no clue what to say.

The first test for the route's safety came shortly after crossing into Islington lands. The two of them and the Russian patrol spotted each other at the same time. No sense in hiding or evading. Yun-mi stiffened and reached for her bow. Laszlo glanced at her sideways, coming to his own conclusions, and touched her elbow. "Let me handle this."

As always, nothing went according to the plan.

"Mister Gabor, Miss Park, how is your day going?" nodded the senior of the Islingtoners once the two groups converged.

"Mister Rudnev," Laszlo greeted back, "how are you?"

Yun-mi said nothing.

Undeterred by her conspicuous silence, the Russian officer, who must've seen her at Kostya's feast, directed his next words at her. "Miss Park, we have instructions to request your presence at the Headquarters."

Her hand slid toward the bow again. "Request? Or demand?"

Laszlo bladed away from the two patrolmen, reaching behind his back.

Rudnev raised his hands, open palms forward. "A humble request, Miss Park. An invitation, if you will. We also have a message to deliver in case you decline." His thin smile hinted that her hostile response had been expected.

"Whose instructions, and what's the message?"

"The instructions are coming directly from Ilya Korenev, our new Chief of Operations, and—"

"What?!" Yun-mi's and Laszlo's simultaneous exclamations blended into one.

"Yes, that's part of the message. Following the untimely passing away last night of the previous Chief, Konstantin Malyshev, Mister Korenev has provisionally assumed the position, pending ratification by the clan's referendum. Chief Korenev has asked anyone who meets you to deliver the news, and to insist that the clan's doors are always open for you." He studied Yun-mi with open curiosity. "Chief Korenev also intimated," he added in a less official tone, "that you've done the clan a great service, and are to be provided with any assistance at any time."

Damn. Yun-mi smiled. Ilya *had* listened, and took the matters into his own hands. That changed everything. The news of the demise of yet another man who had betrayed her trust was oddly satisfying. Racking up a body count of her enemies, eh?

"Thank you, Mister Rudnev, I am delighted. I've got other plans at the moment, but would love to visit when I get a chance. Please pass my thanks and blessings to Chief Korenev."

Rudnev saluted, and the two groups parted ways.

Yun-mi waited for Laszlo to bombard her with a million questions, but he remained silent. After half a hundred steps, she gave up. "Alright, ask away. I know you want to."

"Where do I begin? Who *are* you, woman?"

She giggled, but Laszlo's tone changed when he asked the next question.

"Was it him?"

"Was what whom?"

"Malyshev. Was he the one who 'befriended and betrayed' you?"

Yun-mi sighed. "You are too perceptive for your own good, Las."

Laszlo didn't bat an eye at the contraction of his name. Good, she'd keep using it.

"Did he... hurt you?"

"Not in the way you're implying, no. If he'd tried, I would've killed him myself."

"Just like Parker."

"Just like Parker."

"My Brave Beautiful Flower." His fingers brushed her cheek. "I have to ask. This 'service to the clan'—does it have anything to do with Malyshev's death?"

"Have I already told you you're too perceptive?"

"Wow. You're a dangerous woman, Park Yun-mi. People die around you, left and right."

"Only the wrong sort of people, Laszlo Gabor. Stay in my good graces, and you are safe."

"That sounds suspiciously close to blackmail."

"As intended."

Sauga was more deserted than she'd ever seen an urban area. On the face of it, that had to be a relief. No encounter could go sideways without actually encountering someone. In reality, the effect was deeply unnerving, as if tension suffused the air, and every living soul cowered in its burrow until the danger blew over.

Laszlo checked up on her for the umpteenth time. "You sense it too?"

By way of answer, she dragged an arrow from her quiver and nocked it on her bow's string.

Time went on, and the creepy suspense failed to materialize into a tangible threat. Yun-mi was getting desensitized. She started lowering her bow when a movement caught her eye. In an instant, she was ready to loose once she had the target confirmed. By her side, Laszlo took a knee, aiming his handgun in the same direction.

"Don't shoot! Please don't shoot!" The voice carried panicked and desperate notes. "I'm coming out with my hands up!"

"Don't try anything stupid!" Laszlo yelled back.

A man came around the corner of a house. Middle-aged, brown-skinned, overweight. Bulky clothes, no clear clan identification. His hands were up in the air, as promised, and quivering. "I'm unarmed!"

"We'll see about that," Laszlo muttered, then shouted, "Lean with your hands against the wall! Walk your feet back! Wider!"

The stranger obeyed. Yun-mi and Laszlo approached at different angles, mindful of each other's lines of fire.

Laszlo expertly frisked the man and stepped back. "Who are you?"

"Jamil Khan, I am from The Station—"

In a whirlwind of motion, Laszlo closed the distance again, kicked the man under the knee, dropping him down, grabbed his hair, and put the gun to his temple. "Give me one—one!—reason not to shoot you, slaver!"

The Stationer broke into sobbing, blubbering something unintelligible.

"Reason, dirtbag!" Laszlo jerked the man's head, emphasizing the seriousness of his intentions.

Words came gushing from the prone man underneath him. "I am a merchant, not a slaver! I was going to New Kowloon, but there are armed people everywhere, so many armed people, I was afraid they would shoot me before asking questions! Then I saw you and thought they may let me in with you..."

"Laszlo, wait." Yun-mi touched his shoulder. "Let go of him."

"Why? This is bullshit."

"I don't know what his deal is, but my patron in New Kowloon may be interested in hearing what he's got to say. Hogtie him, so he doesn't pull any dirty tricks. I already had one Stationer trying to trail me before."

"Did he meet an untimely end?"

"Not sure. He was taken back to the Hive for interrogation. If he's still alive, I'd imagine he wishes his end had come sooner."

"No sympathy from me. Fine, I'll follow your lead on this one." Laszlo let go of Jamil's hair, and the Stationer's face dropped into the dirt.

He struggled up onto his haunches, leaning against the wall and panting. "Thank you, young lady! I will make sure your help is well rewarded!"

Yun-mi's stiletto whizzed out of its sheath, and its tip touched the Stationer's throat, forcing his head as far back as the wall behind him permitted.

"I sure as Seven Hells don't need your slaver rewards, you filthy pig, so shut the fuck up!" She spat at his feet.

Laszlo observed her with awe and veneration. "Yeah, I definitely wouldn't want to get on your bad side." He kicked the Stationer's foot. "You, dog's meat. Move it."

Jamil did not lie. The Great Hive bristled with inhospitality. The armed presence around it was by orders of magnitude greater than when she'd left. New Kowloon's full security force must have been under arms.

When Yun-mi and her travel companions showed up on the road to the main entrance, a platoon-sized detachment moved in to intercept.

Paying no heed to the guns pointed at her, Yun-mi stepped forward, keeping her arms where they could be seen by all. "Who's the commanding officer here?"

"Who's asking?" grunted one of the men, answering her question.

"Park Yun-mi. Please inform Golden Dragon Tam Wai Lam that I am here and have a man from The Station with me."

The officer's eyes darted to the two men behind her and unerringly focused on Jamil. The barrel of his gun shifted too, pointing at the Stationer.

"Officer, I am reasonably sure the Golden Dragon would want this man alive. Don't do anything irreversible."

The man's eyes narrowed. "Who do you think you are, to talk to a Kowloonese officer like that?!"

What was it with men in positions of power that led them to question her right to say the things she said? Yun-mi maintained a flat, calm voice, redirecting her anger into the words. "I *think* I am Golden Dragon Tam Wai Lam's agent, on a mission for her. You can either shoot us now and face her guaranteed wrath or stand the fuck down and inform her as I asked."

The officer took a deep breath. "Please follow me," he said with forced ambivalence. "Advise your company not to make any sudden movements."

"Oh, trust me, they know."

Chapter 30

Ka Yi

September 26, 42 PE

Even with a full ten-soldier detail guarding the corridor outside, Wai Lam took no chances. At the knock, she opened the door—this time in her pajamas, not a bathrobe—with a revolver in her hand. The Head of the Hive's Security apologized and reported on his probe into the mystery of bandit training.

Perhaps unsurprisingly, the site of the former boot camp had yielded nothing. It had been cleaned so thoroughly Wu and his best investigators failed to glean a single piece of evidence. Canvassing the nearby villages produced nothing useful either. Yes, the neighbors were aware of something going on in the abandoned cement factory, but had never dared to explore. Wu made sure their fear of New Kowloon exceeded that of the bandits. The locals really knew nothing.

Having hit an impasse in the field, Wu unleashed his sleuths on the archives. The Great Hive was, above all, a bureaucracy. Everything worth registering, potentially worth registering, hardly worth registering, or never warranting a second glance, was meticulously filed and cataloged. If, as the bandits had claimed, they'd been armed with Kowloonese rifles, those should have been easily traceable. Alas, none of the serial numbers matched the registry. Either the firearms had been sourced externally, or—a more troubling hypothesis—someone who knew what they were doing had erased all their tracks. And did this professionally enough to leave no signs of tampering.

"So," Ka Yi asked, "a dead end?"

"Not quite, Golden Dragon. I was about to admit defeat, but remembered to check one last weapon. Along with the rifles, CIU had captured a handgun belonging to the Golden Lions' General. And that's where I hit the jackpot: The gun had been registered to one Yau."

"Siu Ho Fai's confidant?" Ka Yi exchanged dark looks with Wai Lam. This was bad. Bad on too many levels to count. He wished to be proven wrong. Everything would've been much simpler if there weren't traitors in the Hive, and the scheming were solely The Station's.

Dealing with uncertainties was a probabilities game. Yes, he had aced it, but with issues of such importance, having factual information—and not educated guesses—was invaluable. Ka Yi had craved a piece of solid intelligence. Certainty came at a price. No having it both ways. "Is Mister Yau under arrest, Jasper Dragon?"

Wu hesitated. "The matter is too sensitive for me to act on my authority alone. Golden Dragon Siu Ho Fai may argue that his immunity extends to his close associates. I was hoping to get the arrest sanctioned by you, Golden Dragons."

"Sanctioned," Ka Yi and Wai Lam said in unison, and couldn't resist smiling at each other despite the gravity of the situation.

Ka Yi added, "You have preemptive authorization to arrest Siu Ho Fai the moment you get an unequivocal proof of his involvement."

Wu straightened up and bowed formally. "Thank you, Golden Dragons. I will see to this immediately." He shifted his weight but did not leave. "Golden Dragons, I want to bring one more subject to your attention before I go."

"Yes?"

"The rumors regarding your untimely demise, Golden Dragon, and the circumstances leading to it are becoming difficult to contain."

"Doesn't that work to our advantage? Let the enemies stay confused. Throw in some deliberately crafted gossip of your own."

"Understood, Golden Dragon. An implication that Golden Dragon Tam Wai Lam stands behind your death?"

"Brilliant, Jasper Dragon. Make it so."

"Thank you, Golden Dragon. And Golden Dragons... Permission to speak freely?"

"Granted."

"Golden Dragons, forgive me if I am out of line, but once this is over, I would recommend making your, ah, union public before it fuels the next round of gossip."

"Duly noted, Jasper Dragon. That's the plan."

Wu bowed again and left.

Since then, Ka Yi couldn't stop running scenarios in his head. He asked Wai Lam to call the Five Points team for the promised chat. If nothing else, to help keep his mind partially distracted.

Jackson proved to be a sage conversationalist, especially when he picked on the lack of evidence tying Chief Inquisitor to the two attempts on Ka Yi's life. Connecting the fresh scar on Khalifa's neck to possible Kowloonese retribution made Ka Yi further upgrade his estimate of the Fivepointer.

Weinberg's arrival was even more welcome. If there was one person—besides Wai Lam—whom Ka Yi wanted to witness the opening of such a can of worms, it was the captain. If true, the betrayal undoubtedly was New Kowloon's dirtiest laundry. The captain would have learned all about it soon enough. Why not show goodwill and get ahead of the matter while at it?

The news of Marc's abduction by The Station, and of Locksville's treating it as casus belli, had filled Ka Yi with tingling anticipation. The status quo had been broken irrevocably, and the regional power equilibrium was shifting fast. It was, to a great extent, up to Ka Yi to establish the lines along which the future state of affairs would crystalize.

When Wai Lam's personal assistant brought a word of a fresh development from Wu, Ka Yi cut the discussion short. The conversation with Jackson was important. The conversation with Jackson *and* Weinberg—doubly so. But what awaited him in Wu's interrogation room had the potential to shatter the Great Hive's political structure to smithereens and reshape it anew.

Waiting to have his face bandaged to avoid recognition was excruciating, but he didn't argue. To all but a small circle of trust, he was dead, and wanted to keep it that way. But couldn't the guard push his wheelchair faster?

In the interrogation compound, Wu met the Golden Dragons and their two guests. "Yau confessed to conspiring with The Station."

Ka Yi hung his bandaged head. A point of no return. "To what extent?" he asked. Maybe the collusion wasn't too bad?

Wu's report crushed Ka Yi's hopes. "Training of the bandit gangs and your assassination, Golden Dragon. Yet, the man flat-out refused to implicate his patron in the plot. He had been resisting advanced questioning techniques, and even the threat of having his family banished into the wilderness did not move him."

"So, we've got nothing on Siu?" Wai Lam frowned.

Wu afforded one of his rare smiles that made even Ka Yi mildly uncomfortable. "Unbeknownst to him, we brought his wife to observe that phase of inquiry from the next room. She didn't take well to Yau's preference of his patron over her and their children. Madam Yau opened up and spilled plenty of evidence she had overheard at home."

A man entered and whispered into Wu's ear.

The Head of the Hive's Security nodded. "Perfect timing. Golden Dragon Siu Ho Fai just ventured into this compound, to express outrage with his confidant's detention. Conveniently, that spares the embarrassing need to escort him through the Hive."

To his man, he said, "Bring him into the main interrogation room. Wash his assistant's blood off the walls first."

Wu guided the high-ranking observers to their seats on the other side of the one-way window and walked into the room.

The conversation turned entirely anticlimactic. Confronted with the evidence against him, Siu denied nothing. On the contrary, he appeared unapologetic.

Yes, he had conspired with The Station.

Yes, he had arranged for the gangs to be trained.

Yes, having their actions attributed to New Kowloon had been the plan.

Yes, this would be detrimental to New Kowloon's reputation in the short term, but the Hive would reap the benefits in the future.

Yes, this was meant to undermine the authority of certain Golden Dragons in the High Council, and to ultimately remove them from power.

Yes, those were Golden Dragons Shang Ka Yi and Tam Wai Lam.

Yes, when his original plan had fallen short of the expectations, he had agreed to Chief Inquisitor's demands for the physical liquidation of Shang Ka Yi. He had hoped to eliminate Tam Wai Lam too.

Yes, he had been behind the first attempt a year ago, but purely on his own initiative.

Ka Yi glanced at Jackson. Jackson glanced back. Ka Yi inclined his head. No words were necessary.

He drove his wheelchair out of the observation room and into the interrogation chamber. Unhurriedly unwrapping the bandage from his head, Ka Yi watched the traitor's face. He was rewarded with a spark of recognition, followed by a quick flash of horror before the renegade Golden Dragon regained his composure.

"Yes, still alive. No thanks to you."

Siu looked away.

"Why?"

"You were making New Kowloon's trade fleet too strong."

"And that's a bad thing... how?"

"Railroads are the future. We must partner with The Station, not work against them."

"And you needed to weaken New Kowloon to please Khalifa."

"Now you're catching up. New Kowloon is resilient. We can survive a minor downturn, but would thrive tenfold under my influence, once you were removed."

"Yau was to take my place on the Council."

"No, your whore's one."

Ka Yi pushed himself up. Siu observed the painful process with a sneer.

Several things happened in quick succession.

Ka Yi grabbed the handles of his wheelchair and, with a grunt, lifted it into the air.

He heard Wai Lam's scream, "Ka Yi, no!" through the reflective glass.

He noticed Siu's huge eyes and gaping mouth.

He brought the chair down onto the traitor's head.

He blacked out.

The darkness receded. Bright, harsh lights above shone straight into Ka Yi's eyes. He squinted. A face appeared in his field of vision, partially obstructing the lights and making it easier to focus.

Doctor Chen. Stern and unamused. "I would prefer not having to restrain you to your bed, Golden Dragon, but I will if you force me. Do you remember the recuperation regimen I prescribed?"

"I do, doctor. Technically, I broke none of your instructions. I wasn't exercising, and I was fully clothed when fighting."

"Doctor, did he suffer brain damage?" asked Weinberg's disembodied voice. "What is this nonsense he's blabbering?"

"Don't mind him. It's an inside joke." Another voice, trembling with narrowly contained anger. Wai Lam. "He must've been brain-damaged already. If there had been anything to damage in that thick skull of his."

"Hey, I can hear you, you know." Ka Yi attempted to sit up, but Doctor Chen braced him down.

"Good! I mean every word!" Wai Lam still seethed.

"Aw." Weinberg wouldn't be himself if he'd resisted commenting. "Your squabbling is so adorable! Have to say, discovering you two are an item was the highlight of my day. Eclipsed almost drowning, and the enormity of the other revelations in this room."

That reminded Ka Yi where he was, and what had happened. "Where's Siu? Did I..."

"No." Wu, who had abstained from the sensitive parts of the conversation, answered the less loaded question. "Bloody and shaken, scared shitless, if you forgive my bluntness, but not dead. Taken to a solitary cell under triple guard. My people are now running background checks on everyone who might have been involved. We will get to the bottom of this treason, Golden Dragon."

Ka Yi relaxed. As much as he wished the bastard dead, Siu possessed information crucial for repairing the damage. A shame it could only be extracted if he was alive.

Two of Wu's men showed up with a stretcher and transferred Ka Yi under Doctor Chen's close supervision. He had his face re-bandaged and was taken back to Wai Lam's quarters. Not to the reception room where the remaining Fivepointers and Locksvillers were still waiting, but to her private bedroom.

Once everyone else had vacated the room, Wai Lam sat by his side and cupped his cheek. "My stupid, stupid knight. I love you, Ka Yi, you know that, right? But if you ever try something so reckless again, I'll wring your neck myself." Her hand closed on Ka Yi's throat in a graphic demonstration.

"But—"

"No 'buts'. I need you alive, you hear me? He called me a whore, so what? You don't think I've been called worse?"

"He threatened your life."

"And how would your dying of internal bleeding have protected me?"

Ka Yi lowered his eyelids.

"Don't get me wrong, *husband*, it's charming and sexy that you let your hormones get the better of you when my honor is on the line, but—"

"No 'buts'."

She kissed him. Then shifted away and pointed a finger at him. "Don't forget! I'll strangle you! You know I can!"

"Oh yeah. I saw you do that. Will you be naked? Then it may be worth a shot."

"Men." Wai Lam sighed percussively.

"You called me 'husband'."

"I guess I did. Had to get back at you."

"So, that's it? Just like that?"

"Why, are you having second thoughts, Golden Dragon? Or do you doubt my commitment?"

"Gods forbid, Golden Dragon. Neither. I was only curious if you'd like a ceremony of some sort."

"Nah, I'm good. Screw them all."

"I'll drink to that!"

"You won't be drinking to anything until Doctor Chen says you can."

"And so, the family life begins. The wife dictates, the husband obeys."

"You've got *that* right." She nestled against his side and murmured, "I love you, Golden Dragon Shang Ka Yi. Have I already mentioned that?"

"I vaguely recall something along those lines. But it never hurts to hear again, Golden Dragon Tam Wai Lam. As a reminder."

A soft knock on the door elicited a low growl from Wai Lam. "Oh, come on! Really?!"

Mei Yan, Wai Lam's assistant, entered, preemptively bent at the waist. "My most profound apologies, Golden Dragon! It's... Park Yun-mi is here..."

"So? She couldn't wait until I'm available?!"

"Sorry, Golden Dragon, she also brought a trader from The Station with her, and I thought—"

"She what?"

Mei Yan's voice trailed away, down to an imperceptible whisper. Ka Yi barely made out the words. Poor girl was prepared to be torn limb from limb and had resigned to that fate. "A trader, Golden Dragon... From The Station..."

Wai Lam was already at the door. She patted her bowed assistant on the back. "Good call, Mei Yan."

"Hey!" cried Ka Yi. "Where are you going without me?"

Wai Lam turned. "Let me make sense of this first, then I'll loop you in. No reason for a Stationer to see you alive yet."

She left, trailed by Mei Yan.

So many developments he needed to internalize. The new political realities, and the next play against The Station. Weinberg and this tricky Jackson guy. Wu rounding up the remaining conspirators. But none competed against the three words: *Nah, I'm good.* Ka Yi wasn't the same implacable Golden Dragon he used to be. Ever since discovering his feelings for Wai Lam, he was getting sentimental. And did not regret the change.

With the central role traditions played in New Kowloon's society, a couple had to follow a convoluted ritual to pronounce themselves husband and wife. Wai Lam effectively defied all that. "Nah, I'm good" was the weirdest way of saying "I do" Ka Yi could imagine. The most Wai Lam way.

Chapter 31

Yun-mi

September 26, 42 PE

"So, on top of everything else, you're also a magician?" The wrinkles around Laszlo's eyes betrayed a hint of a smile on an otherwise perfectly straight face. "You snap your fingers and a real Golden Dragon appears out of nowhere?"

"Just about," responded a sardonic voice behind their backs. "It helps if you throw a Stationer into the hat."

Yun-mi jumped to her feet, turned, and bowed. Laszlo, not without brief hesitation, followed suit.

"Good to see you, Park Yun-mi," said Wai Lam. "Although I didn't expect you back so soon, and yet with a man from The Station in tow."

Wai Lam was glad to see her. The only part that mattered, the rest was noise. Before Yun-mi realized what she was doing, her legs carried her forward. She hugged the Golden Dragon, squeezing out a surprised yelp. After a momentary delay, Wai Lam returned the hug. Yun-mi released the woman and stepped back. "Please don't break my arm, Golden Dragon," she said with a mischievous grin. She wasn't ashamed in the least.

Laszlo didn't see Yun-mi's face, but heard her words. He moved closer with an obvious intent to intervene if her arm were to be endangered.

"I'll let it slide this one time, Park Yun-mi." Wai Lam allowed a guarded smile, too. "Now, why don't you introduce your overprotective companion?"

"Yes, of course, Golden Dragon. Sorry. Meet Laszlo Gabor, a Humber Bay Raccoons' Triumvir."

"How interesting! Welcome to New Kowloon, Triumvir Gabor. What brings you here? Besides the apparent interest in ensuring Miss Park's wellbeing, that is."

Yun-mi hijacked the conversation before Laszlo could say a word. "The Triumvirate is ready to negotiate with the Great Hive, Golden Dragon! They ask that you send senior officials to clarify the proposed agreement. Laszlo has the details."

Wai Lam and Laszlo regarded her with similar expressions. Like proud but amused parents would an eager youngster. She blushed. "Apologies, Golden Dragon. That was immature. Mister Gabor, please go ahead."

Laszlo graced her with a mocking bow. "Thank you, Miss Park. Golden Dragon, it is an honor. Your emissary here"—he winked at Yun-mi in blatant disregard of proper protocol—"speaks highly of you. I look forward to having an in-depth discussion of your proposals. But with all the unusual activity around, you must be awfully busy. I will gladly accept any proxy negotiators you may deem appropriate to assign."

Wai Lam eyed him benevolently. "Thank you for being so accommodating, Mister Gabor. This is my personal project, and I would love to discuss it with you myself. You are right, a lot is going on here at the moment. What is your schedule like? How long will you be able to stay?"

"It's flexible, Golden Dragon. I've got no pressing commitments elsewhere, and will be happy to stay here with Miss Park until your time becomes available."

"Will you?" A smile touched her lips again. She knew that he knew that she knew. Laszlo held his ground and did not avert his eyes.

Wai Lam nodded to Yun-mi. "Good for you. Now, if you don't mind, may we switch subjects? Tell me about this alleged trader from The Station. Alas, this takes precedence for us here. No disrespect, Mister Gabor, I'm sure you'll understand."

"No problem, Golden Dragon, I do. About that trader..." He succinctly retold their encounter on the outskirts of New Kowloon. "It's obvious he didn't tell us all the truth, Golden Dragon, but whatever he told, I am reasonably sure is the truth."

Wai Lam looked at Yun-mi. "Miss Park, your assessment?"

Yun-mi was flattered to be asked for her opinion. "I agree. He didn't strike me as a type to come up with such elaborate lies when someone puts a gun to his head, and he all but pisses himself."

Laszlo chuckled. "I hoped to spare the juicy details from the Golden Dragon."

"Please don't, Mister Gabor," said Wai Lam. "You'll be surprised how little can make me squeamish. Any detail, on the other hand, may prove crucial. Speaking of which, why was your gun pointed at his head?"

Laszlo looked abashed by the question. "Golden Dragon, when I heard he was from The Station... my instincts got the better of me. I really, really don't like the slavers. It's a clan thing, I guess."

"Excellent. I also really, really don't like the slavers, Mister Gabor. It's a New Kowloon thing, I guess."

Wai Lam examined him with a new regard. "We may find more mutual interests than I had expected, Mister Gabor."

Yun-mi fought back a surge of irrational jealousy. They cannot connect! Laszlo was *hers*!

"As a token of my appreciation," continued Wai Lam, oblivious to Yun-mi's narrowed eyes, "I invite you to observe the interrogation of your Stationer."

"Thank you, Golden Dragon. That exceeds everything I could hope for."

Yun-mi opened her mouth, but Wai Lam preempted her. "Yes, Miss Park, you too."

As they marched down the corridor under heavy guard, Wai Lam said, "Mister Gabor, in the interest of full disclosure, I must inform you I had engaged the services of one Jim Parker from your clan. Will this be an issue?"

"Parker's private dealings were his, and his alone, Golden Dragon. My only concern is that you don't form your opinion of our clan based on him."

"No danger of that with you here, Mister Gabor."

"Then it is settled."

"May he rot in the Seven Hells," added Yun-mi under her breath. They heard.

The Stationer behind the glass wall was sweating. A lot.

"Is it hot in there? Or is he nervous?" Yun-mi asked.

"Both. We pump hot air into the room to make him uncomfortable." The man who responded had been introduced by Wai Lam as Wu, the Head of the Hive's Security. Yun-mi was mortified, and happy she wasn't the one to be questioned by him. She had a vivid memory of the Singh brothers extolling Wu's interrogation skills, as well as the captured Station officer's reaction to his name. His overt disapproval of Yun-mi's and Laszlo's presence did not contribute to her comfort. The topics likely to come up were far too sensitive to be exposed to random outsiders, he said. Even to the people who had brought the subject to him.

Wai Lam agreed with his assessment—and overruled it. Yun-mi's opinion of her, already sky-high, grew by another increment.

Two manifestly non-Kowloonese men were in the room. The Golden Dragon presented them as Weinberg of Locksville and Jackson of Five Points. Meaningless names. But those outsiders were not random, if the Head of the Security had no objections to their presence. Yun-mi was stepping into the middle of something big.

According to Wu's report, the Stationer had been thoroughly searched. No weapons, or anything conceivably weaponizable, were found on him. His clothes were replaced with Hive-issued ones, to rule out the possibility those were suffused with poison. On top of these precautions, Jamil Khan's hands and feet were chained to a metal chair bolted to the floor.

"Doesn't he see us?" Yun-mi tried to catch the captive's eye, but he kept looking through her.

"No," responded the man named Weinberg, sitting to her left. "It's a one-way window. From his side, it's a mirror."

"Huh." An impressive setup.

"Miss... Park, right?"

"Yes?"

"You are what in the City they call a Rat, no?"

"Yes."

"How charming! I always wanted to meet one. Maybe someday—when the dust settles down—you won't mind taking me on a guided tour?"

"Maybe. If Golden Dragon considers that a good idea."

"Ah, so you're a Golden Dragon's Rat."

"That is an oxymoron, Mister Weinberg. I am no one's Rat. Rats can only be affiliated, never owned."

Weinberg's eyebrows crept up. Didn't expect a City Rat to throw around words like *oxymoron* or *affiliated*, huh?

"I see. Apologies if my words have offended you, Miss Park. From my side, I'd be delighted to see you in Locksville when you get a chance. I am sure the Golden Dragon won't mind."

Yun-mi half-closed her eyes. "Mister Weinberg, let me get this straight. Is that a genuine proposal, or are you trying to get into my pants?"

Weinberg coughed, exaggerating his reaction a bit too dramatically. Laszlo, sitting on Yun-mi's other side, snorted. He had a first-hand knowledge of how abrasive she may get. The Locksviller was about to discover.

"As genuine as it gets. What gave you the idea it could be anything else?"

"It's possible I misread the signs. Anyhow, thanks for the invitation. If Mister Gabor finds it interesting, I may consider joining him."

The other foreigner, Jackson, leaned forward to get an unobstructed view of her. "Do you, by any chance, have a long-lost redhead sister? I'm pretty sure I've got your twin on my team."

Yun-mi didn't deign to respond but made a mental mark to check out that redhead twin later.

Weinberg shed his artificial luster. "This conversation started on the wrong foot," he said in a less jovial tone. "I would be interested in having a serious talk with the two of you before we part ways. I'll ask the Golden Dragon to arrange this. In the meantime, the show is about to begin."

He pointed through the window where Wai Lam and Wu took the seats across the table from Khan, and opened a damper in the wall. Sounds from behind the glass filled the observation room.

The Stationer didn't wait to be prompted. His first words left his lips before the interrogators' behinds touched their respective chairs. "Jamil Khan. My name is Jamil Khan. Senior Master of the Trade Guild." He looked at the Kowloonese, gauging the effect of his title, expecting them to introduce themselves. Both stayed silent and kept professionally indifferent expressions.

"I am here of my free will, yes? No need for all this," the Stationer rattled the restraints holding his wrists. "But I understand the precautions. I came to help, yes?"

Still failing to evoke a response, Jamil went on with his blathering. "You must wonder how I can help, and why. And why you should believe a word of what I say. And I can't blame you, yes? I wouldn't believe me either if I were you. Maybe I am a secret agent sent here to poison your minds with misinformation, yes?" He giggled.

His routine of ending each sentence with a "yes?" was becoming irritating.

"Is this going anywhere? You can stop describing what you think we believe and start telling us something we don't know." Wu spoke with minimal use of mimic muscles. In conjunction with his unblinking eyes, this made the Stationer fidget.

"Yes, kind sir, of course! I was getting there, yes. I took a huge, colossal risk coming here. If the Chief Inquisitor found out, he would have had me killed, after torturing me for days. Compared to his basement, this"—he shook his shackles again—"is nothing. I welcome this, because I know I am talking to reasonable people, yes?"

Yun-mi facepalmed. The idiot was not helping his case.

Wu was tiring of the charade, too. "Is this going—"

"Yes, sir, sorry, sir," Jamil rushed to interrupt. "Here's a question. Do you know that The Station was once a Trade Republic, sir?"

"Yes."

"Great, I knew I was talking to knowledgeable people! Did you also know that the institute of lifers and workers was established not fifteen years ago?"

"You mean, slavery. Yes."

"Well, some would call it that."

"Everybody calls it that. Except for The Station."

"Ah, yes, sir, and that is part of the reason I'm here. The Guild is not happy with what has become of The Station. Many of us remember the good old times when the Trade Guild had run our affairs, and not a clique of bloodthirsty Inquisitors. We do not condone the... ah, slavery, yes? We find it detrimental to our reputation among the trade partners. But most of all, we are worried by how the Chief Inquisitor has been spinning out of control lately. This ongoing feud with New Kowloon, the resulting attacks on our trains and the caravan... This doesn't benefit anyone, yes?"

"No, it does not. And you are here because..."

"Our faction is ready to help you remove Chief Inquisitor Khalifa."

"*Remove?*"

"Remove, yes."

"As in..."

"As in, whatever it takes, sir."

Everyone in the observation room held their breath through the long pause. Wai Lam spoke first. "Any proof?"

"Ma'am?" The Stationer looked confused. Yun-mi waited for Wai Lam or Wu to correct him, but both ignored the improper salutation.

"Can you prove the existence of a faction that wants to *remove* Khalifa? That the actual plot is not to draw New Kowloon in? To implicate us as an aggressor meddling in another state's internal affairs? That this is not the Chief Inquisitor's desperate play to recover from his failed schemes with the bandit gangs?"

"Wait... What? Ma'am, what are you talking about? That was *him*?!" Jamil's posture changed. He straightened. His face contorted. "He's gone off the rails completely! He needs to be stopped, immediately!" Droplets of spit flew around.

Did *going off the rails* have a special meaning for the Railroad people?

The primary effect Jamil's reaction had achieved was that Yun-mi believed him now. Much harder to convincingly fake anger than fear.

Wai Lam was not so easily persuaded. "You did not answer my questions, Jamil Khan. If that is your real name."

The detainee wasn't cowering anymore. "I am sorry, Ma'am, I've got no such proof. I am here, though, at your mercy. That should count for something, no?"

He switched from ending his phrases with a "yes" to a "no". Had he resigned to his fate, whatever it might be? Had he reached the end of his rope? Or was he sure his words would eventually be accepted?

"Maybe. Maybe not. Knowing Khalifa for the homicidal maniac he is, would you take it past him to surrender a pawn to win a gambit?"

"I am not a pawn, Ma'am."

Wai Lam kept staring at him coldly. Jamil dropped his eyes. "I see your point. But you have my word, Ma'am."

"Yeah, well. Forgive me if I am unconvinced."

"I understand, Ma'am. I suspected the word of a Stationer might not carry much weight here. So, what is it going to be?"

"We'll need time to verify your information through our channels."

"Of course, Ma'am."

"Now, what kind of help exactly are you offering?"

"We can assist with smuggling people into The Station. We can inform you when Chief Inquisitor leaves the premises, along with his itinerary. Once he's taken out of the picture, the Guild is prepared to step in, to prevent a power vacuum. When we get the reins back, we will be happy to enter negotiations for establishing a mutually beneficial framework of agreements between our states."

"Mutually beneficial, huh?"

"Yes, Golden Dragon."

Yun-mi started. Wai Lam smiled. A smile that could curdle milk.

"Yes, Ma'am," Jamil said, "I've figured out who you are. I did my homework."

"Then you should know not to call me 'Ma'am'."

"Are you going to punish me for that?"

"Nah. I am not petty. But if I decide to punish you in the end, this will count toward your transgressions. In the meantime, Senior Master Jamil Khan, I welcome you to New Kowloon. Enjoy your stay in the most luxurious holding cell the Great Hive has to offer."

She rose and left the interrogation chamber, followed by a silent Wu. Three guards entered, unlocked Jamil's restraints, put his arms and feet in manacles, and escorted him out.

Wai Lam returned to the observation room. "Thoughts?"

Weinberg rubbed his chin. "Tim was the last to visit The Station."

Jackson—whose name was, apparently, Tim—returned the ball. "Your Marc and Rajan were the last. Why don't we ask them?"

"Sure," Weinberg agreed suspiciously easily.

"I see," said Wai Lam. "You two are useless. Miss Park?"

Yun-mi was taken aback.

Scared of being called out on par with the adults? You are an adult. Start acting like one, dammit!

"I believe him." She nodded decisively.

"Mister Gabor?" The Golden Dragon's eyes found the last person in the room.

"Concur." Laszlo used fewer words than Yun-mi.

Wai Lam pursed her lips. "The street smarts say he's legit, while the great paragons of Intelligence Service reserve their judgment. Figures. Alright, Weinberg, let's see what your escapees have got to add. And update Shang Ka Yi, he must be climbing the walls with unsatisfied curiosity."

In the hallways of the Hive, Wai Lam slowed down, letting Weinberg and Jackson go ahead. She wedged between Yun-mi and Laszlo. "Mister Gabor, may I steal your companion for a minute? I promise to return her with all her limbs intact."

Yun-mi matched her stride, and the two fell behind the men. The trailing detail of their armed escort followed at a respectful distance.

"You must think I'm neglecting your accomplishments in the City, Yun-mi."

The thought had not crossed Yun-mi's mind, but with the suggestion voiced, it drew forth a nagging discomfort whose existence she had not acknowledged. Turned out, the Golden Dragon understood her better than she did herself.

"You did amazingly well, Yun-mi. I'm proud of you, and happy I put my trust in you. I can't wait to hear the rest of your report, including that unorthodox alliance deal the Singh brothers informed me about, but we'll have to postpone that. The crisis with The Station takes precedence over everything else right now. Still, I wanted you to know this doesn't diminish your achievements."

"I understand, Golden Dragon. Thank you! I... don't know what to say. No one has ever appreciated what I did."

"Their loss, my gain."

"Would it be too inappropriate if I hug you again? You promised not to break my limbs..."

"I did, but yes, that would be highly inappropriate. Please don't make that a habit. I am still your boss."

"I'm sorry, Golden Dragon."

"No, you aren't. But speaking of hugging... If this Mister Gabor of yours ever crosses any line you don't want him to, let me know. I'll make him disappear, Triumvir or not."

"Oh, nothing of the sort, Golden Dragon. He... he's the best man I've ever met. Really. It took some convincing to *make* him cross a line or two. Also—I know you don't have time—I kind of caused a change of rulership in Islington. Had to do with the previous ruler crossing the wrong line."

"Islington, huh? Aren't you full of surprises?"

"I'm trying my best for you, Golden Dragon."

"Why, thank you, Miss Park!"

"I plan to go back to Islington after we're done here. They invited me and promised help, so we have a better shot at negotiating an agreement now."

"Impressive, Miss Park, very impressive. But Islington will have to wait. I've got a different assignment for you right now."

"You have? What is it?"

"All in due time, Miss Park. You'll know soon."

Chapter 32

Rajan

September 26, 42 PE

Rajan's whole train hauler experience could be summed up as "hurry up and wait". He'd never had a problem with the waiting part. It was the bone-crushing, soul-eating, mind-numbing hurrying up that made him shudder at the recollection.

The wait in New Kowloon was luxurious. Not by comparison to the meager standards of his daily routine as The Station's "worker", but by pretty much anyone's. Quiet, warm room; comfortable seating; plenty of food and drinks to reach out and fetch from the table. And if he'd desired something that wasn't there, it would be provided upon his request.

Rajan did not test that theory. His superstitions whispered that what he had already gotten was too good to be true, and he shouldn't be pressing his luck. Besides, what else could he want? Growing up in a sheepherders' family, then spending his teenage years as a slave, he hadn't developed a taste for anything but the basics. He had yet to get used to being safe, dry, and fed. Once he did—and that was going to take a while—he'd ask Marc for further guidance.

By his side, Marc engaged in a quiet conversation with Buck, enjoying the downtime, sipping apple cider, and nurturing his mutilated hand. Rajan's newly found brother-in-arms had an infinite capacity to wait, from training, if not by nature.

Kossowsky, by contrast, exhibited growing levels of anxiousness. He had his mission, whatever it was, and the detour kept him from completing it. Being forced to sit idly and wait for the higher-ups did not help. The officer sprang to his feet and paced the length of the room. After a while, he would meet a disapproving glance from Janet and force himself to sit back down. Janet would return to her book—until the next burst of the lieutenant's frenetic activity.

The last man, Lundy, brazenly abused Kowloonese hospitality. He had rung the bell several times, and the servants showed up without fail, bowing and listening to new instructions. In short order, the side table by Lundy's armchair was bursting with fruit, drinks, and meats, most of which Rajan couldn't name. Noticing Rajan's attention, Lundy shrugged. "We only live once, eh? Those bastards ain't gonna get any poorer if I take a sample of their pantry."

He raised a cup to toast Rajan. Rajan inclined his head. Should he try some, too? When would he get another chance?

He was rising from his chair when the main doors opened, letting in the big shots—Weinberg, Jackson, the Golden Dragon lady—and two people he hadn't seen before. One was a Chinese girl, the other—a burly man, one sight of whom sent goosebumps up Rajan's arms. There was something of hardened lifers and ruthless supervisors in him at once. Not someone to meet in a dark alley behind the warehouses. The man discreetly scanned the room, taking measure of everyone present. He paused on Lundy longer than the others. Meeting his eyes, Rajan nodded. With a brief delay, the man nodded back, and Rajan remembered to exhale. The Great Hive was a safe place, but that man had unnerved him, and it was oddly relieving to be rendered a non-threat.

The girl was unlike any he'd seen. Not that he'd seen too many Chinese girls. New Hope and The Station had none. The first time he saw one was on a hauling trip, somewhere on the far side of the Niagara River. And then there were the servant girls in New Kowloon. This one looked their age, although guessing Chinese girls' ages was a fool's errand. They all looked too young. Even the Golden Dragon did not appear old enough to hold any office, least of all the highest in the Hive. Unsure, Rajan placed this unknown girl in the same age group with the servants—and with himself. Yet she could be anything but a servant. Head held high, ironic eyes glittering with challenge—and weapons. Lots and lots of weapons. No, definitely not a servant.

"Sorry for keeping you waiting." The Golden Dragon's voice carried around the room with no noticeable effort. Every head turned toward her. "Mister Jackson, Mister Kossowsky." She acknowledged the two with curt nods. "I shall not waste any more of your time. We are grateful to your team for the invaluable service to New Kowloon. You have asked for someone to guide you around Downtown, and I am happy to offer you the help of Park Yun-mi, who knows that area inside out."

Rajan followed the direction of the Golden Dragon's introductory gesture, to discover she was pointing not at the scary man, but at the girl.

"Golden Dragon?" The girl arched her eyebrows, as surprised as Rajan.

"Miss Park, please treat this as a personal assignment."

The girl bowed, not as deep as the servants had, but with enough deference. "Yes, Golden Dragon." She asked no questions.

"Mister Gabor, should you choose to accompany Miss Park, I will understand completely. My door will be open to you whenever you return."

"Thank you, Golden Dragon." The scary man's awkward bow revealed how little practice he'd had. "I am honored."

"I will let the Five Points team brief you on the pertinent details. Mister Jackson, will you be leaving with your team, or staying here to see the resolution of our current crisis?"

Jackson hesitated with an answer. "I'll follow the team, Golden Dragon," he conceded. "But once we're done with our business, I would love to return here."

"Very well. You may leave now to confer with Miss Park. If you decide to postpone your expedition to the morning, your rooms are still at your disposal."

"Thank you, Golden Dragon. Sounds wise." Jackson bowed and waved to his team. Or the lieutenant's team. It was still confusing who exactly was in charge of that odd company.

The Fivepointers plodded out, with Kossowsky thanking the Golden Dragon for her hospitality, and Buck shaking Marc's healthy hand farewell.

Tam Wai Lam turned to Rajan's boss. "Help me bring Shang Ka Yi here?"

Weinberg accompanied her through an inconspicuous side door. A minute later, the two reappeared, pushing a wheeled bed with the other Golden Dragon.

"Company, at last! You can't imagine how glad I am to see you all! I started dreading my wife had placed me in solitary confinement!"

"That would've been only fitting, Golden Dragon, given your erratic behavior. But it's your lucky day, I feel kind and compassionate."

Yeah, right. Not exactly the first words coming to mind to describe her.

Then Rajan heard the wildest story of a defector from The Station.

"Marc, Rajan—your experience with The Station is the freshest," said the lady Dragon. "Thoughts?"

Weinberg nodded to Rajan, encouraging him to answer.

Rajan shrugged. "Sorry, Ma'am... I mean, Golden Dragon. We workers don't mingle with traders. They travel on the trains we haul, but never talk to us. And, vero, what's there to talk about? We know nada about nada, and they care nada how we get them from place to place."

"And what can you say about the traders' relationships with the Inquisitors?"

"Golden Dragon, we workers can see Inquisitors only inside the prison, and sure pray that never happens. Not many saw one and lived to tell."

"I see. Marc, have you anything to add?"

"No, Golden Dragon, I'm afraid not. I had an opportunity to chat with some Inquisitors lately, but we did not discuss the traders. It touched on a few other, dare I say, vitally important things"—he caressed his ribs and winced—"but none related to this subject."

"Sorry to hear you've experienced The Station's infamous hospitality first-hand, Marc," said Shang Ka Yi, then frowned. "Forgive me. That came out wrong. I'll make sure our best doctor examines you once we're done here."

"Now, gentlemen," intervened his wife, "seeing that you won't be able to corroborate Jamil Khan's story, I'd like to ask you a different question. Assuming this is not an elaborate trap—and, I must admit, it sounds too elaborate for that bloody butcher Khalifa—let's grant for a moment that Khan is telling the truth. What do you make of his ideas? Specifically, Rajan, I would be interested to hear your opinion on abolishing slavery. I mean, I'm sure you'd welcome that, same as any sane person, but how will that affect The Station's ability to move goods along their railways?"

Rajan had never considered such a possibility. All he'd ever known was trains hauled by workers and lifers. As appalling as that was, he could picture no other reality. "Golden Dragon, you say they didn't use no slave labor before?"

"Not until fifteen years ago."

"How they moved the trains then?"

"Shang Ka Yi? I wouldn't know, that was before my time."

"I may look feeble at the moment, Golden Dragon, dear, but I am not that old. That was before my time, too. Still, I know they used to employ hired labor, paying for it handsomely and operating with slim margins."

"I suppose they can fall back to that model," Tam Wai Lam stroked her jaw, "but that'll cause an inevitable slowdown while they set this all up and attract enough voluntary labor. Not an easy task, considering their reputation."

"Golden Dragon?" Rajan raised a hand.

"Please, Mister Gupta."

"A year ago, I heard something... I'm sorry if it sounds un poco loco... Hamid, told me he learned... not important how... that the Marshals could build a machine to haul trains. He said a Master was talking about that. And..." His jaw dropped, and his heart skipped a beat. Everyone's eyes were on him, but he couldn't say a word.

"... And, Mister Gupta?" prompted Tam Wai Lam.

Rajan took control of his mouth, but his heart kept racing. "They executed him two weeks after. Tortured and executed, horribly. I still have nightmares, I do. Didn't connect the two things then, but now I see. He told someone else, and that someone snitched on him. When he told me, I didn't believe. I mean, who would? But if Masters killed him for that, means it was all true!"

His revelation was met with a ringing silence.

Shang Ka Yi spoke first. "That may be possible. If we can put engines on our ships, they could do the same with trains. But if they've got the knowledge, why aren't they using it?"

"Because they follow the Faith," responded Weinberg. "They're sitting on the technology until the pragmatists see a chance to prevail. Which may happen any time."

"Have you heard anything about this?" Shang Ka Yi asked Weinberg. "You know everything worth knowing."

The Head of Locksville's Intelligence smiled sadly. "I'm flattered, but there appears to be a glaring gap in the info I'm getting from The Station. Either it's a hoax, or they keep this card too close to their chest. Which explains the summary execution of Rajan's friend, to discourage anyone with the knowledge from running their mouth ever again."

"But if that's true ..." Tam Wai Lam's face darkened. "They'll increase their transportation volumes exponentially."

"Yes," Shang Ka Yi said gravely, "and put us out of business."

"Unless we sign an agreement with The Station, as Khan suggests. Obviously, with Khalifa in power, that's impossible. That leads us to the only plausible conclusion..."

"We take the bait."

"We take the bait. And screw the consequences."

Chapter 33

Buck

September 26, 42 PE

The rooms assigned to the Fivepointers had been plenty spacious until seven people crammed into one. Every surface that could be used for sitting was claimed. Without asking, the Golden Dragon's girl commandeered the chair by the table. Her silent partner towered behind her. Jackson took the other chair; Lundy, faithful to habit, usurped the only armchair in the room; Janet and the lieutenant shared the sofa. Buck was left standing, but didn't mind. The curiosity bubbling inside him wouldn't have let him sit quietly, anyway.

"What shall we call you?" asked Jackson.

"Miss Park will be fine." She didn't bother asking their names.

Not much into familiarity, are we?

The silence that followed stretched beyond the point of Buck's comfort. "You really live in the City?" he blurted.

"Yes." She appeared amused by Buck's disbelief.

"Many Chinese outside New Kowloon?"

The girl drew her chin up, piercing Buck with her eyes. "I am Korean, not Chinese!"

"Cu... Corie-Ann?" Did he hear right?

The man behind Miss Park smirked and patted her on the back of the neck. "Payback for Hungary," he muttered cryptically.

She frowned. "Ko-re-an."

"Oh. Right," said Buck, as if that explained anything, "Ko-re-an. And your home is, uh, Downtown?"

"No one lives Downtown. Not since the E. A small clan on the Centre Island, but they barely survive. And it isn't Downtown proper."

"But you are an urban zombie, no?"

The girl leaned her forehead into her palm, as if attacked by a migraine.

Her companion grimaced. "I know people from outside the City routinely use this name, but we find it offensive." He put a hand on Miss Park's shoulder, and she gratefully covered it with hers.

How could Buck know? "I'm so sor—"

"Do you know where the word 'zombie' comes from?"

Her question caught Buck unprepared. He shook his head, afraid to ask.

"It's an ancient legend. Involves dark magic used to bring people back from the dead. These undead then hunt the living for their brains. *Arrrr!!!*" Her hand clawed at Buck. He recoiled, stumbling.

The girl giggled and looked up at her companion. "To think *these* people consider *us* savages." Then, to Buck, "Do I look like someone who'd want to eat your brain?"

The intimidating man—Gabor? Was that what the Golden Dragon had called him?—hid a crooked smile in his beard and murmured, "Sometimes you very much do, Miss Park. Occasionally, you scare the living daylights out of me."

"Why, thanks for your support," she grumbled.

"Hey, that's a compliment!" The man spread his arms.

"Yeah, right."

Buck finally regained composure. "Again, I'm sorry, Miss Park, I didn't know."

She dismissed him with a wave of a hand. "Don't sweat it, kid."

Kid? Kid?! What did she think... Buck swallowed his indignation and chose the wisdom of silence over confrontation.

Janet picked up the conversation where he had dropped it so ineptly. "If not a zombie, what *do* you call yourself?"

Miss Park... No, no way he kept calling her that! She had to be younger than him! Just an arrogant girl with a big mouth! Like one other girl he knew, the one sitting on the sofa. Park. She'd be Park. That was her name, no? Park You-what? Park You-and-me? No, that couldn't be right. Although... Who knows what kind of strange names they may have in the City? Maybe it was a Ko-re-an thing. Park it was.

Park shrugged. "A human? A person? A woman? What do *you* call yourself?" The point was well made.

The lieutenant joined the verbal melee. "If you don't live Downtown, how do you know your way around it?"

"'Cause I'm a Rat, obviously."

Another pause made the air in the room thick. Buck, Janet, and the lieutenant exchanged puzzled looks. Jackson studied Park with a hint of a smile. And Lundy... Lundy was being Lundy. Sunken in the armchair and indifferent to the goings-on around him. At least not snoring. Yet.

"Let me get this straight." Janet shook her head. "Calling you a zombie is a no-no, but a *rat* is okay?"

"They don't know." Gabor sighed.

"They don't know," agreed Park. "They know fuck all about the City, I can see that now."

"Please enlighten us," suggested Jackson, finally making himself useful.

"Being a Rat is a job," the scar-faced man explained, "and a calling. We explore the City. Scavenge it. Hunt it. Roam it. Know it. *Live* it."

"I see," Jackson replied thoughtfully. "Thank you, Mister Gabor, that's most insightful. Miss Park, you're absolutely right. As you've eloquently put it, we know fuck all about the City. Some other places—a fair bit, but not the City. That is why we need your help. Well, *someone's* help, and the Golden Dragon, in her kindness, offered us your services."

Pretty transparent. Enough with the games.

Park's face grew serious. Her posture changed. A predator tracking the prey right before it pounces.

"Alright," she said, "talk."

Jackson half-turned, inviting Janet to outline the task at hand.

Janet sighed. "We need to find the Seven Hells."

Buck held his breath.

The girl's reaction was anticlimactic. "Huh?" She cocked her head. "Say *what*?"

Her companion, who'd been leaning with his elbows on the back of her chair, straightened up with a disapproving scowl. "Is this some sick joke?"

Jackson angled forward. "I take it you don't know such a place."

Gabor chuckled mirthlessly. "Everybody knows the Seven Hells, even us urban zombies—"

"It's where you can go if you don't quit making fun of us," Park finished for him. Probably not what the man had intended to say, but together they made the sentiment clear.

"Hmm." Jackson scratched his chin. "Let's start over, shall we? Janet?"

Janet sighed deeper. "I have a reason to believe the place *is* real. And it is somewhere Downtown."

Park and Gabor exchanged dark looks. "Go on," said the girl, "what do you know?"

"I found a book." Janet hesitated, staring at Park. "Do you know what a book is?"

The City girl pursed her lips, irately rummaged in the backpack under her feet, produced a book of her own, and dropped it onto the table with a startlingly loud clap. "Yes, bitch," she snarled, tilting her head. "I know what a book is!"

Janet's cheeks turned crimson.

Buck had had enough. He was still seething from the brain-eating humiliation. "Can we stop calling each other names?"

Park opened her mouth—to say something caustic, no doubt—but Gabor's hand squeezed her shoulder and she swallowed the response.

This was easily one of the most important conversations in Buck's life, yet his mind drifted away. This girl... He'd met no one like her. Not even Janet. Not because of her being Korean, whatever that meant, or how she looked. Because of what she was. Janet, a rebel too, knew how to fall back into the mold of society's expectations, when forced. Park—*didn't have* a mold. Feisty. Independent. Cocky. Not pretty—not to Buck's taste. But her amazing *essence* eclipsed everything.

A dangerous line of thinking. Stop.

She already had a partner; one Buck wouldn't dare challenge in his wildest fantasies.

"No names," accepted Park, somewhat reluctantly.

Janet, compelled to stay calm too, continued. "That book had a handwritten note in it, advising that something valuable could be found in the Seven Hells. I can't go into all the details..."

"They're confidential," added Kossowsky.

"Uh, yes." Janet gave him an irritated glance. "But it sounded like the place may be a special sort of... library. Do—"

She bit her lip and looked tentatively at the other girl.

"Yes, I know what a library is," Park articulated in an exaggeratedly flat voice.

Janet's face brightened with relief. "That's pretty much all we've got."

"I..." Buck raised his hand. "I don't know what a library is."

Both girls glared at him. That could have been comical if he hadn't been the target.

"It's a place where books were stored—" started Janet.

"—And where you could come and borrow one to read," finished Park. "Once upon a time. Before the E."

"Yes," picked up Janet, "and before the Faith with all its Simplification bullshit, blaming science for Humanity's downfall, and book-burning."

Buck had been raised on these beliefs. A mere week ago, he would have been appalled by Janet's denigration of the Faith. He was a different man now, and what she said resonated with him.

"M-kay." Park regarded her counterpart. "You may be a bitch, but you're my kind of bitch! Oops..." She elaborately covered her mouth. "Forgot, no name-calling."

"This time, I don't mind." Janet, unwinding from her angry philippic, rewarded Park with a reserved smile.

"Miss Park," said Jackson, "where we come from, Janet's words would be blasphemous." He frowned at Kossowsky, who was about to say something. "Lieutenant, belay!" Jackson's voice, usually lackadaisical, rang with metal.

Everybody in the room looked at the officer. Kossowsky sat on the edge of his seat, red-faced, clenching his fists, but kept his mouth shut.

"See," Jackson explained to the Korean girl in his normal tone as if nothing had happened, "the lieutenant here is the last adherent of the Faith on our team. Please forgive him his unspoken outrage."

Park shrugged. Right. Why would she care either way?

"Back to our original subject." Jackson smiled charmingly. "Can you think of something? Anything at all? Now that you know the Seven Hells may be real?"

"*That's* a scary thought," drawled Park, not appearing frightened in the least. "Las, ideas? Anything of which there are seven?"

"There are other ways to go. Could be a street number. 'Hells' is far more interesting. Does it have some special meaning for the place? A distorted name? Seven Hills? Seven Halls? Seven L's?"

"Hills? No, not in the City. It's too flat. L's... L's. Hm. Something in the shape of the letter L? No, I've got nothing."

"Okay, now hells. The most hellish place I can think of is the Burn. But what is there that's seven?"

"What's the Burn?" asked Buck.

Park reached into her backpack again and fetched a piece of folded paper. She spread the old, frayed, brown-yellow map, held together at the folds by a few threads. She carefully straightened it on the table and pointed at an area outlined by a faded black border. "This. This here is the Burn. An area that had burned out when the E hit. A few of those are scattered across the City, but only one Downtown."

"Eh?" She bent down over the map and counted off points within the black boundary. "... four, five, six... Seven!"

"What?" asked Gabor.

"Blocks! The Burn covers seven city blocks!"

Chapter 34

Yun-mi

September 26, 42 PE

Yun-mi brought Laszlo to the same room she had stayed in last time in New Kowloon. Not home yet, but not a totally strange place, either. *Her* room.

Seated on the sofa, Laszlo observed her confidently milling around and unburdening herself from her everyday carry kit. "Yun-mi, may I ask you a personal question?"

"Always found that lead up stupid. If I don't know what the question is, how can I decide if I want to hear it? And if I say 'no', I'll be dying of curiosity, anyway. Let's agree: you have something to ask me? Just ask."

"You don't cease to amaze me. Are you sure you're only seventeen?"

"Why, do I look much older? Careful now!"

Laszlo chuckled. "But if you don't like my question, please don't bite my head off."

"No promises. Now, out with it."

Laszlo nodded at the firearm leaning against the corner. "Your rifle. I couldn't help but notice: when in danger, you reach for the bow. Does this—"

"Yes. I don't know how to shoot it."

"Then—"

"Why do I carry it around? First, it was Joon-woo's. I've had it since his death. Second, it's intimidating, and people take me seriously. And third... I've got nowhere to leave it."

"You could leave it here. I'm sure your Golden Dragon can arrange for its safe storage. As for the intimidation part, I've got news for you. The people you may need to intimidate won't be awfully impressed by it."

"What are you talking about?"

"It's a 10/22. See how thin its barrel is? Its cartridges? They're tiny. Lethal against small game, with proper shot placement, but humans? You'll have to stuff them full of bullets, or hit an eye, to achieve a meaningful effect. And those people you should be most cautious about—they know. If anything, this gun makes you a target."

"Well then, thank gods I've got you to take care of the intimidation part."

"I hope that isn't the only reason you want me around."

"You've got me there. Hold on, I'll think up something else."

"That hurt." He laughed, but unconvincingly. His eyes remained serious. Questioning.

Yun-mi touched his arm apologetically. "You aren't the only one with lame jokes, Las."

"Aren't we a match made in heaven?"

"We're perfect for each other. Two Rats with an atrocious sense of humor."

"Right?"

"Okay, about that gun. I hear you. Then, what about this?" She brought her backpack from the corner, retrieved the two halves of Parker's rifle, and deposited them into Laszlo's hands.

"Holy..." Laszlo's jaw dropped. "I wondered where it could end up."

"You recognize it?"

Laszlo tilted his head.

Yeah, a stupid question. "Of course, you do." Yun-mi sighed. "I couldn't leave it either."

"Good thing you didn't. That's some heavy artillery!"

"Will it be intimidating if I carry it?"

"Certainly. But..."

"Oh, now what?"

"I'm sure you realize intimidation only goes so far. If you're called on your threats, you've got to follow through on them. I can start teaching you—"

"—but that will take time to master. Don't you think I know?"

"I'm sure you do."

"You... want to have it? That would be less wasteful."

"Yun-mi, I can't. It's yours by rights. If you don't want it, you can fetch a pretty penny for it. And I mean, a lot! But you can't simply give it to me."

She put her hands on her hips. "Laszlo Gabor, I gave *myself* to you, and you're saying I can't give you a stinking rifle? Is it more valuable than I am?"

Laszlo's cheeks reddened. "Yun-mi, you're the most precious thing I have in the world, I hoped you'd know that by now."

"Oh, stop being such a baby, Las! I'm kidding!"

"Park Yun-mi, that was officially the worst joke I've heard from you. The same way you don't want me to laugh about long-term relationships, I don't want you to ever question your value in my life."

"Match made in heaven, eh? Alright, a compromise. I'll *lend* you the rifle. You can have it and use it as you wish, and I'll still own it. Deal?"

"You drive a hard bargain."

"Then surrender now. My next offer will be worse."

Laszlo put the rifle on the floor and raised his hands. "You win. But I get to teach you to shoot."

"If you insist."

With a mix of awe and adoration, she observed him expertly putting the rifle back together.

"Las."

"Yes?"

"How did it happen?"

"How did what happen?"

"Me, becoming the most precious thing for you, all that." She met his startled stare. "Was it because I showed you my vulnerable side? Accepted your help and protection? And now you, a man of honor, feel responsible for me?"

"Yun-mi. Sometimes, you're wiser than a Golden Dragon, expertly reading people's emotions. But other times... you're a silly little girl. Like now."

Laszlo took Yun-mi's hand and pulled her into his lap. He squeezed her in a hug and whispered into her ear, "Do you believe in love at first sight, Brave Flower?"

Yun-mi's experience bore no proof of its existence. None of her short-term boyfriends had qualified. She shrugged, as much as his tight embrace allowed.

"I know I hadn't," Laszlo continued. "Thought it's premium-grade bullshit from old books. Until the moment you walked into the Triumvirate Hall."

She turned to look at his face in disbelief.

"Yes." A firm nod reinforced his words. "And when you gave Francis a piece of your mind... That was it. You had me."

"Damn. Look at you! A romantic hiding in this big, formidable Rat body!"

"Guilty. Your barbed tongue makes it a painful experience, but I think I love you, Yun-mi. No, I *know* I do. There, I said it."

Yun-mi lowered her head onto his shoulder. "And I repay you by torturing you all the time, don't I? Sorry, Las, I... I must be damaged."

"No, but badly hurt."

"Your healing effect is undeniable."

He must have been waiting for her to say she loved him, too. Why couldn't she? The answer was as grim as it was simple. She had never been loved, nor had anyone to love. Laszlo stormed into her life and claimed a huge part of it overnight, but was it love? Without knowing what love was, she couldn't answer. And the last thing she wanted was to lie to this man.

Yun-mi twisted out of Laszlo's embrace, straddled him, put both arms around his neck, and made their foreheads touch. His eyes, blue with green sparks, were a mere inch away.

"You're the best thing to ever happen to me," she whispered, the closest truth she could give him.

He didn't ask for more.

An indeterminate time later, Yun-mi gingerly lifted Laszlo's heavy arm off her ribs and lowered it onto the sofa, trying not to wake him up. She stood and turned to check, only to find his eyes wide open and a grin curving his lips.

"No way I can sneak past you?" Yun-mi sighed. "You're a better Rat."

"Just more experienced."

"Oh? Experienced in having women trying to sneak out of your bed?" Too good an opening to resist.

Laszlo caught her arm and tried to drag her back to the sofa. "You're so sexy when you're trash-talking!"

She resisted, putting her other hand against the backrest. "Wait, let me get some water."

He released her, but not before kissing her neck. "Go, but be right back."

Returning from the kitchenette with two glasses, Yun-mi stopped in front of a mirrored closet door and studied her reflection. A thin but muscular frame, not exactly the standard of femininity most men desired. A mop of raven-black hair, arranged into braids and ponytails on one side, and undershaved on the other temple. A flat face with a small nose and a triangular chin, also far from conventionally beautiful.

"What do you see in me?"

In a flash of noiseless motion, her partner tenderly hugged her from behind. In the mirror, he appeared bulky by comparison, taller and wider. And hairier.

"You're twice my size," she continued, "ten years older—"

"Eight."

"You're a ruler of a powerful clan, and—"

"And scarred and ugly."

"Yes, hideous, but I'm sure you can have any woman you want. Big boobs," she demonstrated with an exaggerated gesture, "wide thighs, long legs, pretty face, blond hair..."

"All true. But I already have the woman I want."

She met his reflection's laughing, adoring eyes. "But why?"

"There's no 'why'. You're the one, that's all. I've never been surer of anything. And yes, you are stunning! How can you not see this?"

She leaned back into him. "You definitely know how to compliment a girl. Lots of practice?"

"Another thing I love about you: you keep me on my toes. Never a dull moment!"

"I can't cook for shit."

"That's fine, I can. At least you can bring a glass of water. By the way, may I have mine?"

Yun-mi was still holding the two forgotten glasses. On the spur of the moment, she splashed their content over her shoulders and, giggling, tried to escape Laszlo's righteous anger. The iron clamps of his arms on her waist made the attempt futile. With a roar, Laszlo lifted Yun-mi off the floor and, ignoring her squealing, kicking, and thrashing, carried her to the bed. There, he gently put her down and leaned over. She touched his dripping face, tracing the slick scar with her fingertips.

"Yun-mi," he said, "you're a stubborn, belligerent, foul-mouthed elemental spirit. You've got a bad temper and an even worse sense of humor. How can I, a mere human, resist such a force of nature?"

Chapter 35

Marc

September 27, 42 PE

Sleep didn't come. Again. A decent shut-eye was a must, if he wanted to be fresh and rested for the day to come—a day that promised to be extra-long. No dice. He had dozed off several times through the night for what had felt like minutes, out and straight back to a groggy, half-awake state.

It wasn't the pain. His head wasn't pounding; his bruised ribs and the hip had stopped pulsating in tune with his heartbeat; the many cuts itched, healing up. It wasn't his hand, checked the evening before by a stern Doctor Chen, as promised by the Golden Dragon.

It wasn't Rajan's deafening snoring, so percussive it would have caused the building to shake, had they not been lodged in such a massive structure.

The reasons lay outside the physical realm.

Outwardly, Marc projected cocky confidence. Up to and including the readiness to jump right back into the fray. But alone in the dark, he'd been cornered by memories, doubts, and fears. The one battle he could never win.

During his CIU service, followed by a year in Weinberg's Intelligence structure, Marc had been through a lot. Rigorous training, firefights, classified missions, whatnot. He'd been shot at too many times to count and killed more people than he cared to remember. But all the while, he'd had his comrades around, and his unit's fearsome reputation. No one but the most screwball thugs would dare confront him. Not because of his personal prowess, but because of what he stood for. Because of what stood behind him. Locksville. Weinberg. CIU. The names instilling fear and respect in any group or individual with a rudimentary sense of self-preservation. Marc had worn Locksville's patch like a flak jacket. It didn't grant protection from a stray bullet, but had shielded him from malicious intent. That had been his world.

Until that protection was ripped away from him.

Until he found himself shackled to a rack in The Station's dungeon.

He had no one but himself to blame for running into a Stationer patrol on his way home. Should have been more alert. He'd been trained better than to rush blindly through the woods. Especially with urgent news to deliver. Still, the legend lent to him by the Fivepointers had all but guaranteed his prompt release... if not for the stupid bad luck. What were the chances of running into the Golden Lions' General? And of him somehow recognizing Marc from the night his gang had been decimated by the CIU?

Even so, Marc had counted on his immunity. Officially, the two powers had maintained a neutral relationship, regardless of the long-standing animosity. The Inquisitors couldn't have known he'd been involved in subversive activities against The Station. Practically, he had expected to be expelled, maybe roughed up a bit, but to return home in one piece. Those were the rules of the game. Had been.

Instead of immunity, being revealed as a Locksville officer had earned him an endless chain of interrogations, beatings, and torture. Marc wasn't broken. Not his spirit, in any case, and his body had been conditioned to take abuse. The Inquisitors had done worse: torn his worldview into shreds.

The conversation with the Chief Inquisitor had turned Marc's perceptions upside down. It had planted the seed of doubt deep in his mind, and yet deeper in his soul.

His torturers weren't to blame for bringing him close to killing himself. That had been his decision, his moment of weakness. Not that he had a death wish, but he'd made his peace with the possibility of sudden violent death a long time ago. The cost of doing business as a CIU operative. Those were the Chief Inquisitor's revelations that had amplified Marc's doubts to the breaking point.

He wasn't afraid of going back. Fights had never scared him, whatever or whoever ended up on the business end of his gun. Failure, that was his greatest fear. A failure to make the right decision when the time comes. Was he adequate for the task?

He, who had always excelled at the waiting game, was counting seconds, lying in the darkness and envying Rajan's carefree snoring. The moment everything came to a head could not arrive too soon.

Finally, footsteps and muted conversations in the hallway hinted at the beginning of a new day. Marc climbed out of the bed, dressed, and tiptoed to the door—though he could fire a cannon over Rajan's head and his roommate wouldn't shift.

He navigated his way through the Hive's labyrinthine corridors to the cantina in the inner yard of the complex.

With a plate loaded with eggs, salted fish, and cooked rice, he scanned the room. Plenty of free tables, but a familiar face would be nice... There. Hunched over the table, Buck was absentmindedly consuming his meal. The young guy started when Marc slid his tray onto the table, then greeted him with a sheepish smile.

"Marc! Good morning. Can't sleep?"

"Nope."

"Me neither. Big day. Can't stop thinking. And worrying."

"Yeah, tell me about that."

"Um-hum. Somebody pierced your bubble?"

You don't know the first thing about it, kid. "Something like that."

They chewed in silence.

"Going back to The Station?" asked Buck.

"Er... Why would you say that?"

"Come on, Marc, I am not that stupid. The Chinese are livid. Something's on. Your Weinberg is here, and I bet he doesn't deal with a lot of ordinary stuff. Seven Hells, Jackson almost gave up on our mission to stay at the Hive! What else can it be? Everything points to a plan to take down the Inquisitor. You show him, Marc! For all of us! And speaking of the Seven Hells..."

"Yeah?"

"That's where *we* are going today."

Marc forgot to swallow. "Come again?" he asked around a mouthful of food.

"You heard me. Only I told you nothing. Your mission is secret, mine's too. And that's that."

"But... Then Seven Hells *is* a place? Not a figure of speech?"

"Looks like. I guess we'll find out today."

"With devils and all?"

"Nah, that part's doubtful. Maybe some urban zombies. Who really don't like to be called that."

"How do you know?"

"Remember that girl from yesterday, Park-something, the guide the Golden Dragon gave us? She's one of them."

"No! Are you serious?"

"Yup. But she prefers to be called a Rat. Go figure."

"Weird."

"Right? And that guy with her, scares the shit out of me."

"I can see why. Gives me the chills, too."

"So, The Station?"

Marc nodded.

"Be careful. Please." Buck's face grew somber. "And take those fuckers down."

"Always am, will do." Confidence. Don't have to feel it to project it. "You keep your eyes peeled too, eh?"

"Take whom down?" asked a cheerful female voice behind Marc's back, and the girl they've just been talking about landed on the bench next to him. "I'm all for taking down fuckers!"

Her imposing companion grabbed a seat opposite her, causing Buck to shift away.

"Speak of the devil..." the kid mumbled. The multiple meanings were not lost on Marc.

"No one," he said. "No one is taking down anyone. It's confidential. Need-to-know."

"Oh," the girl said, "and *he* needs to know?" She pointed at Buck with her chopsticks.

Marc didn't deign that with a response.

"Fine, be like that." She dug into her breakfast.

They ate in silence. Continuing the previous conversation in the City dwellers' presence was out of the question. Small talk? Not in this mood.

"How do you two know each other?" asked the scar-faced man, Gabor.

"Leave them alone, Las," said the girl, all playfulness gone from her voice. "Let them enjoy being jerks."

Marc kept silent. Enough confrontations awaited him later in the day.

Buck, conversely, couldn't keep his mouth shut. "Was that necessary?" he asked, knocking on the table with the butt of his fork. "Why do you always have to be so hostile?"

"Always? What do you know about me, kid, to talk about 'always'?"

"Not much, you're right. But in the short time I've known you, you're the one who's been the jerk."

The girl was about to respond, but Gabor spoke first. "He's not wrong, you know."

She slammed her mouth shut, pursing the lips.

"And stop calling me 'kid'!" added Buck. "You are no older than me, Park!"

Nice. The kid was getting ballsier by the day.

The girl's nostrils flared. She exhaled loudly through the nose and looked at the three men with narrowed eyes. "I see. You've all conspired against me."

Marc cringed preemptively, sure she'd slam her bowl on the table, or do some other impulsive thing, and storm out.

Instead, she laughed. Then raised a fist in front of Buck, who recoiled and stared back in confusion.

"Come on, bump me!" she urged. Buck blinked and kept staring at her, blushing. Easy to imagine what kind of bumping the kid pictured in his mind.

Marc came to the rescue, tapping his fist against the girl's. Buck awkwardly replicated the gesture.

"What, you don't bump fists in whatever backwater you're from?" She looked amused.

Buck shook his head.

"Never mind. You've got guts, that's what counts. I can work with you. What's your name, again? Brennan?"

Buck bent his brows. "Call me Buck. Everyone does."

"Okay, Buck. But don't you dare call me Park again."

"Why? Isn't that your name?"

"My last name, you barbarian."

"Oh. What's your first one?"

"Miss Park would do."

Was she pulling the kid's leg again? Her statement sounded categorical. Enough to stop Buck from further exploring this line of conversation.

This Miss Park reminded him of someone... Of course, Aileen! Little Sis had the same big mouth and did not hesitate to run it, taming everyone around her, no matter the difference in age or size. Even when Marc and his friends had already been sixteen-year-old grown-ups, and she—a miniature girl all of twelve. Aileen... Would he ever see her again after what he was about to do? Would she want to have anything to do with him?

"He-e-e-y!" a sonorous bass roared over Marc's head, easily defeating the cantina's din and bringing the surrounding conversations to a momentary halt. "Park Yun-mi, sister! What a pleasant surprise!"

Marc craned his neck. A group of bearded men crowded the passage between the tables.

With an excited howl, the girl was on her feet in no time and hugged them one by one.

Gabor frowned. Interesting. Her partner didn't know these men or the reason for all the affection.

"Las, meet the Singh brothers! Jihan, Ajinder, Preet, Kulvir, Mankaran, Ranbir. Guys, this is Laszlo Gabor, my man and, coincidentally, Humber Bay Raccoons' Triumvir. These here are Buck Brennan from Five Points and, uh..."

He'd never been introduced to her. Awkward.

"Marc Novak of Locksville," said the oldest-looking brother, Jihan. "You were pointed out to us."

"I was?" said Marc. "Why?"

"We'll be accompanying you today, sir. Pleasure to meet you all, gentlemen!" Jihan flashed a toothy smile.

Ah, the non-Kowloonese assets Tam Wai Lam had promised Weinberg.

Marc studied his teammates-to-be. The fellows all wore the same woodland camo, black turbans—that's what they called those, no?—and sported a broad array of firearms and blades. Wasn't only the local security allowed weapons on the premises? With the elevated threat level and the general frenzy in the Great Hive, that made sense. But Park and Gabor had been carrying their impressive arsenals, too. They all were Golden Dragon's personal *something*—guests, envoys, whatever.

Marc checked the clock on the wall. He had to leave, and soon. If for no other reason than to get his gun back. He could count on one hand all the times in the last five years when he'd been unarmed. Even in the Hive's safety, that mattered.

The brothers left to grab their food, returning to the table and catching up with Yun-mi. Turned out, she'd kept busy, up to and including involvement in a coup in some clan. And she proved to be a fantastic storyteller. There was nothing funny in her misadventures, but she wrapped them in such copious amounts of self-deprecating humor that bursts of laughter regularly interrupted her narration. Marc occasionally grinned, too. And Buck was so captivated by her story, he forgot he was holding a spoon halfway to his mouth. Careful, buddy.

Marc allowed himself to enjoy the moment. His nighttime fears retreated, swept away by the camaraderie. Would he experience something similar ever again?

Chapter 36

Ka Yi

September 27, 42 PE

Ka Yi woke up early. A sign of his body returning to its normal parameters? He tested the theory by taking a few deep breaths. No shortness of breath, no wheezing, no chest pain. Promising. The stab wound still ached when he moved, but he'd be surprised if it hadn't. A vast improvement over the day before. Who knows, Doctor Chen might remove that annoying patch from his ribs. And a few of his restrictions...

He looked at Wai Lam. Despite her boisterous insistence that Ka Yi should follow the doctor's orders to a T, when the time came for them to say good night, she stayed. One of those decisions that go without saying.

Wai Lam looked peaceful. She had finally gotten the rest she had been desperately lacking. With it, the glow returned to her face, replacing the sickly paleness of her skin and the black circles under her eyes. Ka Yi envied her ability to switch off. Convincing her to do this had been an uphill struggle lately, but when she did, she slept like a baby.

"You're doing that creepy thing again," she murmured.

"Sorry, not sorry." Was watching her sleep becoming his fetish? No. Maybe. Who cares? His wife was beautiful, and he was madly in love with her.

"Don't even think about it," she warned, with a twinkle in her squinted eyes. "Doctor's orders."

"Technically, we're somewhat dressed..."

"You expect to sway me with your chicanery?"

Ka Yi let a heavy sigh convey the full tragedy of his situation. "No, I was counting on my irresistible charm. But can you blame me for trying?"

Her cool, dry hand touched his cheek. "I'd be worried if you hadn't. Soon, love. Few more days. I bet we're going to have enough excitement of a different sort today."

Ugh. Why did she have to remind him of the grim and complicated reality impatiently waiting to be addressed outside their chamber? He sat on the edge of the bed, then pushed himself up. The lake behind the window wavered and tilted. "Uh-oh." He dropped back, flailing for something to grab on to. Wai Lam observed his clumsy maneuvers with growing concern.

"They should've fixed the wheelchair you so brutally trashed yesterday. Consider using it today? Please?"

"Undermines my authority. Makes me look like a cripple."

"Not to put too fine a point on it, but... you were stabbed in the chest three days ago, stupid! For crying out loud, you're lucky to be alive! You've got absolutely nothing to be ashamed of!"

Ka Yi defiantly set his jaw. "Don't call me stupid, Golden Dragon!"

She smiled helplessly. "You're the wisest man I know, Golden Dragon. But sometimes you behave so childishly I wonder if someone had secretly switched my husband with his infantile twin!"

Ka Yi painstakingly avoided her eyes. "I can't stand the thought of you seeing me like that. I want to... No, I *have* to be the man you fell in love with, Wai Lam. Not *this*." He pointed at himself in disgust.

Wai Lam scrambled to her knees behind him, put her chin on his shoulder, and whispered into his ear, "But don't you see? I love who you are, what you are. You *are* the man I fell in love with. You make it sound as if I only care about strong male physique or your perceived authority. Don't insult me!"

Ka Yi hung his head. "Sorry," he mouthed voicelessly.

She delicately hugged his shoulders. "Apology begrudgingly accepted. Now, Golden Dragon, stop whining, help me get dressed, and go kick some Stationer ass! With your brains, mind you, not your wheelchair!"

"This Jackson," Ka Yi asked over breakfast, "what do you make of him?"

"A peculiar character. A dark horse. He's sharp. Probably not as sharp as Weinberg—"

"Few people are. And only you and I are sharper."

"Don't butter me up, Golden Dragon." Wai Lam made that sound cold. "I am still mad at you."

"But I apologized! And you accepted!"

"Yes, but I'm allowed to still be mad. As I was saying—"

"Wait, are you serious?" Ka Yi's heart sank.

"Oh, quit being such a baby, Golden Dragon! May I not pretend to be a moody girl for once?"

Ka Yi choked up. "You? A moody girl?"

"Think twice what you're going to say next, Golden Dragon." Wai Lam narrowed her eyes. "You're digging yourself ever deeper."

He shut his mouth with an audible snap.

She shook her head and reached across the table, touching his hand. "Ka Yi, dear. I take it as a compliment that my presence turns you into a drooling idiot, that's adorable, but..." Her voice hardened. "Please pull your head out of your ass, will you? We're at war, and I need you in the game, fully committed!" That was a Golden Dragon talking, not his wife.

Ka Yi leaned back, aghast. It had been a long time since anyone had spoken to him so harshly. The last time, it had been his father. All these years later, the jeers still echoed in his memory. Failure. Mediocrity. Bitterness burned the back of his throat. No! Proving the old man wrong had been Ka Yi's most arduous journey. And it *was* over!

He went, in quick succession, through reflexive anger at such language aimed at him, despondency at how accurate Wai Lam's assessment was, terror of having disappointed her, and finally—acceptance. Wai Lam's words rang true, but they were filled with care, not Father's loveless contempt.

He bent forward and kissed her hand. "Way to keep me real, Golden Dragon."

"Glad to have you back, my love." She smiled so disarmingly his soul melted. Stay sharp. Stay sharp. "Jackson?"

"Yes. As I was saying,"—she pointedly glared at him—"he may not be quite a match for Weinberg, but doesn't lag far behind. Those two are buddies for a reason."

"They are?"

"Yes, you must've missed that part, busy recuperating from your wheelchair stunt."

"You'll never let me live that down, will you?"

"Not a chance. Anyhow, notwithstanding Five Points' isolationist policy, I prefer having him on our side. Their Army, as I'm sure you know in far greater detail, is powerful. Counting them as an ally is better than merely ensuring their neutrality."

"And what's that shady business they've got in the City?"

"That, I can't tell you."

"Can't, or won't?"

"*Seriously,* Ka Yi?" Any traces of her previous barbs' humor evaporated. Worst of all, her eyes weren't laughing anymore. "Did you just use your High Council rhetoric on *me*?! You really think I'd still keep secrets from you?"

Shit. Why? Why did he have to say that? Imbecile.

"And don't start apologizing once again, Shang Ka Yi. Just *please* don't do this again." She dialed down her scalding frown. "I know. Old habits. I forgive you this time, but don't you *ever* use your Dragon claws on me."

He nodded vigorously.

She pursed her lips, then continued, with the residual grudge receding from her tone bit by bit. "I *can't* tell you what the Fivepointers' business in the City is because I don't know. They're secretive about it, and I had no leverage to push Jackson for answers. Needless to say, that makes it all look highly suspicious."

"Yes." Ka Yi finally dared to turn the conversation into a dialog again. "What could drag that ragtag team all the way from Five Points?"

"Very odd. That's why I sent Yun-mi to guide them, with the instructions to watch closely and keep our interests in mind."

"Yun-mi? The Korean Rat you've been telling me about?"

"The same."

"She's that good, eh?"

"Better. She's a jewel. Rough around the edges, but she'll shine yet."

"And how do you endeavor to keep her under control?"

"I don't. I don't believe anyone can. She's a wild thing. A true bona fide Rat. All I can do is nudge her in the general direction that would benefit us. Besides, she seems to see me as a mother figure, and—" Wai Lam stared at Ka Yi point-blank. "Don't even!"

He raised his arms. "Wasn't going to comment, I swear."

She checked his expression for signs of hidden sarcasm and, finding none, continued. "The poor girl had been woefully underappreciated. When I showed interest in her, I thought she was going to offer me her body and her soul."

"You've got mine."

"Yes. Quite a burden." Wai Lam flashed a smile. "She's eager to please me and extraordinarily capable. I'm counting on her."

"Aren't you putting too much faith in a young clansgirl?"

"That young girl snagged a Raccoons' Triumvir for a boyfriend, brokered a formal alliance between two clans, and led to a change of the Russians' rulership. All in two days. After surviving the murder of her mentor, killing her abductor, and finding her way into my reception room. Shall I go on?"

"No, that's more than enough. Wow. I wish I'd met her."

"She's already got a boyfriend, and you're married now."

"Don't be jealous. You know what I mean."

"I'll introduce you when she's back. But don't get any ideas."

"I've got a shrew Dragon all to myself. Why would I want a Rat?"

"Fair point. You'll do well to remember that. And, oh, you're so going to regret that 'shrew'!"

Chapter 37

Buck

September 27, 42 PE

Sailing onboard the *Eastern Star* differed drastically from the precarious adventure with Captain Farley. The massive cargo ship did not heed the lake's futile attempts at rocking it. And the deep, level rumbling of the engine somewhere below the decks was comforting and relaxing.

Engines? Comforting? Shouldn't he be appalled? The requisite revulsion did not flare. Not a Believer anymore. Just like that. Huh. Buck searched for a void that the sudden taking away of such a profound part of his life must've left in his soul. Nope. His soul was disgustingly fine. Excitement was present, to set foot in the City. Apprehension about what they'd find, or *wouldn't* find—and he wasn't sure which development scared him more. Worry about the looming war with The Station, and Marc's chances of surviving it unscathed. But discovering the loss of Faith touched no chords. As if it had never been there.

Late in the morning, the Task Force had assembled on New Kowloon's pier, to find the *Eastern Star*, Golden Dragon Shang Ka Yi's flagship waiting for them. Another gesture from the Chinese, honoring the guests with not just any means of transportation, but the most advanced ship their fleet had on the roster. One that would safely deliver them to their destination. Had the second-hand news he and his team delivered to the Great Hive truly been that valuable? With the original sources, Weinberg and Marc, having arrived shortly thereafter, this smelled of politics. But excessive hospitality wasn't something to be critical of.

The Locksvillers showed up too, accompanied by those Singh brothers he'd met in the cantina. Neither Chinese nor *Ko-re-an*. All wore unfamiliar camo with odd headdresses and were heavily armed. They were sailing back in Captain Farley's boat, tiny and rickety compared to the *Eastern Star*. Surely not because of falling out of the Golden Dragons' graces. Must be the secretive nature of their mission.

Was that all? These few people—against the might of The Station?

Buck perked up. "Be right back!" he muttered to Jackson and dashed toward the warehouses. The local guards tracked him suspiciously but did not interfere. At the port office, Buck inquired about his team's stored goods and emerged onto the docks a few minutes later with the machine gun slung across his chest and two ammo tins pulling at his arms. Slightly out of breath, he jogged up to Marc, placed the tins on the ground and, under awed gazes of the bearded warriors, hung the heavy firearm on his friend's neck. "This should help keep you safe. Put it to good use!"

"Thanks, buddy!" Marc winced in pain, but patted Buck on the shoulder. "Hope it won't be necessary, but nice to have the option."

"It wasn't yours to give, Brennan," Kossowsky grumbled, then met Marc's reproachful eye and relented. "But I approve of the sentiment."

"You can have it back, Lieutenant," the Locksviller smiled wryly. "Once we've taken care of our business. If you are in our area on your way back, come join me for a cup of tea. Or something stronger." The questionable assumption that both men would survive to meet later was left unspoken.

The Golden Dragons were conspicuous in their absence on the pier, but someone else showed up. Choi Cheok Bou, the Portmaster, dressed in more flamboyant garb than on the day of Buck's arrival, was trailed by two aides. Four guards armed with submachine guns followed at a respectful distance.

"On behalf of the Golden Dragons Shang Ka Yi and Tam Wai Lam, I came to wish both your teams safe sailing and the best of luck with your missions." His head bobbed in a curt bow.

He turned to Weinberg and offered a hand, which the captain accepted, searching the Portmaster's face for a hint.

"Captain, I thank you for bringing up my humble name in your conversation with the Golden Dragons. That appears to have been a contributing factor to my promotion. As of last night, I am a Golden Dragon of the High Council. Rest assured, you will never run short of goodwill in New Kowloon."

"Golden Dragon,"—Weinberg bowed with a flourish—"your words are music to my ears. You have my sincerest congratulations."

And then it was time to depart.

Half an hour later, the ship approached a flat, shallow island.

Leaning forward by Buck's side, Janet eagerly drank in the view of the approaching Downtown—and Buck was unable to tear his eyes off of her profile. Damn, she was beautiful. The observation was supposed to be detached, purely aesthetic, but triggered a bittersweet longing in his chest. A missed opportunity? Buck shook his head, forcing himself to focus on something different.

His wandering eye caught on a large cylindrical *something* with small windows along its side and long, thick blades protruding at an angle. Several similar but smaller ones sat nearby. For the life of him, Buck could not guess their purpose. "What *are* they?"

"Not too sure." Janet touched her jaw. "Might be airplanes."

"Air-planes?" Buck tasted the unfamiliar word.

"Yeah. People used to fly around inside them."

"*Fly?!*" Buck's breath caught. "Inside? How?"

"I don't know." Janet sighed, lowering her eyelids.

"So, they're like the satellites you told us about?"

"Uh, no. Satellites fly in space, much higher than airplanes."

"Oh."

"They caused the Burn," Park chimed into the conversation from Janet's other side. "When the E hit, planes fell out of the sky. Some had carried *a lot* of fuel."

Buck's skin crawled. That matter-of-fact depiction sounded too horrifying for words. Plus, maybe the Faith's teachings weren't so abstract, after all? How else could entire city blocks burned by a fallen machine be explained, if not by God's wrath?

A movement on the water interrupted Buck's contemplation. Three longboats emerged from behind the island's promontory. A menacing drumbeat set the rhythm for the paddlers and reverberated in Buck's spine, making his hairs stand on their ends.

"Crap! The Island pirates!" Park grabbed her bow and fetched an arrow from the quiver. Her friend Laszlo materialized nearby with a heavy scoped rifle and dropped to the deck, pushing the barrel over the gunwale. Buck reached for his trusty Garand.

A black-and-white vision seized him, and blinked out of existence a moment later. He relaxed. Everything was going to be alright. Not clear how yet, but it was.

The longboats had completed their wide arc and were fast approaching. Two of them leaped predatorily side by side from wave to wave, the four rows of paddles flashing with beautiful synchronicity. The third split off, aiming for the *Eastern Star*'s stern. A hundred meters away, the first two changed their course, impossibly turning almost on the spot and lunging in opposite directions to the increasing tempo of their drums. The maneuver was masterfully executed but baffling. The explanation for the pirates' change of heart came a moment later. A long series of quick, heavy hammer blows came from the *Eastern Star*'s bow, where two sailors manned a monstrous machine gun. The turret-mounted weapon was larger than the one Buck had given to Marc, with a lower rate of fire, but a devastating effect. One longboat took several hits along its middle, broke in half, and sank in seconds. Its crew, sniped from the *Eastern Star*, followed their boat into the depths. The Kowloonese gave no quarter. Nor did Laszlo, whose formidable rifle barked time after time.

The second boat returned sporadic fire, sending Janet and Park scrambling for cover. Buck, trusting his dissipated vision, discarded the danger and remained standing to have a better view. The pirate vessel absorbed a few bullets in its stern but made good on its escape, briskly rounding the island with less than half its crew left aboard. The third longboat, in the meantime, snuck up close to the Kowloonese ship, into the machine gun's dead zone. Buck leaned forward to check where the pirates had gone...

An aura foreshadowing another vision only started forming when an explosion shook the *Eastern Star*. The deck kicked at Buck's feet, toppling him overboard. He was too stunned by the shock wave to react.

The abrupt immersion in the ice-cold lake cleared Buck's head, but his muscles spasmed, leaving him unable to swim, to call for help, to breathe. What an irony: to come all this way, only to drown an arm's reach away from the City. Stupid.

Strong hands yanked Buck out of the water and hauled him unceremoniously onto a wooden surface. Before he could get his bearings, Buck was hoisted upright by several men crouching behind him at the longboat's aft. Others hit the water with their oars.

"Don't shoot! They've got Buck!" a familiar voice came from up above, through the ringing in his ears and the chattering of his teeth. "Cease fire!"

Buck failed to attach a face to the voice. Odd. If he knew the voice, he should have known its owner. His mind swam, vision blurred, and Buck banked. The snarling men clutching his arms and shoulders didn't let him fall. He smiled at them and passed out.

Buck woke with a sharp inhale. His eyes opened wide, but the blinding sunlight immediately forced his eyelids shut. He tried again, cautiously peering around through thin slits.

He was seated on a concrete surface at the edge of a narrow body of water. A river or a channel, with houses hiding here and there among the trees on the other bank, and several longboats bobbing with the slow current. Buck's lower body was numb, his clothes—dripping wet. What little warmth he had left was quickly seeping into the ground. The moment this realization registered, a violent convulsion shook him. He wasn't going to drown, after all, but freezing to death was not a much more attractive option.

With considerable difficulty, Buck pulled his legs under him and attempted to stand... Unsuccessfully. Something was holding him in place. He peeked over his shoulder. Ah. His hands were tied to a post behind his back. That explained it.

Something shifted to Buck's right. His head jerked there, an impossible mix of hope and panic clamping his chest. Another person was trussed against the next post, two meters away, in a shallow puddle. The crumpled figure twitched again and its limply hanging head moved. Buck gasped, recognizing the familiar profile: Lundy. Shit!

The memories burst through a barrier in Buck's head. The City. The pirates. The firefight. The *Eastern* Star's machine gun decimating the attackers. The disappearing vision that had convinced him of safety, and another one he hadn't had time to see. Whom else had they captured? And where was he?

"Hey!" Buck wheezed, cleared his throat, and tried again. "Hey!"

"Shut your mouth."

Buck *was* seeking to attract someone's attention, but the growl behind him made him jump.

A squat, heavy-set man with a thick black beard and a wild mane of hair entered Buck's field of vision. Two others, taller but younger, followed. The leader stopped in front of Buck, parted the edges of his woolen cloak, and with a meaningful scowl planted his hands on the hilt of a long knife sheathed at his belt. "Ransom," he spewed. "Will your people pay for you?"

Of course. They weren't going to kill him yet.

"Blankets," Buck said, "for me and for him." He leaned his head toward Lundy's unconscious form.

In a short but vicious kick, the pirate's boot swung into Buck's ribs, and for a minute agonizing flames consumed the entire universe. Eventually, the pain subsided. Buck blinked a few times to get rid of the black and white spots floating before his eyes. And of the involuntary tears. He coughed and spit. "We're freezing. Dead, we won't be worth shit."

The stocky man regarded Buck with a hateful glare, and Buck's insides squeezed in anticipation of another blow. But the pirates' leader turned to the guy on his right and bobbed his head. The taller man left, and Buck's tormentor repeated, "Ransom."

A wrong answer would get him killed. Or maybe sold to the highest bidder, such as The Station. But was there a *right* answer? No time for doubts. He'd wanted to be his own person, to have value beyond the usefulness of his visions. Here it was, an opportunity to save his life with his wits. Someone else's life too, even if that someone was a disgusting, hostile slob.

"They'll pay..." Buck paused. "With lead and fire."

The bastard's nascent grin died. He pulled his foot back, winding for another kick, but Buck's frown stopped him.

"You know whose ship you attacked?" Buck infused the words with all the swagger he could scrape together.

The pirate squared his shoulders. "Don't care. These are *our* waters! Whoever enters the harbor pays—in coin or in blood."

Buck curved his lips with a careful measure of contempt. "But do you know?"

The man shrugged. "The squints. Your ship flew the Kowloonese colors."

"Ah." It was Buck's turn to smirk. "Not just *any* Kowloonese. That's the *Eastern Star*, Golden Dragon Shang Ka Yi's own ship."

The pirate did not flinch, but the blood left his face. His remaining sidekick shrunk.

"Do you think"—Buck kept hammering—"the Golden Dragon would look kindly at your attack on his flagship? At kidnapping his guests?"

"Let the squints come! There's enough land on the islands to bury them all!"

Heavy machine guns. Countless rifles. Hundreds of security personnel.

Buck shook his head. "How many have returned from this raid? Half?" The islanders almost deserved his pity. Almost. "That's the toll a single ship took. Imagine what their entire fleet would do."

"Their ships are too big to enter the Cuts." Smugness reclaimed the pirate's face.

"I'm sure if the Golden Dragon asks his pal Weinberg, the CIU will land here in no time."

There. Bull's eye. The leader blinked and averted his gaze.

"Now, release us, and I'll tell the Dragon this was one huge misunderstanding." Buck held his breath. The moment of truth.

The squat pirate clenched his jaw, and his little prickly eyes finally zeroed on Buck. "Murphy!" he bellowed. "Where are those goddamn blankets?!"

Buck quietly exhaled.

Half an hour later, a small group of grumbling islanders deposited Buck and Lundy on a pier facing the City. The *Eastern Star*, which had been hovering halfway between the shores, spewed a cloud of black smoke, turned, and started a careful approach, bristling with weapons. The pirates hastily retreated to the nearby tree line.

Buck was too edgy to sit. He paced the boards, wrapping himself tighter in the blanket against the nasty wind. Lundy sat, awake now, still shivering, miserable, and extra grumpy—but unusually quiet.

The *Star* didn't moor. It came to an almost complete stop, bumped softly and heavily against the creaking pier, and dropped a rope ladder. With the ship's tall side sliding along, Buck pushed Lundy up and climbed right behind him. The acute awareness of how broad his back was, and how easy it would be for someone vengeful to put a bullet through it, made Buck clutch the coarse rungs faster, nudging Lundy to hurry.

The moment Buck rolled over the gunwale and flopped onto the deck, the ship's engine roared and it lurched.

The greetings, the questions, the exclamations—all flew over Buck while he lay face down, enjoying the blessed safety. Hugging the ship. The distant engine's vibrations passed from the deck through Buck's forehead and spread arms, straight to his heart.

When he was reasonably sure he wouldn't break into sobbing, Buck turned over and sat up. Janet was there, and Jackson, and the lieutenant, all talking to him. Gabor and Park stood aside, watching.

The words aimed at him gradually started making sense.

Janet, "Are you okay?"

Jackson, "How did you get away?"

Kossowsky, "Did you tell them anything about our mission?"

Buck's eyelids drooped. "The mission didn't come up. I'm okay. They decided to let us go."

"By the Prophet's threadbare scarf, the boy is a pirate whisperer!" Lundy slapped Buck on the back. "You should've heard him. That stumpy islander didn't stand a chance."

Buck rose to his feet without meeting anyone's eye. "I need to go change into something dry." He squeezed past his teammates. Laszlo offered him a hand and shook firmly. The Korean girl punched Buck in the shoulder and nodded.

Buck retreated under the deck. Thankfully, no one followed him. Way too much interaction for one day. He needed to be alone, to not talk, to digest everything that had happened.

He stayed indoors until the ship docked in the lifeless harbor. A dozen crewmen jumped to the pier. Two caught the ropes and secured them to the mooring cleats; others ran further inland to establish a perimeter. The machine gun's barrel moved from side to side like an enormous wasp's sting.

The members of the expedition assembled, waiting for the gangplank to be lowered.

"Why don't we jump off too?" This close to their goal, Buck's impatience was impossible to curb. He had to leave the accursed lake behind, once and for all.

"That would be undignified," said Jackson. "We are their Flag Admiral's guests of honor. That comes with certain procedural expectations."

As if to prove Jackson's words, the ship's captain descended from the bridge to thank them for their trust, apologize that his crew had been unable to ensure their complete safety, and to bid them farewell. Jackson dismissed the captain's concerns and asked to convey his heartfelt gratitude to the Golden Dragon. The two parted ways, properly satisfied with each other.

The team advanced from the pier to the quay. The guards saluted and retreated to the ship, which promptly took off. Buck tracked the irregular blackened blot on the *Star*'s side. Whatever the pirates had thrown at the ship, the explosion didn't breach the hull, only bent and marred it.

Buck shivered. He'd been standing right above that spot. He was lucky to be alive.

"Why such a hurry to leave?" asked Kossowsky. "The pirates are hiding." He glanced at Buck. "And with this ship's firepower, its crew could leisurely capture half the City before lunchtime."

"The Kowloonese aren't interested in capturing anything," responded Laszlo. The scarred guy was a man of few words, but when he had something to say, it was to the point. Or something only his partner would understand.

"They've got *other* ways of exerting their influence." He shot a sideways look at Park. "But the last thing they'd want is to be caught interfering in the City's affairs. The problem is, sound carries far over the water. Firing that machine gun was the easiest way to announce our arrival. By now, most of the City knows we're here."

"How do they know it's us?" asked Buck.

"Okay, they know *someone* is here."

"And?" asked Kossowsky. "Should we be alarmed? Take a defensive position?"

Laszlo shrugged. "No one cares what happens Downtown."

"Besides the Rats," added his partner.

"Yes. Besides the Rats. And no Rats would ever attack us."

"Because we're opportunists," said the girl.

"Huh?" Kossowsky scratched his ear.

"That means, Lieutenant, our party is too big a prey for a Rat to swallow," interjected Jackson, "and they understand this. Right, Miss Park?"

Their Korean guide sketched an indecipherable gesture, half-nod, half-shrug.

"Yes, Mister Jackson, you're right," Laszlo narrated for her. "Miss Park often has difficulty admitting someone else had nailed the answer."

She burned him with a glare. "You're gonna pay for that, Las. Dearly."

"See, Flower?" Her man looked unperturbed. "You're only proving my point."

Park frowned and turned away.

Buck looked around, and out of nowhere, it hit him. He made it! He was in the City! Whatever was to become of their mission, he had already come further than he could have imagined in his wildest dreams. He had crossed the Boundary into the Wilderness. He had encountered working machines. Visited fabulous Locksville. Been a detainee at The Station, a guest of honor in New Kowloon, and a pirates' captive. He had survived a firefight and sailed across a lake. And finally, he was standing in the streets of the City itself. Buck stared down. Nothing special under his feet, only gray, cracked concrete. Still, Sam and Larry would not believe a word from his mouth.

A year ago, celebrating the E Day, he'd been dreaming of joining the Army. An unbelievably distant memory, as if someone else's. He had changed. He'd learned that the world was far more complex than he'd used to think of it. That Five Points' history hid dark chapters. He'd outgrown his enchantment with a girl, made new friends, and lost his Faith. And—he stole a furtive glance at their two guides, as if they could overhear his thoughts—he met real zombies, who turned out to be just like regular people, only more interesting.

Buck squared his shoulders. *The City, here I come!*

He caught a mocking stare from Janet, an understanding smile hiding in the corners of her eyes. Buck winked back.

Chapter 38

Marc

September 27, 42 PE

Marc traced the unfamiliar contours of the *radio* in his pocket. And again. The temptation of the magical device was impossible to resist. An epitome of New Kowloon's power—in this case, the power to communicate over long distances. Until the briefing that day, something Marc had never considered, let alone considered *possible*. One of those ideas making you wonder, *How on Earth did I not come up with that myself?*

With every tiny aspect of the plan having been deliberated in excruciating detail, the briefing had finally rolled to an end. Tam Wai Lam had left the room, returning with a small briefcase.

"Are you sure?" her husband asked.

"What else would you keep them for? How much more pivotal does the moment have to be?"

Tam placed the case on the desk, released two latches, and lifted the lid. Everyone else moved closer to get a better look. Inside, two brick-shaped items laid emplaced in firm black foam. Each had a small glass window and tiny buttons in a rectangular pattern. Short narrow sticks protruded from the top. An enigmatic word *Baofeng* was inscribed on both. Made of plastic, the items probably had been black once, but faded out into gray with swirly white lines.

The Golden Dragon picked one up and turned a knob, extracting a startling high-pitched sound. She repeated the same actions with the other unit and passed it to Weinberg. Marc's boss took it cautiously, twisted it in his hands, and quizzically looked at Tam Wai Lam. She brought the first brick up to her lips and said into it, "I bet you don't have *these* in Locksville." Her words, crackling and distorted but perfectly recognizable, came out of the second unit in Weinberg's hands with an indiscernible delay. Sharp exhalations filled the room.

Weinberg had enough presence of mind not to drop the device from his hand. "A *radio*? A *working* radio?"

Her triumphant smile confirmed the captain's guess.

"But... how?" Never had Marc seen David Weinberg, the Head of Locksville's Intelligence Service, so astounded. "How did they survive the E?"

"Suffice it to say, a few people had been better prepared for the E. And they'd eventually found their way to New Kowloon. Our Science Lab has ensured the radios stay operational and charged."

"Wow. Just... Wow."

A surviving pre-E tech. Not recreated, not improvised. The original technology. Unbelievable. This could become a game changer.

Marc touched his nape. So many possibilities... "What's their range? How far can we talk?"

"Depends on the terrain," explained Tam, "but should reach between Locksville and The Station."

"But not to New Kowloon?"

"No. Sadly, that's too far."

She showed how to turn the *radios* on and off, where to push to talk, and how to adjust the volume. Rajan and the Singh brothers observed with unfeigned curiosity, waiting for their turns to play with the miraculous piece of ancient engineering.

And then it was time to collect Jamil Khan and leave on their mission.

Captain Farley dropped off Marc, Rajan, the Stationer, and Jihan with his brothers at Grimsby. Weinberg, having established a clandestine arrangement with the shady sailor, continued to Locksville. He was to raise the CIU and head toward The Station to join up with Marc and his recon team. The *radios* were meant to help coordinate the rendezvous, but be kept out of sight until then. No reason to give away this unique force multiplier to people like Khan or, say, Farley. That made perfect sense, but it burned Marc's pocket, begging to be brought out and used. With an effort, Marc shook off the device's spell, caressed it one last time, and pulled his hand out.

He'd never been a believer of the Faith, or any other religion, but having been exposed to advanced technology, he could see how someone might consider it dark magic. Or Satan's appeal.

No. He was a proud infidel.

The team had commandeered the Fivepointers' wagon. Following hushed but fierce instructions from the helpful and obliging Captain Farley, a bunch of locals eagerly brought it to the sleepy little port. Two of the Singh brothers,

Ajinder and Preet, ran the point in a staggered formation. Three others formed a protective detail around the wagon, in which Marc and the rest of the team traveled with comfort. Jihan held the reins, letting the two Locksvillers and the renegade Stationer hide from prying eyes under the tent. Two hours later, Marc directed Jihan to a long-abandoned, overgrown gravel track. With the horses unhitched and the wagon concealed in the thicket, the force advanced through the forest.

Marc was determined not to repeat his erstwhile mistake. The Singhs were more than adequate for the task, even though the woodland terrain was not their natural environment. Still, they moved cautiously and quietly, keeping an appropriate formation to secure the VIP assets.

Odd to be one of those. He'd always been on the other side of this equation—the protector, not the protected. Holding his instincts at bay took considerable willpower. Letting go was the next level of leadership, unprecedented for him and unexpectedly challenging.

Jamil Khan made enough noise for everyone. As if he were deliberately stepping on every dry twig, kicking every small stone, and rustling his clothes. Even Rajan, untrained and clumsy as he was, moved like a feral cat by comparison. Unfortunately, not much could be done about that. Marc signaled to the Stationer to fall back and create some distance between them. Kulvir and Ranbir, the rearguard, trailed further behind.

Being able to rely on others for his safety lured Marc's mind into a reflective mode. He'd been operating mainly on bravado. Deep inside, his very essence revolted against approaching the point of fateful decision he'd been refusing to acknowledge. Triggered by that reluctance, a wave of pain shook his body, a roll call of his injuries. The bruises, the swelling, the ribs, the hand, the head—everything screamed, *I'm hurting! Me too, me too!* Marc silenced the cacophony of pain signals with deep breaths. But any attempt to stop the memories from sweeping in was a lost cause.

Strapped to an iron rack, powerless and agonizing. That had become Marc's reality. He had already received an unhealthy dose of lower-ranking Inquisitors' attention. Blood dripped from the fresher cuts and crusted over the older ones. One of his eyes was swollen shut.

The Chief Inquisitor lounged comfortably in a leather chair and studied Marc with unconcealed curiosity. After a while, The Station's dictator broke the prolonged silence.

"One thing I still can't make sense of, is what interest might those Five-pointers possibly have in harboring a Locksviller. They *were* real Fivepointers, weren't they? Never mind, don't bother answering. Or not answering. I'll ask *them* on their way back. Now, to you, Officer... Again, never mind. You'll tell me your name yourself when we are friends. Oh, such revulsion! We *will* be friends, have no doubt!"

The Inquisitor chuckled and crossed his legs.

"You're an experienced man, I see that. We can keep going through the mo-tions. I'll threaten you; you'll hold your head defiantly high. I'll have my people apply various degrees of physical persuasion, and you will stoically withstand it... until you can't anymore. Trust me, everybody breaks. My specialists may not be as exquisite in their art as Wu's crew in New Kowloon, but they deliver. We may find ourselves back in this room in a day, or two, or five. You seem tough, so I'm willing to bet... say, four days."

The Chief Inquisitor squinted.

"Yes, four days until you break and surrender. We will have wasted four days, and you will have lost some less-essential limbs and organs. How would you like losing an eye? I see you were already given a chance to practice that. Or the testicles? In my experience, the manliest men find it difficult to have the balls when they don't have the actual balls. I am not trying to scare you into submission, just outlining one way we can go. A way that would be quite uncomfortable for you, and somewhat unpleasant for me. Not because I resent such drastic measures—I enjoy inflicting pain, I'm sure you've heard that much about me. No, I find having to break you unpleasant because broken people are much less useful assets than those cooperating willingly."

"Assets?" Marc had been sure he'd continue to be tortured for the secrets he knew. This turn of the conversation took him into uncharted territory. "What exactly is it you want of me?"

"Ah, see? You *are* a reasonable man. Not one of those self-professed heroes who disdainfully spit into my face, only to have their tongues cut off. Yes, I'd like you to become my asset. A double agent, if you will. And before you object, I don't need you to betray your precious Weinberg with whatever paltry information you may have. All I need is a man who may happen to be in the right place at the right time to make an important decision. The *right* decision. I'm going to let you go, and you'll continue with your usual activities as if nothing had happened. But you'll keep my interests in mind. That's all."

"That's all," repeated Marc. "Right. And what's preventing me from agree-ing now to save my hide, and then double-crossing you?"

"Heh, aren't you an astute one! The more pleasure it will be to work with you."

"You didn't answer my question."

"Didn't I? You're right, I didn't. Well, it's simple. I'm going to convince you we're the proverbial good guys."

"Are you?"

"The good guys? But of course!"

Finally, the team approached the wide clearing around The Station. Gnashing his teeth to not groan, Marc crawled the last twenty meters, with Jihan on his heels. Ajinder joined them, unfolded the bipod under his rifle, and scanned the area through the scope. Marc pulled his binoculars out of their pouch, awkwardly adjusted the focus with his bandaged hand, and surveyed the painfully familiar scene. Unlike New Kowloon, The Station was not abuzz with activity. Regular teams manned the guard towers, and The Station did not appear any less hospitable than its usual self. The good old Station, pretty fucking unwelcoming as it was.

But something *had* changed since his last visit. Strange decorations lined the sides of the railroad leading into The Station. At first, Marc's brain refused to process what his eyes were showing, but gradually the images took shape.

"Oh," said Marc. "Oh, no, you didn't. Fuck, no. Sick motherfucking inbred murderous *cabrónes hijos de perra...*" He continued cursing until eventually running out of cuss words in the five languages he spoke. Good guys. Yeah, right.

Jihan, who'd been patiently waiting for the stream of obscenities to peter out, extended a hand. What? Ah. Marc passed the binoculars. Jihan growled something in a language Marc did not understand, but his tone echoed Marc's own. A mental note to ask the man to teach him later. In the meantime, he had unpleasant business to attend to.

Marc waved for Jamil and Rajan to approach. He cringed, watching the trader's clumsy attempts to approximate a crawl. When the two men got close, Marc took the binos from a grim Jihan and offered them to the Stationer. The trader struggled with the optics, finally figuring out the way to adjust them, and peered in the direction Marc pointed to. A second later, he yelped, gurgled, and hastily turned away to puke all over the forest floor. Not something to hold against him. Seeing a dozen men impaled on stakes could produce such an effect on the most hardened person. Especially if, as Marc suspected, that person knew these men.

Marc offered Jamil water. The Stationer gratefully accepted the canteen, sloshed the water in his mouth, took several gulps, and returned it. His shaking subsided. The man deserved respect for recovering so remarkably fast.

"Are they who I think they are?" Marc asked in a low voice.

Jamil nodded morosely. "Ten of them. My Guild. I don't recognize the other two."

"The lifers' pack leaders, Mendoza and Horseradish." It was Rajan's turn to use the binoculars. "I played them off each other to cover our escape, Marc."

Was Marc supposed to feel responsible? No. These men's blood was not on his hands, and he couldn't care less about the lifer scum.

"Don't feel bad about them," Rajan echoed his thoughts. "Motherfuckers were bad to the bone, both. They had it coming. Not... Not this way." He shivered. "I have no regrets. The others..." he allowed Jamil Khan to pick up the conversation.

"The others are ten out of the fifteen members of our faction," the trader confirmed. "I'm here, and the remaining four had been traveling when I left. There's a chance we can save them if Khalifa doesn't get to them first."

"When are they due back?" Marc was already running through the options.

"Let me think. The double-stacker from the west should be here tomorrow. The three-boxcar train from Rochester—in two days."

"The one from Rochester isn't coming. Your friends are safe."

"Not coming? You know something I don't?"

"Locksville has closed the passage for The Station's trains."

"I see. Funny. Your hostile action may have saved their lives."

"Yeah. Fate is a fickle bitch, isn't she? Now, with the other train, let's think how we can kill two birds with one stone. Or kill one and save two others."

Chief Inquisitor Moctar Khalifa delivered on his promise. Sort of. He couldn't persuade Marc that The Stationers were the *good* guys. The Inquisitor himself did not truly believe that. What he believed, Marc had learned, was that the Railroad people were *not worse* guys than everyone else. That the game had no good guys, and whoever claimed the contrary was lying—to others, and possibly to themselves, too.

Khalifa returned after Marc had been untied, washed, dressed, and fed. He sent the guards away and said, "Ask me anything."

Finding the right questions turned out unexpectedly challenging.

The Chief Inquisitor grinned. "Difficult when you aren't bound by any restrictions, isn't it? I'll help you out. Why do you consider us bad? Why are we the enemy?"

"Duh. Because you're slavers."

"That's one possible answer. This subject comes up most often. But are we, really?"

"What are you saying? You claim you are not?"

"Absolutely. That's what I claim. The workers? They aren't slaves, as much as they whine to the contrary. They are merely bound by contracts. Which they accept with full knowledge of what they're signing up for. Is it hard work? Damn right it is, but we've never made a secret of that. And if they still sign up with that knowledge, it's because they've got no better options. Their choice is between working for us and starving to death."

"But the children?"

"Worse. The children are sent to us by their families, the very societal institution that's supposed to have their best interests in mind. Whether out of greed or dire need, it is their call. We're providing the employment opportunity, and a promise to let them go when the time comes. Let's face it: if we didn't take those children in, most of them would never have lived to see adulthood. If there are any bad guys in this story, it's their parents."

"You're saving these children."

"Yes, we are. You're being sarcastic, but that's what we do. We're a business, not a charity, and they have to work hard for a living. But it's honest work—unlike, say, being sold to a brothel, or joining a gang."

"Which brings us to the lifers."

"Yes. And your question is?"

"Isn't *that* slavery?"

"No. That's justice. Life in prison with hard labor. What's the alternative? Kill the criminals? An option too, but a wasteful one. Why not make them work to repay some value to society?"

"And the value ends up in your coffers."

"We're a part of society too." A shadow of a smile touched the Inquisitor's lips.

"What about the punishments?"

"No state can function without rules and discipline. Ours may just be harsher than the others'."

"And you're basically a dictatorship."

"So what? This is our internal matter. You'll find many political systems out there, the entire spectrum. Does this make us the worst? Would you rather prefer a Dark Island-style theocracy? I see you shudder at the thought. Then why are we singled out? Plenty of authoritarian regimes around masquerade as democracies. At least we aren't pretending. And, unlike them, we help the world move on."

"You do? How?"

"Don't be daft. Trade, of course! We connect societies. We connect people. Now let me ask *you* a question. What's your precious Locksville's contribution to the world?"

Marc's head involuntarily jerked up under the Inquisitor's curious regard. How could Khalifa hit the nail on the head so precisely? Marc had never as much as hinted at his doubts to anyone!

"Order?" he posited, tentatively.

"Meh. I mean, sure, order is better than anarchy. But we would have managed without your help, somehow. And anyway, are you proud of being, effectively, muscle for hire?"

Marc shifted uncomfortably. He *was* a proud third-generation Locksviller, born and raised. A patriot. And yet... he could not name a single manifest achievement his homeland had contributed to the world.

The Inquisitor interpreted Marc's silence correctly. "I don't doubt your loyalty, and I am not convincing you to betray your state. But be honest with yourself, for once. What else has Locksville got to offer? Passable wines? Not much to brag about. The inevitable conclusion is that it's a parasite, leeching on major trade routes and gorging on the passersby's blood."

Marc found no logical flaw in the unsettling comparison. Weinberg, a sophisticated debater, would have come up with plenty of arguments to counter Khalifa's point, but... He wasn't Weinberg. He hated to admit the Inquisitor was making good on the promise to persuade him. One last ace remained up his sleeve.

"What about the attacks on trains and a caravan? Are you going to deny those were of your own doing?"

"No. I'm impressed you've figured that out, and won't deny that. Yes, we've had a hand in that. See? I'm perfectly honest with you. That's collateral damage."

"I was in that caravan!"

"Tough luck."

"But people died!"

"People die every day. Most of them die stupidly, or of natural causes. At least those died for a good reason."

"Which is?" That was a cheap ruse. But if they already were being honest, allegedly...

Khalifa ignored the hook. "The end justifies the means. When you play at this level, it always does. And if someone tells you otherwise, know they're lying. You think the Chinese care about a few lives lost here and there if it's for the greater good?"

"And what end are you justifying?" Marc kept pushing.

"Joining forces with New Kowloon."

Marc opened his mouth and shut it again. He had *so* many questions. But before he could ask, the "host" took the conversation further.

"Look, Marc. People generally fall into two categories: the sheep, and the wolves."

"And you're the wolf."

Khalifa grimaced, irritated. "Let me finish. No, bandits are the wolves. There's a third category, the sheepdogs. Your so misleadingly named Counter Insurgency Unit, for example."

"Alright. So, where do *you* fit in?"

"Think, Marc, think. What—or who—is missing in this picture?"

Marc imagined a pasture with a herd of sheep, a pack of wolves lurking at the edge of the forest, and a bunch of guard dogs patrolling in between. And then a human figure walked in. "A shepherd," he said.

"A shepherd." The Inquisitor nodded, satisfied. "He who cultivates the sheep, commands the dogs, and occasionally tames some wolves."

"And you're one such."

"I am," Khalifa agreed, humbly downcast. "As are your beloved Weinberg, and Five Points' Colonel, and a couple of New Kowloon's Golden Dragons. We look into the future, capable of seeing the bigger picture. We may not always see it eye to eye, and that's the root of our disagreements. I'm inviting you to join this exclusive club. You're almost there, anyway. Your last step will be to start thinking independently. Challenge your perceptions. Draw your own conclusions. You owe that to yourself."

Marc leaned back, overwhelmed but trying to follow the advice. "You want to change the playing field by introducing a new player."

"I'm glad I wasn't wrong about you." The Inquisitor smiled one of those carnivorous grins that must have given goosebumps to the *sheep*.

"But you know Weinberg will never work with you. Nor will the Chinese. You're... tainted."

"And now we're coming to the crux of the issue. What's the alternative?"

Marc shrugged.

Khalifa kept pushing. "Say, I *am* removed. What happens next?"

"One of your deputies steps in. Or a trader."

"No. They're all sheep, or sheepdogs at best. Some—wolves in disguise. It will be total chaos. The Station will fall apart and disintegrate."

"Will anyone shed a tear?"

"Marc. Marc, Marc, Marc. You've got so much to learn yet. What did I tell you we do? We enable trade. We connect. *That* is the future, the reconnected world! New Kowloon does the same, only by water. We complement each other. Neither of us can do this on our own. This world needs The Station, and The Station needs me." He let the statement sink.

Marc raised his eyes to meet Khalifa's.

The Chief Inquisitor nodded emphatically. "Shepherds do not have to like each other. But they need to understand each other's value. Am I a good person? Yes. No. Who cares? That is not what matters."

Marc nodded back. "I still think you aren't, but I see your point."

"Great. Now. I'm sure you'll figure out a way to sneak back to Weinberg. I'll even let it slide if you slay a few of my dogs, to make your escape convincing. Just don't go overboard. See? All for the greater good. The only favor I'm asking in return is that when the time comes for you to make an important decision, you make it with your eyes wide open. As a true shepherd. How's that for a deal? Oh, and sorry about all the torture. It had to look authentic enough."

"Gee, thanks. It sure *feels* authentic enough. You realize what Weinberg will do when he finds out you've tortured me?"

"I'm counting on it."

Chapter 39

Yun-mi

September 27, 42 PE

Happiness, plain and simple. It did exist! Back where she belonged, check. Needed, check. Loved? Ooh. Such a check!

Downtown. The place where she'd spent most of the last two years. Where she was more at home than anywhere else in the world.

It welcomed her return. *It* opened up to her, via that private connection they shared since that day when the City had first admitted her as a part of itself.

Yun-mi did not believe in the supernatural. There had to be a simpler, mundane explanation. Maybe the intuition she had developed with practice. But it was comforting to think of the City as a benevolent, omniscient creature.

That day, when she'd first experienced *the knowledge*, she'd been so awed she didn't tell Joon-woo. She couldn't bring herself to share this intimate connection later, either. It was *her* secret. One of the very few truly private things she'd ever possessed. If her mentor had noticed the change, he'd kept his observations to himself. And now it was too late to ask him.

Since then, whatever location he had tasked her with reaching, she'd hit the ground running. She would not have been able to describe that sense of direction, to put it into words, if asked to. She simply *knew*: this street was a dead end; taking that detour would bring her to the target faster; and that tunnel she should never-ever enter! She had obediently followed the guidance and had not regretted it once.

Thank you, old friend, great to see you too!

She had a goal. An interesting, challenging goal. Not a training drill or a foraging expedition. The Golden Dragon herself relied on her skills and knowledge to accomplish something significant. If Wai Lam had as much as wiggled her brows, let alone tasked her with a personal assignment, Yun-mi would have gone to the end of the world and back. To Seven Hells.

Last but very far from least, she had Laszlo. Whether he hovered behind her shoulder like a blood-curdling guardian angel or closed the file she led, his presence was tangible. Not only was he there, he was there *for her*. *With* her. Her man. Her rock to lean against. To trust blindly. Finally.

The mere thought of him sent sparks through her nerves. The thought, and the sweet buzz that had been filling her body since last night. Her treacherous cheeks tingled, blushing, but that was okay. No one would notice in the shadows.

Happiness. In the extra springiness of her steps; in how high she held her head; in the smile that kept creeping onto her face.

Hadn't she learned from the past? Hadn't life taught her good times never last? A small voice in her head desperately tried to talk her back into her habitual preparedness for the worst. Tried—and failed, shattering against her resolve to enjoy the moment.

Buck, who'd been hanging around her in the lead like an eager pup, struck a conversation. They were in an underground passageway. She and Laszlo stepped silently, out of a professional habit rather than any practical concern. The others, apparently, had never trained in such arts, and the noise of their footfalls echoed and bounced in the tunnel, sounding as if a huge, lame centipede was out for a lazy stroll. Three lamps dispelled the darkness, carried by her, Kossowsky in the middle of the line, and Laszlo in the back. The three moving spots of light, temporarily reclaimed from the lifeless murkiness, seemed to be further apart than they really were. That must have given the boy the false sense that the others wouldn't overhear. That, or he was ready to break his quiet spell.

"Isn't he too old for you?"

What was that about? Oh. You little jerk. "Excuse me?"

Buck shrunk under her scathing glare, stumbled, and fell a step behind into the shadows, but quickly caught up. "I'm worried he may be using you, is all," he mumbled in a reconciliatory tone.

"Big question, who's using whom," Yun-mi muttered. "Regardless, thank you for your concern, but that's none of your goddamn business, k—" He'd asked not to be called kid. And he'd escaped the pirates. Fine. "Buck. I *am* happy with him. And we won't discuss this any further, clear?"

"Clear…"

Great. Now the idiot looked miserable, as if she were to blame. She beckoned him to come closer. Grab him by the scruff? Tempting, but no. "Tell me, are you fucking insane? Hit your head hard on the island?" she whispered, ferociously but quietly enough to *really* not be overheard.

He flinched away. "N-no... Why?"

"If Laszlo gets a whiff of any ideas you may have about me, he'd tear you a new one. You know that, right? And you're still trying? You don't strike me as suicidal, so must be nuts, or dull as a bag of stones."

"I... I'm..." Whatever Buck planned to say remained unsaid. He walked on dejectedly, looking away, until finally uttering, "I meant nothing like that."

Alright, magnanimous Miss Park would accept this half-assed non-apology.

Buck visibly forced himself to switch to a different topic. "Why are we taking these tunnels? Can't we walk in the streets? We are in this famous Downtown but don't get to see any of it."

Why, indeed? Yun-mi didn't have a ready answer. *It* had led her into the Path, the complex system connecting dozens of buildings without the need to climb to the surface. She had a reasonably good idea of what awaited them on the ground, but... Sure, why not?

"Follow me," Yun-mi said louder, and the centipede obediently slinked after her into a side corridor. She took the stairs up. These were the odd ones, built into a narrow trench with crumbling rubber handrails on either side. She could swear these stairs had been created to move, but was unsure why, where to, or how. Upstairs, Yun-mi led the group through a set of glass doors into a wide lobby. She stepped aside, letting the foreigners go ahead and take the view in.

Laszlo came up and pulled her further away. "What are we doing here?"

"He wanted to know why we weren't taking the streets." Yun-mi pointed at Buck with a thumb, leaving out the sensitive part of their conversation. She didn't want the kid's blood on her hands.

"I see. And that's all? He wasn't trying to flirt with you?" Such an innocent question.

Too perceptive, yes. Yun-mi grabbed the collar of Laszlo's jacket, pulled his face down to her height, and kissed him. "Please don't hurt him. He's just a stupid country kid. He's been through a lot today."

Laszlo arched an eyebrow. "Hurt him? Is that what the love of my life thinks of me? How sad. I am not a monster. I don't hurt little children."

She kissed him again. "*That's* what the love of your life thinks of you."

A smile undermined Laszlo's effort to appear wounded. "Flower, my dear, I trust you, and won't be threatened by competition I know you can handle. Now, if you can't... Let me know, and *then* you'll meet the monster."

Yun-mi rested her head on his shoulder. "Love you too, Mister Monster."

Laszlo's muscles tensed under her cheek.

Oops. The playful words escaped her mouth on their own. Or did they? Certainly not contrived, but were they true? Not sure... yet. "I said it, didn't I?"

His hand brushed her hair.

"Yun-mi?" Janet's call echoed in the hollow space. "Why are we here? What's all this? Is this the way to the Burn?"

Yun-mi grunted, wishing the Fivepointers vanished, leaving the two of them alone. "No."

Daylight seeped into the lobby through what once had been immense, two-man tall windows. These days, their frames were filled with what looked like piles of greenish ice invading the building.

"Brennan asked why we aren't traveling on the surface. This is why. Come." Yun-mi led them up another flight of dead, once-moving stairs to the next floor and cautiously approached the opening—a former window too—overlooking the street level. They were in a high-rise building, with its mind-blowingly tall brethren crowding the Downtown Core around. "All these towers had once been covered in glass. All the way to the top. Hard to believe, I know. Over time, the glass fell and shattered. That's how we've ended up with this." She gestured to where the shards below had formed a landscape of their own. The skinless structures loomed amid a frozen sea, complete with waves and valleys. "Gets better once we make it out of the Core. Lower buildings, less glass. Especially in the side streets. But for now, back down we go."

Yun-mi allowed the travelers another minute to take in the surreal view, the likes of which they wouldn't find outside the City. Janet, the most emotional of all, held a hand at her throat as if stifling a cry. Buck looked stupefied, Jackson and Kossowsky—stern. Even Lundy, the only one she couldn't puzzle out yet, gawked, letting complex emotions wash over his usually skeptical face.

"What a waste," whispered Jackson.

"The amount of skill, the knowledge it took to build this—all gone now." Janet's voice was small and thin. "How far behind we have fallen. They were giants! And we... we're nothing more than pests, living off of the rotting left-overs. Rats, stripping the last pieces of the carcass off the bones." She shot an apologetic glance at Yun-mi and Laszlo. "No offense!"

Yun-mi shrugged. "None taken. It *is* true."

The metaphor resonated with her own thoughts. She had heard the stories from the times of the first Rats, in the early years after the E. Millions of people who had lived in and around the City had escaped or perished, leaving countless treasures to the paltry thousands of survivors in the urban area. Usable—*re*usable—items. Clothing and footwear, tools and raw materials, kitchenware and furniture. Jewelry and other useless trinkets. Coins. All could be found in abundance. If she were to believe the legends, one had used to go to an abandoned store or a warehouse, and pick up whatever they desired off the shelves. Apartments and houses had been brimming with stuff. Kick down any door and walk away with full sacks. There had been food to be found, the most precious of all prizes. With everyone going half-hungry all the time, unsure of when, or what, their next meal would be, non-perishables had been worth a premium price. That was then.

As time had gone by, the pickings had grown scarcer and thinner. The food-stuffs that hadn't spoiled had long since been eaten. An increasing number of the clothes she was finding crumbled, falling apart at a touch. And she was one of the best. Many of her less capable colleagues were returning from their City runs empty-handed more often than not. Her generation's Rats were picking the last useful morsels off the already clean skeleton. What would they—*all* the City folk—do once their inheritance had been fully and irreversibly squan-dered? Her only hope was New Kowloon. While the Rats fought for the meager leftovers, the Dragons had been building. Slowly but surely, from the ground up, and up, and up.

Yearning to be a part of that, she'd bet on the Dragons. That was why she had eagerly accepted Wai Lam's vision of uniting the clans into a trade network. The only way forward—from their barbarian existence driven by the day's sustenance, and into the future of something meaningful. Not at once, not tomorrow, step by excruciatingly slow step. New Kowloon offered a promise. Without it, they were doomed to remain... urban zombies.

"I so hope what we find will change this." Janet's quiet words weren't in-tended for the others' ears, but in the eerie calm of early afternoon Downtown, Yun-mi heard her. Everyone did.

"Shush!" Kossowsky's exclamation was too loud. "Don't—" He cut himself and looked at Yun-mi and Laszlo. What *was* it they were after?

Chapter 40

Rajan

September 27, 42 PE

Stop. Stop!

Sure, he'd told Marc not to blame himself for the horrific deaths of the two lifers. Neither should he. And yet, something still gnawed at him. Yes, the two had been as bad as lifers come. With plenty of blood on their hands and zero regrets. With a trail of victims and suffering left behind. Likely to shed more blood if they had lived through that day. All true. But *he* wasn't like them. *He* wasn't a lifer. *He* wasn't a natural-born killer. He was bad, but not as bad. And now their deaths were on him. Not the execution, but if he hadn't started that riot...

Stop. Stop these thoughts!

Bene. Forget the lifers. But he also killed a man with his own hands, beating him to a pulp. He wasn't much better than Horseradish or Mendoza. And if that was true, why did they deserve to die—and he didn't?

"Rajan?" Marc's voice jerked him out of that dark place.

"Qué?"

"What you said is true, sí? You said that was not my fault. Neither was it yours, buddy."

Was Marc reading his mind?

"Don't you dare go down that path. Been there, done that. Got nothing but pain and depression. Snap out of it, brother. We're soldiers. We shoot bad people for a living. They die. If not, we do. It's that simple. But we're the good guys in this story."

"Are we?" Much worse words were ready at the tip of his tongue. But he would have regretted them later.

Until last week, the Universe had had no good people. Since then, he'd met Marc and Weinberg. And Buck. And those two Dragons. None of them fairytale-good, but not totally bad like the lifers.

"Are we the good guys? Ha! Ye of little faith!" Marc presented two hands, imitating scales. "Lifers and slavers," he named his bandaged hand, "you and me," the healthy one. The hands wavered around the equilibrium, then the first one went up, the second—way down. Marc looked to the left, to the right, shrugged, and nodded. "Questions?"

Rajan sighed. Ridiculous. He smiled. "Bene. You win, Marc."

"Always!" Too cheerful. Suspicious. "The good guys always do."

"That makes me the bad guy, no?"

"Er... Shit. Oh, well. You know what I mean."

A squawking sound from Marc's pocket startled them. "*Marc, you there?*" asked Weinberg's distorted voice. That *radio* thingie.

Marc fumbled with the zipper, fished the device out, and pushed a button on its side. "I'm here, boss. What's up?"

"*What's up?!* Under different circumstances, I would've disciplined you for insubordination, Lieutenant Novak."

Marc rolled his eyes but added deference to his tone. "We're in position, sir. They've blocked the bridge and placed an ambush on both sides. We're observing from point-six klick due northeast. Khalifa is here too."

"Is he? Interesting. We're about an hour away. Keep watching."

"Yes, sir."

The radio paused, then squeaked again. "I can't see your face, Marc. But if I find out you're mocking me..."

"No, boss. No mocking, sir."

"I'll know."

Marc met Rajan's eyes. "How does he do that?"

Rajan shrugged. His experience with superiors had been based on shouts, punishments, and threats of punishments. He understood that language well and had learned to navigate The Station's natural order with minimal friction. Weinberg had shown himself to be an altogether different sort of boss. He smiled. He acknowledged. He asked for Rajan's opinion. All new and weird.

There was the flip side. Back at The Station, the supervisors didn't see the "workers" as persons. They cared nothing for what Rajan thought or felt, as long as the work was done and he made no trouble. Weinberg paid attention to his subordinates. Saw their mood swings and doubts. Made Rajan nervous. But that was a fair price to pay. He was developing a taste for being noticed.

Everything went according to the plan. At first.

From their observation point on the old water tower roof, Rajan and Marc watched the two-pronged CIU force stalking through the forested banks of Twenty Mile Creek and taking their positions. The Station's ambush remained oblivious to anyone else's presence. Arrogant as usual. The top dogs on their home turf.

An hour later, the two-car train appeared on the horizon. A painfully familiar boxcar with the traders' and supervisors' quarters, followed by a double-stacker carrying two containers. At that speed, at least another half hour before it reached the creek. Did they always move that slowly? Crawling with agonizing sluggishness, the train got closer, and the haulers' faces became discernible. Team Three.

What was that feeling? Guilt for having escaped while they were still suffering? Or pride for the same, and gratitude for his luck? Homesickness, for a place that had never been his home? Yearning for something he'd gotten used to, however painful that life had been? No. No. No. Yes. Yes. Yes. A hauler's life had been much simpler. Do the back-breaking job, hate everyone. Straightforward. No thinking, no doubts, no mixed emotions. Was he better off now? Fuck, yeah! How was that even a question?

Finally, the wheels rattled over the bridge. The Station's ambush sprang, blocking both ends. The haulers stopped, blank-faced, showing neither surprise nor fear, but always welcoming an extra break.

He'd used to be like that, empty eyes, numb brain. Yes, definitely better off now.

The supervisors disembarked and joined the soldiers without fuss.

Only one trader caused a hiccup. He read the situation correctly and jumped off the bridge. His head never resurfaced over the shallow water. That was unexpectedly courageous. And dumb. Or not. Beats being impaled. Quicker.

The other trader surrendered, bawling, and was escorted to the command post where the Chief Inquisitor waited, surrounded by a small retinue.

A burst of automatic fire interrupted the conversation. The bullets wheezed over the Stationers. From this far away, the words couldn't be heard, but the CIU must have announced its presence. At the Chief Inquisitor's wave of a hand, the Station soldiers complied, laying down their weapons and dropping to their knees with the hands behind their heads.

Rajan and Marc climbed down from the tower and hiked to the bridge, leaving Jamil Khan with the Singh brothers behind. Weinberg, accompanied by a CIU detail, headed in the same direction.

The Chief Inquisitor greeted everyone with a broad smile.

Chapter 41

Buck

September 27, 42 PE

The Burn was, in fact, hellish. But an old, retired, *has-been* variety of hell. At the time it had burned, it must have been a real inferno. Four decades later, it was... unassuming. Creepy, but not exceptionally terrifying.

Elsewhere in the City, skyscrapers, supermarkets, and multilevel parking lots were the norm, mostly remaining upright, if in various degrees of disrepair. They could have no windows, busted doors, or caved in roofs, but were easily identifiable as buildings. So many of them Buck had stopped gawking.

The Burn had only a few remnants of buildings left standing. The rest had collapsed into heaps of charred bricks, or nothing at all. When he'd heard the name *Burn* the other night, his imagination had painted a scarred landscape in shades of black and gray. Maybe that's how the Burn had looked early on, after it had, well, burned. But time and the elements had exacted their inescapable toll on the traces of the disaster. Washed by the rain, eroded by the seasons, the Burn had nothing extraordinary about its colors. Same as its surroundings, just *deader*, in everything related to people.

Wildlife, however, had claimed a firm hold of it. The ashes must have served as extra fertilizer, because the Burn was overgrown. Car skeletons turned into bushes. Trees formed such thick walls, they forced the travelers to detour. Marginally thinner greenery hinted at the former streets. Bird and animal sounds filled the forest, and vague shapes escaping practically from under Buck's feet found refuge not five steps away. Humans were rare guests here, judging by how little fear they instilled in the local fauna.

Park confirmed his suspicions. "Nights here must be interesting."

"What can we expect?" Buck's hand squeezed his rifle. No more surprises, if he could help it.

"What not? Raccoons, skunks, possums, foxes, feral cats. Coyotes. Deer and moose. Maybe bears. But wild dog packs are the most dangerous."

"Uh, okay. Have you been here before?"

"Once, in daytime, out of curiosity. The Burn is not a place for a Rat. Nothing of value survived the fire. Laszlo, you?"

"A couple of times. Hunting."

"What were you hunting?" Buck regretted the question as soon as it left his lips.

Laszlo turned to him. "Bounty," he said, deadpan, unblinking.

Buck averted his eyes, swallowed, and lost all desire to further probe the unnerving Rat.

Kossowsky came up. "Where exactly are we going? Do you have any idea where to search? How can we find anything in *this*?"

Park beckoned to Janet. "This library of yours, was it created after the E? Otherwise, we may as well call it quits and go home, because it turned into ashes a long time ago."

"You're right. The E was what drove someone to create it."

"That note you found," chimed in Buck, "did it mention anything else? Anything at all that may prove useful to us?"

Janet hesitated, and he pushed on. "Look around. If it's a crate or a box, we may search for months, and still end up empty-handed. We've come this far, why insist on secrecy?"

Janet's eyes darted to Kossowsky. Jackson didn't wait for the lieutenant's response. "Buck's right. We're all in this together now. Read us the goddamn note already."

She pulled a piece of paper out of her jacket's inner pocket.

"Only the relevant part," warned Kossowsky, ever vigilant.

Buck rolled his eyes. No sense arguing. Something was better than nothing. The *irrelevant* parts would come to light soon enough.

Janet unfolded the page, cleared her throat, and read aloud, "*If you're looking for*—uh, never mind... Blah, blah, blah... Here. *You'll find it in the First Circle of the Seven Hells, where the crown had fallen.*"

Everyone waited for her to continue, but she stayed silent.

"That's it?" asked Park. "This was enough to send your expedition? You people are *so* strange. A miracle you've made it this far."

Kossowsky scowled. "Miss Park, please concentrate on the task at hand. First Circle. What can that mean?"

"Fine, let's concentrate."

"No need," said Laszlo. "I know the place."

Chapter 42

Marc

September 27, 42 PE

"Captain Weinberg!" gleefully exclaimed the Chief Inquisitor. "How nice of you to join us today!"

Weinberg stopped, scrapping and reevaluating whatever opening statement he had prepared. The Inquisitor's greeting was not a reaction that could be conceivably expected from a man in his situation.

"Come on, Captain, don't be shy!" continued Khalifa. "What were you planning to do? Arrest me? Execute me on the spot? Make me disappear?"

Weinberg signaled to the soldiers accompanying him to lead the other Stationers away, outside the hearing range. Four people stayed in the shadow of an ancient oak—Marc, Rajan, Weinberg, and the Inquisitor.

The captain tilted his head. "And what would *you* have me do with you, Khalifa?"

The Stationer shook his head. "Oh no, Captain, you don't get to shift this onto me. You made the move, you take the responsibility. I am but your humble prisoner."

"Very well," said Weinberg, nonplussed. "We're at war, and I hold you personally culpable. You broke the neutrality between our two states. You captured and tortured my man."

"This man here?" The Inquisitor smiled, nodding at Marc. Butterflies in Marc's stomach took wing. The moment of truth was swiftly approaching.

"Yes, this man. For that alone, I should kill you right here and now."

"Will you have the decency to do it yourself? Or will you, as always, delegate your dirty work to others?"

"If you insist." Weinberg pulled a pistol from the holster and pointed it at Khalifa's head. "Chief Inquisitor Moctar Khalifa, by the power vested in me by the Defense Council of the Free City of Locksville, I proclaim—"

Marc sighed and forced his suddenly disobedient legs to step forward, putting himself between the two men. This was it. Time for some shepherding.

"Sorry, Captain, can't let you do this."

Exhilarating energy surged through Marc's veins. Was this moment the sole purpose of his life? Why was it so important to defend one shepherd from another? To become a shepherd himself? Power? He'd never craved it and still didn't. The hole in his heart, that's why. The emptiness left by losing his parents. He knew first-hand what it was, to have no one to look after him. No one to protect, to feed, to guide him. If he could fill that void for someone else—for an entire society!—what better goal could he ever wish for?

Assuming, of course, he survived the next few minutes.

"Marc?"

Interesting times. In the last few days, he'd witnessed Weinberg surprised more than anyone probably had ever.

"What is the meaning of this?" The captain frowned and lowered his gun. "Care to explain yourself?"

"Boss, he's a shepherd. You are a shepherd. Shepherds don't kill each other. If they do, who will tend the flock? Who will command the dogs? Who will keep the wolves at bay?"

Weinberg stared at him for a long minute. "I could court-martial you for this."

Marc did not look away. "You could."

"And execute you for treason."

"You could," Marc repeated and spread his arms, inviting the captain to proceed if he was so inclined. His heart was trying to escape his doomed body.

Weinberg holstered the handgun. "Okay," he said. "Alright. I see you had arranged all of this, Khalifa. I'm listening."

Marc stepped aside, barely concealing his relief. His hands, pushed deep into his pockets, shook violently.

"Always a pleasure to deal with a shrewd man." The Chief Inquisitor, unperturbed by coming dangerously close to being shot in the face, grinned from ear to ear. "From one manipulator to another, admit, this was well-played, ha?"

With a bit of a stretch, the captain's grunt could be taken for an agreement. "I found it odd that you didn't wait for the traders' return to The Station. Your decision to venture out yourself, even odder."

"But not odd enough to suspect a set-up?"

"No, not odd enough. Now stop gloating, you aren't out of the woods yet. Figuratively"—Weinberg looked around—"or literally. You've got my attention, but I can still shoot you and go home with the warm memory of a day well spent."

"Granted."

"What's your angle? And don't feed me that 'shepherd' bullshit. It may have worked on Marc, but won't sway me."

"As you wish, Captain, though I believe this metaphor is accurate. Let's establish some ground understanding. First, without me, The Station would disintegrate."

"Naturally. Especially after you had eleven Guild traders killed."

Khalifa didn't bat an eye. "Traitors, as you must well know."

Weinberg did not confirm, but neither did he object, and the Inquisitor continued. "Why act all sanctimonious, Captain? Don't you Locksvillers execute your traitors?"

"We don't have traitors." The hairs on the back of Marc's neck stood on their ends under Weinberg's glance. Whether his actions constituted treason was debatable, but they had passed the watershed moment. That much was clear. Marc would never enjoy the same level of trust as he had before. No way back. He had just lost his job.

"Everybody has traitors!" The Inquisitor chuckled. "But if that's your blind spot, fine. Take the Chinese. Do they treat their turncoats any better?"

Weinberg remained silent.

"Great. We've established that I am instrumental to The Station's survival. Do you agree its survival is important?"

Weinberg kept staring at his counterpart.

"Come on, Captain. You aren't contemplating splitting our assets and clients between Locksville and New Kowloon, are you?"

"Huh," said Weinberg, "there's a thought."

"You can't be serious."

"I am not."

"Good. So. You need The Station, and The Station needs me. Where does this leave us?"

"I expect you're prepared to enlighten me."

"Right you are. See, I am a pragmatic man. The status quo is not working. I want to move forward. To break the established patterns."

"To abolish slavery and start using engines," Weinberg said.

Khalifa inclined his head. "You know? Of course you do. Yes. But I couldn't openly come out against the Faith orthodoxy. I needed an external shock to shake things up. Which you have so obligingly provided."

"New Kowloon would never allow this."

"I am prepared to work with them."

"They aren't prepared to work with you, Chief Inquisitor. Not after the attempt on Shang Ka Yi's life."

"Which was a retaliation for his attempt on mine." The Inquisitor touched the scar on his neck. "His completely unprovoked attempt, I must add. Yes, we'd been meddling in each other's affairs, but that had been fair game. Until he'd crossed the line."

"Last fall's assassin doesn't count?"

"What, now?" Khalifa's face puckered in convincing puzzlement.

"I see. Then that was Siu Ho Fai's own initiative."

"You know about him, too. You live up to your reputation, Captain. I'm impressed. And I am not impressed by too many people. On that subject... Yes, gambling on Siu has proved unfortunate. I underestimated his ambitions and resentment toward Shang. You're saying Siu tried to kill him last fall?"

"Yes."

"Ah, now it all makes sense. Whom would Shang blame? The usual suspect. I'll set the record straight with the Hive, if you can broker a meeting."

"That can be arranged."

"Then—"

Marc recoiled from a spray of blood over his face. A fraction of the second later, a distant report of a shot followed. Khalifa's head swung to the side, and he collapsed. Fuck! Fuck-fuck-fuck!

Marc dropped to his knees and checked on the Stationer. The bullet entered his mouth and tore a hole in his cheek, taking a few teeth with it. Blood gushed from his tongue. Khalifa was alive but unconscious.

Marc peered up at Weinberg. "The Singh brothers! Tam's Plan B!"

"Vengeful bitch!" the captain spewed and sprinted toward the water tower, frantically waving his hands. A CIU squad rushed to provide him protection.

"Rajan, help me!" Marc called. "Rajan!"

Rajan remained motionless, his eyes riveted to the prone man.

"Rajan!" Marc yelled for the third time. "For fuck's sake, I know you hate his guts, but I need your help now! We must keep him alive!"

Rajan lingered for a moment longer, finally stepping forward, and together they turned the Inquisitor on his side. Marc pulled a bandage from his vest and started stuffing it into Khalifa's mouth to stem the bleeding.

"Ain't his guts I hate," Rajan said levelly. "Yours."

Chapter 43

Yun-mi

September 27, 42 PE

"The epicenter of the Burn," Laszlo said, "where the plane had crashed. You know where it is?"

Yun-mi shook her head.

"It was called Queen's Park. Queen, the crown, get it?"

Now it started making sense. "And it's the First Circle 'cause that's where the Burn was ignited!"

"Bingo."

"What's there now?"

"Same as everywhere in the Burn. But! The subway tunnel underneath collapsed from the crash, blocking it in several places."

"I know! It's unpassable between the Chrystal and Saint Patrick!" Unraveling the mystery, thread by thread. Yun-mi's pulse picked up.

"Right? Now, what if there's an access point—a sinkhole, or some such—from what was once Queen's Park to that section of the tunnel? Underground, in the heart of the Burn, a perfect hiding place!"

"Okay," Kossowsky said, "sounds convincing. Lead the way."

"Easier said than done." Laszlo shook his head. "Neither of us is familiar with these blocks. No detailed maps. Dense shrubbery. We may be better off cutting laterally, going through the next neighborhood, and then reentering the northern end of the Burn."

"Great idea!" Yun-mi agreed, a little too eagerly. She took her bearings relative to the CN Tower and pointed west. "That way."

She was happy to leave the Burn. She couldn't *feel* the City there, and that kept her on edge. A hundred steps into the Burn, she had lost her sense of direction. The City's guidance, its gentle and friendly touch on her shoulder, had been first muffled, then disappeared altogether.

The lieutenant eyed her and Laszlo suspiciously. "This better not be some trick. Need I remind you of the Golden Dragon's orders?"

The jackass didn't know the half of it.

Wai Lam's orders weren't limited to being a glorified tour guide for the weird team. Mistrustful of the secretive foreigners, the Golden Dragon had tasked Yun-mi with discovering their true goals, what side effects those goals might have on New Kowloon, and specifically on Wai Lam's personal interests.

Laszlo gave the officer the friendliest fake smile, equal parts funny and creepy on his scarred face.

"No tricks, Lieutenant," Yun-mi answered for both of them.

Leaving the Burn took much less time than crawling through it. Once outside, the warmth of the restored connection with the City washed over Yun-mi. "Gonna get dark in two hours. I'd rather get it over with before that. Who's up for a jog?"

The men didn't object. Either they didn't mind or were reluctant to show their weakness in front of a woman. Only Janet's face soured. No worries, girl, we'll get you into shape yet!

Yun-mi tightened up the straps holding her equipment and ran. She settled into an energy-conserving pace, only sprinting to cross major streets out of habit. She didn't look back for two blocks until hearing, "Miss Park!" She stopped and turned around. "Wait!" Buck caught up and pointed at the ridiculously stretched line. Kossowsky wasn't far behind, followed by Jackson and Lundy at a distance. It was Janet, bent over and holding her side a hundred meters away. Laszlo, having volunteered once again to close the file, supported her.

Jan might take a bit of training. "Don't stop, keep walking!" Yun-mi shouted and resumed her run. Less than a block left.

With the familiar shape of the Crystal looming up ahead, she waited again for the laggards. Janet breathed noisily and sweated like a horse.

"Can you walk for a bit longer, or do you need a break?" Yun-mi asked.

"Are you kidding?" Janet huffed. "You'll have to tie me up if you don't want me to follow!"

Yun-mi high-fived her. "That's my girl!" Not a long-lost twin, as Jackson had suggested, but definitely a kindred spirit. "Okay, let's move. Should be a short walk." She stopped on the border of the Burn and took a breath before crossing the imaginary line. See you soon, City.

Having a concrete destination and knowing it was close made the going easier. The team did not stretch anymore, bunching together and pushing forward with determination. Yun-mi settled into the rhythm... and almost fell into the hole.

"Back!" she gasped, throwing her arms to her sides and balancing on the edge for infinitely long seconds, until someone grabbed her bow and pulled her back. She exhaled loudly and produced a string of profanities that made even Lundy cock his head. "Phew. That was close. Thanks, Buck."

Laszlo touched her shoulder, insisting on an eye contact. "All good?"

Yun-mi puffed, waiting for her heart to stop palpitating. "Yes. Yeah, all good." She firmly nodded, mainly to convince herself.

Laszlo fished a hank of rope from his backpack and started tying it around her thighs and waist. She smiled. "You know me too well, Las."

He looked around. "Did anyone doubt she'd insist on climbing down first?"

The Fivepointers giggled.

Janet stepped forward. "I'm second."

Jackson murmured, "Nobody doubted that either," causing another burst of laughter.

While waiting for Laszlo to finish, Yun-mi surveyed the surroundings. Would her adventures ever bring her into the Burn again? Doubtful. Might use the opportunity to study it. To her right stood the remains of a building that, burned out and half in ruins, still reminded her of a palace from old illustrated books. To her left, the vegetation had overrun a massive tubular shape—the crashed plane.

Laszlo tightened the knots, tugged at the rope, and grunted in satisfaction. "Good to go. No, wait." He cupped her face in his palms and kissed her. "Now you are. Careful down there, eh?"

"Aw," said Jackson, "how romantic!"

Without looking back, Laszlo growled, "Another word from you, and—"

"Gotcha. My lips are sealed."

This stretch of the subway tunnel ran close to the surface—probably why it had collapsed on impact. A short descent brought Yun-mi to a mound of broken concrete and soil. She cautiously slid to the tracks level and shone the light around. Not that she'd expected to see racks of books lining the walls, but *something* standing out would've been nice. A trace. A clue. A goddamn *That way to the library!* sign with a big arrow. Instead, only garbage and animal skeletons. Yun-mi stepped out of the improvised harness and pulled on it twice. The rope disappeared into the opening above. A short time later, a pair of legs entered the hemisphere of her light, followed by the rest of Janet. The girl lit her own lamp and joined Yun-mi, furtively scanning the surroundings. The corners of her lips curled down.

"No library," Yun-mi narrated.

"No library," echoed Janet.

"Tell you what. If I was hiding something here, I wouldn't place the hoard right near the entrance, where someone may get a glimpse of it from above."

"Makes sense."

"We're roughly in the middle of the blocked tunnel section. Let's split. I'll go there," she pointed north, "you—there. Meet back here."

"" Janet's voice almost did not quaver. "Or... *not* animals?"

As if on cue, a noise of rolling gravel behind Janet spooked her. She gulped. But it was only Kossowsky.

"Change of plans." Yun-mi was all matter-of-fact. "We'll send *him* south. You and I are going together. How's that sound?"

"Better." Janet gratefully touched Yun-mi's arm.

"Yo!" Yun-mi raised her voice to attract Kossowsky's attention. "You there! We go this way, you go that way. Meet here. Understand?"

"Last I checked, I was in command."

Crap. Not this bullshit again. "Last *I* checked, you couldn't tell your left from your right in the City. So shut up, shove your ego up your ass, and do as I say!"

"Whoa," whispered Janet, "I don't think he's gonna like that tone."

Whether he liked it or not, the officer chose not to argue. Without saying a word, he turned and climbed down the far side of the heap that once had been the tunnel's ceiling.

Janet giggled nervously. "You really don't care what people think about you, do you?"

"Nah. Tried that once, wasn't impressed."

Janet elbowed her. "You're not too bad for a zombie, you know."

Yun-mi elbowed her back. "You're not too bad yourself, for a barbarian princess."

Three hundred paces in, she stopped in her tracks. "Well. I'll. Be. Damned."

Dozens of hard-shell plastic boxes, stacked three to four tall, crowded the abandoned station's platform. Yun-mi bent to study the faded, dusty labels. *Languages. Geology. Math 3. Microbiology. Chemical Engineering 1. Medicine 2. Sociology. Power Generation. Literature 5.* She shone the light up and read the station name on the wall. *Museum.* How fitting. "To think of the countless times I've been up in the Crystal, not a hundred meters from here, and never even suspected." Yun-mi shook her head and, after a brief struggle with the locks, pulled the lid off a crate marked with a mysterious *Parts & Components 8.* A mess of electronics greeted her, all wrapped and labeled. She picked one up. The neatly handwritten text, *Motherboard*, added zero clarity about the nature or purpose of the device. Unlike the garbage she'd seen before, though, it looked pristine. No burned or melted patches, no blackened wires. Whatever this *part*—or *component?*—was supposed to do, it could, in fact, work. Otherwise, why would anyone have bothered to stash it in this confusing, but evidently well thought out, cache?

Janet stood over a crate she'd opened and caressed the books inside. Her cheeks glistened with tears in the amber light of the lamps.

Yun-mi approached. "That's what you've been after?"

Janet vehemently nodded. Many more times than a simple affirmation required. She frowned, bit her lips, wrinkled her forehead. And sniffed, a lot. Then closed the lid and snapped the latches. For another minute, she stood unmoving, holding her palms on the top of the box.

Yun-mi wrapped an arm around Janet's shoulders.

"'Phar-ma-co-lo-gy.' What's that? I don't recognize most of the names on these boxes."

Janet pulled away, giving Yun-mi a haggard, wet-eyed look. "Me neither. And that's what's so sad."

"Hey, no one knows everything."

"You don't get it. I couldn't imagine *how much* I didn't know. These"—she pointed—"are entire *sciences* I've never heard about! Do you understand what this means?"

Yun-mi's voice betrayed her. "I do," she said, barely above the hearing threshold. In the surreal silence of the tunnel, even that sounded too loud.

Janet opened her mouth and closed it without saying a word. And again. Finally, she responded with a question of her own, "What do *you* think this is?"

A treasure. The most valuable treasure in the world. "Civilization."

"Yes."

"A game changer."

"Yes."

"And whoever gets their hands on it will have decades of head start over everyone else. Enough to rule the world."

"Yes."

Yun-mi pulled the girl closer into a hug. "Don't tell your team we found it," she whispered into Janet's ear. "This has to belong to all!"

Janet gingerly freed herself from Yun-mi's embrace and backed off. "Don't you think I know? But I can't. Colonel... I just can't." She wouldn't meet Yun-mi's eyes.

Yun-mi fixed her with a dark gaze. "You realize they'll kill Laszlo and me, yes?" Her voice came out flat. "You and I, we are writing a history book now, and it has no ending in which your team lets outsiders walk away with this knowledge."

Janet's face paled. Her lips moved, but produced no audible words. At a guess, "I didn't think about that."

"Or we can kill *them*." Yun-mi's voice got lower and harsher. "But I suspect you won't like that either. Particularly, where it comes to a certain officer with no sense of humor and a stick up his ass."

"No. I would not like that."

"The choice is yours."

"The choice?" Janet stared at her feet. Her dry cough must have been a mirthless chuckle. "There's no choice. You are right. We can't tell them."

Yun-mi put a hand around Janet's shoulders once more, prodding her toward the exit. The girl flinched at the touch, then relaxed.

"We'll figure out what to do later. Now," said Yun-mi, deathly exhausted, "let's go lie to your friends."

They walked back toward the bright spot glowing with a warm evening light from above. After a few minutes of silence, dispelled only by their steps, Janet glanced at Yun-mi. "Or, you could kill me down here, and no one would be the wiser. That would make everything much simpler. You can craft a convincing story."

Yun-mi slapped her stupid redhead twin upside the head. Not hard, but with gusto. Caught off guard, Janet yelped and rewarded Yun-mi with a guilty smile—despite all.

Chapter 44

Buck

September 27, 42 PE

The hole in the ground beckoned, its call irresistible. Buck had to be there when the goal of their expedition was revealed. He stepped toward the ledge after the lieutenant, but Jackson shook his head.

"No. You stay here."

Buck glowered back. Unfair!

Jackson approached and whispered into Buck's ear. "We are not here for sightseeing, remember? Colonel sent you with a purpose. Fulfill it! This is a critical point. If something is about to go sideways, I need your warning. Now quit being a drama queen and make yourself useful."

Still unfair. Buck was not a walking alarm. Not a freak with a handy quality. He was a man in his own right, and he'd proven that already! Fine, he'd do what was asked of him one more time, but that was it. No more jerking him around.

Buck settled above the opening. If he was prevented from finding the library, at least he'd be the first to hear the news.

The exchange between Park and Kossowsky brought a grin to his face. Buck glanced at Laszlo, who returned an understanding smirk.

This similarity of their reactions had an unexpected effect. It turned a creepy killer into a real, complex human being who cared a lot about that coarse little wild thing. The transformation was striking and spiked the urge to set the record straight. A few hours ago, he'd faced off with a pirate. How much worse could this be?

"Look, about before, underground... I wasn't trying anything—"

"It's all cool."

"—I just wanted to look out for her... Wait, what?"

"We're good, Buck."

Buck shut his eyes and took a deep breath, calming his racing heart. The scary Rat wasn't planning to mutilate him for now, but the silence grew awkward.

"How did you get that scar?" Buck blurted.

Laszlo frowned. "It was a *huge* bear who surprised me. We fought for hours until I tore out his claw and stabbed him with it in the eye!"

Buck searched the man's expression for signs of mockery. "You're shitting me, right?"

"Naturally!" Laszlo admitted easily. "The true story is that I was once competing with a dirtbag for a girl's attention, and he had a *huge* axe, and—"

"Let me guess. You fought for hours until you tore the axe from his hands and stabbed him with it in the eye. Am I in the ballpark?"

"More or less. I was going to add some juicy details, but you've got the gist of it."

"I will not hear the truth, will I?"

"The truth? The truth, Buck, is almost always boring. Mundane. It rarely involves dramatic adventures. Most often, it's your average everyday crap. Someone's stupidity or overconfidence. Failure to plan, and no contingencies. Stuff like that, you know. My scar? Nothing heroic about it. I was about your age. Strong, arrogant, all-knowing. Fell out of a window. Wasn't a particularly long fall, the second floor. But my cheek was lucky to find a rebar sticking from the ground. Could've lost an eye. Seven Hells—" He looked around and chuckled at the irony, shaking his head. "Could've had my stupid brains splashed all over. See? Nothing to impress a girl with."

"But you impressed at least one girl somehow."

The Rat gave Buck a longer look. "Yes. *The* girl. Don't ask me how, I don't kiss-and-tell."

Recalling *the* girl's gesture from the morning, Buck extended a fisted hand toward the man. Laszlo bumped him. "You're a quick learner, I'll give you that."

"Yo, Kossowsky!" an outrageously impudent yell sounded from down below, and Buck turned his attention to the sinkhole.

"Over here," echoed the lieutenant's muted response. "Coming back."

"Las," called the girl, "start hauling us up. Jan is ready."

Buck helped Gabor pull at the rope and gave Janet a hand to climb onto the surface. One glance at her dejected face told him everything. A dead end.

Park was next up. Buck suspected the girl would reject his help, but she took his hand and thanked him. She moved aside, ruffling Janet's fiery hair to cheer her up.

Laszlo glanced questioningly at his partner. She shook her head while her fingers brushed her bow. The scar-faced man responded with a reassuring smile, but his hand bumped, as if accidentally, into his fearsome knife, easing it in its scabbard. Alarming signs, but Buck's senses remained blissfully calm.

Jackson bent over the hole. "Anything on your end, Lieutenant?"

"Nothing at all. Just bats and bat shit."

Jackson turned to the girls. "Janet? What did you find?"

"Nothing in the north either," Park answered for her.

"Janet?" the veteran insisted.

"You heard her," Janet replied, not meeting his eyes.

"You're an awful liar, Janet." Jackson continued outstaring her.

The brutal vision threw Buck onto his knees. He almost toppled into the sinkhole. A *dark* one. Clutching his head, he met Lundy's cold eyes. "No. No-o-o! Don't! Please!"

The events that followed blended together.

Lundy pointed his gun at Laszlo.

Park was already tearing the bow off her shoulder, but not nearly fast enough. The realization flickered in her eyes: too late.

A smeared shape of Laszlo's knife streaked toward Lundy, and the Rat was already pulling a handgun from behind his back.

Jackson was raising his gun, too.

Buck squeezed his eyes shut. A shot, deafening even through the roar of his pulse. Two other shots, lagging by a fraction of a heartbeat. And then silence. Long, long silence. Endless silence beyond the ringing in his ears. Buck refused to look. If what he would see around him was half as bad as his vision...

Dark visions were rare, one in ten, and offered no happy outcome. If he did nothing, people died. Because that's when he got his visions. And if he tried to prevent the carnage, people still died. The same people could die differently, or other people would suffer the damage. With *dark* visions, there was no winning. Damned if you do, damned if you don't. He hated them. And hated himself for having them, as if he were to blame. Would've been much easier not to know. To let events happen, as normal people do.

Eventually, Buck gathered the courage to open his eyes. It was bad. Different from the vision—because he had interfered—but bad.

A crumpled heap that used to be Lundy laid on the ground with a bloodstain spreading on his chest and a knife stuck in his eye. Park kneeled over unmoving Laszlo, shaking him and calling his name. Janet, pale, stood nearby, trembling.

"What's going on up there?!" Kossowsky bellowed in the pit, his voice angry and worried.

Jackson stepped forward. Buck brought his gun up, aiming at the veteran's center of mass. He was through with allowing people to be shot at. Jackson froze, put his rifle down, lifted both hands, and walked toward the two Rats under Buck's watchful eye. He pulled the Korean up and directed her into Janet's embrace. Park despondently gazed at Laszlo, biting her lip.

Jackson touched Laszlo's neck, turned him over with a grunt, opened the man's jacket, and checked the wound.

"Yun-mi," he said, "he's alive. Help me bandage him."

She was at his side in a blink of an eye. The anxious little girl was gone, yielding again to a determined Rat. In a heartbeat, she was packing her man's wounds in the stomach and the lower back.

"He needs medical attention. The sooner the better." Jackson showed an enviable ability to keep his calm. "Any place nearby that could help somehow? Closer than New Kowloon, I mean?"

"Yes, I know exactly the place. JCC, the Israelites. Famous for their doctors. Right around the corner."

"Will someone tell me what happened?!" yelled Kossowsky.

Jackson tiredly lowered his eyelids, walked to the edge, and picked up the rope. "Are you gonna help, or keep daydreaming?" he asked Buck. "Oh, and for crying out loud, put that gun down, before someone else gets hurt!"

Buck looked at the rifle in his hands as if seeing it for the first time. Why was he holding it? Why was he pointing it at Jackson all this time? Then he remembered. "Who shot whom?" he demanded.

Ignoring the gun, Jackson came close. "Lundy shot at Laszlo Gabor."

"W-why?" Buck's head was spinning.

"Laszlo and I shot Lundy. We were too slow."

"Why?!" repeated Buck, stupefied by the sheer absurdity of the senseless violence.

Jackson tousled Buck's hair the way Park did to Janet not two minutes ago. "It's complicated. No time to explain now, kid, we must help this poor guy. I'll tell you once we're there. Now we need to decide what to do with Tony."

He raised his voice. "Listen, Kossowsky. I'll pull you up on one condition. Promise not to ask questions and do exactly as I say. Do we have a deal?"

"What were those shots? Was anyone hurt?"

"Lieutenant, which part of not asking questions did you not understand?" This time Kossowsky obediently kept his mouth shut.

"That's better. To put your mind at ease, Miss MacPherson is fine. Buck, grab that rope."

"Jackson, stop yammering and move your ass!" hollered Park. "We must go! Now!"

Buck's heart was thumping in his chest. Not at all surprising after the mad dash with the unconscious Rat dragged between him and the lieutenant like a sack of potatoes. Jackson panted behind, carrying the Rat's kit. Park led the way, pulling a breathless Janet by the hand.

They made it shortly before sunset.

Approaching a long squat building, not unlike a *supermarket* but two or three stories tall, the Korean girl yelled to the people gawking at the strange group, "Medic! Get a medic!" By the time Buck and Kossowsky reached the entrance, the doors burst open and two men ran out to meet them, with a narrow bed on large wheels. They helped load Laszlo and rolled it back in at a run. Park followed closely, clutching the prone man's limp hand. She was denied entry through the inner doors. An older man wearing a white robe looked at her with a spark of recognition. "You're Kim Joon-woo's student, yes?"

"Yes, Doctor Levin. Please save him! Please, please, please!" Plaintiveness distorted her voice. "I'll get you anything you want! Money! Food! Medications from New Kowloon! You've got to believe me, I can!"

The doctor put a calming hand on her arm. "That won't be necessary. I'll do my best. Now, let me go check the patient. Wait here. I'll update you as soon as I can."

He left, but a group of very serious people stepped into the small waiting room, instantly crowding it. One, presumably the commander, singled out Jackson as the most senior among the visitors. "Is there a security situation we need to be aware of?"

"No, Mister Alon, everything is... contained," replied Park instead, nervously wringing her hands.

The man she called Alon studied her. "Have we met, Miss?"

"Park Yun-mi, of Little Korea. Formerly. I met you while accompanying Kim Joon-woo."

"Ah, yes. I remember now. You were younger then. What happened? Who are these people?"

"They're with me. We had... a disagreement. A... a man..." She steeled herself and pushed her hands into her pockets. "A man was shot. But there is no danger to the JCC. You have my word. We were nearby and needed urgent medical help."

"I see. Can we do anything else, Miss Park?"

Didn't take Jackson's skills to see her head was elsewhere. She kept gravitating to the inner doors, but had enough presence of mind to respond. "Thank you, Mister Alon. My friends will require a place to spend the night. And transportation tomorrow."

Alon nodded. "That can be arranged. Find me in the morning. As for the accommodations, guest suites are available upstairs. Your friends are welcome to them."

"What's the rate?"

The local chief, whatever his title was, smiled tightly. "On the house, Miss Park."

The girl stopped pacing. "Thank you, Mister Alon, that's most generous. I'll owe you one."

"You'll owe nothing if you satisfy my curiosity. Why did you say 'formerly of Little Korea'? Are you not Kim Joon-woo's second anymore?"

Buck had asked himself the same question, but too many other subjects had competed for his attention.

"Kim Joon-woo is dead," the girl replied. Oh, her strength...

Alon pursed his lips. "My sincerest condolences, Miss Park." He shook his head. "Never thought I'd live to hear those words. I will take my leave now. Nathan"—he pointed at one of his men—"will show your friends to their rooms. I hope your man gets through it. He is in excellent hands, you know. There's no one better than Doctor Levin in the City. *Refuah shlemah*. I'll see you tomorrow."

The security left, and Park sagged onto the bench. Janet moved closer. The young Korean rested her head on Janet's shoulder and closed her eyes.

After a minute of silence, Kossowsky's soft voice inquired, "May I ask questions now?"

Buck nodded. "Me too." No more delays.

"Alright, but..." Jackson looked pointedly at the local guy.

"Nathan, could you please give us the room?" asked Park, without opening her eyes.

"Sure, Miss. I'll be outside if you need me."

"Okay," said Jackson when the doors closed behind the guard, "shoot. Ugh, sorry. That came out wrong."

"About that." The lieutenant accepted the pun. "What in the Seven Hells happened... in the Seven Hells?"

Chapter 45

Yun-mi

September 27, 42 PE

What was happening to her? Laszlo was just a man, someone she'd met mere two days ago. Two days?! More like two eternities! So much had been crammed into these days, enough for half a lifetime: events, actions, words, laughter; closeness, physical and spiritual; and his eyes, those adoring eyes, so out of place on the scarred, weather-beaten face of a seasoned Rat. No one had ever looked at her the way he did. No one had ever *seen* her as he did. No one had ever admitted to loving her, crazy and wild and freakish as she was. Not just *a man*. *The* man.

Parker and Kostya had taught her painful lessons, and she'd been prepared to stay alone forever... Until Laszlo proved she can trust someone besides herself. She cherished his presence in her life; his appreciation; his unconditional siding with Team Yun-mi—against Team The-rest-of-the-world. Did she love him back? She wanted to. And maybe she did, but there was no way to answer that question definitively without knowing what love was. Laszlo's disarming smile made her melt on the inside, underneath all her gruff posturing. She had pulled down her defenses, letting him in. If that was what falling in love meant—so be it.

The time refused to move. She was an insect, trapped in a drop of resin drifting down the tree trunk but unable to control anything. Not the direction of the movement, not the speed, not the destination. Nor the fate. People around were saying things. To her, about her, but it was all background noise. She was not there. A thick wadding surrounded her, many layers of space that made the voices echo dully and pushed everyone miles away, even though they were still in the same cramped waiting room. She didn't mind the distance. All those people were strangers. They mattered not. Only one person in the world mattered, and that person was somewhere behind these white doors. Hidden from her. Too far to touch. To kiss. To hold.

"That was my fault, to some extent," the stranger called Jackson was saying. "I pushed Janet too hard, and Lundy figured it out."

"Figured what out?" asked the stranger called Buck. "Stop talking in riddles already!"

"Figured out that Miss MacPherson and Miss Park had found what we were looking for, but decided not to tell."

"Is this true?" asked the stranger called Kossowsky. His voice vibrated with edginess. "You found the... *it*? Why in the Seven... uh, why on Earth did you try to hide that?!"

The stranger—no, the warm presence under Yun-mi's cheek—called Janet sighed and didn't answer. A part of Yun-mi understood the need to say something, but she was utterly disinterested. The effort of thinking of a response and then spending the energy to shout it all the way out of her cocoon to reach those distant strangers... Too much. And completely unnecessary.

The warm presence called Janet gave out another anguished sigh and said, "Yes. Yes, we found the library." With every word, her voice gained defiance. "And Yun-mi knew what would happen. That you'd kill her and her boyfriend to keep it a secret! She could kill you all, but refused! And you... You..." She sobbed.

Jackson raised mollifying hands. "The only one with such orders was Lundy. I tried to stop him but was too late. Sadly, my reflexes are not what they used to be."

"*Orders?*" Buck's jaw went slack. "From Colonel?"

"Who else? See, Lundy's actual mission was not to protect me. Or not *just* to protect me. He was sent with us to ensure no one goes rogue and disobeys orders. Including me."

"Weren't you friends?" With each revelation, Buck's eyes bulged further out of his head. That could have been funny, had Yun-mi cared to be entertained.

"Friends? No. Buddies, at most. Time spent together does that, even to people having nothing in common. Sure wasn't his endearing personality." His face stayed unreadable. "I always knew he wouldn't hesitate to put a bullet in the back of my head if I ever misstepped."

"Shouldn't have saved him, back on the pirate island," muttered Buck, burying his head in his hands.

"And you killed him?!" It was stranger Kossowsky's turn to express outrage. "For *following* Colonel's orders?! This is mutiny! I shall execute you myself!"

In her semi-catatonic state, a simple thought lit Yun-mi's bubble. *Kossowsky—bad. Jackson—not as bad.* She let her instincts drive. One moment she was leaning into Janet, the next she was on her feet with the bowstring drawn. Still miles away, she knew exactly where the arrow would pierce Kossowsky's skin. The unwavering, razor-sharp broadhead looked straight into the small depression under his chin, right between the collarbones. A tiny vein pulsated—slowly, very slowly—on the man's neck.

Because of Yun-mi's complicated relationship with time, her actions must have been fast. The collective gasp from all the strangers came long after she completed the sequence.

"Say a word."

No one spoke. Was he deaf?

"Jackson, say a word," she repeated. Would that make her already obvious request any clearer?

"Ahem," stranger Jackson cleared his throat. "No, Miss Park, please lower your weapon. Thank you for coming to my defense, but, er, my life is in no danger. Isn't that right, Lieutenant?"

"Yes," whispered the stranger called Kossowsky—or was he called Lieutenant? Only lips moved on his ghostly pale face. "That's right. No danger."

Yun-mi's intervention was no longer needed. With the same practiced efficiency, she re-sheathed the arrow and sat back, leaning on Janet like she had ten heartbeats before.

The stunned silence stretched on. Yun-mi didn't care. That changed nothing in the rate of the resin drop's movement.

After a while, stranger Lieutenant Kossowsky asked, eying her apprehensively, "So, what happens now?"

"Now?" The not-as-bad Jackson scratched the silver stubble on his chin. "Now we wait for good news from Doctor Levin. And since you're a man of the Faith, Lieutenant, I suggest you pray to the God Almighty, Mother Earth, the Prophet, and whoever else is in your pantheon, that Laszlo Gabor comes through. Because"—he too glanced at Yun-mi—"you have associated yourself with the wrong side." He stared at Kossowsky meaningfully. "And there will be Seven Hells to pay."

The lieutenant frowned. "That's 'now' now. I was asking about the library. You were given the same orders as the rest of us. Will you disobey Colonel? Betray Five Points? The Army?"

"'Betray'? As isolated as Five Points is, we're a part of a broader society. If our actions benefit that broader society, they'll benefit Five Points too, don't you think?"

"I am a soldier. I don't think. I've got my orders, and I intend to follow them."

"Even if this turns you against your friends?"

"Friends? We are a team. *Were* a team. You aren't my *friend*." It was as if that word disgusted him. "Brennan isn't my *friend*. You're my subordinates! And you'll obey my command, or face the consequences!"

"And Miss MacPherson?" inquired Jackson innocently. "What is she to you? Also a subordinate? Not a friend? Not an ex-fiancée?"

Was he talking about Janet? Wasn't she Lieutenant's wife?

Kossowsky pressed his lips into a thin line. His cheeks attained a tint of pink. He remained silent. The warm shoulder behind Yun-mi stirred, and its owner spoke. Calmly, emotionlessly. Delivering information. "This is it, Tony. The crossroads. Until today, I hoped we had a chance. But now you must choose, me or Colonel."

Absentmindedly, Yun-mi decided she didn't like that Colonel. He was, as Jackson put it, *on the wrong side.*

"Why can't it be both?!" The exasperated lieutenant—or Tony? which was it?—threw his hands up.

"Do you really not understand? Or do you need me to spell it out? Alright, tell me, Tony, why is this mission so important to Colonel? Why all the secrecy?"

"I don't question Colonel's reasons. As for the secrecy, it's obvious. To not let anyone else get their hands on that cache."

"Why? Why would he care about books? I know this word is hard for you to utter, but grow a pair already. Books! An abomination, something to burn on a pyre. Do you think Colonel wants to grace his subjects with a windfall of blessings on the next E Day? A free book for every Fivepointer to make a wish by the Simplification fire and praise Colonel's generosity? Is that it?"

"Maybe." Stubborn. Still bad.

Yun-mi craned her neck to check Janet's face. "Why do you bother?"

"Shut up," replied the girl, her eyes locked with the lieutenant's.

Yun-mi rested her head back on Janet's shoulder. Could she end up in the same situation? Never. No way Laszlo would get anything so wrong and then persist in his ways. Naturally, not everyone got so lucky. One chance in a million. Janet could fight tooth and nail for her happiness, but the contempt in her words was a sign her love had already died. She was closing the chapter, leaving nothing unsaid.

"It's the power." The young, stupid stranger called Buck spoke, attracting everyone's attention. He'd been staying out of the conversation for so long Yun-mi had forgotten about his presence. Ignored him as another negligible feature of the room. And now he echoed her own words, said ages ago back in the abandoned tunnel. "The books, the knowledge. Whoever has them holds the power to control the future. That's why Colonel wants them. To be in the center of what is coming."

"Or," added Jackson quietly, "to destroy them. And deny that power to everyone else."

"No one asked you two," grumbled Janet. "I wanted Tony to figure that out on his own."

"Colonel is the Protector of the Faith! He'd never use books!" The lieutenant hotly threw his head up, curving his lips in distaste. "That power you apostates are talking about, leave it to the infidels, to dig their own graves!"

"And that's exactly my point." Jackson remained calm. "On our way here, you've seen the same things we have. Pelham, Locksville, New Kowloon. The City. And yet, somehow, you failed to draw the same conclusions. We—all of us living today—we're the leftovers. The rotting trash our ancestors had left behind. Someone who'd seen this coming has given us a unique gift, a second chance. And you want to let Colonel destroy it? Squander the opportunity to spare hundreds of years of languishing in this misery? Why, so that your children can live in caves? Don't you see what a crime that would be? A crime against what's left of humanity!"

The lieutenant scowled. "And what would *you* do with it? Leave it to the zombies?" He burned Yun-mi with a hateful glare. "To the Kowloonese? The Station? So you can work together to bring the Second E upon us?"

Janet sprang to her feet, closed the distance, and delivered a resounding slap on Kossowsky's cheek. The ringing reverberated through Yun-mi's cocoon, and she couldn't help but smile.

"Screw you, Tony!" The redhead slapped him again. "We're done! You don't exist for me anymore!" She stomped back, breathing heavily through flaring nostrils, but her eyes glistened. She yanked Yun-mi's kukri from its sheath and touched the lieutenant's chest with the sharp tip. Ridiculous with that awkward grip, and awesome in her rage.

"Try to stop us, and I'll slit your throat myself!" Janet resolutely returned to her seat, meeting no one's eye, and slid the wicked knife in its place.

"*That* went well." Jackson's sardonic chuckle sounded inappropriately loud in the silent room. "Miss Park, the locals seem to listen to you. Could you please ask them to detain Lieutenant Kossowsky for a few days?"

Yun-mi shrugged. Whatever. She opened her mouth to call Nathan when the inner doors parted and Doctor Levin walked in. One glance at him sufficed. The grimly set jaw. The corners of his lips, tragically angled down. The sorrow welling in his eyes. The dejection in his posture.

A cold fire whooshed through Yun-mi, extinguishing her hopes, feelings, emotions. A black Abyss broke loose in her stomach and swallowed her. She slipped to the floor and curled up, pulling her knees to her chin and squeezing her eyes shut.

She wanted to die. No, she was already dead. Why still so much pain? Wasn't death supposed to cure everything, once and for all?

What did you expect? The nasty world snickered, spitting into the Abyss. *You were far too happy. Should've known it never lasts. People you care about the most, they all die. First Joon-woo, now Laszlo. Misery is the way of life. Get yourself together and move on.*

Yun-mi *wanted* to suffer the pain, to be miserable, but failed even in that. She couldn't be *anything*. She couldn't *be*. The world shrugged and dissolved, leaving her alone in the universe. Her body, empty on the inside, was no more than another layer of the wadding in the center of the infinite emptiness outside.

Someone—Janet?—kneeled nearby, gently lifted Yun-mi's head, and snuggled it in her lap.

A voice—Doctor Levin?—continued verbalizing random sounds far above, somewhere over the edge of the Abyss, miles and miles away. Meaningless words fell like flakes of hot ash, burned their way through her, and kept on tumbling into the darkness below. There were "so sorry", and "everything we could." "I wish we had" followed closely and bounced off her. The long, awkward "condolences" broke into a myriad of tiny shards. None of that mattered. None of *anything* mattered. The Abyss offered no images, no sounds, no touches, no smells. No memories. It tasted bitter, but that was to be expected. It offered nothing and wanted nothing of Yun-mi. Promised nothing, and thus could not disappoint. She let it pull her. Envelop her. Hug her. Was it her new lover?

Even in the blessed darkness, she would not be left alone. A remote commotion spoiled her solitude. Someone gave instructions. Someone argued. Strong arms picked her up and carried her somewhere. Abyss? You? No, the hold was too strong, too physical. Las?! The crazy, irrational hope, the unmitigated desire for that to be true blazed through her like a lightning bolt, forcing the Abyss to heave her all the way up into the material world. She flung open her eyes, willing to see Laszlo's face, his beard cloven by the scar, his... It was only Buck, carrying her up the stairs. Still alone. A moan escaped her, conveying the full depth of her despair. Deflated, she slid back into the bottomless pit.

Chapter 46

Ka Yi

September 28, 42 PE

"You went behind my back, Tam Wai Lam!"

She didn't flinch. Unsurprising. His wife had faced an assassin—and prevailed. "When you swung that wheelchair, you didn't consult me either, Ka Yi."

Their dining room darkened. Or was it his vision? "That was different!"

"Was it? Then consider the Singhs *my* imaginary wheelchair." She let him digest the idea. "But look beyond your hurt feelings. Didn't we agree Khalifa must go?"

"Not like that!"

"Why? What difference does it make? Your preference for indirect action, is that it? Well, I do things my way. And I get them done. Bluntly, not as elegantly as you. But often faster and more efficiently."

"That was a low blow." Ka Yi scowled. She didn't avert her eyes. So strikingly beautiful with that aloof face! And... so right. What was he about to say? All desire to continue arguing dissipated. He sighed and asked with a smidge of residual grudge, "How could you know?"

"Know what? That the Singh brothers may need to intervene? Khalifa's a devious bastard. I expected him to weasel his way out through a separate agreement with Locksville."

"What is it with you and Weinberg? You've never made a secret of your dislike of him."

"Nothing to do with dislike. Weinberg does what's good for Weinberg, first and foremost. Locksville comes at a close second. Everyone else's goals are optional. Weinberg doesn't have friends, only interests."

"Same as us."

"Yes, same as us. But I prioritize our interests over Weinberg's. I hope you do too. Admit it, I wasn't too far off. It was Weinberg's lieutenant that Khalifa succeeded to turn."

"Not exactly 'turn', let's be fair..."

"Turn. Recruit. Convince. Whatever you call it. He poisoned that young man's mind. Enough to prevent his commanding officer from executing the creep on the spot."

"Didn't you hear what Weinberg said? The Inquisitor is ready to make peace with us. To reform The Station. To work together."

"And you bought into that? The famously sharp Shang Ka Yi, the Golden Dragon who can plan ten steps ahead, outsmart five warlords at a time, and overthinks everything, was swayed by sweet-talking from the Chief Sadist? Second-hand sweet-talking, mind you, assuming your buddy Weinberg didn't convey a selectively narrated interpretation of the encounter. Or edited, to make it sound closer to what you'd want to hear."

"Why is it that every time Weinberg's name comes up, we end up fighting?"

"Good question. Can it be because he's your blind spot?"

"How so?"

"You see in Weinberg a Locksville version of yourself. He isn't. But he's a part of your old boys' club, and you let that cloud your judgment. It's easier for me to see because I am not a boy, as you might have noticed, nor am I old."

"Clearly." Ka Yi closed his eyes. This was tiresome. He could continue churning up counterarguments, but the effort seemed futile. His wife had repeatedly beaten him on the playing field he'd considered his own. She ridiculed his strategic capabilities, the subject of his particular pride. And yet, none of that invoked his anger. Had the same words come from his father, he would have been so mad! What was different? Was *she* his blind spot, too? Most definitely not an old boy—but even that didn't cloud his judgement. Her reprimand came from love. Unlike Father's, who had mastered the art of not caring. Always being the first, the best, the smartest had been Ka Yi's way to prove Father wrong. Being second to Wai Lam? Happily.

She figured out she'd pushed too far. "Regardless. Whatever happened, happened. Much to my chagrin, your friend Moctar is still alive. Six-hundred-meter shots are tricky that way. We may as well try to hear everything straight from the mouth of the horse. If its mouth is not too badly mutilated. I admit I am mildly curious to meet him in person."

"Assuming he won't bullshit us in your presence."

"Isn't that a reasonable assumption? You tell me."

The prone figure of the person who had caused Ka Yi much pain and trouble didn't look too menacing. It projected no particular strength or imposition. Must be his charisma that had elevated him to power. And his cruelty that had kept him afloat.

Thick bandages left only one eye visible, obscuring the Inquisitor's face. His sickly, ashen skin looked gray. A sharp cheekbone. Wrinkles in the corner of the eye. Not evil incarnate. Just a man, missing half his venomous tongue. How poetic.

Ka Yi almost asked Wai Lam if he'd looked as serene when he'd been unconscious, but kept his mouth shut. He was supposed to still be angry with her.

His wife towered silently behind his back, leaning on the wheelchair's handles.

As if sensing the attention aimed at him, Khalifa woke up. The uncovered eye opened, scanned the room, and closed again. What was that? Exasperation? He tried to say something but produced only muffled, unintelligible sounds.

Doctor Chen approached and enunciated, "Do not talk. You were shot through the mouth. You're missing a part of your tongue, and there's a hole in your cheek. Use this." He offered a small blackboard and a piece of chalk.

The patient reluctantly took both, scribbled on the board, and turned it toward Ka Yi.

"new kowloon?"

Ka Yi nodded. "Welcome to the Great Hive, Chief Inquisitor."

The man erased the text with the edge of his hand and scribbled more.

"welcome???"

Ka Yi chuckled. "You're alive, aren't you? And not even chained to the bed. Isn't that welcome enough?"

"shang ka yi?"

"In the flesh. And this here," he pointed behind him, "is my wife, Golden Dragon Tam Wai Lam."

"congratulations"

"Why, thank you, Chief Inquisitor. Though our honeymoon was almost ruined by your friends here."

"why alive?"

"Me? Or you?"

The man in bed pointed at himself.

"You can thank Captain Weinberg for that. And Marc Novak, whom, I understand, you know well enough."

Khalifa tried to smile and groaned in pain.

"Also," Ka Yi continued, "you should be eternally grateful that my wife's curiosity outweighs her bloodlust."

A nod. *"order to shoot?"*

Wai Lam's voice was frosty. "Are you asking if it was my order to shoot you?" Another nod.

"Yes."

"thank you"

"'Thank you'? Really? That's rich, even for you."

"veracity"

Khalifa showed them the board, then erased the word and briskly wrote, *"my claim"*

Then, *"forced to reform"*

"Ah," said Ka Yi. "Got it. This allows you to tell The Station's orthodoxy that you have to bow to the external pressure and change the course."

"Never let a crisis go to waste," sniggered Wai Lam.

"yes and yes"

A minute passed in silence while Ka Yi and Khalifa studied each other. He couldn't see Wai Lam's face, but had little doubt she was staring their adversary down. The Inquisitor lifted the board again.

"sorry"

Ka Yi arched an eyebrow.

"look at us"

Ka Yi should have hated the evil, repugnant person lying in the bed. A homicidal sadist, by all accounts. His archenemy. And yet, all he saw was just a man. A complex, smart man with a dangerous mind, but still—not Satan himself. Instead of scoffing, Ka Yi grinned. "Yes. One stabbed, another shot."

"got out of hand"

"You think?" Wai Lam's sarcasm was so sharp it could cut.

"apologize"

"peace?"

"You'll understand our reluctance to trust anything you say... er, write." As usual, Wai Lam didn't mince words. "Even in better times. Now, when you're at our mercy, you'll promise anything, whatever we'd want to hear, to save your hide."

"of course"

"ask weinberg"

A sardonic cackle behind Ka Yi's back. "We did."

"I offered peace"

"before shot"

The word *before* was underscored twice. Ka Yi looked up, first time since this awkward "conversation" had begun. "He's got a point."

Wai Lam frowned. "Assurances?" She wasted no breath on pointless arguing.

"anything"

"Signed trade cooperation agreement," Wai Lam demanded.

"done"

"Share the know-how of your engines," ventured Ka Yi.

The Inquisitor paused, but only for a few seconds. *"fine"*

"You stay in our custody, and rule from here," Wai Lam pressed, "until further notice."

Khalifa rolled his one eye and waved the board with the last written word. Then he wrote his longest sentence yet. *"who will run the station?"*

"Marc Novak. Jamil Khan. Rajan Gupta." Ka Yi hurried to propose before his wife came up with something more preposterous.

"who?"

"Rajan? An escaped worker. Weinberg's man now."

"I see"

"insane"

"may work"

Then, *"need to visit"*

"Visit The Station?" Ka Yi asked. "So you can dig in there, and it will take a full-blown siege to smoke you out? Forget about that. But I understand, you must endorse your proxies and show your people you aren't our puppet. I'll get Weinberg to arrange a meeting on a neutral ground. In a day or two, once you recuperate a little."

"*Weinberg*, Golden Dragon?" Wai Lam made the name sound derogatory.

"Yes, Golden Dragon, Weinberg. Don't worry, we'll have leverage over him too."

She pursed her lips, but refrained from commenting.

"my prognosis?" Khalifa raised the board. Ka Yi pointed to the other side of the bed.

"Unless the bleeding from your tongue reopens, you are out of the immediate danger," said Doctor Chen. "You won't be able to chew on your left side, and will have an ugly scar on the cheek."

"beauty!"

"speech?"

"Once your tongue heals, and that may take some time, you will regain that ability, but with a bad lisp. Your speech will not be very intelligible at first, so hold on to that blackboard."

The Chief Inquisitor wrote *"still worth it"*, emphasized the message with a thumbs up, and groaned. He was smiling under the bandages, for sure. Had their roles been switched, Ka Yi knew he would.

Did he just reach an agreement with the Devil?

Chapter 47

Yun-mi

September 28, 42 PE

Part-awake, yet mostly still in the clutches of sleep, Yun-mi stretched and reached to hug Laszlo. Only... something felt wrong. Strange shape under her touch. Muscle tone way off.

Her eyes flicked open. Fully present, she sat with a start.

Janet, bleary-eyed, took Yun-mi's hand. "You slept," she said. "Good."

The memories rushed back, and the world lost its colors.

"I didn't want to leave you alone," said Janet.

Regret was plainly written on her face and oozed from her eyes. Her hair, highlighted by the warm rays of the morning sun, shone like a funeral pyre. "I... Yun-mi..."

Why struggle to find the right words? Yun-mi didn't need her words. Didn't need anyone's words. She needed neither sorrow nor compassion. She needed nothing and no one. She was hollow, squeaky clean on the inside. The shining, unblemished polished metal that was her heart beat with a perfect rhythm, indifferent to the world. She wasn't sad, or angry, or miserable. She wasn't tired, or cold, or hungry. She was a machine. An orphan machine without a purpose that had somehow survived its personal E.

"Yun-mi, I'm sorry. If I had lied better, Jackson wouldn't have figured everything out, and then Lundy wouldn't—" her voice trailed off under Yun-mi's unblinking, dispassionate gaze.

Yun-mi stood and headed to the door. Before opening it, she remembered to say, "Thank you for staying with me," because that was what people did. Right? So much superfluous communication to express emotions or to cater to other people's feelings. Weird. Why bother? They all die in the end.

She found herself in an unfamiliar hallway and randomly turned right. It didn't matter. All the ways led to... She stopped. Where *was* she going? Why? What for? What did she have left to justify going anywhere? Why not sit, or better lay down where she was, and wait for the end of time? She did. The split porcelain tile pleasantly cooled her cheek. Cobwebs of cracks spread from a dark, irregular hole in the middle. Yun-mi peek into it but saw nothing. Abyss, is that you, my friend, my lover? It did not respond, but its reassuring presence was never too far, amiably indifferent. Like her. A perfect match. Match made in heaven. Right, Laszlo?

A shadow fell over her. She frowned.

"Yun-mi, please," said a vaguely familiar voice from above. "Tell me how I can help. Talk to me, I beg you!"

Where had she heard that voice? Ah, yes. The one with the red hair. What was her name, again? Janet? Janet. Poor thing, so much sadness. Why did people torture themselves like that? Didn't they understand? No one cared. No—one—ever—cared. Oh, well. Yun-mi reluctantly diverted her attention from the peephole into the Abyss. Janet crouched, extending both hands forward, palms up. What did she want? Yun-mi had got nothing to give her. Ah. A help offer. To pull her up. Fine, if that was important to Janet, why not?

Yun-mi gave Janet her hands and allowed herself to be lifted upright. She didn't mind standing. She could peer into the Abyss from any point. Janet fruitlessly tried to catch Yun-mi's eye. Yun-mi looked right through her. Staying unfocused helped keep the Abyss real close, right at the periphery of her vision.

"Hey!" the other girl raised her voice and snapped her fingers in front of Yun-mi's face. That wasn't very nice. No one gets between her and her Abyss! On reflexes, she caught Janet's wrist and twisted it, sending the rude intruder nose-diving into the floor.

Janet struggled to her knees, stood up, and turned back to Yun-mi. A grimace of fury contorted her face. She smeared the blood from a fresh cut on her cheek with the tail of her hand and snarled. "Oh, no, you don't! You don't get to bask in your self-pity!"

Self-pity? What was she talking about? Yun-mi was perfectly content.

"You won't get rid of me so easily!" continued the angry human. "And you know what? You're stubborn, I am stubborn too. Your kind of bitch, remember? Now, you may not need us—or *think* you don't need us—but *we* need *you*."

"So what?" Speaking out loud felt clumsy. Redundant. Talking to the Abyss was infinitely simpler.

"What do you mean, 'so what', you selfish little bitch?! You stinking piece of rat shit, filthy zombie ass! You—"

The profanities touched nothing inside her. Like everything else, they didn't matter. Why was the annoying redhead so agitated? Trying to grab Yun-mi's attention, that's why. To pull her away from the Abyss's comforting embrace. Oh, well. Not like the Abyss was going anywhere.

Yun-mi cocked her head and finally let her eyes focus on Janet. "I know what you're doing."

"You... You do?" Janet rushed to Yun-mi and squeezed her in a hug. "Sorry, sorry, sorry," her anxious whispering tickled the skin on Yun-mi's neck. "I didn't mean any of that, you know, right?"

"You didn't?"

"A wee bit..." Janet pushed away from Yun-mi, peering into her face. "Bitch." The girl grinned, but her eyes still brimmed with worry. Yun-mi rewarded her efforts with a wan smile.

"Oh, God, finally, you're back!" Janet pulled Yun-mi closer again.

"You said you needed me," mumbled Yun-mi into her chest. "What for?"

Janet stepped back but kept holding Yun-mi's hands. "The library? Remember?"

"What about it?"

"We need to take it to New Kowloon, to the Golden Dragon. His lab in the Hive... I want to *live* in that lab! He'll know what to do with the library. It will fill the gap."

The Golden Dragon... Wai Lam! The memory shook Yun-mi. How could she forget? There *was* someone in the world who cared about her! Someone whom she still cared about, too! Sorry, Abyss, my love, you'll have to wait a little longer. I'm yours, just... not yet, okay? I know you are patient.

"Also..." Janet averted her eyes. "Laszlo... I thought you'd want to bury him? I don't know what's appropriate for a Rat." Apologetic face didn't suit her.

Yun-mi inclined her head. The words tried to cause her pain, to jab a hot stiletto under her sternum. She didn't let them. Polished metal. "We'll leave him on the platform where the library is. That would be fitting."

"Leave? Just like that?"

"We're Rats. Tunnels are where we belong. Alive *and* dead."

Seeing Janet's long face, Yun-mi added, "We can leave your ex there too if you'd like."

Even the Abyss chuckled.

Chapter 48

Buck

September 28, 42 PE

Jackson unceremoniously woke Buck up and dragged him downstairs. Buck had no objections. He didn't mind finding something to eat.

Luckily, Nathan was there and led them to a cafeteria. Toward the end of his night shift, the guy was bored half to death and welcomed any distraction.

A rather scarce selection of food was available at exorbitant prices.

"My treat," graciously offered Jackson, noticing Buck's hesitation. Uncomfortable with someone else paying, Buck settled for a modest breakfast, half the size he'd normally have. He'd be hungry again long before lunchtime.

At the table, Nathan was waiting with another man. "This is Shahnaz. He'll be taking care of your transportation needs."

"Gentlemen," Shahnaz exposed two rows of bright white teeth. "What kind of vehicle will you require?"

"Nothing fancy," said Jackson. "A wagon with a single horse would do. But tell me this, Mister Shahnaz—"

"Just Shahnaz, please."

"Sure. We'll be traveling west, out of the City, and have no plans to return. How will your wagon get back here?"

"Simple," Nathan answered. "I'll be driving it. Alon's instructions. My presence will also grant you immunity along the way. Bloor Corridor Treaty."

"Aha. And how much will this cost us, Shahnaz?"

"Hundred twenty coins."

Buck whistled.

"Our services aren't cheap, yes. But they are famous throughout the City for their reliability." The man was positively beaming with pride. "Also," he added in a lower key, "your group was marked as a security risk, and a different tariff applies. Of course," he smiled conspiratorially, "nothing prevents you from hiring a wagon at any of the stations west from here. Little Korea, High Park, the Raccoons—I'm sure they all will be happy to lend you one. But if you get a better price from them, that would be a first. We're more reliable too, did I mention that?"

This Shahnaz was far less scary than Laszlo, may he rest in peace, or the pirates' leader. If Buck had courage to stand up to them... "Seventy coins, and we run our own security," he blurted, remembering Master Flanagan's teachings.

Shahnaz took measure of him. "A hundred, but Nathan's participation is non-negotiable."

"Eighty."

"Hundred is the lowest I can go. And a free friendly advice, young man? Learn when to stop bargaining and lock in your achievement. You've no leverage. You need transportation, and we're the only ones who can provide it."

Buck made a show of scratching under the chin. "Say, Tim, why don't we walk to Little Korea and hire a wagon from them? Shouldn't be too far, I reckon, and Miss Park must be able to negotiate a locals' price."

Before Jackson could respond, Shahnaz waved his hands. "Okay, ninety coins! A onetime special for valued customers!"

Buck glanced at his companion, who responded with a slight nod.

"Great." The warmth of a well-deserved pride spread in Buck's chest. "You've got yourself a deal, Shahnaz."

"Please have it ready for us outside," added Jackson.

Janet and Park joined the table.

Buck searched both girls' faces for signs of distress, or any indication of their mood at all. He was prepared to see—and apprehensive of the prospect of coping with—grief, anger, blame, dejection. What he was not prepared for was this matter-of-fact composure. Austere yet present, Park wasn't her usual boisterous, badmouth, in-your-face self she'd been at the breakfast the other day—but neither was she in last night's vegetative state.

Buck wasn't a stranger to grief. After Mom's death, he had fallen apart, and it took him weeks, if not months, to return to more or less normal functioning. But this girl... He covered her hand with his. Hopefully, she'd recognize the gesture for what it was—compassion, support—and not as a disastrously timed, untoward advance.

She did. Her eyes met his, and she responded with a sad little smile. "Thank you," was all she said.

Those eyes! The old eyes of someone who'd seen everything shook Buck to his core, but he steeled himself to not look away until she did, releasing him.

At the Burn, Buck, Park, Janet, and Jackson left Nathan outside with the wagon, bringing Laszlo's wrapped body with them. Lundy lay where they had abandoned him the evening before, but worse for wear. Buck shivered at Park's calm explanation that birds and small night predators had taken their toll for his passage into the Afterworld. A figure of speech, or a part of her religious beliefs, whatever those might be? Buck did not ask.

He knelt by Laszlo's side and touched the swaddled shoulder. "You stabbed him in the eye, man. I'm proud to have known you."

The Korean girl pulled Laszlo's knife out of Lundy's skull, wiped it, and offered it to Buck hilt-first. "He'd want you to have it," she said.

It took all Buck's willpower to keep his eyes dry. If *she* could, he had to, too.

Laszlo was carefully lowered into the pit, followed by Park, Janet, and Tim. This time, Buck volunteered to stay above ground, to haul everyone back up. He didn't mind. Creepy on the surface, the place must be creepier underground. Once alone, Buck approached what was left of Lundy. By an unspoken agreement, no one touched the Fivepointer's remains. "Not turning into you," Buck whispered to the lifeless, half-eaten face.

After a while, the voices in the tunnel returned. The team down below brought crates to the opening and went back for more. It took time to stage all of them. Then came pulling up everything and everyone.

With the last crate on the surface, Buck surveyed his dusty, panting companions with a challenge. "We're taking this to New Kowloon." He wasn't asking. He was prepared to fight if it came to that, but had an ironclad certainty that wouldn't be necessary. "It's the missing piece. With this library, their lab will..." Buck lacked the words, the knowledge, and the vision to finish that phrase. But conviction, he had to spare.

Park nodded. Jackson winked.

Janet touched his arm. "Of course we are. I'm sure they'll be excited if you stay at the lab too. You've already showed—er..." As usual, she almost said too much.

Jackson raised an eyebrow.

Park's face remained unreadable, but no way such a slip of the tongue could go unnoticed.

Janet smiled guiltily. "I wouldn't mind a familiar face either."

Shuttling the cargo to the wagon was excruciating. Not trusting the outsider, Jackson stayed with Nathan, leaving the running back and forth to Buck and the girls. The crates were heavy even for Buck. Janet and Park must've been on their last leg by the time there remained nothing to carry.

The wagon returned to the JCC, where they picked up Kossowsky, tied and gagged, and pushed him between the crates.

"What's the JCC?" Buck asked Nathan when they departed.

"The name? Short for Jewish Community Center. The building you spent the night in? That was it."

"But Miss Park also called you Israelites. Which is it?"

"Both!" Nathan laughed. "We have some others too, like Shahnaz—he's Persian, but the majority are Jewish."

"Then why Israelites?"

"After Israel, the Jewish State. See?" The driver pointed at the blue-and-white canvas on the wagon's side, with a peculiar six-pointed star in the middle.

"But didn't you say *you* are the Jewish State?"

"No, dummy, that was an Old World state, before the E!"

"Too complicated."

Nathan laughed again. "Welcome to our history, thousands of years of complicated. The important thing for you is, with this flag, no one will dare mess with us."

The wagon passed through no-man's-land and rolled into an inhabited area. "Little Korea," the driver announced.

Park's home. Or former home.

Curious, Buck jumped off to walk alongside her, a dozen steps ahead of the wagon. She acknowledged his presence with a sideways look and a curt nod. Neither spoke.

In a sprawling vegetable garden, a few youths picking the late tomatoes straightened up.

"Isn't that Park Yun-mi?" one called.

"Yeah, look what the cat dragged in!" answered another.

Without sparing them a glance, she flipped the audience with both middle fingers. That earned her a fresh round of catcalls, which she calmly ignored.

"You don't seem to be very popular here," Buck said. "Is that why you left?"

The girl shrugged. "Not much of an accomplishment to be popular among assholes and idiots."

"Amen to that." Buck had known his share of both back home.

They continued in silence until Park broke it. "Yesterday in the Burn, how did you know what Lundy was going to do?"

Buck's first urge was to deny everything, as he had done for years. But it was impossible to lie to this girl. Not after all she'd been through. The irrational guilt for the dire consequences of his dark vision gnawed at him.

"I *see* things," Buck said, "when something bad is about to happen. I've told no one about this, other than my parents. And Janet."

That earned him a doubtful look. "No one has ever found your behavior suspicious?"

Not a question he'd expected. Buck shrugged. "A few people had figured out. Jackson. Colonel. But I have *told* no one else."

"Why tell me?"

"I... don't know." Buck couldn't meet her eyes.

"Thank you."

Her attention lingered on Buck, and he stuttered. "Y-you believe me?"

"Of course. There's... something I too have told no one. When I'm in the City, it *talks* to me. Not 'talks' talks, not with words, but that's how I sense it. It's *there*, helping me find my way around. Could be nothing. Maybe I've learned the maps, and it's my intuition talking."

"That is so cool! Much better than mine. Useful."

"You believe me too? I don't sound crazy to you?"

"Are you kidding me?"

"Wow. Didn't expect this to be so liberating, to stop keeping the secret to myself. And..." She glanced at him. "Sorry for being a jerk to you before. You're okay."

Heat flashed Buck's cheeks. Didn't see that coming.

"Will you stay in New Kowloon?" asked Park.

"Don't know yet. Need to discuss with Jackson and Janet. Why?"

"If you stay, may I tell Wai Lam about your ability? It's important."

"If you have to." Buck still couldn't say "no" to her.

They kept walking in silence, but of a different sort. A shared secret connected them now.

Crossing High Park in the early afternoon, with the liveliest traffic along the street Buck had seen in the City, the travelers attracted little interest.

Entering the Humber Bay territory, Park stiffened. Under Buck's questioning look, she divulged only, "Now there are two Raccoons dead because of me." So much pain splashed out with these words, Buck bit his tongue and only adjusted the rifle on his shoulder. He ached to comfort her but didn't know how, and wouldn't have dared even if he did.

Islington Clan was the next. A shadow ran over her face when she announced its name. Twenty minutes into the Russians' lands, a small delegation awaited on the road. Buck looked at Park for guidance, but she appeared unsure herself.

One figure detached from the group and approached. "Miss Park," said the man, tipping his black hat, "it is an honor and a pleasure to welcome you."

"Spare the formalities, Ilya. Or is it Chief Korenev?"

"You, Miss Park, may call me anything you want. Call me a cowardly jackal, if you'd like."

That earned him a surprised, appreciative glance from her. "Looks like I was wrong about you, Chief. Apparently, the way things work in your clan *may* change, given a suitable push."

"They may, and they have, Miss Park. And I will be eternally grateful to you for providing such a push." He inclined his head. "Would you introduce your companion?"

"Companion?" A shadow of pain twisted her face before she looked at Buck, as if only then noticing his presence. "Ah. No, these are my, uh, business associates."

"I see. May I offer you and your associates our hospitality for the night, before you continue your travels? It's going to get dark in a few hours."

"You understand why I may be leery of Islington's hospitality, Ilya."

"Islington is a very different clan now, Miss Park, I assure you."

She stared at him for long seconds. Buck would have become uncomfortable, but this guy, Ilya, held his ground. Satisfied, Park said, "I will take your word, Ilya. Your hospitality is welcome. We won't make it to our destination before dark."

Ilya ceremoniously bowed again. "Your trust deeply honors me. Thank you, Miss Park."

Following that cryptic exchange filled with references only these two understood, the team was provided accommodations for the night but preferred to stay with the wagon. To Buck's deep satisfaction, copious amounts of food compensated for giving up on the indoor sleeping arrangements. Even the lieutenant had his hands untied and the gag removed. Buck had feared they may get an earful from his former commander, but Kossowsky stayed quiet. Maybe all his rage had burned out through the day, or he considered talking to the traitors beneath him. Either way, a blessed break. Buck had no internal resources left for arguing.

Chapter 49

Marc

September 28, 42 PE

"You can't do this! Sir, please, I beg you! No! Please, sir, no!"

The Inquisitor wriggled between two troopers. They were visibly uncomfortable, but it was hard to tell with what. Could be the verdict itself, intended to put the most hardened among the Stationers ill at ease. Or being pressed into the prison guard duty; professional soldiers with a modicum of self-respect, always and everywhere, preferred a good fight over escorting prisoners. Or, possibly, the tumultuous changes in their way of life. Marc couldn't blame them. The breakneck pace of events demanded all his wits to keep up.

The pathetic creature before him used to be a senior Inquisitor, the one who had tortured Marc on Khalifa's behalf three days ago. Last night, having learned of his boss's fall from grace, he and a small group of colleagues had tried to quietly abscond but were apprehended by the soldiers. When the Inquisitor saw Marc in his erstwhile boss's chair, the spark of recognition in his eyes was followed by a swift disintegration. The amazing transformation of the self-important, arrogant Master into a squirming worm took less than a minute. A revulsive mix of tears, snot, and spit dripped from the Inquisitor's face to the floor. As if that wasn't bad enough, he peed himself.

"Not much of a hero now, are you? With our roles reversed?"

The disposition was anticlimactic. Marc was disgusted with himself for giving the order. He didn't like the idea one bit, despite the knowledge that this single death would save countless lives in these volatile days of transition. The summary execution presented a perversely optimal solution, striking the balance between the minimal necessary violence and maximum achieved deterrence. A one-off action to close the circle and leave the past to the past. A loud and clear statement that would bring the remaining Inquisitors into line, show the surviving traders that their peers' persecution didn't go unpunished, and ensure no one suspected the new regime of weakness. Keep the sheep at bay; teach the dogs who holds the stick.

And who would be a more suitable candidate than the Staff Executioner? A purely tactical choice, unrelated to Marc's personal grudges. At least, that was what he tried to convince himself.

A change of mind came abruptly. Nothing wrong with satisfying personal grudges if doing so aligned with the practical decision made for political reasons.

Marc placed his bandaged hand on the desk and studied it. The prisoner's eyes widened. He already knew what awaited him.

"Put his arm on the table," Marc ordered the soldier on the left. "Hold it."

The Inquisitor screamed. Ignoring him, Marc looked around in search of a hammer, or an improvised substitute. Finding none, he unholstered his handgun, grabbed it awkwardly with his left hand by the barrel, and gauged the heft. Not heavy enough. Ah, what the hell. The revenge didn't have to be symmetrical. He gripped the gun properly, pressed it to the Inquisitor's palm, and pulled the trigger. The shot in the enclosed space made Marc's ears ring, but the Inquisitor's squeal was louder.

Marc waited patiently for the condemned man's mad-white eyes to regain a degree of consciousness. "That will give you something to think about while you're awaiting the execution." The words were supposed to have weight, to sound appropriately cruel. But they fell flat and only made Marc feel worse.

This wasn't him. This was Khalifa, speaking through his mouth. What a disappointment... and a relief.

Being a Shepherd without turning into a Chief Inquisitor was shaping up to be the greatest challenge of Marc's life. But he finally had a purpose.

Chapter 50

Buck

September 29, 42 PE

In the morning, another enigmatic conversation took place when the local Chief came to bid the team farewell.

"Miss Park," he said, "I understand, you will always take anything I say with a grain of salt. But allow me to tell you once again: I am forever in your debt. Anytime you need anything, ask, and I'll make that my clan's top priority. Any way I can assist now? An armed escort, perhaps?"

"We are fine, Ilya, but thank you, I'll keep your offer in mind. For now, one thing I'd like you to do. Whenever your schedule permits, come visit New Kowloon. Tell them I sent you. Ask for Golden Dragon Tam Wai Lam. She'll make you a proposal. Think about it, that's all I ask."

"Consider it done. Safe travels, Miss Park. Hope to see you again soon." The man saluted formally.

A tall blond woman that came with him stepped forward and, without breaking her silence, hugged Park. The girl reciprocated and, though shorter, patted the woman's head in a motherly gesture. "Sorry about everything, Svetlana."

"Don't be! Thanks to you, I am a human again."

When Park pulled away, a single tear ran down the woman's cheek. She didn't wipe it, letting it drop to the ground. Or maybe she didn't notice.

This time, Janet joined Park in scouting the road, while Buck and Jackson provided the rear guard. That allowed them to have a much-needed private conversation before they reached New Kowloon.

"What about Colonel, Tim?" Oddly, it felt okay to call Jackson by his—shortened—first name again. With his former sinister role likely left in the past, Jackson had lost his intimidation. Not an all-powerful clandestine Five Points officer anymore, but a fellow outcast. "He promised that if we don't deliver the *artifact* or run away, he'll find us and we'll be very sorry. Aren't you afraid at all?"

"You should've realized by now, Colonel's reach outside the Boundary is limited. Who do you think has been taking care of his sensitive business in the Wilderness?"

"You?"

"None other."

"He can hire someone. Bounty hunters? Spread the word that he's looking for us, that there's a price attached to our heads?"

"Unlikely. First, that would draw unwanted attention. The attention he had tried to avoid by keeping our mission secret. And second... Naturally, you don't know Colonel as well as I do. He is not a very vengeful man. He's pragmatic, above all, and doesn't easily give in to emotions."

"Are you saying he'll let it slide?"

"Not at all. We're done for. You, I, Janet. No way back for us. The only question is where we'd like to spend our exile. He may seek an opportunity to talk to us discreetly, but I don't expect he'll come after our heads."

"What if—"

"That's a possibility too."

"You don't know what I was about to ask."

"Believe me, I do. I've been thinking the exact same thing."

"The lieutenant?"

"The lieutenant. If he disappears, Colonel would never know we've found the library. We'd be back from an unsuccessful expedition, having exhausted all the options. The problem is—"

"—that sooner or later he'll learn that the library had surfaced in New Kowloon," Buck finished the sentence for him. "And Janet."

"Yes. That, and Janet. Despite all the breakup drama, she won't be ready to sign off on Kossowsky's life yet."

"Even if this means exile."

"Even so."

"She doesn't need to know..."

"Kid. Come on. When have you become this callous?"

"Did you miss last week? I thought you were around through most of it."

"Ha. You've grown up. Not sure I like the new Buck more, but he's better adjusted to life Outside. Be careful not to lose your soul, though. Unless you want to turn into Lundy."

"Look who's talking. Didn't you shoot the man, what, not two days ago?"

"You have a point." Tim winced. "But you don't want to turn into me either."

Buck instantly regretted broaching the subject. "How do you know what I want?"

"Fine. I know *I* don't want you to turn into me. Too many ghosts. But tell me, why are you so eager to return?"

"My Dad, for one. My friends too."

"And how do you see your life at home, assuming everything goes smoothly? Back to being a private in the Army? To finish the training and be posted at a God-forsaken tower on the Boundary? To look forward to Marketplace duty as a wonderful stroke of luck? To view marching through the square on the E Day as the highlight of your year?"

Buck's imagination readily rendered the pictures, and he remained silent. Jackson was right, and that was that.

"Sad, eh?" Tim continued. "After everything you've seen and experienced out here, to be reduced to what are, basically, menial duties... You'll do yourself in. Or mutiny. Based on what I've learned about you, the latter sounds more probable. I'd give it a year, tops. Am I right?"

Buck nodded.

Jackson kept pressing. "How will you be able to go through the boring, sleepy life in Five Points, knowing that out there—out *here*—someone is busy rebuilding the *real* future, and you aren't a part of that? And don't forget about the Faith," he added as an afterthought. "You're a Creekpointer, not a Hillcrester. How do you think your neighbors would react when you skip Sunday sermons?"

Buck spread his arms and shrugged. "Okay, you got me. But I'd like to have *an option*. To leave some bridges unburned."

"How do you imagine that? Return to Colonel, resign from the Army, and go travel? Become a merchant? To come for a visit occasionally?"

"I don't know. But there's also Janet. She too has got family in Five Points."

"Let's ask her what she wants."

"Let's. But don't mention Kossowsky."

"Of course not. I'll take care of him. Maybe in a... non-lethal way. But the less you know, the better you'll sleep."

"Alright." Buck sighed heavily. "Tim?"

"Yeah?"

"If that works, what about you? Back to your job? After all, *you* had not been confined by the Boundary before."

Jackson threw a perceptive look at Buck. "Your next question will be if I can take you with me."

Buck grinned sheepishly.

"Not a bad idea, kid. The more I think about that option, the more I like it."

"If you keep your post, will you pull me from the Base to your... structure?"

"I don't have a structure, Buck. I am not Weinberg, and sure not Shang Ka Yi. It's just me, myself and I. And now, possibly, you."

The words took a second to sink in. Buck wanted to hug the man, but instead offered his hand in a dignified manner. Jackson laughed and shook it.

"One more question, Tim."

"Don't you always have 'one more question'?"

"I guess. What about the Chinese having the library? How will we sell that to Colonel?"

"The easiest explanation is usually the most believable one. Obviously, they found it before us. That's why we came back empty-handed."

"Hm."

"Hm?"

"Janet is a terrible liar. No one knows that better than you."

"Thanks for the reminder."

"Sorry. But Colonel will see right through her. Through me, too, even the new me."

"Give yourself some credit, kid. I'm sure the new you can handle Colonel better than you think. You've stood before the Chief Inquisitor, Weinberg, two Golden Dragons, urban zombies. You killed and were shot at. Seven bloody Hells, you negotiated your release from a bunch of pirates! And, speaking of, you found and visited the actual Seven Hells! After all this, Colonel will not seem as terrifying as last time. As for Janet... Say, what if she had a nervous breakdown right before reporting to Colonel?"

When New Kowloon appeared above the cityscape, it still inspired a proper amount of awe, yet Buck welcomed the view as an old friend. Not the alien megastructure he'd seen the first time.

As the wagon pulled through the Hive's gates into its inner court, the two Golden Dragons showed up, surrounded by a large protective detail. The female Dragon needed only one glance at Park's face to understand—maybe not everything that had happened, but enough. She opened her arms, and the girl stepped into the embrace, pressing her face into the side of the woman's neck. Her shoulders shook. Tam Wai Lam exchanged meaningful looks with her husband and led Park inside.

Buck was left with a bittersweet feeling. The girl had finally let the grief catch up with her, but there was someone who'd take good care of her while she mourned.

Shang Ka Yi approached Jackson. "I gather your mission was at least partly successful?" he asked, eying the heavily laden wagon.

"Yes, Golden Dragon. Barring the unnecessary loss of life... We found what we were looking for, thanks to Miss Park's invaluable help and her, uh, late companion's insights. But it isn't *our* mission anymore." His gesture encompassed himself, Buck, and Janet. "It's *ours* now." The second circular motion of his hand included the Golden Dragon and the Great Hive compound.

"Shall we retreat to a more private location?" asked Shang Ka Yi.

"Yes, Golden Dragon, that would be prudent. In the meantime, may I suggest unloading the wagon's content into *very* secure storage, under heavy guard, and releasing the driver?"

Shang Ka Yi beckoned a security officer and gave him hushed instructions. The guard saluted and ran off.

"Please follow me." The Golden Dragon headed for the entrance. The host's physical condition showed signs of marked improvement, but he was still carrying himself with caution, maintaining a particular posture.

"I'm all ears, Mister Jackson," he said, tête-à-tête with the three Fivepointers in a large chamber.

Jackson looked at Janet, then at Buck, and finally straight at the host, but Janet spoke before he opened his mouth. She tilted her head to the side, and a cunning smile touched her lips. "Say, Golden Dragon, may we interest you in leading the restoration of civilization?"

Buck splashed water on his face. Not so much to clean it as to wash off the fatigue.

It had been a long couple of days, among the longest he'd known. The most significant, too. The choices he'd made were going to define the rest of his life. Were those the right ones? Only time would tell. But Buck was calm, at peace with himself. He might come to regret his decisions later, but hey, that's how it works, yes?

He was spent, physically and emotionally, but the anticipation of the things to come kept him afloat. Not a bubbling spike of excitement that would pass as soon as it met reality. No, a solid feeling nestled in Buck's stomach. The joy of having accomplished something important, and of greater goals yet awaiting ahead. The sense of having grown up.

Buck raised his eyes. So did his reflection in the mirror. Then came the recognition. Those eyes. That face. The unfamiliar man from Buck's dream at the Boundary all those days ago... It was him. An older, wiser, much more cynical him.

A wry, crooked smile curved the reflection's lips. Yes, there. Smiles never change. How could he not recognize it?

Buck saluted his reflection. "I'll see you when I see you, old man! Until then, take care."

Chapter 51

Jihan

October 19, 42 PE (three weeks later)

Before responding, Jihan reached into his jacket's pocket, pulled out a pipe, and compacted the tobacco with his thumb. This habit had been helpful in keeping his calm over the last weeks, but... he wasn't at The Station anymore.

Jihan hastily glanced up at Tam Wai Lam and met her mocking gaze.

"Beg your pardon, Golden Dragon! Would you mind if I...?" He raised his pipe.

"Smoke away, Mister Singh. By all means, rub in your extortion."

Blood rushed to Jihan's cheeks. New Kowloon paid handsomely, but the pungent weed was priced prohibitively even for Jihan's plump wallet. Demanding a pack of the precious stuff from the Golden Dragon as a sign-up bonus for such a long and unusual engagement had been an audacious but worthwhile move. Until this point. Tam Wai Lam was known to never forget a spite, and the last thing he needed was to end up on her naughty list.

"I'm joking, Mister Singh. You were in a position to bargain and didn't miss the opportunity. I can only respect that. Now, light your pipe and kindly proceed with the report."

Jihan forced himself to go through the ritual. His hands almost didn't shake. He leaned back in his chair and took three puffs. Those first ones were always the most satisfying.

"Thank you, Golden Dragon. Where should I start?"

"From the beginning, Mister Singh. Start from the beginning."

This assignment was over. Finally! Report out and go home. His previous contracts with New Kowloon had kept him occupied for days; a week, tops. Being stuck in that hellhole for almost a month without seeing his wife and kids, and with only two of his brothers to accompany him? He had nearly declined the contract, but reconsidered. The money was too good to say "no". It would keep his family more than comfortable through the lean and thin winter. Also, Tam Wai Lam had assigned much importance to this project, and he couldn't let her down. Not without causing irreparable damage to the family business. And he respected her too much to reject her request.

"In the first days, the direction which The Station was going to take had been uncertain. The volatile situation had kept everyone on edge. A lot could go wrong... But didn't."

"I've heard about Marc's unorthodox opening statement."

"Yeah. The shock and awe caused by putting the second most notorious Inquisitor on a spike bought him a few days of quiet. The workers and the free folk had openly cheered, the traders weren't too unhappy either, and whoever had held a grudge had kept to themselves."

"Were there many of those?"

"Not really. The Preachers grumbled about godless infidels but have not attempted to stir unrest. After a series of interviews, most of the Inquisitors were set free and left. Only two stayed behind. 'Every self-respecting state needs a few good Inquisitors,' Marc said. 'Keep your friends close, and your Inquisitors closer.' Cynical, but not wrong."

"I'd be worried if he hadn't shown a healthy measure of cynicism. And the military?"

"The Station's military remained scrupulously neutral, Golden Dragon, keeping to themselves in their barracks and pointedly staying out of the CIU soldiers' way. Until the third day."

"Did they make a move?"

"No. Marc did. Bold and risky, if you ask me, but played out perfectly. He sent Locksville's occupation contingent back home."

"Bold indeed."

"That earned him a visit from The Station's commanding officer. The captain declared his unit's *alignment* with Marc. Not loyalty or allegiance, that would have been too much to expect, but good enough. At least, until the situation became clearer with the Chief Inquisitor's *convalescence*."

Which, as had been clear to everyone, was captivity in all but name. Jihan pointedly glanced at the Golden Dragon. She rewarded him with one of her hallmark cold smiles that filled his veins with ice. "We allowed Khalifa to address The Station's elites."

"That helped, Golden Dragon. The unsaid truths were obvious, but the decorum was observed, enough to quell potential dissent. Once the unofficially exiled leader had publicly authorized Marc to act as his proxy 'until the Chief Inquisitor's health allowed him to return', Marc's position had solidified."

Tam Wai Lam did not acknowledge his sarcasm, and Jihan hurried to wipe the grin off his face.

"Please expand on that, Mister Singh."

In a briefing before Jihan's departure on the mission, the Golden Dragon had tasked him with two objectives. Outwardly, he and his two brothers were to provide the executive security for Marc Novak. Preferably through intimidation, but using lethal force if need be. His main and more sensitive order, though, was to monitor Marc and ensure... what, exactly? That was where things had become fuzzier. Marc was to use his judgement, and not to serve as a simple conduit for Khalifa's wishes. But not to usurp the power either. He was not to be allowed to lean too strongly to any one alliance, including Locksville and his former boss, Weinberg, in particular. With a twinkle in her eye, Tam Wai Lam had hinted that a minor bias toward New Kowloon's interests would not be frowned upon, but the optics of overall neutrality must be preserved.

"Marc got Jamil Khan working with the surviving members of the Trade Guild on a bilateral cooperation agreement with New Kowloon. Traders being traders, they disagreed on every single clause and kept badgering Marc for arbitrage. They were rarely happy with the outcome, but that's great. A deal can be fair only if it leaves both sides grumbling, right?"

"Are you grumbling about our deal, Mister Singh?"

Jihan bit his lip.

"It's okay, Mister Singh, you don't have to answer."

"There is one thing, Golden Dragon. Marc's sister. When were you planning to tell me?"

"I wasn't." Tam Wai Lam did not blink. "At this level, Mister Singh, the game is played by different rules. Those don't include sentiments, kindness, or clemency. Only cold calculation. You don't expect me to apologize, do you?"

"Of course not, Golden Dragon!"

"Back to The Station, then. What else can you tell me?"

"The Marshals. The other major development. Marc had given them the go-ahead to build their self-propelled train engines. The Marshals rushed to work, only to come back with urgent demands for this part or that, unquestionably necessary for the technological process, if he didn't want them to sit idly on their hands through the winter. But the work's coming along. They may have up to five engines by the springtime."

"No pushback?"

"Some. The Preachers regularly threaten to maledict Marc if those apostate Marshals don't stop their heretical activities right away. As far as I am concerned, target practice would have been the best use for those self-important asses, but Marc keeps insisting on taking no more lives unless he absolutely has to. Making a scapegoat out of the Staff Executioner for Khalifa's sins... It didn't sit well with Marc. He understands it had to be done, but has shifted to non-violent solutions. A promising sign, in terms of your mission parameters."

"Your forecast, Mister Singh?"

"Things have been progressing well. Better than I had expected. With all that crazy Shepherd talk, I still cannot predict how Marc's personality will evolve, or whether he'd agree to give up the reins when—if?—the Chief Inquisitor is released. With every passing day, he's becoming more of a Stationer than some locals. At this stage, it is anyone's guess where he'll lead The Station."

"Well, thank you, Mister Singh, for accepting this unusual assignment. I won't hold you any longer from rejoining your family. Here." Tam Wai Lam placed a small bag on her desktop and pushed it toward Jihan. "A little something to make your winter warmer."

Jihan's eyes moved from the bag to the Golden Dragon and back. "Is this..."

"Yes, Mister Singh. Tobacco."

"Looks like I'm getting the better end of the bargain, Golden Dragon. What's the catch?"

A smile—a genuine one, for a change—brightened Tam Wai Lam's face. "I expect to see you in the spring."

Chapter 52

Weinberg

October 19, 42 PE (three weeks later)

"An excellent question." Dave spun the karambit on its ring. He had no plans to use the exotic knife as a weapon, but fidgeting with Shang Ka Yi's gift helped him concentrate. Nothing had been mentioned aloud, but Dave strongly suspected that was the Dragon's attempt to mollify him after Tam's escapades.

Dave was drawing a blank; not a state he was used to. "Any thoughts? What would you suggest?"

Rajan tracked the blade's movement. "Me, sir?"

What would it take for the guy to show initiative? Four years of indentured labor would teach anyone to obey and wait for the next command, or they wouldn't survive. But the time had come for Rajan to change his ways.

Rajan wasn't Marc, for damn sure. Not as quick-witted, but also not as unreliable. You lose some, you gain some.

"Yes, Rajan, you. What do you think is the right thing to do?"

"Uh. Lemme see, sir. The zombies, Marc let go home. The rest are assholes, each one. Shoot 'em all, I don't care."

Rajan's communication skills had improved immensely over the last month. He was taking pains to avoid using the mix of languages he'd picked up during his years at The Station. The ex-hauler had gradually started exhibiting emotions and establishing relationships in Locksville. Not friendships, god forbid, that would be a long time coming. But at least he didn't think all people were bad anymore and wasn't afraid to open up. Progress! His maximalism and lack of subtlety were still an issue, and addressing those would be an arduous, bumpy road.

"Who'll do the shooting? You? Me? The Station's military?"

"No, they won't do it. Marc won't let 'em. Too soft."

"How many of the lifers are left, anyway?"

"Thirty-eight, last count."

"That's a lot."

"It is, sir."

"How about... Okay, here's a thought. We take them all off The Station's hands and give them a fair trial. Those with blood on their hands will hang, the rest may go free. Whatever their crimes had been, we'll say they've worked off their debts."

"A fine plan, sir. If you convince Marc, that is."

"Shouldn't be a problem. I'm sure he'd be happy to have one less issue to deal with."

"Yes, sir. If you say so."

"You've got reservations."

"Thought I knew the man, sir. Now I don't."

"Ah. I see. That was tough for me too. A subject for a different conversation."

Marc, Marc. What have you done? The first person Rajan had connected to. The first person he'd learned to trust. And you betrayed that trust in the worst possible way, by conspiring with Khalifa! Then again... What a brilliant move!

"Anyhow, that's the lifers. What about the workers?"

"Yeah, the workers. Marc spoke to them. Said the right things. Said, if you want to go, go. But if you've nowhere to go, stay. If you stay, The Station will pay well. Better working conditions, he promised, too. Larger teams. For another year. Then..."

"Then?"

"Then, he'll have enough engine-trains before next summer's end."

"Aha. And where will the workers go?"

"Dunno."

"He didn't say?"

"No, sir."

Dave swung the karambit a few more times. "I'll tell you what. Over the winter, I expect those researchers in New Kowloon to churn out practical plans. By this time next year, we'll be setting up workshops, maybe some manufacturing. We'll need workers. *Real* workers, I mean, not slaves, yes? By then, everyone will compete for the workforce. New Kowloon, the clans, maybe even Five Points and The Station itself, who knows. So... You think you can go back to The Station and persuade enough people to choose us?" Dave winked.

Rajan considered the offer. "Yes, boss," he nodded with determination, "I think I can."

"Good man. And while there, keep an eye on our friend, will you?"

"Friend? You mean Marc?"

"I mean Marc."

"Fucking traitor," grumbled Rajan.

"Don't say that. It is not as simple as that. In the end, we may yet thank him."

"I won't."

"Fine, I'll thank him for both of us. In the meantime," Dave rose and dropped the knife into the desk drawer, "there's someone who wants to meet you."

"Me?" Rajan's face contorted, ruining his efforts to maintain the grave expression he considered an attribute of manliness and professionalism. "Who?"

Dave opened the door and sidestepped. "Madam Gupta, come on in."

A haggard woman with a broad smile on a dark, wrinkled face tiptoed in. Rajan's eyes grew wide, and lips trembled. He managed a breaking, raspy whisper. "Mom?"

Chapter 53

Wu

October 19, 42 PE (three weeks later)

Golden Dragon Tam Wai Lam walked into the brightly lit hall, and the hum of the crowd died down. She had a unique quality—one of many making her who she was—to draw everyone's attention. The heads of over three dozen guests, mainly men but also a few women, turned as if by command. She raised her hands in a dignified salute.

"Clansfolk! Welcome to New Kowloon! I am humbled and honored by the opportunity to host so many of the City's finest! I trust your travels through the rain and the mud were safe and not too arduous, and that you found our hospitality satisfactory."

Heads nodded in response, with "Yes" and "Thank you".

"Great! Before we proceed to the reason we're all here, I would like to express my profound gratitude to my emissary, Park Yun-mi, whose tireless efforts have made this impressive gathering possible." Tam Wai Lam turned and gestured at the quiet girl behind her.

The object of attention, eyes downcast, kept an implacable expression through a wave of calls, whistles, and scattered clapping. Judging by the crowd's reaction, she'd garnered a greater acceptance than the Golden Dragon. That was bound to change once Tam Wai Lam presented her case, but still thoroughly impressive.

"Impressive" was the word of the month for Wu, in everything related to Park Yun-mi.

At first, he was unamused by the Golden Dragon's decision to assign the Korean Rat to his special unit. Of course, he bowed and responded with the obligatory "Yes, Golden Dragon!", keeping his reservations to himself. Park

Yun-mi's being a girl bore no importance—Wu had female operatives. But admitting someone foreign-born to the Hive Security's inner circle? The idea went strongly against his grain. A City Rat? In Security?

Yet, he was not in the habit of second-guessing the Golden Dragon's orders. Unlike a few of her peers, past and present, under whom he'd had a dubious privilege of serving, she'd proven her mettle beyond all doubt. Sharp of both the brain and the tongue, often unconventional, no-nonsense and efficient, she kept even him on his toes. And she rarely was wrong about anything. The girl, Wu had concluded, must be worth something.

He was not disappointed.

Tam Wai Lam had cautioned him that Park Yun-mi had experienced a recent loss. Wu was unsure what to do with that information and had no plans to cut the girl any slack. He needed associates he could rely on, regardless of what went on in their personal lives.

Park Yun-mi required no slack. She channeled her grief into frenetic activity. She wore herself down through exhaustive training, early morning to the late evening, crashed for the night, and repeated the cycle all over again the next day.

After the first week, Wu's uncharacteristically overwhelmed instructors had trickled into his office with reports. He had learned that she'd picked up rifle shooting in two days and was improving faster than anyone they'd ever trained. In hand-to-hand combat and bladed weapons, whatever she lacked in skill and finesse, she more than compensated with determined ferocity. And when it came to archery... The instructor begrudgingly admitted he'd got nothing to teach her, and could probably take a few lessons himself.

By then, Wu had been sufficiently convinced of the girl's adequacy for his Security Service. As always, the Golden Dragon's unorthodox decision had panned out spectacularly.

After ten days of this insane schedule, Tam Wai Lam had given Park a new job. The ex-Rat was to tour the City far and wide, convincing as many clans as she could to attend the Golden Dragon's planned conference. Tam Wai Lam had offered her protégé any necessary resources. What happened next exceeded everyone's wildest expectations, including the Golden Dragon's.

Park Yun-mi selected two of the Singh brothers, had Wong recalled from Dixie, and requisitioned Shang Ka Yi's senior trade officer.

Three days later, she returned with four additional people accompanying her, representing High Park, JCC, and Islington. After visiting the North, she came back trailed by five representatives of the York clans. Then she brazenly commandeered one of Shang Ka Yi's smaller ships and sailed west, calling communities as far down the shore as Burlington. Everywhere she went, she had deputized local ambassadors to spread the word. As a result, Tam Wai

Lam's conference was attended by a jaw-dropping fourteen clans, including "The Other Chinese" from the northeast. Park Yun-mi's patchwork entourage, grown to twenty strong, was an interesting side effect of her travels. The group had become so loyal to her they did not hesitate to push back against anyone, including Wu himself. Almost her own mini-clan. That, presumably, was part of the reason she received a rowdier welcome than the Golden Dragon.

Tam Wai Lam's face beamed with pride and satisfaction. "Thank you, everyone! I am happy to witness your love and respect for Park Yun-mi, which I share wholeheartedly. That is why it gives me such great pleasure to use this momentous occasion to announce Miss Park's promotion to the rank of Iron Dragon!"

A momentary stunned silence exploded with cheers and applause.

The girl finally raised her eyes, and an impish smile touched her lips.

First smile in a month. First smile to make Wu uneasy.

Chapter 54

Wai Lam

October 20, 42 PE (three weeks later)

Wai Lam leaned toward the window until her forehead met the glass. Its chill pleasantly contrasted with the enveloping warmth of the bathrobe and the heat of the exotic beverage cup cradled in her palms.

Behind her back, Ka Yi was chattering, but she only half-listened.

"...talked to the Chief Scientist, to pick his brain on those special abilities Yun-mi had told you about, hers and Brennan's. To say he was astonished would be an understatement of the year. After the initial shock wore off, he peppered me with so much scientific jargon, I could become a scientist myself, if I understood a word. Something about population bottleneck, evolutionary pressure, and some such. Bottom line, in his opinion, it may be hyper-developed intuition. Whatever it is, we need to find other people like them. Imagine the edge that would give New Kowloon! We— Are you listening, dear?"

The subject was fascinating, but Wai Lam had a more important matter to discuss. She relished another sip of coffee and turned to Ka Yi, not bothering to keep her face. She imagined childish delight written all over it. "I can't believe you've kept coffee secret from me for a year!"

"I didn't think we were at that stage of our relationship yet."

Wai Lam was way past doubts and insecurities. "And the real reason is? You do nothing without a reason. Is it a part of some elaborate, multi-step scheme to... to do what, exactly? I'm at a loss."

"A single step, really, my love. I waited for a perfect moment for you to experience it. When the weather is cold enough to appreciate the warmth. When you aren't too tired or preoccupied, so you could properly concentrate on the coffee."

"What makes you think I am not preoccupied?" She looked up from the cup, letting the mischievous bangs conceal half her face.

"You are? With what? Yun-mi has made your dream of the Citywide Trade League come true. Our scientists are analyzing the new books twenty-four-seven and promise an actionable plan within weeks. And the tech gets us decades ahead. The Station is no longer a threat, at least not—"

Under her unyielding stare, Ka Yi trailed off. His doubtful face said he was frantically running through a mental checklist, figuring out if he needed to be aware of something else, but woefully wasn't. Until his eyes finally zeroed in on her hand resting meaningfully on her belly. Men. So unobservant.

His eyebrows climbed up, and his lips slid into the widest, goofiest smile. "What? No way. Really? You sure?"

"I'm two weeks late. And I'm never late." She also just *knew*, but there was no explaining that to her oh-so-rational man.

Without taking his eyes off her, Ka Yi put down his coffee cup—and missed the table. Paying no attention to the spill, he stepped forward and squeezed Wai Lam into a hug. She extended away the hand with her own cup. "Watch it, oaf! Don't you dare spill mine too! You may be already used to coffee, but for me, it's the first!"

Ka Yi's face beamed. "The timing is perfect! Our offspring will inherit a better world than we did!"

"You think?"

"I know! That library, it changed everything!"

"You almost sound more excited about the library than my news."

"I reject those baseless allegations, Golden Dragon!"

"Then think about the name."

"The name?"

"For the baby, stupid."

"Ah. Coffee?"

"I am not finished with this cup yet... Wait. You mean, as the name? *Coffee?*"

"Why not? It's unique. And unisex."

She giggled. "You're so weird sometimes, husband."

"We can consult the books. Ask the analysts studying the History section. They'll come up with something meaningful." He was positively bubbling with ideas. "Or... let's ask the godfather!"

"Little Coffee already has a godfather? You're freaking me out. Who?"

"Why, your favorite man, Weinberg, of course!"

"Ew! Gross. Not cool, Golden Dragon, not cool."

"But consider—"

Wai Lam stared deep into his eyes. "Tell me, Golden Dragon," she drew her most formidable suaveness, "do you count on ever having more than one progeny?"

"Er... Not sure I like where this is going... Why?"

"It takes all my willpower, my dear, not to kick you right now, and only because I'm concerned about the long-term effects on your reproductive capabilities."

"Ouch. Got it. Shutting up now."

"Fine, you may ask Weinberg. I will allow that. Don't say I always have to have the last word."

"What a gracious wife I've got."

"This will cost you a top-up of the coffee."

"Despite the preoccupation?"

"Because of it."

Chapter 55

Janet

October 20, 42 PE (three weeks later)

Colonel descended into another bout of coughing, so painful to observe Janet's own throat itched.

A young officer hurried in and placed a steaming clay mug before the commander. Strong herbal aroma filled the room. Colonel took two sips, cautiously exhaled, and sagged against his chair's back.

"Thank you, Jarvis." His voice came out low and hoarse. He dismissed the lieutenant with a nod and cleared his throat. "Apologies. Seasonal flu. Even I am not immune to its sneaky offensive."

His condition changed Janet's perception of the man. Not weaker, only more... human? Careful. Human or not, he still was the same perceptive bastard!

Jackson had drilled them on what to say and especially what not to; how to behave and how not to; and how to see through Colonel's traps. The tedious coaching had lasted through their entire trip home.

Home. Home? Yes, still was. Reevaluating the meaning of pretty much everything, her new hobby of late. Five Points remained her home. Its scale had changed, though. Before the expedition, it had been the only part of the universe she'd seen first-hand, with the rest being abstract, bookish knowledge. Now it had become a small bubble on the outskirts of the enormous world. Still *her* bubble, though, where her family was.

Yes, her family had extended, to include a new best friend, feisty Yun-mi, and goofy but infallibly reliable Buck, and even Tim Jackson, the irritating clown. After everything they'd been through together, how could she see them in any other way?

Yes, she'd travel to New Kowloon again the moment she got a chance.

And yes, she'd stay in the Hive for as long as they'd let her, to be in the midst of the events, to witness first-hand all that mattered.

But she'd always have Hillcrest Point to come back to.

"Well." Colonel concluded his quiet study of the three returned travelers.

The silent treatment, Tim had warned, was the man's favorite technique to make the audience uncomfortable and loosen their tongues. Janet looked away and shifted in her seat, as would be expected of her.

Jackson had offered her an out, to simulate a nervous breakdown, but Janet insisted on attending the debriefing. After all, she was the one who had stirred up this whole mess. It took Jackson's trickery and pulling rank to get a permit for Janet to enter the Base.

"You're back. Two men short and, by the looks of it, empty-handed."

It was Jackson's turn to clear his throat. "Yes, sir, but not quite. I mean the last part, of course."

"Out with it, Tim." Colonel coughed and took a swallow of his drink to stop another feat.

"Long story short, sir, we were late. Turned out, the Chinese had already discovered the library."

"The Chinese." Colonel's skeptical eyebrow rose a smidge.

"It's in New Kowloon now, sir. But we reached an agreement with their Golden Dragon, one named Shang Ka Yi, and secured access to the books. Lieutenant Kossowsky stayed behind to liaise."

Unlike her, Jackson was a good liar. He delivered partial truths sprinkled with horse manure with the sincerest expression on his straight face. *To liaise*, right. From the house arrest in New Kowloon.

"Hm. And Lundy?"

"Unfortunately, Chuck is dead, sir. A hostile encounter. He fulfilled his duty to the last."

Janet didn't need to fake sadness. That awful day still haunted her nightmares.

"Hm," said Colonel again and stood up, filling half the space in the cabinet with his dominant presence. "Hm. You know what I think, Tim? You are full of shit."

With the Marketplace vacant until the Winter Holidays, he had moved to the Base in their absence. Colonel's small cabinet amplified its owner's intimidation. Or maybe that was the effect of his words. Whatever the case, Janet's heart rate picked up.

"Sir?" Jackson, innocence personified, acted hurt by the accusations.

"I am disappointed, Tim. You've had ample time to conjure a better story. I trust you to be my people reader, and the best you can manage is this sloppy pile of crap? Not only is it not believable, it's insulting. Do you think so little of *me*?"

"N-no, sir." Jackson looked puzzled.

"Fine. You want to do it the hard way? Let's do it the hard way." Colonel shrugged, not releasing Jackson's eyes for a second. "Simple stuff first. Okay, you're an old apostate, that's no secret. Miss McPherson is, well, *her*." Colonel acknowledged Janet with a shallow nod. "But Brennan? You kept mentioning the books, and he didn't make a single Sign of Faith?"

Buck blushed. His fault, but also Jackson's oversight.

"Whatever it is you've got going, he's in on it. Next, Kossowsky. The one man who would sooner sell his mother into slavery than compromise on the Faith. And you expect me to believe he'd agreed to have anything to do with books? 'Liaising'? Liaising my ass, Tim!"

The words hung heavily in the silent room. Fair point. Tony would never...

"You ought to satisfy my curiosity," Colonel continued. "Why on Earth did you think I'd be interested in mere *access* to the books when I had clearly ordered them delivered to me?"

He stopped pacing, returned to his seat, and sipped from the mug.

"Permission to speak freely, sir." Jackson's hoarse voice matched that of his commander.

"Oh, come now, Tim! We go back—how long? Why the sudden formality? Fine. Permission granted, Sergeant Jackson."

"That's exactly my point, sir. I've known you long enough to suspect that this Protector of the Faith shtick is just that. You've been going along with it because you have to. Comes with the territory. I can't imagine you wanted these books to destroy them. Which means your interest was to use them instead. Hence, access. Is your curiosity satisfied... sir?" Jackson allowed a tiny smile.

Colonel reciprocated. "You're not wrong, Tim." He abruptly turned deadly serious. "If a word of this leaves the room..."

"No danger of that, sir. Besides, who would believe a green private and a known troublemaker? Now, about the rest..."

"Hold on. You've got one other hole in your story. How did the Chinese get hold of the library?"

"Maybe the note Janet had found wasn't the only one? Could there be more, and someone in New Kowloon had stumbled upon another copy?"

"Enough, Tim. I'll spare you the need to devise new lies. There are no other notes. Janet's was the only one."

Jackson, searching for words. That was a first. But... "How can you be so sure?" Janet was beyond the point where asking for permissions would still be a thing. Deep inside her, the answers had already crystallized.

"Because you wrote it, didn't you, sir?" Buck perked up in his chair.

Colonel responded with a wry smile. "Quite a team you three have become."

No further confirmation was needed. Yet something still bothered Janet. "Why didn't you simply tell us?"

"I'm beginning to think that could've been not a bad idea. I needed deniability. In case you bunch had fallen into the wrong hands and gotten your tongues loosened."

"What a cheerful thought." Janet wasn't amused.

"But," Buck scratched his new beard, "how did *you* know, sir? About the library and all."

"The first Colonel had created it before coming to Five Points. He'd hoped to establish a base of operations from which to use the technology and the knowledge in these books, once the dust had settled. But the Faith had swept the entire region off its feet before he could act. Then came the invasions, the crusades, all the good stuff. The time was never right. The previous Colonels had to handpick their successors accordingly, and to pass this knowledge."

"Why not transfer the books to someone else? Someone powerful enough and not influenced by the Faith?" Jackson gave up the last pretenses.

"Like the Kowloonese? Is that why you delivered the library to them?"

"Yes, sir. And also..."

"Because you weren't sure of my intentions."

"That too, sir."

"I wanted Five Points to lead the reconstruction, of course. Call it patriotism, but also power, control, diplomacy. Shall I go on?"

Jackson, always impeccably unperturbed, shrunk under the ruler's stare.

"What now, sir?" Buck asked the question that weighed on Janet, too.

"Now?" Colonel's fists tightened. "By rights, I should summarily punish you three for disobeying my orders."

Janet swallowed around the lump clogging her throat. Yet that "by rights" provided a sliver of hope.

"Go." Colonel turned to the window and waved his hand. "Go home, spend a couple of days with your families. Then return to New Kowloon while the roads are still passable. You were planning to sneak off anyway, don't bother denying. Be there. Be a part. And forge an alliance with Five Points. If anyone can, it's you, and I'll hold you personally responsible. Nothing short of full partnership, understood?"

Jackson stood up and shook Colonel's hand.

"Oh, and Tim?" The man behind the table didn't seem so big anymore.
"Yes, sir?"

"Don't you ever dare lie to me again."

"You've got it, sir."

"One last thing. Send Kossowsky back, will you? You won't need him, anyway." Colonel winked at Janet and glanced at Buck. "He's a better aide-de-camp than Jarvis. But don't tell either I said so."

On the way out, Janet pondered the meaning of Colonel's hint. Obviously, he'd known about their broken engagement. But Buck? Was there anything else, or did *she* want it to be the case? For someone to nudge her toward this loyal, handsome guy who'd grown up so much in the last month. Who'd been there for her without fail, expecting nothing in return. Whom she turned down and, *by rights*, shouldn't expect to win back.

Janet, Buck, and Tim left the Base in silence and walked to the crossroads.

"That went sideways." Jackson sighed. "Yet, surprisingly, we're better off now than I had any reason to hope."

"Yeah," said Buck, "didn't see *that* coming."

They all chuckled.

"Meet in 'Firkin and Boot' two days from now?" Jackson suggested.

"That works," said Buck. "Janet?"

"Fine by me. Not my fondest memories, that place, but sure. Firkin, two days."

None of them moved. Were the men as reluctant to part as she was?

"Alright, I'll leave you two to it. Got a few matters to take care of at the Base." Jackson slapped their shoulders and sauntered off.

Janet turned to Buck. "That's it, ha? This is the other side."

"Feels good. But there'll be more. More other sides, I mean. And I'll see you there."

She stepped in, hugged him awkwardly, and planted a kiss on his cheek. His beard felt as soft as she'd imagined it. "See you there."

The End

2019 – 2021

Afterword

If you are reading this, you likely have made it through the entire book. Yay! I cannot overstate how happy this makes me. But there's one thing that would make me even happier: if you left an honest review!

This may sound minor, merely playing to the author's ego—and it does, of course, I will not deny the obvious. But it's *so* much more than that! **Every single review counts.** Those are worth their weight... well, not in gold, being virtual, but, say, cryptocurrency. Especially for the self-published indie writers such as yours truly. The more reviews a book has, the more favorably the mysterious Amazon algorithms are going to treat it. So, if you've enjoyed this novel, please help fellow readers discover it! A nice side effect is that knowing I've done something right alleviates the inevitable author anxiety (hint: that's where your positive reviews come into play). Less positive (but constructive) reviews point out the shortcomings, ensuring each next book is even better. Rest assured, I read them all. Did I mention that every single review counts?

I appreciate your time!

Be sure to check the ***Also By*** to see my other books.

P.S. Oh, and don't forget Goodreads! https://www.goodreads.com/author/show/27317704.Alex_Andre

Find more, follow, and get in touch:
https://alexandre.ink/
https://www.facebook.com/AlexAndreWriting
https://www.instagram.com/alexandrewriting/
author@alexandre.ink

Acknowledgements

My special thanks to the early readers who took the time to go through the entire book or its parts, provided their constructive critique, and helped shape it the way it is today.

This book would not have been the same without you.

Roman, Jaime, Gennady, Katya, Cindy, Evan, Ben, Ella, Lev – you know who you are, the unsung heroes!

About Author

Alex has lived on three continents, is fluent in three languages, suffers an unhealthy interest in linguistics, and never has enough time to get to all the books on his ever-growing To Read list.

He has always appreciated (and envied) select authors' ability to string words into elegant sentences and tie those sentences into intricate plots.

The time has come for him to try his own hand in the craft.

The E Apocrypha is his first series of novels.

Also By

LESSON NUMBER SIX
A short story prequel (Book 0.5), providing a glimpse into the past of one of the *Lost & Found* protagonists, a year before the events of Book 1 of *The E Apocrypha*.

Yun-mi, a young scavenger aspiring to become her clan's best Rat, is cornered.
Has she bitten more than she can chew? Had she sharpened her skills enough to survive the ambush? Or... Wait... Not everything may be what it seems.

LOST & FOUND
Book 1 of *The E Apocrypha* series
Available as an ebook, paperback, or audio book on Audible

In a world shattered by loss of technology, survivors live off the scraps of the fallen civilization.

Ambitious young scavenger **Yun-mi** is thrilled that her mentor is finally taking her trading. Events take a horrific turn when his murder leads to her being sold to slavers. Driven by her ferocious determination, Yun-mi fights against her abductor. Survival depends on aligning herself with powerful allies, yet whom can she trust in the fractured society?

His first assignment as a recruit in the religious confederation military leads **Buck** into the fabled City. The brutal reality he finds along the way destroys any fairy-tale notions he clings to. Rocked by the revelations, Buck sees all the fundamental ideas he's been raised on crumbling before his eyes. Is he truly one of the good guys? Or part of the problem plaguing the land?

As Yun-mi and Buck's paths cross, they must work together on a mission that could alter the course of history. Forced to rely on one another, can they grant their decaying world another chance? Or will Yun-mi and Buck become collateral damage?

AS & WHEN
Book 2 of *The E Apocrypha* series
Available as an ebook, paperback, or audio book on Audible

They've messed with the wrong woman. **Aileen**'s got a city to run—its shady part, in any case. Abducted and whisked away from Locksville, she refuses to be a pawn in powerful players' games. She most definitely is not a damsel in distress and needs no freakin knights in shining armor to come to her rescue. Alas, her best-laid escape plans misfire, landing her in even hotter waters far away from home. Aileen must find her footing in an unfamiliar, unforgiving society, fighting tooth and nail to survive.

Bo, Aileen's sharp and grumpy advisor, would move mountains to find her, his limp and aversion to violence be damned to the Seven Hells! He wouldn't trust anyone else with the impossible search for the most important person in his life.

Ajinder, executive protection specialist, won't tolerate his principal being taken—by someone other than himself. He is no stranger to dispensing violence and doesn't shy away from being on its receiving end. With his motivation stretching beyond pure professionalism, woe to those who question his skills and determination.

Will their grit, smarts, ruthless single-mindedness, and game-changing technology be enough to find Aileen before it's too late?

Meet familiar faces from *Lost & Found*. Return to Locksville, New Kowloon, The Station, as well as discover new corners of the world that had lost all technology.

HERE BE DRAGONS
Book 3 of *The E Apocrypha* series

Technology is power. More so, in the world where both are sparse. But would those possessing the former share the vision of the latter?

Kat, a fierce pirate with a lot to prove, disowned for insubordination and left ashore to face certain death.

Karim, an officer with demons to fight and revenge to exact, struggling with reconciling his homeland's troubling past.

Denny, a young smuggler and wannabe criminal mastermind, forced to flip to the legit side by a betrayal at the peak of his career.

The three find themselves, through a sequence of unrelated events, unwilling participants of an irrational journey beyond the edge of the known map, where be dragons. Will their skills, smarts, and sacrifice be enough to stave off the disaster and save the day? Is the day even worth saving, or is their visionary leader's obsession with technology misplaced?

www.ingramcontent.com/pod-product-compliance
Lightning Source LLC
Chambersburg PA
CBHW051058030726
47504CB00006B/1688